DOGEATERS

ALSO BY JESSICA HAGEDORN

Dangerous Music
Pet Food and Tropical Apparitions

DOGEATERS

Jessica Hagedorn

PANTHEON BOOKS · NEW YORK

Portions of this work were originally published in the following publications: *Conditions: Thirteen, Everyday Life, Rolling Stock, The Seattle Review, TYOUONYI* and *ZYZZYVA*.

Grateful acknowledgment is made to the following for permission to reprint previously published material:
Associated Press: Associated Press bulletin entitled "Insect Bounty," dated September 20, 1988. Reprinted by permission.
National Historical Institute and Pura Santillan-Castrence: Excerpts from *Philippines . . . (1846)* by Jean Mallat, translated by Pura and Lina S. Castrence. Reprinted by permission.

Library of Congress Cataloging-in-Publication Data

Hagedorn, Jessica
Dogeaters / by Jessica Hagedorn.
p.   cm.
ISBN 0-394-57498-2
I. Title.
PS3558.A3228D64   1990
813'.54—dc20   89-16195

Book Design & Illustrations by Stephanie Bart-Horvath

Manufactured in the United States of America

First Edition

for John and Paloma

and
in memory of

James Emanuel McCall
(1889–1962)

and

Tecla Ibañez McCall
(1889–1969)

Contents

Contents

ACKNOWLEDGMENTS

The author wishes to acknowledge the MacDowell Colony, the Writer's Room, and the Center for American Culture Studies at Columbia University for space, support, and sustenance during the writing of this book. The New York State Council for the Arts provided several writer-in-residence grants which are deeply appreciated.

Special thanks to my friend and agent, Harold Schmidt, for believing in this book, and to my wonderful editor, Helena Franklin, for her fussing, caring, and attention to detail.

And to Luis Cabalquinto for his poem "The Dog-Eater," which appeared in the *American Poetry Review*, Nov.–Dec. 1984: *salamat*.

I am also grateful to Santiago Bose, Thulani Davis, Luis H. Francia, Ramon Hodel, Erlinda Cortes Brobston, and Renee Montagne. There are many other people I wish to thank, both here and in the Philippines, for their assistance on this project; life being what it is these days, I think it would be wiser to be discreet.

AUTHOR'S NOTE

This is a work of fiction. The characters, incidents, and dialogue are products of the author's imagination and are not to be construed as real. Where the names of actual persons, living or dead, are used, the situations, incidents, and dialogue concerning those persons are entirely fictional and are not intended to depict any actual events or change the entirely fictional character of the work.

This book includes actual quotations from *The Philippines* by Jean Mallat (though the titles I have given them are my own), from the Associated Press, from a poem by Jose Rizal, and from a speech by President William McKinley. All other material presented as quotations from newspapers are fictional, as is *The Metro Manila Daily* itself.

PART ONE:
COCONUT PALACE

They have the greatest respect for sleeping persons, and the greatest curse they can pronounce against anybody is to wish that he die in his sleep. They can not abide the idea of waking a sleeping person, or when they are obliged to do it, it is always done as gently as possible; they carry this repugnance so far that one can hardly expect them to wake up a priest or doctor to come to the aid of a sick person.

—Jean Mallat, The Philippines *(1846)*

Love Letters

1956. The air-conditioned darkness of the Avenue Theater smells of flowery pomade, sugary chocolates, cigarette smoke, and sweat. *All That Heaven Allows* is playing in Cinemascope and Technicolor. Starring Jane Wyman as the rich widow, Rock Hudson as the handsome young gardener, and Agnes Moorehead as Jane's faithful friend, the movie also features the unsung starlet Gloria Talbott as Jane's spoiled teenage daughter, a feisty brunette with catlike features and an innocent ponytail.

Rock Hudson's rustic gardener's cottage stands next to a frozen lake. The sky is a garish baby-blue, the clouds are ethereal wads of fluffy white cotton. In this perfect picture-book American tableau, plaid hunting jackets, roaring cellophane fires, smoking chimneys, and stark winter forests of skeletal trees provide costume and setting for Hollywood's version of a typical rural Christmas. Huddled with our chaperone Lorenza, my cousin Pucha Gonzaga and I sit enthralled in the upper section of the balcony in Manila's "Foremost! First-Run! English Movies Only!" theater, ignoring the furtive lovers stealing noisy kisses in the pitch-black darkness all around us.

Jane Wyman's soft putty face. Rock Hudson's singular, pitying expression. Flared skirts, wide cinch belts, prim white blouses, a single strand of delicate, blue-white pearls. Thick penciled eyebrows and blood-red vampire lips; the virginal, pastel-pink cashmere cardigan draped over Gloria Talbott's shoulders. Cousin Pucha and I are impressed by her brash style; we gasp at Gloria's cool indifference, the offhand way she treats her grieving mother. Her casual arrogance seems inherently American, modern, and enviable.

We compare notes after the movie, sipping our TruColas under the watchful gaze of the taciturn servant Lorenza. "I don't like her face," Pucha complains about Jane Wyman, "I hate when Rock starts kissing her!" "What's wrong with it?" I want to know, irritated by my blond cousin's constant criticisms. She wrinkles her mestiza nose, the nose she is so proud of because it's so pointy and straight. "AY! Que corny! I dunno what Rock sees in her—" she wails. "It's a love story," I say in my driest tone of voice. Although I'm four years younger than Pucha, I always feel older. "It's a *corny* love story, when you think about it," Pucha snorts. Being corny is the worst sin you can commit in her eyes.

"What about Gloria Talbott? You liked her, didn't you? She's so . . ."—I search frantically through my limited vocabulary for just the right adjective to describe my feline heroine—"interesting." Pucha rolls her eyes. "AY! *Puwede ba*, you have weird taste! She's really *cara de achay*, if you ask me." She purses her lips to emphasize her distaste, comparing the starlet to an ugly servant without, as usual, giving a thought to Lorenza's presence. I avoid Lorenza's eyes. "She looks like a cat—that's why she's so strange and interesting," I go on, hating my cousin for being four years older than me, for being so blond, fair-skinned, and cruel.

Pucha laughs in disdain. "She looks like a *cat*, aw-right," she says, with her thick, singsong accent. "But if you ask me, *prima*, Gloria Talbott looks like a *trapo*. And what's more, Kim Novak should've been in this movie instead of Jane Wyman. Jane's too old," Pucha sighs. "*Pobre* Rock! Everytime he had to kiss her—" Pucha shudders at the thought. Her breasts, which are already an overdeveloped 36B and still growing, jiggle under her ruffled blouse.

It is *merienda* time at the popular Cafe España, and the tiny restaurant is quickly filling up with more customers flocking out of the Avenue Theater across the street. I am acutely aware of the table of teenage boys next to us, craning their necks and staring lewdly at my cousin Pucha. Pucha plays with her hair, affecting a coy pose as she, too, suddenly becomes aware of the boys' attention. "Psst . . . pssst," the loudest and largest of the boys hisses lazily at my cousin, who makes a big show of pretending not to hear. I glare at him angrily. I want Lorenza to save us, pay our bill, escort us out of the crowded restaurant, and take us home in a taxi.

Lorenza catches my eye. "Señorita Pucha," she murmurs to my cousin, who refuses to acknowledge her. Pucha is flattered by the hissing boy's grossness and has other plans. She orders another round of TruCola, including one for the frowning Lorenza, who pointedly does not drink it. In her loud voice, Pucha professes to still be hungry and orders a second slice of *bibingka*, which she eats very slowly. She is a changed person, smiling and chattering about Rock Hudson, Ava Gardner, and her latest favorite, Debbie Reynolds. She is suddenly solicitous, oozing sweetness and consideration. "Don't you wanna eat something, *prima*?" She asks me. "A sandwich, maybe? Some cake? Is okay—I got my allowance."

The teenage boy starts to hiss again. Then he starts making kissing sounds with his fat lips. I am disgusted by his obscene display and the giggling reaction of my flustered cousin. I stick my tongue out at him, this flat-eyed snake who makes a fool out of Pucha in public. He is oblivious to me, his shining flat eyes fixed on my dim-witted cousin. His friends are laughing. I am powerless; I am only ten years old. I remember to this day how I longed to run out of the fluorescent Cafe España back into the anonymous darkness of the Avenue Theater, where I could bask in the soothing, projected glow of Color by De Luxe.

"I'm not hungry, and I think we should leave," I mutter through clenched teeth. The gang of boys nudge each other with their elbows, making faces at us. My overripe cousin bats her pale eyelashes at their leader the snake while she sips her drink with a straw, lost in thought. He leers at her; she smiles back, blushing prettily. Lorenza starts to get up from our table. "*Tayo na*, Señorita Pucha. Your mother will be very angry if we stay out too late," she threatens Pucha gently. Pucha is visibly annoyed. She gives Lorenza one of her contemptuous looks. "What about my dessert?" she whines, then turns to me. "Lorenza is your *yaya*, Rio—not mine. I'm too old for a *yaya*, *puwede ba*." I glare at her. "Señorita Pucha, your mother ordered us to bring you home early," Lorenza insists. Pucha ignores her and keeps eating. "I have to finish my dessert," she repeats, her voice louder and more impatient. "Pucha," I say with some desperation, "let's get out of here. What are you going to do—give him your phone number? You mustn't give him your phone number. Your parents will kill you! Your parents will kill me," I start blithering. "He's only a boy. A homely, fat boy . . . He looks like he smells bad." Pucha gives me a withering look. "*Prima*, shut up. Don't be so *tanga*! Remember, Rio—I'm older than you, and you better not say anything to anybody!" She turns to Lorenza: "Did you hear me, Lorenza?" Lorenza sits back down, defeated. Pucha turns to me once more and speaks in a whisper. "I don't care if he's a little *gordito*, or *pangit*, or smells like a dead goat. That's Boomboom Alacran, stupid. He's cute enough for me."

The cashmere scarf is gracefully draped around Jane Wyman's head to keep her warm. In her full-length, mahogany sable coat, she drives her dependable dark green Buick, the color of old money. It is how I remember the movie: a determined woman alone in the winter, driving a big green car on a desolate country road, on the way to see her young lover. *Pobre* Rock, indeed. A woman like Jane Wyman baffles Pucha. Why does she choose to drive her own car, when she can obviously afford a chauffeur? Pucha wants to know. And who plays Jane Wyman's spoiled son and Gloria Talbott's brother? Pucha insists he's Tab Hunter, her second favorite after Rock Hudson. I shake my head and don't have the heart to argue with her. The role of Jane Wyman's son is a minor one, completely forgettable. The character's name is "Ned"—that much I remember. Ned Nickerson is the name of Nancy Drew's boyfriend in those books the American Consul's wife gives me the following Christmas. Now, after all these years in America, I have yet to meet a man named "Ned" or anyone with the surname "Nickerson."

1956. Long before my mother Dolores leaves my father Freddie and takes me to North America. Long before my brother Raul decides to stay behind, renounce his worldly possessions, and become a faith healer. Long before my father Freddie Gonzaga, out of fear, announces he is moving to Spain for good. He makes pronouncements but rarely lives up to them, according to my cynical mother, who should know. She envisions him a recluse, living out his last days in some rotting villa in Manila, abandoned by his mistresses and surrounded by all his packed belongings. Bulging suitcases reinforced with rope, sealed cartons the size of refrigerators stuffed with obsolete Betamax machines, rusting tape recorders, and unused Japanese microwave ovens. "Any day now!" he'll say. "I'm packed and ready to go!" He waves his passport defiantly at anyone who challenges him. Rumors abound: My father suffers from a terminal disease, my father has a few months to live. Much to everyone's surprise—including his doctors' and his own—he lives to be a very old man.

It's been years now since my cousin Pucha reported in one of her numerous letters to me, spelling errors intact: "RIO—I wish you never left us but if God wills I will perhapps be joineing you soon over there, *primma*. I need a US divorse, *sabes ya*—its still not okay here its a mortal sin. Well maybe I could do it in Honkong and go shopping too but I rather the US we could go shopping together! Or maybe Reno ITS MORE FUN plus with you there *primma* it wont be so lonley! Your Papi is not so good he just came out of hospital again why dont you come see him? Hes always joking you know how he is, life of the party, *pobre tambien*! Raul was with him everyday, thanks be to God your brother is here. Write to me why dont you I always do the writeing its not fair. I miss you LOVE always, PUCHA."

I never worry about my father. He has connections and believes in paying bribes. In his later years he is often broke, but when he really wants or needs it, he finds the money. There will always be a way out for him. I am still not sure what sort of passport he waves in the air, if he owns one or two. Maybe Spanish, maybe British, maybe Filipino, maybe anything. It is the sort of business he keeps to himself. He believes in dual citizenships, dual passports, as many allegiances to as many countries as possible at any one given time. My father is a cautious man, and refers to himself as a "guest" in his own country.

My mother, who carries American papers because of her father, feels more viscerally connected to the Philippines than he ever could. She used to argue with him. "I don't understand, Freddie. You were born here. Both your parents and most of your brothers were born here. I was born here, so were our children. You are definitely a Filipino! A mestizo, yes—but definitely a Filipino."

My father smiles a complacent smile. It usually means the discussion is over. He shrugs. "Two generations, three generations, it really doesn't matter. What matters is I feel like a visitor. After all, my great-grandfather came from Sevilla," he reminds my mother. "And your great-grandmother came from Cebu!" she snaps back. There is a brief silence before my father repeats, "It doesn't matter. It doesn't matter what you say—it's how I feel." My mother throws up her hands and curses magnificently. His stubborn evasiveness is something my mother will never understand about my noncommital father; it never fails to infuriate her.

My father and uncles are smug, mysterious men together, especially at the dinner table. "Let's be on the safe side," my father might say to Pucha's father, Uncle Agustin. "We're not fools, and we're not cowards. But we are typical Gonzagas who want to stay alive at all costs. Nothing to be ashamed of." My father could be discussing anything—real estate or politics—it's all the same to him. Uncle Agustin puffs on a Cuban cigar and says nothing for a moment, assessing in his small mind what his younger brother has just said. He is even more noncommital than my father. "Well," Uncle Agustin finally says, clearing his throat. "Well, Freddie. Perhaps."

My father brings up one of his favorite topics, the eldest and most successful Gonzaga brother, my Uncle Cristobal who lives in Spain. Uncle Cristobal flies a *Falangista* flag above his front door to show his allegiance to Franco during the Spanish Civil War. He flies the flag not because he really is a fascist, but because he is a wily opportunist; like my father and Uncle Agustin, he is a practical Gonzaga, a man who always knows which side is winning. After the war, Uncle Cristobal is rewarded with a prosperous import-export firm based in Madrid. My father has said that if Uncle Cristobal had lived in Russia in 1917, he would have been a Marxist. "Adaptability is the simple secret of survival," my father always maintains. It is another of his well-worn Gonzaga clichés, but also a rule he lives by.

1956. My *Lola* Narcisa Divino's room is filled with the sweet gunpowder smell and toxic smoke of Elephant brand *katol*, a coil-shaped mosquito-repellent incense. Narcisa Divino is my mother's mother, a small brown-skinned woman with faded gray eyes. She is from Davao, in the southern region where I have never been. While my grandfather Whitman Logan lies ill in bed at the American Hospital, my grandmother stays in the guest room next to the kitchen in the back of our house in Manila.

Besides my grandmother, who is treated with a certain deference and referred to as "eccentric," I am the only one who doesn't mind the incense she burns all afternoon and into the night. My brother Raul complains about the whole house stinking and makes fun of *Lola* behind her back, imitating her stoop-shouldered walk and soft, childish giggles. When his rowdy friends come over, Raul acts ashamed of her and avoids introducing her to them. She becomes invisible, some tiny woman who happens to be visiting, content to listen to her radio dramas in the back room. *Lola* Narcisa ignores the rest of the family as much as it ignores her. She acts surprised by my daily visits. There are times she seems confused about who I am, but she is always pleased to see me. Some days, she calls me by my mother's name.

My father Freddie is polite and even solicitous in my *Lola* Narcisa's presence. He is willing to pay all of my grandfather's mounting hospital bills, and makes sure *Lola* Narcisa's basic needs are met. Once a month, the fashionable Dr. Ernesto Katigbak is sent for to examine her weak lungs; my father pays for Dr. Katigbak's expensive house calls without complaining. He even calls her "Mama," but she, my brown-skinned, gray-eyed grandmother, is not asked to sit at our dinner table. When guests inquire after her, my Rita Hayworth mother simply says *Lola* Narcisa prefers eating alone in her room. Actually, my *lola* prefers eating her meals with the servants in the kitchen. She prefers to eat what the servants cook for themselves, after everyone else in the house has been served their food. While they eat *kamayan* with their hands, she and the servants go over the intricate plots of their favorite radio serial, *Love Letters*, which they listen to after dinner in my grandmother's cozy room. I know. When my cousin Pucha isn't visiting or spending the night, I've joined my *Lola* Narcisa and her friends many times.

On the wall above her bed hangs a large crucifix, with the tormented face of Christ rendered in bloody, loving detail. Russet ringlets of horsehair hang from Christ's bent head, crowned with a miniature wreath of thorns. Next to the crucifix hangs a framed painting on velvet of the Madonna and Child, which my *lola* brought with her from Davao. The Madonna is depicted as a native woman wearing the traditional *patadyong*; the infant Jesus has the brown skin of my *Lola* Narcisa and straight black hair. Below the velvet painting, my *lola* has arranged votive candles in a neat row on a shelf meant for books. Her bed is covered with a white crocheted bedspread, which gives off a faint odor of mothballs. The bedspread and what seem like hundreds of doilies scattered around the room were all made by *Lola* Narcisa. A black steamer trunk containing my grandparents' clothes stands at the foot of the huge bed, where my tiny *lola* sleeps alone and waits.

She is eating, always eating, like an agitated, captive animal. She holds a bowl of rice with *dilis*, anchovy-size dried salted fish, on her lap. She likes to eat with her hands, and is comfortable enough around me to do so. She gestures toward the ivory-colored, U-shaped Philco radio on the table by her bed. "Turn it on for me, *hija*—my hands are greasy," she says. The radio was once my brother Raul's, but he now owns a sleek black transistor model my father brought from Hong Kong. Next to her radio, my *lola* has placed a chipped, crudely painted clay statue of San Martin de Porres.

"What's on, *Lola*?" I ask, although I know the answer. She smiles at me, a hint of mischief in her twinkling eyes, which sweep over my skinny body. I am almost as tall as she is, and this amuses her greatly. "*Love Letters! Love Letters* is coming on, in exactly three and a half minutes," *Lola* Narcisa replies. "Sit down, Rio—get comfortable and don't ask too many questions. The others will be coming as soon as their chores are done." This is one of her lucid nights; she recognizes me as her granddaughter and affectionately orders me around. I turn the knob on the radio to get clearer reception. She takes a handful of rice and fish and pops it expertly into her mouth. Then she chews with a worried look on her face, temporarily forgetting I am there. I wonder if she is thinking about my grandfather. Just as abruptly, she focuses on me again. "Rio, does your mother know you're here?" She asks. I nod. "Did you finish your homework?" I hesitate, then nod my head again. *Lola* Narcisa looks sternly at me. "I don't believe you, Rio." She pauses and studies my disappointed face before sighing and patting my hand. "All right, *hija*—you can stay. But if your mother comes to get you, I won't stop her. You understand? It's very late, and you have school tomorrow. Tomorrow is Monday, isn't it? Uh-hmm! I don't want your mother making *sumpung* and blaming me for your bad habits!" She wheezes and clears her throat, putting the now empty bowl next to San Martin de Porres. "Uh-hmm. *Sige, hija*—I'm going to wash my hands. Then when I come back, you can sit down near me, right here on the bed . . ."

Love Letters has been on the air for years, the most popular radio serial in Manila. Even the President boasts of being an avid fan. Many of the episodes have been adapted into successful movies by Mabuhay Studios. Top movie stars still perform as guests on the show, including the biggest and most beloved—Nestor Noralez and Barbara Villanueva. Nestor and Barbara are engaged to marry in real life but keep postponing the wedding. Nestor sadly admits in numerous interviews that for him, "Hard work and Lady Success come first." Barbara is just as understanding and loyal to Nestor as the characters she portrays.

My grandmother's crazy for *Love Letters* because the plots are so sad and complicated. Every week, there's a new story, which always involves a love letter. An episode comes on every night of the week, each story beginning on a Sunday and ending on a Saturday. Everyone weeps at the inevitable, tragic conclusion on the seventh night.

According to my father, *Love Letters* appeals to the lowest common denominator. My Uncle Agustin's version of the lowest common denominator is the *"bakya* crowd." It's the same reason the Gonzagas refuse to listen to Tagalog songs, or go to Tagalog movies. I don't care about any of that. As far as *Love Letters* goes, I'm hooked—and though I'd definitely die if cousin Pucha ever found out, I cry unabashedly in the company of *Lola* Narcisa and all the servants.

Without fail, someone dies on *Love Letters*. There's always a lesson to be learned, and it's always a painful one. Just like our Tagalog movies, the serial is heavy with pure love, blood debts, luscious revenge, the wisdom of mothers, and the enduring sorrow of Our Blessed Virgin Barbara Villanueva. It's a delicious tradition, the way we weep without shame. If Pucha could see me, I'd never hear the end of it. She has no use for Barbara Villanueva, Patsy Pimentel, or Nestor Noralez, whom she calls "The King Of Corny." She has no use for anyone who isn't Kim Novak, or Rock Hudson.

L O V E L E T T E R #99

Dalisay (Barbara Villanueva) is a beautiful young servant who's been deflowered by the handsome Mario (Cesar Carmelo), the son of wealthy landowner Don Pedro de Leon (Nestor Noralez) and his wife, the haughty mestiza Doña Hilda (Patsy Pimentel).

Dalisay writes Mario a love letter as soon as she discovers she is pregnant. Mario is away at a military school in Baguio. To make matters worse, Dalisay must function in her role as servant in Don Pedro's hacienda as if nothing has happened, especially under the suspicious scrutiny of the arrogant and possessive Doña Hilda, who calls her only son "a gift from God." Dalisay, of course, has no one to turn to or confide in.

The letter is intercepted by the snoopy headmaster Pating (Nestor Noralez) at Mario's military school. Pating doesn't tell Mario about the letter, but instead sends it back to Mario's horrified parents. Don Pedro and Doña Hilda have their hearts set on their son marrying Elvira (Patsy Pimentel), the daughter of the town mayor. Elvira is actually in love with a soldier of humble origins, but she is willing to marry Mario to please her parents.

The beautiful young servant is cruelly thrown out of the house on a stormy night, and there is no place she can run to but her widower father's hut on the outskirts of town. Dalisay's father, Mang Berto (Nestor Noralez), is a poor tenant farmer who works Don Pedro's land. Mang Berto vows to take care of his innocent daughter, and accepts responsibility for the care of her unborn child. Everyone in the small town is scandalized, and treats the miserable Dalisay with scorn.

Mario wants to come home for Christmas and profess his love for the poor servant girl at the risk of being disowned by his powerful father. He still has no idea about Dalisay's condition. Doña Hilda is worried about the possible outcome of her beloved son's impending visit, and decides the only practical solution is to get rid of Dalisay by staging an accident. The unsuspecting young girl awaits the birth of her child, meekly resigned to the fact that Mario refuses to see her.

Meanwhile. . . .

Barbara Villanueva's melodious voice sings an ominous invocation against witches: "*Asin, suca / get-teng, luya / bawang, lasona*" . . . "Salt, vinegar / scissors, ginger / garlic, onion" . . . An invocation against death, to protect her unborn child.

It is raining outside, a torrential rain, a sign that the typhoon season is about to begin. I can smell the rain, a thickness in the air. The furious downpour clatters against the tiles on our roof, beating a mist up from the ground. I pray the streets will flood and there will be no school tomorrow. It is a godsend, this sudden storm, this lightning and thunder and static on the radio. My *yaya* Lorenza is terrified and cowers in the kitchen every time the thunder crackles and explodes. She is tearfully cleaning grains of rice, picking out the tiny pebbles and white worms before the rice can be cooked by Pacita. "*Dios ko, dios ko, dios ko*," she mutters, biting her lip and making signs of the cross. She will be the last to join us in my grandmother's room, where we are all concentrating hard on the story inside the radio. My parents and brother seem distant and harmless, although they are only a few rooms away. My mother has forgotten all about me and assumes Lorenza has put me to bed. I am curled up under the crocheted bedspread on my *lola*'s bed. *Lola* Narcisa rocks in her chair. Aida, Pacita, Fely, and the chauffeur Macario sit or stand in various corners of the room, straining to listen.

I try to blot from my mind the image of my grandfather Whitman sick in the hospital, the shabby American Hospital with its drab green walls, drab green smells, and the hovering presence of the hospital's supervising staff of melancholy American doctors. Like my grandfather, they are leftovers from recent wars, voluntary exiles whose fair skin is tinged a blotchy red from the tropical sun or too much alcohol; like his, their clothes and skin reek of rum and Lucky Strikes. It is not an unpleasant scent, something soothing I associate with old American men and my grandfather Whitman, whom I love.

My *Lola* Narcisa claims that her husband is the first white man stricken with *bangungot*. She seems almost proud of his nightmare sickness, a delirious fever in which he sweats, sleeps, and screams. Most *bangungot* victims die overnight in their sleep. It is a mysterious illness which usually claims men. My grandfather's case is even stranger than most—he's been sick like this for weeks. At first, the American doctors diagnosed malaria. After a week, they patroled the corridor outside my grandfather's private room, consulting each other worriedly and coming up with more far-fetched theories. *Bangungot* is ruled out of the picture by the chief of staff, Dr. Leary, who dismisses the tropical malady as native superstition, a figment of the overwrought Filipino imagination.

I have been to the hospital only once, with my *lola* and the cook Pacita. My parents have forbidden me to go back; when I ask why, my father replies, "You are much too young to be around sick people. It's best to remember your grandfather as a healthy man." What they don't seem to understand is that unlike Raul, I'm not afraid.

When *Love Letters* is over, the servants file out of the room, murmuring good-night and thanks to my grandmother. Lorenza even comes back with another bowl of snacks for *Lola* Narcisa: minced red salted duck eggs dabbed with vinegar, more rice with crunchy *dilis*. Happy and lost in her radio reverie, my grandmother nods and smiles at no one in particular. Lorenza turns to give me one last warning before leaving the room. "Rio, if you don't go to bed in your own room, your mother will chop my head off." I grin at her and put my finger to my lips. "I won't tell, Lorenza. Promise."

My grandmother dabs her eyes with one of my grandfather's oversized handkerchiefs. The *Love Letters* theme song is playing, a saccharine instrumental melody replete with organ and violins. The somber voice of the male announcer intones, "Tune in for the next episode of *Love Letters* at the same time tomorrow night. And so, until then . . ."

Hunching her bony shoulders, *Lola* Narcisa leans in closer to the radio, as if by doing so she can prolong her precious drama one more second. An eerie, high-pitched sound is followed by the voice of the same radio announcer, this time more cheery and impersonal. "This is DZRK, Radiomanila, signing off for the evening. At the sound of the tone, it's exactly twelve midnight, in the Blessed Year of the Family Rosary. Remember: The family that prays together, stays together."

Forgotten not just by my mother but by everyone, I sit drowsily on the lumpy bed watching my grandmother eat and cry. Tomorrow they'll find me asleep, next to her. I know I should go down the hallway to my own room, but the house is too big and dark, all the lights turned off by the reliable Fely and Lorenza. As I watch my rapt grandmother, I too begin to cry.

It's another movie. *A Place in the Sun*—condemned by the Archdiocese of Manila as vile and obscene. I don't understand the commotion, why Pucha and I have to sneak off and pretend we're going to see Debbie Reynolds in *Bundle of Joy*. Fortunately for us, Pucha's older brother Mikey is our chaperone for the day. He wants to see Elizabeth Taylor naked.

We are all bewildered by the movie, which is probably too American for us. Mikey falls asleep halfway through it, after Shelley Winters drowns. I decide that even if I don't understand it, I *like* this movie. In my eyes, it is unjust that Montgomery Clift is executed for Shelley Winters' murder. While Mikey snores away, Pucha and I sit tensely in the dark, waiting for the obscene images that never appear. Pucha is enthralled, although I don't think she gets it either. She has found a new idol in Montgomery Clift. All she can say afterward at the Cafe España is, "Shelley Winters is so ordinary. She deserves to die. *Que pobrecito*, Montgomery!" All Mikey can say is, "You owe me one, girls . . ."

The back of Montgomery Clift's shoulder in giant close-up on the movie screen. Elizabeth Taylor's breathtaking face is turned up toward him, imploring a forbidden kiss. They are drunk with their own beauty and love, that much I understand. Only half of Elizabeth Taylor's face is visible—one violet eye, one arched black eyebrow framed by her short, glossy black hair. She is glowing, on fire in soft focus.

Jane Wyman bends over a comatose Rock Hudson. She tells him she loves him, she will be with him forever in the rustic cottage by the frozen lake. He finally opens his eyes. A deer wanders up to the picture window. Sentimental music interrupts the pastoral silence, swelling to a poignant crescendo as the closing credits roll along. As no doctor ever could, the power of Jane Wyman's love has cured Rock Hudson and pulled him from death, like Sleeping Beauty.

I try to imagine *Lola* Narcisa bending over my grandfather's bed like Jane, an angel of mercy whispering so softly in his ear that none of us can make out what she is saying. My grandfather the white man tosses his head from side to side, still locked in his eternal nightmare after all these years. He barks like a dog, grunts and sputters like an old car. My grandmother wipes the drool from the corners of his mouth while my Rita Hayworth mother, Dolores Logan Gonzaga, stands as far away from her father's bed as possible. She seems terrified and bewildered by this image of her dying father.

He groans *Chicago, Chicago, Chicago*, with such longing I shut my eyes and the movie projector goes off in my head. Concrete, glass, and in the background, cardboard cut-out skyscrapers. June Allyson descends from a winding staircase, wearing a ballgown made of gold-flecked, plastic shower curtains. My grandfather mutters repeatedly in his frenzied sleep: *Chicago, Chica-go . . .*

He shrieks, as if someone or something has finally caught up with him. The anguish in his voice, in the way his body twists and jerks epileptically on the hospital bed, is unbearable. The anxious American doctors have been waiting for a sign. They rush into the room, trailed by eager nurses ready with gleaming, stainless steel bedpans, ominous catheters, and intravenous attachments bursting with glucose and pints of fresh black blood. My mother Dolores covers her eyes. She is shaking and sobbing with grief. "DON'T TOUCH HIM!" my *Lola*

Narcisa screams in English at Doctor Leary. Everyone stops dead in their tracks, stunned that the shriveled brown woman has so loudly and finally spoken.

I am confused by the thought of Elizabeth Taylor's one violet eye luminous in black and white, the pristine illusion of elegant deer peacefully grazing outside Rock Hudson's picture window. In this hospital room, there is only our sense of foreboding, heightened by the grayness of bedsheets and medical uniforms, the dim fluorescent lights, the lizards watching from the corners of the ceiling. My grandfather is dying. My mother has been tranquilized and waits for my father, who has telephoned the nurse's station to let her know he is on his way. Our family priest, Father Manuel, has been summoned. No one seems to remember or care that my grandfather Whitman is an avowed atheist, that his hatred for the Catholic clergy runs deep. "Don't wake him," *Lola* Narcisa keeps pleading in English. "If you wake him, he dies. Uh-hmmm." She nods her head. "Better to leave him dreaming."

Typhoon rages outside. She waits in the chair next to the bed, eyes glazed and gone. Buzzing static emanates from the radio. She rocks, ever so slightly. It is a rhythm only she can feel and hear. The air is crackling, electric. I feel a chill, and cover myself with one of my grandmother's shawls. Above my *lola*'s head, a speckled lizard disappears behind the safety of the velvet painting. On a tin plate resting on the windowsill, the *katol* incense has burned down into an ashy, smoldering heap, the smoke still dense and fragrant. The ancient Philco radio is alive, hissing and humming to my *Lola* Narcisa, its dreadful music somehow soothing her.

The King
of Coconuts

BECAUSE, they would say. Simply because.

Because he tells the President what to do. Because he dances well. Because he tells the First Lady off. Because he dances well and collects art. Because he calls the General *Nicky*. Because he owns a 10,000-acre hacienda named *Las Palmas*. Because he employs a private army of mercenaries. Because he collects primitive art, renaissance art, and modern art. Because he owns silver madonnas, rotting statues of unknown saints, and jeweled altars lifted intact from the bowels of bombed-out churches. Because his house is not a home but a museum. Because he smokes cigars. Because he flies his own yellow helicopter. Because he plays golf with a five handicap. Because he plays polo and breeds horses. Because he breeds horses for fun and profit. Because he is a greedy man, a generous man. Because his wealth is self-made, not inherited. Because he owns everything we need, including a munitions factory. Because he dances well: the boogie, the fox-trot, the waltz, the cha-cha, the mambo, the hustle, the bump. Because he dances a competent tango. Because he owns *The Metro Manila Daily*, *Celebrity Pinoy Weekly*, Radiomanila, TruCola Soft Drinks, plus controlling interests in Mabuhay Movie Studios, Apollo Records, and the Monte Vista Golf and Country Club. Because he conceived and constructed SPORTEX, a futuristic department store in the suburb of Makati. Because he was once nominated for president and declined to run. Because he plays poker and wins. Because he is short, and smells like expensive citrus. Because he has elegant silver hair, big ears, slanted Japanese eyes, and the aquiline nose of a Spanish mestizo.

usually begins. A witty exchange explodes into a shouting match, objects are thrown around the room. Breaking glass and shattering plates exhilarate her; no one really gets physically hurt. Their mutual contempt is a bond; they would never consider leaving each other. Their daughter is the burden they share, secretly sure she is the price for all their sins. They do not admit this to each other. They are exemplary Catholics, and donate large sums of money to the Church.

To a renowned American correspondent sent by a prominent American news magazine, Severo Alacran is gracious and self-effacing. "Please don't call me a visionary," he insists, "I'm really just a businessman."

Amiably, he poses for pictures. Eyes twinkling, his face friendly one moment and stern the next, he is photographed seated behind his massive desk, surrounded by mementos and awards, framed photographs of his wife and daughter, the President shaking his hand, the President and First Lady at some palace function laughing with him, a smiling group shot with the golf team he sponsors, "Manila Junior Champions." A creased snapshot of General Douglas MacArthur, Severo Alacran, and an anonymous Filipino man is displayed in a pewter frame on the wall above his desk.

He is thoughtful and relaxed in a solitary portrait which shows him standing next to one of his treasured paintings, "Farmers Harvesting Rice" by Amorsolo. "My enemies claim it's a forgery, that I can no longer tell what's authentic from what's fake," he admits casually. The correspondent frowns; he genuinely *likes* Severo Alacran. He hopes the rich man will elaborate. But the rich man breezily changes the subject, inviting the journalist to a private showing of his recent acquisitions later that afternoon.

Asked about his last name, he laughs heartily. He addresses the famous correspondent by his first name. *Steve.* A young man's name. Alacran, he explains, means "scorpion" in Spanish. "How about that, Steve? What's in a name?"

That same week, he is interviewed by Cora Camacho, the Barbara Walters of the Philippines, on her popular TV show, *Girl Talk*. He flirts and disarms her. "My dear Cora, of course I'm happily married!

Aren't you?" He knows, as do most people in Manila, that Cora Camacho is single. She stifles a giggle, her overly made-up face feigning shock and dismay. "Mr. Alacran! I'm here to interview *you*— not the other way around." She smiles brightly at him.

He has decided she is hard as nails. "Of course," he agrees, smoothly. "How could I forget? Ask me anything. You know," he says, leaning closer to her, "I'm flattered to be on your show. You're our most celebrated media personality—a positive role model for all Filipinas."

Fuck you too, Cora Camacho thinks, her smile widening. "Why, thank you, Mr. Alacran!"

"Cora dear, you make me feel so *old*. You must stop calling me Mister!" He is aware that the age difference between them is slight.

Cora squirms in her TV chair, leaning forward for a camera close-up. "What shall I call you then—Sir?" She winks at her invisible TV audience, devoted millions who identify with her totally. Like them, she is a fan. Like them, she is demanding and devouring.

"You must call me by my first name. Severo."

"Se-ve-ro," Cora Camacho repeats, huskily.

"There, you see? You make me feel young again," Severo Alacran lies on national television.

She hopes he will linger after the taping ends, maybe offer her a ride home in his limousine. She hopes her "Tigress" perfume isn't too overpowering. Maybe he drove himself to the studio today, in one of those fancy sports cars. A Maserati or Ferrari, something Italian and phallic. A young man's car. They could be alone, speeding on the highway, like in those American commercials where the road is endless and smooth, empty of other cars, trucks, buses, jeepneys, pedicabs, barefoot boys riding slow, plodding *carabao*. Cora Camacho loves the obvious, thinks she deserves to ride in an open sports car just once in her life, with the wind undoing her lacquered hair and one of the world's richest men driving beside her.

Cora Camacho moves closer to Severo Alacran. The camera closes in on her determined face. She is glad she always carries an extra toothbrush in her briefcase. The interview is about to end, and she only has time for one more question.

The White Bouquet

Announcing her intention to marry Pepe Carreon, Baby Alacran breaks the customary silence at the dinner table with her quavering voice.

"What a strange idea," her father says. He is preoccupied with the salad on his plate, fresh wild spinach and red Spanish onions tossed with vinegar and a dab of olive oil. "I want more vinegar," he demands, suddenly. "Vinegar and some salt. I can't taste anything!" The servant leans over to pick up his plate, then hesitates.

"You can't," his wife says. "Doctor's orders."

He groans. He longs for red meat, the peppery, greasy taste of pork *adobo*. He imagines the piquant flavor of shrimp wrapped in taro leaves, stewed in a mixture of hot chili and coconut milk.

His daughter repeats her announcement.

"NEVER!" her mother snaps. "He's much too old for you." She eyes Baby with suspicion. "How long has this been going on?"

"Don't be absurd—Pepe's a perfectly nice fellow," her husband interrupts. "His father manages our soft drink plant."

"No, that's Pepe's *uncle*. Pepe's father's in the army," Baby gently corrects her father.

"*Que* horror! I detest army men," Isabel Alacran says.

"You like Nicky," her husband reminds her.

"Nicky's Nicky. The army's vulgar," she retorts.

Severo Alacran is secretly pleased. Perhaps his daughter isn't so hopeless, after all. He drinks thirstily from a glass of Swiss mineral water. This unquenchable thirst is constant, a symptom that has

23

appeared in recent months. "Cut out all salt," Dr. Ernesto Katigbak has advised, "especially soy sauce and *patis*."

"I need my *patis*," Severo Alacran insisted.

"You'll be sorry," Dr. Katigbak warned him.

Severo Alacran asks the hovering servant to fetch him another bottle of mineral water and more ice. He follows her with his curious, detached gaze as she exits briskly into the kitchen. She is young enough, not too homely. She is new at her job. He must remember to corner her later and ask her name.

"That boy is no boy," his wife is saying. "He's at least thirty-five!" She observes the way her husband studies the new maid, and resolves to get rid of her first thing in the morning.

"He's only twenty-seven," Baby squeaks.

Her mother glares at her. "So? You're not even eighteen! I won't allow it. He's some kind of army man or cop, isn't he? How humiliating!"

"Isabel, don't be a bore. He's a perfectly nice fellow. He's been coming to our house since he was a boy—"

"If I had known, I wouldn't have allowed him in my house!" Isabel says to her husband.

"I do business with him," he tells her, coolly.

"He's just been promoted," Baby says to her mother, hastily. "He'll be working with General Ledesma. Don't you remember? Uncle Nick told us about it at dinner—"

Her father nods. "That's right. The other night—"

"I don't remember a thing," her mother snaps.

"It's astonishing, how fast and far the boy has risen in his career," Severo Alacran says, with satisfaction.

"His *army* career," his wife snorts in disdain.

"Don't underestimate the military," Severo Alacran says, finishing his second glass of imported water.

"How long has this been going on?" Isabel asks her daughter.

Baby blushes. "He proposed, last night."

Isabel looks puzzled and annoyed. "When? Where? You never leave that room of yours," she adds, in an accusing tone.

"On the telephone," Baby answers.

"The telephone," Isabel murmurs.

"Ingenious! I like that in a man!" Severo Alacran pats his daughter on the arm. She cringes at his touch, tries not to show it. "How nice for you," he continues, awkwardly. "How nice." He signals for the dishes to be removed.

Isabel disagrees, vehemently. "Disgusting! An army man. Those uniforms . . . He's ugly, besides. One of the ugliest men in Manila. How can you do this to me?" she asks her daughter. "Between the two of you, I see nothing but more ugly children." She shudders. "Dwarves! Hydrocephalics! Harelips! A legacy of bad blood and bad skin . . ."

"For godsake, Isabel. The boy only has a mild case of eczema. Don't get hysterical," Severo Alacran says. "Those things can be treated, with a little cortisone." He remembers with a grimace the time his face broke out in boils, after one day's sunbathing on a private beach in Spain.

"Oh sure, cortisone," Isabel sneers. She gestures toward her daughter, who blushes deeper. "What about her? She has a chronic case of eczema, seborrhea, and God knows what else! What do we do about that?"

"For godsake," Severo Alacran stammers. "He's a nice fellow."

"*Nice*," Isabel mutters to herself. She wishes it were Saturday, and she were in bed with a lover in some anonymous hotel room.

Baby hangs her head in shame. She has been repeatedly reminded that she is not blessed with her mother's presence and feline allure. She is unbearably shy, soft, plump, short like her father, without any hard edges. Her complexion is marred by tiny patches of acne. Her breasts are flat, her waist narrow, her hips much too wide and out of proportion to the rest of her. Her legs are thick and muscular— "peasant legs," her mother calls them—in contrast to her feet, small and delicate. Her only fine points are her melancholy eyes, dark and erotic as the mass of unruly, luxurious black hair that grows down past her tiny waist. Her hair hangs with a sensuous heaviness that suggests something wild buried within her. Baby's mother nags her to tie her hair back, pin it away from her face, wear it up in a bun, braid it, cover it with a scarf, a hat, or a veil, straighten it, cut it all off.

"Whose baby are you?" her mother croons, a lullaby of exasperation. Baby conjures up a powerful childhood memory, envisioning her ornate gold and white crib in all its baroque, overwrought splendor. A canopy of lace, organdy, and pink satin ribbons. Fat, Florentine cupids dance above her, their mischievous faces frozen in permanent glee. Her mother gazes down at her, curious but indifferent. Her father preoccupied, mysterious.

Coffee is served. Baby fidgets in her chair, fighting back the urge to chew her nails. She desperately wants to excuse herself from the table, jump up, and disappear into her room. Wait for Pepe Carreon to call on her private telephone. One ring, hang up. Call again. Listen to him whisper how much he loves her, no matter what. Nothing can stop them, he will say. He is not afraid of her father. Her mother makes him laugh. He speaks in a low, self-assured voice. He thrills her with his dark voice and persistence. She is not sure why he has chosen her, if he means what he says.

Her parents argue the merits of Pepe's proposal. *Doesn't she want to go to finishing school first?* her father asks, without enthusiasm. He'll send her to Switzerland, which he's sure she'll enjoy. She can meet cousin Girlie in Paris. The Swiss are rich and hygienic, their houses sparkle on the Alps, they have window boxes filled with blooming geraniums. It is a picturesque country without poverty or suffering. Even the cows look rich, and are fed chocolates. Don't you adore Swiss chocolates? *How can you discuss chocolates at a time like this?* her mother interrupts. I won't allow it, I won't allow it, I won't allow it, she keeps repeating. *What about college?* her father asks. He is trying to be kind. COLLEGE! Her mother laughs. Your daughter is dimwitted, she tells him. Have you seen her grades? She can barely read.

"You're her mother," he reminds her.

"I certainly am!" Isabel Alacran says, lighting a cigarette. Her hands are shaking. It is strange. Baby has never seen her mother become distraught or lose her composure.

Baby's hands lie in her lap. She is ashamed of their clammy dampness, the gnawed tips of her fingers. She hides them under the table. Mortified, she feels the wetness under her armpits, the sweat darkening the long sleeves of her new dress. She tries to recall if she remembered to spray herself with deodorant this morning, after taking the first of her daily showers. She bathes three times a day, sometimes four in a frantic effort to ward off the nervous sweat that breaks out automatically in her parents' ominous presence. Lately, she's been forgetting to apply the men's deodorant she's forced to use. She is ashamed, sure her mother will make a comment any second. Her mother is impeccable; her mother never sweats.

Her parents continue bickering, oblivious to her. Baby sits very still. It is almost ten o'clock, the time when Pepe usually calls. Soon the phone will ring. She will have to remain in her chair, unable to answer her phone, until her parents excuse her. They insist on an audience for most of their quarrels. Baby tries not to think of Pepe. He will call her later, after midnight. She prefers that; she likes talking to him when she is drowsy, her sleepy voice as husky as his. She pretends she is another woman, someone like her mother. Full of sexual mystery, Baby whispers back into her telephone . . .

She isn't sure she wants to marry Pepe Carreon, but she will. She derives no actual pleasure from the touch of his lean, scarred flesh; she recoils from his gruff, aggressive kisses. She wishes they could remain suspended forever, their only real contact on the telephone. Furtive conversations, late at night. It's his voice she truly loves.

He speaks to her in a language she barely comprehends, using words like *desire, adoration*. It confuses her. *Love* is the only word to which she fully responds, and Pepe uses it freely. Baby decides it is her duty to love him in return. He never calls her stupid. He loves her, even when he hurts her with his touch, his face hovering over hers, a grim mask of flaws and scars as familiar as her own. He loves her no matter what, that's what he says.

She clenches her hands into small fists. As a child, the servants had painted her nails with iodine that burned her mouth every time she chewed them. When that failed, they rubbed her fingertips with fiery chili peppers. Then, the sweating started. Dark patches of salty sweat under her arms. "She sweats like a man!" her mother exclaims, horrified. Baby wears pads under her arms to protect her clothes. She is nine years old. She fears that one day the sweating won't stop, that the perspiration will travel across her chest and back, working its way down, soaking her underwear and skirt, dripping in puddles at her feet. She lives in perpetual shame, and learns early how to make herself sick enough not to have to go to school and confront the cruel stares of the nuns and her classmates.

Dr. Ernesto Katigbak is brought in to examine her. "It's plain and simple anxiety," he tells her parents. "The child must learn to relax . . ." To control her perspiration he prescribes fragrance-free powders, astronomically expensive powders they order from a pharmaceutical firm in California.

Months later, Baby's fingers and toes develop an itchy rash. The rash develops into hideous, watery blisters and open sores. Isabel Alacran is sure her daughter has contracted leprosy, and won't go near her. With her feet swollen and deformed, wrapped in bandages, Baby is forced to spend most of her time in bed or in a wheelchair. She is unable to go to school for more than a year. Dr. Katigbak sends Baby to his wife Emilia, a skin specialist. "I'm just a heart surgeon, after all," he confesses. Severo Alacran threatens to sue him.

Diagnosed as suffering from an extreme case of nonspecific tropical fungus, Baby is bathed daily in ultraviolet solutions that leave a vaguely sulphuric, medicinal smell on her raw skin. The effect is cool, and strangely soothing. The servants paint Baby lavender twice a day, wrapping her hands and feet afterward with fresh bandages. Baby lives in her bed and wheelchair until after her tenth birthday—bathed, changed, and fed by a succession of servants and nurses who don't seem to mind the sight and smell of pus. She reads comic books voraciously, and movie magazines. She memorizes all the lyrics to the latest Tagalog songs in the cheap little "Song Hits" booklets the nurses bring her every week. She sings earnestly, making the nurses laugh. With her or at her, it doesn't matter; it is the first and only time Baby Alacran is indulged by anyone. Her parents sometimes make a show of checking on her progress, standing awkwardly in her doorway on their way to a nightclub. "And how do you feel today?" her father would inquire, cheerfully.

"The same," Baby would always answer.

"What is this nonspecific fungus?" Her parents would ask Dr. Emilia Katigbak impatiently. "How much longer before it goes away?"

"It could dry up and vanish tomorrow. It could last a few more months. Think of your daughter's body as a landscape, a tropical jungle whose moistness breeds this fungus, like moss on trees," the doctor explains.

Six months later, the wheelchair is gone. The sores dry up, but the sweating and nervousness persist. Baby's nail-biting habit returns.

Baby cannot help herself; her hand creeps up to her face, touching her cheek. It moves toward her mouth, rests there. She wonders if she will hear the phone ring, even here, in this room. "Why don't we compromise?" she hears her father saying. "Why don't you at least finish high school? You only have a few weeks left to go before you graduate, then you can think of marriage . . ."

Her mind goes blank. Baby starts to chew.

Exactly three days later, on her way to school, Baby Alacran elopes with Pepe Carreon. It's been carefully planned by Pepe, down to the last detail; the chauffeur and Baby's *yaya* quietly paid off. Baby disappears with her lover to an undisclosed retreat in Baguio. A note is sent to her parents, setting out terms. Baby reveals that she is pregnant.

In her absence, the scandalized nuns have expelled Baby from school. Her mother is placed under sedation by Dr. Ernesto Katigbak. Her father retreats alone to his coconut plantation. More days pass, another note is sent. A phone call is made, late at night: "Your daughter is alive and well," says a male voice. Rumors fly around Manila. The tabloids scream:

BABY KIDNAPPED BY COMMIE INSURGENTS!!!

General Nicasio Ledesma visits the Alacran mansion to offer aid and sympathy. His wife Leonor offers to make novenas. Baby's paternal grandmother, Doña Serafina Alacran, suffers a mild heart attack. When she recovers, she refuses to leave the hospital from shame.

A wedding is hastily arranged. It is Baby's small triumph, her only revenge. Everyone who is anyone is invited. The bride wears a spectacular white gown of silk and chantilly lace, designed with an empire waist to conceal her swollen belly. A tulle veil embroidered with seed pearls crowns her head. Her long black hair has been brushed away from her face, which seems unblemished and almost pretty in the soft evening light. Her gaze is steady and serene.

It is sunset. The Archbishop presides. The crowded cathedral is hot, the air thick with frankincense and the fragrance of assorted perfumes. In the front row, Baby's grandmother Doña Serafina threatens to faint. She wears black, a disapproving frown on her powdered face. The altar is ablaze with candles, the music solemn and ethereal. A hush falls over the crowd. Someone coughs. Others crane their necks to get a better view. It's the wedding of the decade. The women fan themselves and pray, rosaries of onyx and rosewood wound loosely around their wrists. The bride's mother stands erect and dry-eyed, her rage plain for all to see. The groom wears an ill-fitting tuxedo. His bewildered family are lost in the row of spectators jammed against the walls of the church. General Ledesma stands next to him, stiff and impressive in his formal uniform, his chest covered with medals. He is Pepe Carreon's best man.

Severo Alacran beams in the aisle where he waits for his daughter. He offers an elbow to Baby, who staggers under the weight of her belly, her opulent gown, the enormous bouquet of flowers she is carrying: White lilies, white roses, white orchids. "It's bad luck," Doña Serafina mutters to herself. No one hears her.

The bride takes her father's arm. The ringbearer, a frightened little boy of six in velvet jacket and knickers, stumbles on the edge of the bride's endless veil. A murmur runs through the crowd. The boy catches himself, clutching the satin pillow bearing two gold wedding bands. The slow procession begins.

Mister Heartbreak

I make it down to CocoRico around four in the afternoon, before it officially opens. Andres looks surprised. "Oy, Joey. *Kumusta?* What brings you here so early?" He asks me, distracted. Behind the counter, he wipes his precious liquor bottles and glasses, rearranging them over and over again; Andres is never satisfied. "HURRY UP!" He suddenly yells to the unseen Pedro. "It's almost five o'clock! What do you think I'm paying you for! The toilets are a health hazard! Do you think I'm running a cheap whorehouse?" Andres looks at me meaningfully, then frowns when I start laughing. "*Baboy*," he sneers, calling me a pig. I blow him a kiss.

I'm here early because I have nowhere else to go. I slip off my sunglasses, sliding into my usual stool at the bar by the cash register. I am facing the empty dance floor, painted black—my idea and my creation. In a few hours the small black square will be packed with hundreds of gyrating men and boys. Giant speakers crowd the space, but they look good—beautiful, black, and cool. Andres balked at first—he hates to part with money—but I bought them hot from some American guy with connections at the PX. Andres was pleased with the bargain.

"What a horrible day. I'm melting," Andres complains, fanning himself with the latest issue of *Celebrity Pinoy*. He speaks with a Spanish lisp, his high-pitched voice constantly wavering on the brink of hysteria. He's a bundle of exasperation and wrecked nerves, a genuine Manila queen. He rolls his eyes and places one hand at the base of his throat. "This heat is going to kill me. Make it stop—

Dios mio, I wish it would rain! Typhoons bring my blood pressure down. *Puñieta!* If things don't improve, I'll have to see a doctor—"

"You need to stop being so cheap and have the air conditioner fixed. And stop eating so much," I add, watching him gobble roasted peanuts. His mouth never stops working; he gulps down handfuls at a time, and when the peanuts are gone he starts on some Cheez Curls.

He ignores my comments. "My blood is boiling from shouting so much at that idiot! He can't do anything right. I never should've hired that savage—to think I sent him to that missionary school! I should've listened to my instincts. Here I am, an Alacran—always trying to be charitable—"

"Pedro's okay. He works for nothing," I remind him, sipping my Coke. Ice-cold, the way I like it. Andres pours me a shot of white rum, his face flushed. "He's Igorot—what did I expect?" he asks himself, muttering in Tagalog and Spanish. "He eats dogmeat." I've heard all this before, and throw one of my cassettes into the spectacular sound system. James Brown grunts "I Got the Feeling," drowning out Andres's litany of complaints. "I should've known better, Joey. You know me. I'm fussy. CocoRico isn't just some disco, *di ba?* It's my home away from home—and I can't run a place I'm ashamed of! It's a reflection on my family name . . ."

There he goes again, never letting you forget he's an Alacran. Andres Alacran the Queen of Mabini—a relation from the poor side of the family, forced to earn his living. I nod automatically to please Andres, who pours me another shot of rum. I savor its burning sensation on my tongue, feeling snug and fed like a baby. When Andres gets going with one of his tirades, it's easy enough to shut him out. But I also know what he means. CocoRico is home for me too—a safe place, cool and dark and easy on the eyes.

It's only ten past four. I'll wait another hour. I'm on my own special diet these days, longer intervals between times. I've devised it to stay in control; it's become a little game for me, watching the clock, keeping score. I see how well I do, if I can top myself. *I do very well.* It's all filed away in my head, my scorecard. Day one, two, three . . . I don't tell anyone about my new game, except Uncle. Uncle approves of my discipline. I'm careful. If Andres knew, he'd fire me for sure. He'd be sorry to see me go, but he'd fire me anyway. Andres is an old-fashioned man. Junkies make Andres really hysterical.

"PEDRO!" Andres shouts again. "When you're finished with the toilet, I want you to mop these floors one more time! Do you think I'm blind? I can still see dirt, dirt everywhere!" Andres shouts improvised curses at the janitor: *Pedrong Tamad*, Pedrong Headhunter, Pedro the Pagan Dogeater with the Prick of a Monkey and the Brain of a Flea. Then he throws in the usual *gago, tanga, walanghiya, ulol*: stupid, stupid, shameless, stupid, and variations of stupid like dumbfoolidiot. Andres's ranting disgusts me, his shrill voice cuts through my James Brown and pisses me off. "Calm down before you have another heart attack," I growl at Andres, who finally shuts up.

The janitor peers at us from the other side of the dance floor. He wears an old SPORTEX T-shirt I've passed on to him, and Andres's khaki pants several sizes too big for him and torn at the knees. His placid face betrays nothing. "*Señorito* Andres Sir," he begins in a very polite tone of voice, "what about toilet paper?"

"What about it?"

"Toilet paper, *Señorito* Sir."

Grumbling, Andres reaches under the counter where he keeps his supplies under lock and key. "Just one," Andres says, holding out a roll of rough, brand-X toilet paper. "And it better last all night!" I declare, imitating Andres's indignant tone of voice. He shoots me one of those poisonous looks.

The man from Abra limps across the floor, mop in hand, to take the roll of toilet paper from Andres. "*Señorito* Sir," Pedro says, staring at both of us.

"What now?" Andres responds with his customary impatience.

"*Señorito, 'yun kwan, ho.*" Pedro needs something else from his boss, he refers to it without naming it, which infuriates Andres even more.

"*KWAN?* What *kwan* are you talking about?"

Pedro points in the direction of the men's room with his chin. "*Ano ba*, Pedro—am I supposed to read your goddam mind?" Andres shouts. I can't stop laughing. If Andres had his way, toilet paper would be rationed out piece by piece, or better yet, he'd charge his customers for every sheet. Andres believes Filipinos enjoy stealing toilet paper from public bathrooms, that's why there's never any left. "No one shits at my disco," I actually heard him once say to Chiquiting Moreno, trying to justify his miserly ways.

"Paper towels," I say to Andres. "Pedro wants paper towels for CocoRico's toilet, so your customers can wash up . . . Don't you, Pedro?" Pedro nods. Andres has had enough. He pulls out another packet of stiff brown paper and throws it on the floor. "There. Is everybody happy?" Andres glares at us, his hands resting imperiously on his hips. Pedro bends over and picks up the packet without saying a word. When he has disappeared back into the men's room to finish cleaning up, I turn to Andres. "You're really an asshole, boss." It's Andres's turn to blow me a kiss. "Takes one to know one," he answers smugly.

"Mister Heartbreak"—Andres nicknamed me, the first and only time he ever propositioned me. He didn't seem to mind when I turned him down. Sometimes I don't understand him. When I told him about my father, he shook his head in admiration. "You're lucky you have Negro blood," he said, "a little black is good for the soul." This is the miser who treats Pedro like a slave. What a weirdo—a man of contradictions! He makes novenas to Tina Turner and Donna Summer: "Divine *putas* with juicy lips," he calls them. "Immortal women, the way I like them."

"Just like your mother," I tease. Andres, who is notoriously thin-skinned, calls me a black bastard. But I like him just the same.

"DON'T FORGET THE LYSOL!" he yells. Andres leans forward and lights my cigarette. He pours himself some awful Spanish brandy. His puffy mestizo face with its prominent nose and broken blood vessels is tinged pink with excitement; Andres can't wait for his bar to open so he can reign over his establishment, all that really matters to him now. He could never accept the fact that I'm CocoRico's main attraction, the DJ and real star of the show. I'm sure Andres considers me one of his charity cases, just like Pedro.

Andres wears his long, dyed black hair swept back into a greased ponytail. "My gaucho hair, my tango hair," he proudly calls it, adjusting his signature Basque beret. In his youth, Andres Alacran was known as the best tango dancer in Manila. He was so good, they brought him in to teach all the old movie stars at Mabuhay Studios; he even made cameo appearances in quite a few musicals. The Fred Astaire of the Philippines, "El Professor de Tango"—Andres has all the clippings in his scrapbooks from bygone days to prove it.

Andres discovered his one true love, a genuine hermaphrodite named Eugenio/Eugenia, starring in a traveling freak show—the kind I saw as a child in those sleazy carnivals that pitched their tents on the outskirts of Manila. Uncle used to take me. We'd see The Bearded Woman from Mexico, a stocky wonder with glittering eyes, thick wavy hair like Jesus, and a full-length beard. The Borneo Man, a terrifying spectacle with his forlorn eyes and python's body curled up on the makeshift stage. Seven Little Dwarves Direct from Zamboanga, asleep in matching cribs, unfortunate infants with the wrinkled faces of old men, dressed in red jester's caps and matching red booties with tiny bells on the tips of their curled toes. The Man from Java knew Uncle personally and proudly made his living tearing the heads off live chickens with his teeth. The gloomy, dusty carnivals thrilled me. I could never get enough.

Eugenio/Eugenia. Andres talks about him all the time. I've seen pictures. Faded sepia photographs inscribed: "Yours truly, E. 1937. Love, Always." Andres and Eugenio/Eugenia dancing the tango together, Eugenio/Eugenia's head thrown back in a graceful swoon: 1938. *Corny*, but that's a Spaniard for you. 1939: Andres in a striped, boatneck French sweater, the kind he still wears from time to time. "My Apache look," he giggles. He wasn't bad-looking then, I'll have to admit, except for that parrot's beak of a nose. He wore his ridiculous beret in every picture.

Holding a long cigarette holder, Eugenio/Eugenia poses in a beaded flapper dress, his square-jawed, unsmiling face and pretty Chinese eyes heavily made up. Some of the photos are tinted, the hermaphrodite's lips painted a bright red, his cheeks pink and rosy. Everything is slightly off, carefully posed and artificial. "Wasn't he   *35* beautiful?" Andres moans, taking one last look before putting away his snapshots in a treasure chest of souvenirs he preserves in the mini-fridge under the counter. I don't respond.

"He could look like Valentino, dressed to the nines as a man," Andres would reminisce dreamily. "Those were the days! We'd go to town and have dinner with my friends. Then—off to the nightclubs! I even took him home to meet my parents. 'Mama, Papa—meet Eugenio Villarosa, son of Dr. Epifanio Villarosa of Cebu,' I said, making it up as I went along. My father shook his hand. 'I'm sure I know your father,' he said, Mama nodding her head in agreement. They never suspected a thing, invited him to stay for dinner . . ." Andres shakes his head slowly. "I tried to get him in the movies, but failed. That's what he wanted most of all—to be a movie star in one of those Mabuhay musicals. He got so jealous of me and my cameos. 'I can sing and dance better than any woman!' He would say. Poor darling. Mabuhay Studios knew his true identity, and wouldn't give him a chance."

They were Fred Astaire and Ginger Rogers, winning first prize in all the dance contests. It's all true. I've seen pictures of Andres grinning like a fool next to a deadpan Eugenio/Eugenia, now dressed as a woman, both of them holding up trophies and awards. Their stormy love affair lasted on and off for two years. When Andres failed to land him a movie contract, Eugenio/Eugenia left the apartment they shared without warning. It happened right after the Japs occupied Manila. Eugenio/Eugenia disappeared without a trace and was never heard from again. Andres is heartbroken to this day. "There are rumors," he once said, "so many rumors. He was in Macao, singing in a nightclub. Consorting with a Japanese General. Working as a spy for British Intelligence, smuggling bullets in his brassiere. Captured by Chinese guerrillas and executed for alleged war crimes. Can you imagine? They must've died when the autopsy was performed—"

"Autopsy?" Andres likes to impress me with big English words.

"Idiot! Aren't you always watching TV?" he roars impatiently. "Those cop shows you're so crazy about—they're always having autopsies performed on dead people to see why they died!" Andres takes a deep breath, then calms down. "What the hell, Joey. I believe all the *tsismis* about him. He was absolutely capable of anything. He had no morals. The last rumor I heard is probably closest to the truth: that he is very much alive, still living in Macao as a woman, married to some wealthy Portugese."

I toast the memory of the hermaphrodite. "To the love of your life, El Professor—"

Andres nods, finishing his brandy. "To love, *period*—" he adds, grimly.

When I'm not at the bar, I stay in all day, sleeping. I love to sleep. I could sleep for ten, twelve hours at a time. I come alive at twilight, refreshed by my sleep and the cooling effects of the oncoming darkness, the setting sun. I'm energized and electric, a vampire ready for action.

"Night time / is the right / time," as the old song goes, if I'm not with some stranger whose name I have to strain to remember. It's a surprise, waking up like I do, trying to make out the form asleep beside me. Frantically assembling little details in my mind, so I can remember something, anything. So I can say the right thing, collect my money, and say goodbye. Sometimes it's pleasant—waking up like I do, in fancy hotel rooms with clean sheets and the air conditioner always on. What I like best is waking up alone in bachelor apartments—the kind rich guys rent in Makati—surrounded by invisible servants, elaborate stereo systems, bottles of imported cologne and aftershave arranged in gleaming bathrooms Andres would die for, my money waiting for me in an envelope discreetly left on a table near the front door. My steady clients, my one-night stands. Some more thoughtful than others, surprising me with an extra cash bonus, or a chain bracelet with my name engraved in gold. Sometimes I'll steal from them, just to make a point. A bottle of cologne, a Rolex left carelessly next to the bathroom sink. It keeps that element of danger alive in their luxurious rooms. I never keep what's given to me as a gift; I like to let them know how little their trinkets are really worth, what kind of dope I bought with their money. It's a warning, my philosophy of life—keeping things slightly off-balance. It's how I survive.

CocoRico: Andres takes care of introductions at the bar. "You must meet Joey," he'll tell some foreigner, calling me over during a break. "Our famous DJ, he'll keep you dancing." Andres might wink if he's drunk enough, before turning away and letting things happen. He's not a bad boss. I'm paid in cash every night for playing my music. I can play anything I want, as long as the crowd keeps dancing and buying drinks. Andres wants nothing else from me. Everything on the side is mine to keep, as long as I'm discreet, as long as the crowd keeps dancing.

I go home to sleep on the floor of Uncle's shack in Tondo, his square box of odds and ends with its tin roof and plywood walls. The toilet's a hole in the ground Uncle dug outside, with a lean-to roof and a makeshift door. Andres would faint at the sight and smell of it, but it suits me fine.

It's a cozy shelter from the rain, a step above a squatter's hut. I'd never tell Uncle that, of course. He'd slit my throat. I could never insult the house he built with his own hands, it's where I go when I need to get away. It's where I grew up—Uncle's orphanage for wayward boys. I sleep right next to chickens, pigs, goats, and dogs.

Hey, I'm just kidding. Uncle has one mongrel, that's all. An ancient rice hound, probably older than Uncle, with yellow-brown teeth and mangy fur. Ugly as sin. Uncle named the dog Taruk.

One time, when I was around thirteen years old, me and Boy-Boy got drunk and mean on *tuba*. Prodding the dog's scrawny butt with the tips of our shoes, we made it growl by pretending we were going to kick it. The dog was tied up; we kept lunging at it and laughing. Actually, I wouldn't have minded kicking it for real. I'd been tempted, many times. That beast was so mean and ugly, there was no love lost between us. I knew better than to hurt him; that dog is part of Uncle. Boy-Boy and I were just teasing.

Uncle walked in and surprised us. "Don't you bastards have anything better to do? If you'd think with your brains rather than your pricks—GET AWAY FROM THAT ANIMAL! If you touch a hair on his head—"

"That's the ugliest dog in Manila," Boy-Boy snickered, slurring his words. "I'm not even sure it's a dog. Are you sure it's a dog, Joey? See, Uncle—Joey isn't sure!" he hiccuped. "You should have that poor dog put to sleep. That's an ugly, sorry animal—"

Oh shit, I thought. Boy-Boy was asking for it. His face was red and splotchy, his eyes cloudy with alcohol. Like a Chinaman, Boy-Boy couldn't hold his liquor too well. He was a dummy besides, and never knew when to shut up. I could see it all coming, as the old man flew at him.

Uncle slapped Boy-Boy, hard. Boy-Boy's head snapped sideways with the force of the blow. Uncle lifted his arm to hit him again. Boy-Boy said nothing, just stared at him—one cheek redder than the other, his eyes watering with pain. "Uncle," I said softly. I could see Boy-Boy trying to suppress his own anger, fighting back tears. "He didn't mean it," I said.

"You boys are dumb shits. Think you know everything. Bigshots! You don't even know how to drink," the old man sneered, relaxing enough to let his arm drop. He stroked the back of the dog's neck. "Taruk is my dog, you understand? My dog. And this is my house. If you don't like it, get out!"

In silence, we finished the rest of our *tuba*, puffing nervously on harsh, local-made Marlboros. The animal crouched near Uncle's feet, eyeing us with suspicion and growling from time to time. It's hard to challenge Uncle and win. There's always that moment when Uncle loses his sense of humor. His face sets and hardens. He refuses to budge; it's no use arguing with him. He'd just as soon kill you.

As for chickens, goats, and pigs—you can forget it. It's just another one of my jokes. Uncle's no peasant—he's a city man, born and bred in Manila. Busy with schemes and hustles, his various transactions with the Chinese and the cops, he functions in an opium haze, most days. But his mind stays sharp and cunning, no matter what. Don't make a mistake and underestimate the old man. You'll be in for an unpleasant surprise.

There are those who resent Uncle, who call him a pusher and common pimp. There's nothing common about him. When you think about it, the old man's been my savior. Raised me like his own son, along with Boy-Boy, Chito, and Carding. We've outgrown him, but we come back to visit whenever we can. Everyone else has a place of their own. To tell you the truth, I'm the only one who hasn't really left.

Soon.

I'll have it all worked out, soon. I know I will. I have to. I'll hit the jackpot with one of these guys. Leave town. I'll get lucky like Junior. Some foreign woman will sponsor me and take me to the States. Maybe she'll marry me. I'll get my green card. Wouldn't that be something?

I love it when everything falls into place. Don't you?

Soon.

Everything will change, soon.

Jungle Chronicle

The most inaccessible lairs of these wild mountains are inhabited by a great number of those small Negroes called "Negritoes" whom we spoke about earlier; sometimes they are chased out of their homes, taken prisoners, the youngest among them being chosen to be raised by inhabitants in their homes until the age of reason, in the meantime being used for diverse chores, after which they are set free. One of our friends owned one which he gave to us; he was called Panchote, was not lacking in intelligence and was most of all very mischievous.

—*Jean Mallat,* The Philippines *(1846)*

His Mother,
the Whore

There are those who say my poor whore of a mother sold me to
Uncle for fifty pesos. *Zenaida*: desperate, half-crazy, unable to feed
me and herself those last few months. They say she was still young
and still beautiful, they shake their heads solemnly at the terrible
waste. I'm not sure they're telling the whole truth; maybe she was
more ordinary than they remember, an ordinary whore with a ravaged
face. They describe how she jumped in the river, a watery grave black
with human shit, every dead thing and piece of garbage imaginable:
the rotting carcasses of wild dogs and cats, enormous rats with heads
blown off by bullets, broken tree branches and the tangled bouquets
of wilted banana leaves, palm fronds, and *kalachuchi* flowers. When
they pulled out my mother's blue corpse, they say her long black hair
was entwined in this mass of slimy foliage and decay, a gruesome veil
of refuse dragging on the mud beneath her.

This is what they tell me, this is what I've chosen to believe. They
say Zenaida's ghost still haunts that section of the river, a mournful
apparition in the moonlight. Boy-Boy claims he's seen her more than
once, but I don't believe him.

Zenaida. She was a legendary whore, my mother. Disgraced and
abandoned, just like in the movies. Driven to take her own life. My
father was not the first man to promise her anything, that much I
know for sure. Uncle identified her bloated body, arranged for her
pauper's burial. That's why I owe him. No one knew her last name,
what province she came from, if she had any other family besides me.
They say I was five or six years old, that I was mute for months after

her death. I was so dark, small, and thin, they called me *"Gagamba"*—little spider. I went home with Uncle and never shed a tear. I don't want to remember anything else about my sad whore of a mother. I've heard enough. That's why I never ask Uncle. That's why he never brings her up.

He started me doing odd jobs on the street. I sold cigarettes, boiled peanuts, Chiclets, *sampaguita* garlands, *The Metro Manila Daily*, and movie magazines. Legitimate little things that never got me anywhere; I had to compete with all the other kids on the street, running up to cars and buses, pestering tourists, hawking our wares. I hated every minute of it. Then there were times when Uncle pretended he was crippled and blind. I would lead him up to the air-conditioned Toyotas and Mercedes-Benzes where rich people and foreigners sat with their doors locked, trying hard to ignore my outstretched hand at their windows. But Uncle had no patience and little time for begging. "That's for lazy people," he would say.

When I was seven, Uncle taught me to steal. I was wiry, fast, and fearless. A natural talent, according to him. More daring than Boy-Boy, who was two years older than me and cried all the time. I was one of the best pickpockets in Manila; just ask anyone around here. Ask Uncle. I enjoyed stealing, the heady rush that hit me as I disappeared into a crowd, stolen goods burning in my hand. A ring, a watch, a chain around someone's neck. The money sometimes still warm from someone's back pocket. A heady rush of triumph like dope, a pleasure so private, delicious, and powerful. I never once got caught—that's how good I was.

I would do anything for Uncle in those days. We all would—grateful orphans who earned our keep, eager to please and turn our loot over to Uncle. I was the youngest and the smartest, Uncle's favorite.

What they say about me and Uncle isn't true. Just ask Boy and Carding, or Chito at that dress shop in Mabini where he works. The only thing about Uncle is he made things possible. He taught me everything I know.

One of Uncle's whores fucked me when I was ten. I don't remember her name—only her sour smell. A smell that clung to me for days. She looked weary, her movements slow and lumbering, like an ox's. Her broad, ox-face and dark, bloody lipstick repulsed me. I turned my face away, wouldn't let her kiss me.

Sitting at the only table in the middle of the one-room shack, Uncle watched us fuck on the mat a few feet away from him. He was smoking opium, leaning down to scratch behind Taruk's ear while the dog slept. I remember feeling ugly because all my hair had been shaved off by Uncle after he discovered lice. But the ox-woman didn't seem to care, or notice.

Uncle watched us hump and writhe as if it was the most ordinary thing in the world, his expression benign and serene. The woman never spoke, grunting occasionally and shifting my body on top of her with rough hands. With my bald head, I felt ludicrous and smaller than ever, poised on top of the ox-woman's hefty body. I rode her as I would a horse or *carabao*. In the dusty light, her flesh quivered, covered by a film of sweat. I shut my eyes, imagining her giving in to my earnest, awkward thrusts. She may or may not have actually moaned, but I heard what I wanted to hear. Then I forgot about my bald head, my small, skinny body. The pleasure I suddenly felt was extreme and overwhelming. I came quickly. To my surprise, I was eager to fuck the ox-woman again.

Maybe she did it as a favor to Uncle; maybe he had to pay her. I don't know. After the second time fucking her, I fell into a deep sleep. When I woke up, she was long gone. Uncle and his dog were nowhere to be found. All that was left was her smell.

I've had my share of women since, but they don't really interest me. Don't ask me why. To tell you the truth, not much interests me at all. I learned early that men go for me; I like that about them. I don't have to work at being sexy. Ha-ha. Maybe it's my Negro blood.

Uncle says I prefer men because I know them best. I take advantage of the situation, run men around, make them give me money. For me, men are easy. I'm open to anything, though. If I met a rich woman, for example . . . If I met a rich woman, a rich woman who was willing to support me . . . TO LOVE ME NO MATTER WHAT . . . You'd better believe I'd get it up for her too . . . Be her pretty baby. I know how to do that. Make them love me even when I break their hearts, steal, or spend all their money. Sometimes, you'd be amazed.

Maybe I'm lying. Uncle says I was born a liar, that I can't help myself. Lies pour out of my mouth even when I'm sleeping. The truth is, maybe I really like men but just won't admit it. Shit. What's the difference? At least Uncle's proud of me. I know it, though he'd never say so.

Hell. Sometimes I feel the days go by too fast. I get worried. I won't be young forever, and then what? I don't want to end up a shower dancer like Boy-Boy, working nights in some shithole rubbing soap all over my body just so a bunch of fat old men can drool, turning twenty tricks after that, giving away my hard-earned profits to the goddam cops or clubowner! *I'm nobody's slave.* Look at Carding—already finished at nineteen. He'll do anything for money. They've got him by the balls.

Much as I respect him, I don't want to end up like Uncle. With all his brains and experience, he's still small-time. Just an old junkie who rules Tondo, with nothing to show for it. It's not enough for me. Not anymore.

I know I deserve something better. Right now I'm biding my time. I take good care of myself, I'm in control, my life is simple. I do okay spinning my records and turning a few tricks. I'm dressed, fed, and high. I can take it or leave it, break hearts wherever I go. Life can be so sweet, sometimes.

FLOATING BODIES

MAKUPIT, Pangasinan—Three bodies, one headless, were found in Makupit River earlier this week, police said yesterday.

Major Anacleto Rivera, Makupit's police station commander, was visited by General Nicasio Ledesma recently as part of the continuing investigation by the Chief of Staff of turmoil and insurgency in the troubled area. Only last month the body of a woman was found washed up on the banks of the same river. The woman had been beheaded, and her hands and feet were also missing. She has never been identified.

In this week's gruesome discovery, the bloated bodies belonged to two women and a teenage boy. Major Rivera said that the body of the beheaded teenager had been identified as Boy Maytubig, who has been missing since Holy Week. The other two bodies have still not been reclaimed. Rivera also said the victims could have been dumped somewhere else and carried down the Makupit River.

There were unverified reports of two more bodies in advanced states of decomposition found on the riverbank of the neighboring town of Lazaro.

According to a government survey, the frequency of headless and dismembered cadavers washing up on shore has reduced demand for fish in Makupit, which was one of the centers of a thriving fishing industry until these recent alarming discoveries. "It is unfortunate," Major Rivera said to reporters at a press conference hastily called on the steps of Makupit's Church of the Sacred Heart. "Housewives refuse to buy fish caught in Makupit River. We trust that this will prove a temporary situation."

—*The Metro Manila Daily*

Serenade

Romeo Rosales was sulking. Lately, Trinidad Gamboa couldn't seem to pull him out of his dark moods or make him laugh. She had known Romeo for almost a year, and was the only woman besides his widowed mother Gregoria who knew his real name: *Orlando*. Trinidad Gamboa had fallen madly in love the moment she laid eyes on Romeo from the window of her cashier's booth at the Odeon Theater.

They were sitting in a shabby Chinese restaurant on Ongpin Street, at 2:35 on a stifling Saturday afternoon. Before Romeo had met the determined cashier at the Odeon Theater, he had gone to the movies as often as his modest salary allowed, spending all the tips he made as a waiter at the exclusive Monte Vista Country Club. He would see anything: comedies, Tagalog melodramas, westerns, musicals, and religious extravaganzas like *The Ten Commandments*, which played to packed houses in Manila for what seemed an eternity. Audiences never failed to clap and cheer each time the Red Sea parted on the giant screen.

Whenever something miraculous occurred in one of his Hollywood epics, Romeo would turn to Trinidad in awe and say, "Did you see *that*?"

A solemn look on her face, Trinidad would nod as if she were privy to some secret information. "*Camera tricks*," she would inform him, smugly. Romeo was often dumbfounded by how much Trinidad would take for granted; she had answers for everything. It was part of her power over the husky young man.

Today, nothing seemed to be working. Romeo sat in a slump,   *47* staring at his plate of dim sum, occasionally taking wistful sips of his bottle of TruCola. "Let's go see the new Lolita Luna movie, *A Candle Is Burning*," Trinidad said, eagerly. "I'll treat—I just got paid." She had been taught by strict parents to insist that the man pay the bills; to do otherwise meant a woman was easy and desperate. "Having a man pay your way is the only advantage of being born a woman," Trinidad's mother had preached like a broken record, one of the main reasons Trinidad, on the pretext of enrolling at the university, had moved to Manila.

"Didn't you hear me?" Trinidad's tone was indignant. It was noisy and hot in the fast-food restaurant, and flies were buzzing around their table. She fanned herself with a stained and battered cardboard menu, swatting at the energetic flies at every opportunity.

"Yes—I heard you!" Romeo groaned, reaching for Trinidad's hand. "Will you STOP THAT . . . You're driving me crazy!" He took the menu away from her.

"I was only trying to get rid of them," Trinidad said, frowning. "It's not sanitary. *Ano ba*—what's wrong with you? I thought you were a big Lolita Luna fan. It's her latest *bomba* movie, at the Avenue Theater. This time she stars opposite that new guy, Tito Alvarez. *Di ba*, he's your old friend?"

"I don't like the Avenue Theater—it's crawling with rats."

"So what, it's air conditioned, and it's so hot today I think I'm going to faint." A thought occurred to Trinidad. "What's the matter? Are you afraid to see Tito in this movie?"

Romeo finished his soda pop, sucking up the sweet liquid through a straw as noisily as he could. He knew it got on Trinidad's nerves. "Why?" he asked innocently. "Why should I be afraid to see my old *kumpadre* star in his first movie?"

"Because you're jealous. He hasn't answered your letters," Trinidad said.

Romeo slowly got up from the table, making a great show of putting on his SPORTEX jean jacket, the prefaded one with metal studs Trinidad had given him for Christmas. "Don't be an idiot," he said, managing a smile for her. "Tito's a busy man—and I understand he may not have time for his buddy right now. I've got a lot on my mind, Trini—that's all. If you *must* see this movie, then let's go—" Romeo tried to sound casual.

They jumped into the first beat-up taxi that passed in front of the restaurant. Cheered up by getting her way, Trinidad gazed at her pouting lover's face with unconcealed affection. "Wow, Romeo— you're even handsome when you frown!" she teased. "You're my one and only star," she added, cuddling closer to him. Romeo ignored her comment. They rode along the bumpy streets in the clattering, hot, tin box on wheels, beads of perspiration dripping down their faces.

The first time Trinidad Gamboa had set eyes on Romeo Rosales, she was flabbergasted. He was much younger and better looking than her idol, Nestor Noralez, and certainly more available. Romeo definitely belonged in the movies, something she would tell him over and over again during the course of their tempestuous relationship.

Romeo Rosales had pulled out his worn peso bills and shoved them into the cashier's window, oblivious to the smiling cashier with the heavily powdered face and bright lipstick. Her one gold tooth gleamed as she eyed him discreetly, carefully counting out the change before handing it over to him with his ticket.

He wished she'd hurry up. Lolita Luna was starring in *The Agony of Love*, one of her first *bomba* pictures from Mabuhay Studios. He'd seen it twice before, at another theater in Quiapo: Lolita was practically naked in the movie's climactic scene, where she was rescued from drowning by the handsome young fisherman played by the suave, middle-aged Nestor Noralez. If you looked closely enough, you could catch a glimpse of Lolita Luna's erect nipples pressing against the clinging, wet, white nightgown she happened to be wearing when she plunged into the Agno River to kill herself.

Romeo was anxious to see the movie again. He was not only Lolita Luna's biggest fan, but an admirer of the director Max Rodriguez as well; Nestor Noralez he simply put up with as his glorious Lolita's leading man. He would sit back in the comfortable darkness of the air-conditioned Odeon Theater, paying extra for the privilege of sitting in the first-class loge section. He would imagine himself in the Nestor

Noralez role: resisting the sex goddess Lolita Luna's formidable charms while attempting to stay faithful to his loyal, self-effacing wife, portrayed sympathetically by the always dependable Barbara Villanueva.

The smiling cashier was waiting for him when the movie was over. "You must be a real Nestor Noralez fan—just like me!" she said. Romeo grimaced. He stood there awkwardly without saying anything, then turned abruptly and started walking toward his jeepney stop. "Wait!" Trinidad called after him, running to keep up. Romeo stopped to look at her. "My name is Trinidad," she said, suddenly shy but determined to go on. "Trinidad Gamboa. I'm new in Manila . . . What's your name?" When he told her, she asked him in the same friendly tone if he was hungry. Romeo nodded. Romeo Rosales was always hungry and always broke.

"Would you like to join me for *merienda* over there?" she invited him, pointing to the Hong Kong Cafe with her eyebrows.

"I don't eat Chinese food," Romeo said, making a face.

"Have you ever tried it?"

Romeo shook his head. Unperturbed, Trinidad took his arm and led him to the café. He was so *adorable* and *cute*, she thought, like a puppy. "It's okay, Romeo—" she said gaily, "if you don't like what I order, they have other things you can eat."

She was certainly aggressive, which intrigued Romeo.

"Do they have cheeseburgers?" He grinned, flirting back and endearing himself to her. But who would pay the bill? He asked himself. He barely had enough money to pay for the long jeepney ride back to his apartment, the one he shared with his cousin Tomas. Tomorrow morning he would have to borrow money from the frugal Tomas for an even longer jeepney ride to work. Romeo Rosales was in no hurry to go home. He cast a sidelong glance in the cashier's direction as they walked down the street. She wasn't too bad looking, except for too much powder and that flashy gold tooth. She was a little on the thin side, something that would take getting used to; Romeo preferred the voluptuous appeal of Lolita Luna.

"*Dios ko!*" Trinidad squealed, pretending to be exasperated with the young man. "You can have anything you want—cheeseburgers,

Coca-Cola, ice cream—" She couldn't believe it had happened so fast. The man of her dreams was walking next to her, his muscular arm entwined in hers, his sullen profile set off by thick, jet black hair. Perfumed and glossy with pomade, Romeo's hair was carefully combed and arranged so that his natural curls tumbled carelessly down his forehead. Like Sal Mineo in *Rebel Without a Cause.* Elvis Presley in *Jailhouse Rock.* Or that daredevil Nestor Noralez in *Tormented.*

They sat down in the crowded café, next to a booth jammed with giggling schoolgirls in plaid uniforms. Trinidad could feel their curious eyes on Romeo Rosales, and sat proud and erect in her booth. *Look, but don't touch*—she thought.

"By the way," she said to Romeo, "I'll treat."

Romeo made a feeble show of protest: "No, no, I insist, Trini—"

He had called her *Trini.* Blushing, Trinidad waved her hand in a grand, dismissive gesture. "No, no, Romeo. I'll treat. You can help me celebrate my birthday," she lied, surprised by her own boldness.

Romeo gave her a puzzled look, then brightened considerably. This girl might be crazy, he said to himself, but what do I have to lose. He wondered how old she was, guessing she was in her late twenties or early thirties. He wondered if she would lie to him when he felt comfortable enough to ask her. He figured she probably would. He relaxed in his seat, and let her persuade him to try Chinese food. She ordered noodles stir-fried with shrimp and pork. *Not bad*, Romeo admitted to himself, eating with gusto. The noodles tasted just like his mother's *pancit.* Trinidad giggled. "Of course! Who do you think invented *pancit*? The Chinese!" She informed him, merrily. Romeo wolfed down the food Trinidad served him, while she ate demurely, picking at her food and professing a lack of appetite. Actually Trinidad was quite hungry herself, but she remembered her mother saying that truly feminine women hardly ate at all, at least not in public.

Romeo watched the coy and smiling cashier with a great deal of amusement. When the meal was over he confessed to feeling dizzy with "fascination" for Trinidad—an English word which he confused with "infatuation." Trinidad didn't bother to correct him. Without too much effort, he convinced her to go home with him to his one-room apartment. Trinidad Gamboa paid for the expensive taxi ride to Pasay City. She was devirginated at exactly 11:47 P.M. on a Thursday evening, on Romeo's creaking cot. The anxious, sweating couple was separated from Romeo's sleeping cousin Tomas by a flimsy curtain draped over a wire strung from both ends of the room. For Romeo, it was a surprising experience. He had never been with a virgin, and he found it rather bewildering. For Trinidad, it was bloody, painful, and a profound relief. She had been waiting for this exact moment all her life.

The thought of Romeo with another woman was enough to drive Trinidad Gamboa insane. She wrote her parents in Cebu, hinting at a possible engagement to her nineteen-year-old lover. Her mother wrote back: "What about your studies? Why haven't you enrolled at the university? WHO IS ROMEO ROSALES? What town is he from? How old is he? Does he have a job? Make sure your Aunt Teresing writes me . . ."

Her father, a retired tax collector, was not impressed with his daughter's romantic illusions. He wrote tersely: "COME HOME. I did not give you permission to go to Manila to live a life of sin. WHO IS ROMEO ROSALES? You have disappointed us greatly by postponing your enrollment at the university. Your mother is sick with worry, and I will not tolerate any of your escapades! Come home soon, or I will cut off your monthly allowance. Romeo Rosales is not worthy of you . . ." Trinidad Gamboa's father signed his letter with a forbidding, emphatic flourish.

Trinidad was twenty-eight years old, and the thought of life as a spinster back in her home town terrified her. She would be subject to shame and humiliation, considered a failure in her parents' unforgiving eyes. It looked as if enrolling at the university in Manila really would be her last chance to make something of her uneventful life, if she didn't quickly find a husband. She had been grasping at straws when she first arrived in Manila, but now she had Romeo Rosales, a bright star in her hazy constellation.

Weeks went by. She didn't respond to her father's letter. If her father cut off her stipend, she would just have to work full-time as a cashier at the Odeon. Or supplement her income by taking a second job as salesgirl at SPORTEX, the department store owned by the prominent Alacran family. It was something Trinidad actually wanted to do. She spent long hours browsing through the chilly, air-conditioned floors, avoiding the scorching heat outside. She fingered the overpriced dresses and tried on patent leather shoes, dreaming of the day she could use a salesgirl's twenty-percent discount.

Trinidad Gamboa was elated by her plans. She was sure she could always manage. She had never defied her father and had always placed her parents' concerns above her own. It was time for a change. She felt giddy with her newfound freedom, yet still unsure about her momentary happiness with Romeo. There were days her uncertainty gnawed away at her.

Romeo Rosales was not living up to all her expectations. In unsubtle ways, Trinidad hinted she would like to take him home to Cebu to meet her parents. All expenses paid, of course. Romeo refused, not even attempting to make any excuses. She then reminded him that she was anxious to meet his widowed mother, that she would like to accompany him on his monthly visits to the tiny village in Batangas where she lived with his younger brother. Romeo diverted Trinidad with his boundless capacity for sweet talk, something he'd learned from countless hours of studying Nestor Noralez movies.

"Your eyes are mysterious, deep, dark pools that never fail to hypnotize me," Romeo would whisper, taking the frail Trinidad in his arms. She would allow herself to be led to the big round bed covered by a red satin sheet, the only piece of furniture in their regular meeting place, the mirrored Room #223 in the seedy and inexpensive Motel Tropicana.

Her face might be plain, and her body much too slender; Romeo had never gotten used to her sharp, bony angles and gold front tooth. But Trinidad Gamboa was receptive and eager in bed, and he would simply close his eyes and imagine the torrid siren Lolita Luna, ecstatic beneath his own pumping body. He could hear Lolita Luna moaning as he murmured in Trinidad's ear: "My sweet, perfumed flower— my darling madonna—my whore—"

His insatiable lust made Trinidad Gamboa feel like the most desirable woman in the world. She forgave him everything, even his erratic moods and reluctance to meet her family. Every Friday, she went to confession at the old Santa Mesa Church, one block away from her Aunt Teresing's boarding house. The swarthy priest always said the same things to her: "You are committing mortal sin. You will definitely burn in hell if you don't put a stop to your impure relationship. For penance, say the rosary seven times."

Obediently, Trinidad Gamboa would say her rosaries and light votive candles at the foot of a life-size statue of a fair-skinned, fair-haired Virgin Mary. The statue looked down at her with an impassive, blue glass gaze, which Trinidad mistook for divine compassion. Always sure her heart was in the right place and that she would eventually go to heaven, Trinidad Gamboa would leave the church at peace.

She waited patiently for the moment when Romeo Rosales would come to his senses. He would fall on his knees, repentant. He would bury his pretty face in her skirt and weep, begging her forgiveness and thanking her for all she had done for him. He would praise her selflessness and ask her to marry him. Just as Nestor Noralez finally asked the saintly and equally generous Barbara Villanueva, in that memorable Mabuhay Studios musical *Serenade*.

Tsismis

(Hoy, bruja! Kumusta? Ano ba—long time no hear! What's the latest *balita? Sige na*—sit down let's make *tsismis.* You want Sarsi or TruCola? Diet Coke or San Miguel? *Dios ko 'day,* it's too hot for coffee . . . Too much beer, *bruja*—you're gonna end up fat like your brother if you don't watch out.)

We blame everything on the heat. It's been a typical Saturday, not much is accomplished. My mother Dolores spends hours at SPOR-TEX with Pucha's mother, my *Tita* Florence. As usual, they will return without any purchases, complaining loudly of crowds, snooty salesgirls, and exhaustion. *"Que ba,* I think those people just mill around the store because it's air-conditioned!" Tita Florence sniffs in disgust. She is an older, plumper version of Pucha, with the same sharp nose and flaring nostrils.

My cousin Pucha and I get our weekly manicure, pedicure, and complimentary foot massage at Jojo's New Yorker, right across the street from the Foodarama Supermarket and ten times cheaper than Chiquiting Moreno's Makati "salon"—*a saloon of a salon,* as my father describes it, strictly for society matrons and high-priced whores. My father thinks women are constantly being duped, especially by *baklas* who run trendy beauty parlors.

"Why can't we go to Makati just this once?" Pucha whines. "We have the car and driver, it's not so far—" Pucha hates it every time we go to Jojo's. "Because Jojo's right around the corner," I sigh, "and I've only got one hundred pesos to spend for *both* of us. That won't even get you a shampoo at Chiquiting's." That shuts Pucha up. Pucha never has enough money, and she's stingy besides. It depresses her to sit in Jojo's unpretentious beauty parlor with its modest neighborhood clientele, several steps down the social ladder Pucha's been climbing so fiercely since the day she was born. Jojo waits on most of her customers herself and has no time for idle chatter. She's an enterprising woman with frosted tips in her short hair and a large mole on her nose. Pucha's sure Jojo's a lesbian, and mistakes all of Jojo's gestures toward her as passionate come-ons.

There is only one other unglamourous patron this early Saturday morning, wearing a faded house dress and rubber slippers; she dozes with her mouth open, slumped under Jojo's prehistoric hair dryer. "*Que horror*," Pucha mutters, as we walk past the sleeping woman.

(*Hoy,* and how do you think that *alembong* Nestor used to pay his rent? *Aba, sino pa*—who do you think told me? Max himself, that's who. *Chica,* they went to the same school and no matter what Nestor says, Nestor is definitely the same age as Max! Exactly, *doña* . . . Max happened to be right there in the lobby of the Manila Hotel and saw the whole thing with his own eyes . . .)

One of Pucha's goals in life is to be able to afford going to Chiquiting Moreno's whenever she wants. Like when she feels too lazy to wash her own hair, for example. The first and only time either one of us ever went to Chiquiting's was when we all got our hair done for my cousin Ricky's wedding—Pucha, *Tita* Florence, my mother, and me. My mother paid the exorbitant bill. Pucha still brags about it to this day. I can't tell what's more important to her: being invited to debutante parties or having Chiquiting lacquer her hair. She thinks marrying that creepy Boomboom will insure her social standing. She's probably right. Ahhhh, people will whisper, here comes Mrs. Doña Pucha Alacran with a new hairdo. Plus, money will never be a problem. Pucha imagines countless hours of pleasure decorating and redecorating the fabulous rococo palace of her dreams. When she gets carried away with her high and mighty plans, she describes her fantasy future wedding to Boomboom in gory detail, the gown her mother will order from some Frenchman, and all the guests she's planning to invite, including the President. "I'll insist we can't live in

Greenhills," Pucha says, with authority. "Too many Chinese." "What do you care," I respond, bored to death, "so long as they're *rich*?" Pucha frowns. "But Rio—even the rich ones contaminate the water with hepatitis! Boomboom said so." "Be careful he doesn't find out about our family history," I warn her, trying my best to look solemn. Pucha is mystified by my remark. "*Que ba*—what family history?" I react with a combination of innocence and surprise. "Didn't your father tell you about our great-great-grandmother Assumpta Gonzaga? Her real name was Assumpta Ching Ming Soong, and she was from the only Christian family in Shanghai." Pucha Gonzaga gasps in horror, her elaborate wedding plans temporarily ruined.

(*Naku!* Doña Booding was sitting there having her *merienda,* you know how she likes her ice cream and sweets . . . The chamber orchestra was playing *merienda* music—a little Strauss waltz mixed in with the "Jealousy" tango, maybe some *kundiman* mixed in with the cha-cha—*alam mo na,* real *halo-halo* stuff. Doña Booding was waiting for Nestor in the lobby, waiting to spy on him and catch him by surprise . . . She was sitting partially hidden by some potted palm . . . From what Max told me, she waited for hours—stuffing her face with *halo-halo* sundaes and chocolate cake . . . *Bruja,* will you stop laughing?)

When my grandfather Whitman died, everyone expected me to cry, but I didn't. My *Lola* Narcisa went back to Davao after the funeral, to sell her house and pick up the rest of her things. My mother Dolores picked me up at school the day it happened. I knew something was wrong because she was alone in the car, except for our driver Macario. Where was Lorenza? My mother was wearing black, and her eyes were swollen from crying. *He died in his sleep,* she said, looking out the window and avoiding my gaze. *He never woke up. It was a good thing—he didn't suffer,* she was sure of it. All the American doctors were sure of it. Everything started to change after his death. My mother fell in love with the Brazilian ambassador, Jaime Oliveira. My father got promoted to Vice President In Charge Of Acquisitions for Severo Alacran's conglomerate, International Coconut Investments. Intercoco, for short. He was jokingly referred to as Severo Alacran's head *bugaw* or chief pimp by Pucha's father, my joker of an uncle, Agustin. My father thought it was funny, but no one else in the family did.

Part of my father's job includes playing golf from dawn until dusk every Saturday, and Sundays after Mass, gambling for high stakes with his boss Severo Alacran, the nearsighted Judge Peter Ramos, Congressman Diosdado "Cyanide" Abad, Dr. Ernesto Katigbak, and occasionally even General Nicasio Ledesma. Congressman Abad cheats to win, and doesn't care who knows it. The caddies are in cahoots with the flamboyant politician and Severo Alacran, who is less blatant about his cheating. The Congressman is president of the board at Monte Vista, and Severo Alacran is Severo Alacran; both men are therefore untouchable.

My mother Dolores is indifferent to golf and the women like Dr. Emilia Katigbak who play it on the women's course, a segregated area back there somewhere behind the club. My mother only comes to the Monte Vista to sit in the clubhouse dining room and watch Jaime Oliveira playing tennis on the courts below her window. She always sits at the same table, with Mrs. Goldenberg the American consul's wife, Mimi Pelayo, or Cherry Pie Lozano's mother.

(Nestor finally strolls in with someone else, some skinny mestizo *daw,* some boy in tight pants, according to Max. Doña Booding jumps up from her chair, knocking over the potted palm and spilling cake and *halo-halo* sundae all over the carpet . . . She starts screaming at the top of her lungs: "I want my money back! I want my Rolex! My car! My apartment!" The orchestra keeps right on playing—*alam mo na,* no one in the Manila Hotel would dare to stop Doña Booding! She screams and claws at Nestor, she rips the Rolex off his wrist, she curses his dead mother . . . Then she accuses him of being a *bakla*—that's right, in front of the whole world . . .)

My father is a privileged member and stockholder in the sprawling country club, where the magnificent greens are rumored to be infested with cobras, and the high-beamed ceilings of the open-air dining pavilions are a nesting-place for bats. Uncle Agustin claims the bats are useful for keeping away mosquitoes, and the snakes are useful for keeping away Japanese tourists. Uncle Agustin hates the Japanese, and is not a member of the Monte Vista. He is a frequent guest of my father's, who also secured him a job with Intercoco. When Uncle Agustin gambled away his inheritance, my father went to Severo Alacran and begged him to hire his older brother. Fortunately, Severo Alacran repays favors. Though he was well aware of Uncle Agustin's abrasive personality, a job was especially created for him, and he became Associate Vice President in Charge of Shuffling Papers at the Quezon City branch of Intercoco. It is a bogus position which pays him enough to maintain a modest bungalow and two hardworking servants who shop, cook, clean, launder, garden, chauffeur, and look after his lazy, demanding children. "Nothing to be ashamed of!" Uncle Agustin once declared to my father, "We have everything we need."

My father knows perfectly well his brother resents him for all he's done. It doesn't matter. We spend every Saturday together—Pucha's family and mine. Pucha and I come home from Jojo's beauty parlor, our nails filed and painted "Tangerine Tango" or "Jungle Red." We shut ourselves in my dismal bedroom, surrounded by copies of *Celebrity Pinoy* magazine and trays of food. It's a dead weekend for the social butterfly Pucha. No parties to attend, no boys panting on the telephone. She's been punished by her mother for giving Boomboom Alacran her valuable pearl ring, which Boomboom wears dangling from a chain around his fat neck. Pucha got the idea from an Elvis Presley song. While *Tita* Florence is pleased by the attention her daughter is getting from an Alacran, she's no fool—Pucha looks older than her age, but she's still quite a few years younger than Boomboom. *Tita* Florence is determined to preserve Pucha's precious virginity.

My mother and *Tita* Florence are having *merienda* in my mother's sitting room. When my father and Uncle Agustin finish their golf, they'll come home and we'll all sit down to one of my mother's lavish Saturday night dinners. Pucha's brother Mikey and my brother Raul will show up just in time to eat—they always do, they're like animals, they can smell food from miles away.

(How should I know? Nestor was a nobody then, that's why . . . Only Max remembers. Nestor stood there, cool as cool *daw*, then unzipped his pants. "I owe you nothing," he said, taking out his *titing* and waving it at Doña Booding and all the people watching in the lobby. "I paid

for everything with *this.*" Then he stuffed it back in his pants and walked
away.)

My father orders us to call Severo and Isabel Alacran "*Tito*" and
"*Tita,*" as if we're related by blood. "We're related by money," Uncle
Agustin snickers, proud of his connection, however marginal, to the
king. My cousin Pucha is just like her father; she leaps at every
chance to call Severo Alacran "uncle," says it loud enough for everyone to hear. She flirts with him in her coy, petulant way. I've caught
the old man looking at her, sizing her up slowly. I can tell he finds
my silly cousin desirable; her eagerness amuses him. I've told her it's
disgusting, she should lie down on a bed of money and die, the way
she acts these days. She pisses me off so much, sometimes I'm embarrassed to be seen with her—wiggling and strutting all over the
place. It's a wonder she's still a virgin. "*Ay, prima!*" Pucha laughs,
feigning shock at my sour observations, "for such a baby, you have
a dirty mind." "Severo Alacran keeps staring at your boobs," I
complain, "and you keep leading him on!" Pucha actually looks
pleased. "Rio, take my advice," she says, in that condescending tone
of hers. "Go to confession and stop being so *corny.*"

(Max is Max but I believe him when it comes to Nestor's *kalokohan.*
You know what happened to Doña Booding? How she gave up everything for God and took to calling herself La Sultana and telling fortunes?
The boy with Nestor? how should I know? *Dios ko,* you ask too many
questions. He's probably dead, according to Max . . . And Nestor—
puwede ba, just look at him! *Wala nang* sex appeal—*kawawa naman,*
it's Nestor's turn to have to pay for it now.)

Sometimes Pucha and I go swimming at the club. We go Saturdays
after lunch, or Sundays we'll go have *merienda*—eat German hot dogs
so long and thick Pucha can't stop giggling. The waiters stare at her
and grin, it's awful—everything reminds Pucha of sex. We put on
our bathing suits and lounge by the pool deck after eating, so Pucha
can scan the horizon for the arrival of Boomboom Alacran and his
foulmouthed friends. As soon as she spots them, Pucha starts posing.
Pucha doesn't really know how to swim and thinks bathing suits have
been created for the sole purpose of showing off her body. I jump in

the pool and swim as far from them as I can, relieved that my job of keeping my ambitious cousin company is over.

The sign by the Monte Vista pool reads:

NO YAYAS ALLOWED TO SWIM

Which means that when Congressman Abad's daughter Peachy was five years old, her *yaya* Ana had no business jumping in the pool to save her from drowning. Ana jumped in anyway, dressed in her spotless white uniform and matching white plastic slippers. She pulled Peachy out of the pool before the stupid lifeguard even noticed anything was wrong. My mother told us all about it—she was sitting right there by the pool and would've jumped in herself except that like Pucha, my mother can't swim.

Sprikitik

Here we are at dinner, the Gonzaga clan on a Saturday night. My bombastic Uncle Agustin goes on about the General, complaining endlessly about the day's golf game, the money he lost because Congressman Abad cheated and no one did anything about it. It's the same old story, every time *Tito* Agustin loses a game. He'd rather blame it on someone else than admit he's a shitty golfer—the butt of many jokes at the Monte Vista.

Pacita serves us peppery sweet *lechon kawali*, grilled *bangus*, and her specialty, an Ilocano-inspired *pinakbet* with bitter-melon, squash, okra, and stringbeans stewed with cloves of garlic, bits of pork fat, and salty fermented shrimp *bagoong*. Pucha won't eat *pinakbet*, she says it gives her bad breath. Neither will Uncle Agustin. They ask Pacita to open and heat up a can of Heinz Pork'n'Beans instead. Pucha loves her canned beans because they're gooey with molasses, but most of all because they're expensive and imported. We eat in happy silence, our insides swimming in sugar, grease, and vinegar.

The ancient ceiling fan squeaks, twirling at medium speed. Between mouthfuls, Uncle Agustin predicts monsoon rain, a disastrous early typhoon season. "It's much too hot to go on this way—we need relief." Aida and Lorenza stand by with homemade contraptions the gardener Godofredo has constructed: long wooden sticks with newspaper streamers attached to the ends, designed to fan away flying insects the way a *carabao* or horse flicks its tail.

"I can't imagine him doing it," *Tita* Florence says, about the Congressman. "He's such a darling man, so kind and charitable, so darling—are you sure, Agustin?" She shakes her head slowly at the awful thought—she shakes her head slowly and eats more than anyone else at the table. A dainty predator, she devours tiny portions bit by bit, chewing methodically with a rapturous look on her face. Uncle Agustin looks at his wife with murder in his eyes. He says nothing, then turns to my father and begins recounting Severo Alacran's latest escapade with some foreigner's wife. "He's fond of her red hair," Uncle Agustin says, winking obscenely. Mikey and Raul grin; Pucha kicks me under the table. *Tita* Florence is aghast, and puts down her fork and spoon long enough to say: "Agustin, *por dios*—haven't I warned you? You will learn wisdom on your deathbed and then—it will be much too late."

After dinner we drag ourselves to the adjoining living room for coffee, cigars, and Spanish brandy. "We're out of French cognac, I'm afraid," my mother apologizes. "Excellent, excellent. The French are over-rated! Spanish brandy is actually the best in the world," Uncle Agustin says, anxiously waiting as my father pours him a double. Pucha and I sit next to each other on the rattan couch, drowsy and overfed. "Johnny Walker Black, on the rocks for me," my cousin Mikey says to Aida. My father gives him a curious glance. "Miguel. I didn't know you drank—since when?" Mikey shrugs, avoiding his mother's worried look. Emboldened by Mikey, my brother asks for a beer and is handed a TruCola by my mother instead. "Shit," he mutters, under his breath. "Excuse me, Raul—what did you say?" My mother asks sweetly.

"Genuine *ba ito*, or *putok*?" Mikey asks Aida when she returns with his drink. It is a reference to the common practice of selling deadly mixtures of rubbing alcohol and brown tea in brand-name bottles as imported liquor. Aida is confused by my insolent cousin's tone. She answers in a meek voice. "Johnny *Lumalakad, ho.*" "Genuine *ba ito*, or *putok*?" Mikey repeats, growing impatient. He addresses her in a loud voice, as if she were retarded. Aida's face flushes crimson and I want to leave the room, which suddenly makes me feel stifled. Raul joins in the fun. "That Johnny Walker is *sprikitik*, boss!" Mikey cracks up. My mother rescues Aida from further embarrassment. "Never mind, Aida. The boys are just teasing—you can go now and have your dinner. Just ask Fely or Pacita to make more coffee for us." Relieved, Aida hurries out of the room. My mother turns to my father. "I don't get it, Freddie. What's the difference between *putok* and *sprikitik*? Don't they both mean fake?"

My father thinks for a moment. "You might say Congressman Abad *sprikitiks* when he plays golf, but General Ledesma rewards his army with cases of *putok* liquor."

Tita Florence fans herself with a woven *pye-pye*. "*Dios mio*, Freddie. What are you making *bola-bola* about?"

"It's a known fact, Florence," *Tito* Agustin informs her. *Tita* Florence rolls her eyes in disbelief, fanning herself with renewed vigor.

"Papi," Mikey says to his father, "they say the soldiers don't know the difference, and they're grateful! They say that's why the soldiers are so loyal to the General. He gives them cases and cases of *putok* labeled Dewar's Scotch, or Johnny Walker. The *putok* is so terrible, their guts rot and burn, and they wake up with killer hangovers. They say that's why Ledesma's men stay mean-spirited and ready to kill—" My cousin Mikey says all this with admiration. My brother looks impressed. Pucha leans over to whisper in my ear. "This is boring. I think I'm going to vomit."

"The General is from a good family," *Tito* Agustin says to my mother. "Do you remember the Ledesmas from Tarlac?" My mother shakes her head. *Tita* Florence puts down her fan to correct her husband. "Wrong, Agustin, as usual. Nicasio is the outside son of Don Amado Avila and the laundress Catalina. I know because my mother is from the same town as the Avilas—"

My mother's eyes widen. "You mean he's actually Senator Avila's half-brother?"

"And the president's former chauffeur," *Tita* Florence nods triumphantly. "That's why the General hates the Senator so much."

Uncle Agustin looks irritated. "You're all wrong! Severo once told me that the Ledesmas and the Avilas are cousins, from feuding families in Tarlac."

We are all ears—it's better than any episode of *Love Letters*, and even Pucha perks up.

"What about those camps?" my brother Raul suddenly asks.

"What camps?" My father is annoyed. *Tita* Florence and my mother seem perplexed, while Pucha looks bored. Uncle Agustin keeps drinking.

"The camps," Raul repeats. "The General runs the main one, *di ba*?" He turns to my father. "You know—for subversives. Senator Avila's always denouncing them—he calls them torture camps."

"Senator Avila," Uncle Agustin groans. "*Por favor*, Freddie—how about another drink?"

"Senator Avila has no proof. It's those foreign newspapers again—"

"American sensationalism," Uncle Agustin agrees.

"Does anyone want more coffee?" my mother wants to know.

"How about you, Agustin?" *Tita* Florence gives my uncle a meaningful look. Uncle Agustin ignores her.

"Boomboom Alacran went to the main camp, just to see for himself. *Di ba*, Mikey? You told me," Raul says. Mikey nods.

"It's right there, a few kilometers outside Manila. Looks like an ordinary army barracks *daw*, but if you're ever arrested—" Mikey gives us an exaggerated shiver. "It's true," he insists, "Boomboom tells me everything."

"Boomboom's full of shit," Uncle Agustin says, smiling. He lights a fresh cigar.

"AGUSTIN!" *Tita* Florence's hand flies to her watermelon breasts in a gesture of dismay. "Your language—the children!"

"All the Alacrans are full of shit," my father adds. "Severo Alacran built his empire on shit: bullshit." The men can't stop laughing, including my brother. He feels extremely grown-up, I can tell.

My father leaves to make one of his important phone calls in his private study. It is past ten o'clock. My mother watches him close the door to his study with a peculiar look on her face. I am the only one who seems to notice; everyone else is busy chattering or getting drunk. "Would anyone care for coffee?" my mother asks wearily. "No thank you, Dolores—that's the third time you've asked!" *Tita* Florence says. She starts to get up from her chair, smoothing the wrinkles on her rayon skirt. "Come along, Agustin—it's late." Uncle Agustin starts to say something to her then thinks the better of it. He gets up slowly, a satisfied smirk on his face. "A lovely evening, Dolores—you're the best hostess in town! Isn't she the best, Florence?" My *Tita* Florence is silent. Uncle Agustin barely avoids crashing through the furniture as he makes his way to the foyer. "Mikey," he barks, "go find that sister of yours! What's she doing in the bathroom? Putting on more makeup?"

I dutifully kiss one of *Tita* Florence's rouged cheeks. She smells like garlic and "Evening in Paris." For the first time in the entire evening, *Tita* Florence focuses on me. "And how is your *Lola* Narcisa these days, Rio?" She pats me on the head.

Mikey leads a sullen Pucha back into the foyer where we all stand, waiting uneasily for my father to finish his mysterious phone call and join us in saying good-night. Pucha signals me with her eyebrows, then whispers she'll call me first thing in the morning. We'll go over the night's *tsismis*, the juicy gossip that is the center of our lives. If the laundress Catalina is really the General's mother, then who is Apolinaria Cuevas? Who is the red-haired foreigner's wife *Tito* Severo is fucking? "Shit," Pucha will say, impressed. "Did you hear the way my father and your father both said *shit*?"

Her Eminent Ascent into Heaven

On Bougainvillea Road, located within one of the posh Makati sub-divisions patrolled by men in blue uniforms, a jeep full of restless soldiers is parked at the top of General Nicasio Ledesma's hilltop driveway. The soldiers smoke and laugh softly among themselves; it is very late, after all, and they know enough not to draw attention to themselves by making too much noise. The youngest complains of being hungry. "Should I knock on the back door and tell the old woman to bring us some food?" he asks his companions. "*Sige, 'bro*—wake her up," one of them tells him. Another soldier climbs out of the jeep, yawns and stretches his arms, then saunters up to a wall of the General's windowless villa to take a piss. The soldiers find it hard to stay awake. It has been a long, uneventful night, with only the vibrating cicadas filling the sultry silence. In the encyclopedia-lined study of the fortresslike house, General Ledesma has been in conference with his protégé Pepe Carreon for hours.

Upstairs, the General's wife tosses and turns on her spartan bed, a regulation army cot she once asked her husband to send over from one of the barracks. The General found her request perfectly understandable, in light of her devotion to an austere, forbidding God and her earnest struggles to earn sainthood through denial. A former piano teacher and distant cousin of the General, Leonor Bautista was forced to marry Nicasio Ledesma by her elderly parents. After much initial resistance and the intervention of her parish priest, Leonor Bautista succumbed and married the General. She found life with the much-decorated war hero undemanding and rather tranquil, except for the strangers frequently trooping in and out of her house. She is not expected to accompany the General to the social functions he attends; for this she is eternally grateful. The General seems to want nothing from her at all after their marriage. He showed no reaction when the reclusive Leonor immediately asked for her own bedroom down the hall from where he slept. "The smaller the better," Leonor said. "Leave the walls unpainted. I want no air conditioning, no electric fans, no mirrors. I would like to be as far away from you as possible," she added, with a cryptic smile. It was their wedding night, one of the rare occasions when Leonor spoke to her husband directly. From then on, Leonor Ledesma divided her life evenly between "good days" and "bad."

Good days are spent collecting and sorting old clothes, toys, medicine, and canned goods for the Sisters Of Mercy Orphanage. "Bad" she spends locked in her narrow room, fasting on water and praying prostrate on the cold cement floor to her beloved Santo Niño statue, a three-foot tall Holy Child dressed in a red velvet robe embroidered with real pearls and semiprecious gems. Every few months, the General's wife retreats to a Carmelite nunnery in Baguio for rigorous meditation and more prayer in an atmosphere heavy with imposed silence. The General encourages her spiritual odysseys and asks her to pray for him. "The Lord listens to you and only you," he tells her. "Beg the Lord's forgiveness on my behalf." Leonor Ledesma gives her husband a pitying look, almost tempted to speak. After her parents die, the General arranges for her piano to be brought to Manila by army truck, but she refuses to acknowledge its presence in her living room. In frustration, the General finally donates the dusty, out-of-tune piano to the Sisters Of Mercy Orphanage, which pleases Leonor immensely. She writes him a note, which is brought to him on his breakfast tray by the gray-haired servant Hortensia: "You have atoned for some of your sins, Nicasio—but only some. The Sisters were grateful for your gift, as were the poor children of the *hospicio*. I will make a novena in your honor this Wednesday."

Leonor Ledesma sees her husband as a curious toad disturbing the solitude of her tropical fortress with endless midnight meetings. "Who are those men outside making noise?" she asks Hortensia.

"His soldiers, *Señora*," Hortensia replies, "only his soldiers."

"Are we at war again?"

Hortensia shakes her head. *"Hindi, ho."*

"Tell them they should be quiet or go home!" Leonor Ledesma pauses before asking her next question. "And who is that bloodsucker always eating at my dinner table?"

Hortensia wants to laugh, but knows better. *"Si* Mister Carreon, *Señora."*

"The eldest son?" Leonor Ledesma has always suspected the General's bastards are hiding somewhere in the villa.

Hortensia sighs, bracing herself for the confrontation she knows will follow. *"Señora*, you have no children."

"I know *that*. I'm not a madwoman like they say—you're blind, Hortensia! You can't see what's right in front of you!" Leonor Ledesma lowers her trembling voice. "It doesn't matter to me, any of his children. I wish they'd just crawl out from under the sofa, say good-night, and leave! They've desecrated this house long enough."

"Yes, *Señora*." Hortensia's stony expression remains unchanged. She believes the General is too much of a cold fish to have any bastards—unless the *tsismis* was true and he was making one with that movie star Lolita Luna.

"Would you sing this hymn with me?" Leonor Ledesma asks, her tone softening. She takes the older woman's hand. "The Lord is my shepherd, I shall not want . . ." Hortensia hesitates before joining in, praying silently to her own God to rescue her from another unbearable night with her proselytizing mistress.

Much later, after several hymns and an interminable rosary led by the General's wife in a halting voice, an exhausted Hortensia bids her mistress good-night. The General's wife falls into a fitful sleep, grinding her teeth in anguish. She wakes with a start, her eyes frantically trying to make out objects in the dark. Aside from her bed, the only piece of furniture in her narrow cell is a wooden chair on which her threadbare robe is draped. She convinces herself no one else is in the room, that the Santo Niño is watching over her. She breathes deeply as she lies back down. She reproaches herself for not demanding that Hortensia bring her mat and sleep on the floor next to her bed. Leonor

Ledesma's eyes open and close, then open again. The low ceiling reminds her of the lid of a coffin, the exact shape of her tiny bedroom. "How fitting," her husband once said.

She lies in the suffocating dark, waiting for the ceiling to fall and seal her away forever. She imagines that being smothered might be a sweet death; she waits for this death to claim her every night. This yearning for a sudden, painless death is her most selfish desire, her greatest sin. Father Manuel has warned her about this many times, in confession.

The General's wife, out of sheer habit, recites the "Hail Mary" in a whisper. Outside her screened window, the leaves of an acacia tree rustle in the wind, lulling her back gently to the red landscape of her dreams.

President William McKinley Addresses a Delegation of Methodist Churchmen, 1898

I thought first we would take only Manila; then Luzon; then other islands, perhaps, also. I walked the floor of the White House night after night until midnight; and I am not ashamed to tell you, gentlemen, that I went down on my knees and prayed Almighty God for light and guidance more than one night . . . And one night it came to me this way—I don't know how it was, but it came: one, that we could not give them back to Spain—that would be cowardly and dishonorable; two, that we could not turn them over to France or Germany—our commercial rivals in the Orient—that would be bad business and discreditable; three, that we could not leave them to themselves—they were unfit for self-government—and they would soon have anarchy and misrule over there worse than Spain's was; and four, that there was nothing left for us to do but to take them all, and to educate the Filipinos, and uplift and civilize and Christianize them, and by God's grace do the very best we could by them, as our fellow men for whom Christ also died. And then I went to bed, and went to sleep and slept soundly.

Heroin

Joey Sands. Do you like it? Like a crooner, don't you think? That's where I got my last name. "The Sands." A casino in Las Vegas. This old drunk fuck was telling me about it. "HEY, little pretty black boy . . . ain't seen nothin' like you since I left Detroit . . ."

He couldn't get over it, touched me when he got the chance. Did I have a daddy? Was my daddy an American? Shit, I laughed back at him, imitating his drawl: SHEE-IT, man, I said. Mocking him. You must be kidding! Man, I don't even have a *mother*. Laying it on real thick, so he'd feel sorry for me.

He started coming around CocoRico all the time. I'd be at the bar up front, checking things out. Actually, he wasn't bad looking. When he wasn't drunk, his face and eyes didn't droop as much, and you'd notice his big body and muscular arms, pretty strong and firm for a man his age. I'd always act surprised to see him.

That was before the disco craze, before I talked Andres into hiring me as a DJ for the back room. "What do I need you for?" Andres used to say, pointing to the jukebox. It seemed like forever before Andres let me give it a shot, and look at him now: he's making money, the place is jammed until all hours of the night—even *girls* want to come here and dance, the music's so good.

"You're kind of young, aren't you?" the American once observed. But I could tell he was fascinated, just like all the rest of them. Joey Taboo: my head of tight, kinky curls, my pretty hazel eyes, my sleek brown skin. "Where's the little GI baby?" he'd ask Andres, if I wasn't around. Andres would shrug in that bored way of his. "He'll be here any moment now, I'm sure." The American would buy more drinks, sitting close by the door. Sometimes I'd get there, let him buy me dinner. Sometimes I'd just stay away.

"Call me Neil," he said, his eyes fixed on me in that sad, funny way of his. It was one of his sober days. "NEIL. What kind of name is that?" I loved making fun of him.

"Good sport," he'd laugh with me, jabbing at his own chest with one of his large hands.

I spit on the floor in contempt. "Man, you don't have to talk to me like I don't know anything! *Puwede ba*—good sport," I mimic, rolling my eyes. "What do you think this is? The Lone Ranger and Tonto?"

I sulk, look away from him. Scan the room for a pretty face. Make him feel real bad.

Embarrassed, he looks lost. "Joey, I'm sorry." He means it. I like that best. I could make him do anything.

I keep at it for just a little while longer. "Man, I'm no savage." When he looks like he's going to cry, I stop. Touch his leg under the table. Soothe him with my voice. "NEIL," I tease, gently now. "Neil Sedaka—ahhh . . ."

One time he asks me a favor. "For my buddy—" Some younger guy named Phil. I didn't like Phil as soon as I met him. "Phil wants to see a live show—" Phil is standing there, next to Neil. Staring at me and not saying anything.

"You mean a sex show?" I take my time drinking my beer, ignoring Phil's piercing gaze.

"Yeah, that's right. One of those . . ." Neil is uncomfortable. Andres stands behind the bar, within earshot. He seems absorbed in the magazine he's reading, another article about his rich cousin Alacran. But I know Andres—one ear's cocked in our direction.

"You want boys, girls, or both? Maybe you want children?"

"How much?" It's the first and only time Phil opens his mouth.

"Depends," I say. I'll negotiate with Uncle privately, take my cut. "We have a car," Neil says.

We drive down Roxas Boulevard slowly, looking for the street. It's early, around eleven at night. I sit in the front seat with Neil, giving directions. Across the boulevard I can see Manila Bay, black and still. "Is that your ship?" I point to the ghostly carrier floating in the middle of the dark sea. The men don't respond.

Uncle's waiting for us with Emiliano the night watchman, hired by Congressman Abad to guard his property from vandals and thieves. Uncle deals with me directly, talking in Tagalog and ignoring the two white men. He orders Emiliano to stay outside to watch the car, after I tell Neil to give Emiliano some money.

The abandoned Lido Supper Club is a white building with fake marble columns on the outside. Statues of half-naked nymphs and satyrs hold unlit torches. Uncle ushers us in through the back door. It's cavernous inside, and eerie. Everything's been left as it was— dozens of little tables and chairs, all with stained white tablecloths still on them, ashtrays filled with cigarette butts, empty bottles of San Miguel beer. The enormous dance floor is tiled with blue and white mosaics. There is a thick coat of dust on everything we touch.

Uncle looks for the main switch, stumbling and pointing his flashlight at the cobwebs on the walls. Finally he turns on the dim chandelier that hangs in the room. He motions to a table in the front row, facing a large stage. Not too long ago, Johnny Buenaventura and His Amazing Orchestra used to play "The Girl from Ipanema" here. Now, a bare mattress lies dead center, a roll of toilet paper and a bottle of alcohol next to it.

I leave the two Americans at the table, take Uncle aside and tell him what they want. He is gone approximately ten minutes. A skinny young girl enters, followed by a well-built young man, close to my age. She wears a flimsy, loose-fitting dress, her eyes lowered. She is barefoot, and I notice her manicured toenails sharpened to a point, her black nail polish dotted with tiny crescent moons. The young man is also barefoot. He wears khaki pants, nothing else. There are intricate tattoos of spiders and cobwebs up and down his sinewy body. A weeping Madonna is tattooed across his back. He is beautiful. The two Americans sit up in their chairs, attentive now. I stay in the back of the cavernous room, smoking my cigarette in the shadows. This way, I can watch them all, the two Americans, the young girl with her face turned away, the young man with the magnificent tattoos. Uncle has quietly disappeared. When it is over, the young man looks up at the white men while the girl tears off some toilet paper, dabs it in alcohol, and wipes herself off. "Okay, boss?" the young man asks eagerly, grinning at the stunned Americans. "You want us to do that again?"

We are in a room at the Hilton. "You ought to sing," Neil is saying, "you have a great voice. Good way to make some money, even here in Manila." I grunt in response. What does he know—I've heard all this before. I turn on the giant color TV.

I have just taken a bath *and* a shower. If the water stayed hot, I'd be in there all day. Afterward I stuff the plastic shower cap and slippers with the Manila Hilton insignia, complimentary robe and two bars of Cashmere Bouquet soap into one of Neil's SPORTEX shopping bags. He hates it when I do that. "You don't need to take that cheap shit. I'll buy you whatever you need . . ." He just doesn't understand. I love the newness and cleanness of my little souvenirs, the smell and touch of the glossy plastic. I would live in a hotel room forever, if I could.

"I'm hungry," I say to him. "Call room service."

We are sprawled on the king-size bed. It's two in the afternoon— *Tawag Ng Tanghalan* is on. A young girl is singing "Evergreen." She is earnest and terrified, but her voice booms out in spite of her, from somewhere inside that frail body. Neil shakes his head in admiration. "Not bad. Wow! She's not bad at all . . ."

The TV audience claps and whistles enthusiastically when she finishes the song. She blinks into the camera, startled by their response. She is last week's winner, and an audience favorite. She stands tensely in front of the cheering crowd, fidgeting with her hands. I can't bear to watch her, it's too painful. Her awkwardness makes me angry. "Look at her—how stupid!"

"Poor thing," Neil sighs, "she needs to be rescued—quick."

Impatient, I make a face. There he goes again, upset: he identifies with everyone and everything. Probably why he likes to stay drunk. I can't be like that. If I was on TV, I'd be the coolest guy. Mister Heartbreak, *talaga*: the one that got away. Cool, calm, collected.

Lopito appears on the TV screen, waving to the noisy audience. Before he can even thank her, the young girl rushes off the stage. Lopito throws up his arms in mock exasperation. He gestures toward her departing back. *"HOY*, GIVE HER A BIG HAND *NAMAN*, LADIES AND GENTLEMEN! LET'S HEAR IT FOR CONNIE LIM, OUR REIGNING CHAMPION! THE BARBRA STREISAND OF THE PHILIPPINES!"

Before announcing the next contestant, Lopito rattles off the different prizes: a twelve-inch Motorola color television, a clock-radio, a year's supply of Magnolia Ice Cream. The grand prize is a screen test and a chance to appear in Mabuhay Studios' next musical, starring everyone's favorite sweethearts, Nestor Noralez and Barbara Villanueva. Lopito reminds us, once again, that Nestor and Barbara were discovered on *his* show. "DAT WAS MANY MOONS AGO, *DI BA?*" The audience in the studio cheers.

"Why don't you audition for this?" Neil asks me for the hundreth time. "You'd be great—" *He can't be serious.* I give him one of my withering looks.

"Come on, Neil. Call room service—I'm starving to death!" I'm starting to get irritable.

The next contestant is a young guy named Romeo something. Nice biceps, pretty cute, but corny. I poke Neil in the ribs, playfully. "Not bad—huh Neil? Your type . . . Look at those thighs and those lips!" Neil ignores me. "What a hairdo!" I moan, pretending to faint.

Neil gets up from the bed. "What do you want to eat?"

Romeo whoever-he-is starts belting out "Feelings," only he sounds like he's saying "*Peelings.*" He's trying very hard, and he's making me sick. No *karisma*, as Andres would say. I switch the channel.

There's an old black and white movie with Leopoldo Salcedo fighting the Japs. I lean back against the pillows, my arms behind my head. My tight black curls are still wet, framing my face. Neil is looking at me, ready to dial room service. "Well?" He's annoyed, I can tell.

I am still naked. We both pretend not to notice how hard I'm getting. "Cheeseburger deluxe," I say, dreamily. "French fries with ketchup . . . Mango ice cream . . . and a Coke."

When Neil got stationed back in the States, he sent me a postcard: JOEY SANDS c/o Andres Alacran "COCORICO" 4461 Balimbing Street Ermita Manila Philippines.

"JOEY: I thought you'd appreciate this. Wish you were here. . . ."

The postcard was from Las Vegas: a color photo of the Sands Casino, with Sammy Davis Jr.'s name in lights. NOW APPEARING.

"You got mail," Andres said, handing me the postcard. "You're lucky I didn't throw it away . . . Where've you been? Joey—you can't just not show up for work without calling me!"

With that buddha-face of his, Andres watched as I held the card in my hands, pretending I could read. "Let me," he finally said, snatching the card. When he finished reading it to me, I smiled. Put the card back in my jeans pocket. Carried it around for days after that, maybe months. I don't remember now.

I asked Andres if he'd write a letter on my behalf, someday. I have Neil's APO box number, whatever that means. I have to figure out what it is I want, before I dictate my letter. It's gonna be good. I know how to get to Neil. He'll send for me: We can live in Vegas or L.A.

"Sure—why not?" Andres said, in that easygoing way of his. He looks past me at the door. A couple of Australians have walked in. Middle-aged, okay bodies. They've never been here before. They hesitate—they could turn around and leave and never come back. Andres sizes up the situation. They aren't servicemen. They look classy, yet casual. What Andres calls "old money"—his favorite kind.

It's early. CocoRico's empty except for me and a couple of other young guys. There won't be a rush for another hour. "Good afternoon," Andres greets the Australians, in his best English and most courteous tone of voice. His shrewd eyes stay fixed on them. I perk up. This is going to be interesting. I am tingling, the dope in my veins has run its course and settled peacefully.

The Australians are reassured by Andres's politeness. They smile and sit down at the bar, not far from me. Andres stands under a poster of a matador and bull, brought to him all the way from Barcelona by one of his rich lovers. He is chatting amiably with the Australians, asking innocent little questions: *Where are you from? Really? And how do you like Manila?*

The Australians loosen up. One of them, the older one, eyes me boldly. I ignore him, smiling to myself. Andres will pick just the right moment to make his introductions. I listen to Andres go on and on, prying information out of them. He can be so cordial when he wants.

That's what I like about him. He's so slick.

Her Mother,
Rita Hayworth

"Was it an angel who sat on my chest? Or that demonic *kapre* again?"
My mother isn't sure. "Like the night Rio was born—smoking his
damn cigar, the only light in my hospital room at that time of night
. . . He watches me from the dark corner of the room . . . He's
familiar, and not so terrifying now. He's been with me since Raul
was born, perched at the foot of my bed in another hospital—which
one, I can't remember . . ."

"San Juan De Dios, I think you said once," Salvador reminds her.

"He is my secret guardian angel, the only thing I can hold on to
in that shabby Catholic hospital. *Where is my husband?* I keep asking
the nuns. *He's on his way,* they keep telling me, the liars. I don't
believe them, and start screaming for my mother. No one hears. The
nuns are chanting *Dominus Agnus Dei* in the chapel down the hall, it's
dark and hot and the baby's coming, I know it's a girl this time, but
no one is there to help me—not my husband, not my son, not my
doctor who is detained. The sirens are going—is it typhoon signal
number three or an air-raid alert? Are the Japs bombing us? I'm
screaming for help—where is my charming husband? The angel-
gorilla soothes me, he looks familiar, he looks like Freddie's brother
Agustin, he puffs on his fat supernatural cigar and strokes my hair.
Talk to me! I beg him. *Talk to me!*" She pauses. "It's not exactly an
ape, you understand. Not exactly a baboon with wings. More like a
big hairy angel—the size of a house."

"King Kong," Salvador murmurs. He holds up a bottle of Revlon's
latest shade, "Frosted Dew."

My mother makes a face. "Put that away, it looks like something Florence would wear."

"Kangkong!" Uncle Panchito laughs. They all join in the nonsense: wordplay, lewd jokes, *tsismis*. I am forgotten in my mother's dressing room, seated at the vanity table, inspecting her perfume bottles. The manicurist Salvador is filing my mother's long, oval nails with an emery board. He sees my mother once a week, on Fridays. Usually Panchito the dressmaker comes along. He pores over my mother's fashion magazines for new ideas while Salvador soaks my mother's hands and feet in lukewarm water; they are massaged in scented oils, rinsed and dried carefully by the fastidious Salvador before the actual manicure and pedicure begin. It is an elaborate process which intrigues me, and I always make sure I'm around during Salvador's visits. He fascinates me too. In spite of his effeminate gestures, Salvador is married, the hardworking father of seven. I know he has eyes for my brother Raul.

"I hate pink," my mother says, as Salvador puts away the "Frosted Dew" and shows her bottle after bottle of different colors. "Pink is an insipid color."

Uncle Panchito looks up from the current issue of *Vanidades*, which *Abuelita* Socorro has sent my mother from Spain. Panchito isn't really my uncle, but I call him that out of respect, because I like him and he is twenty years older than me. I would call Salvador that too, if he would ever acknowledge my presence and act less patronizing to me. My mother calls Panchito "Chito." He is her personal dressmaker, her *modista*, and probably her closest friend. He is always at our house, sewing away on an antique Singer my mother bought especially for him; he and Salvador come only when my father is at his office or playing golf at Monte Vista. My father loathes Salvador and Panchito, and refers to my mother and her pals as "The Three (dis)Graces." He hates it when I call Panchito uncle, and nags my mother to hire a new dressmaker, preferably a "real" woman. My mother is stubborn and loyal; on the rare occasions when my father stays home on weekends, she visits Uncle Panchito in the small dress shop in Ermita where he lives and works. Salvador and his family live nearby, packed into a rundown but clean three-room hovel near the San Andres Market.

It is easy for my mother to pick up Salvador in our car on the way to Uncle Panchito's, then the three of them can have *merienda* at one of those coffee shops in Mabini. Sometimes my mother takes me along. One of her favorite haunts is the *Taza de Oro*, next door to the painter Horacio's studio. Horacio often joins Salvador and Uncle Panchito for their endless coffee breaks with my mother at the *Taza*. "Come on, Rio—we're going to meet some artists," my mother used to say, motioning me into the car.

Uncle Panchito likes to wear dresses and other women's clothes from time to time. He often wins "Most Original" at those transvestite beauty contests he goes to with my mother. Like the time he wore my mother's leopard-print shirt tied in a knot at the waist and her black capri pants, for example. He calls it his "Calypso look." He'll say: "I'm feeling very Caribbean today. Put on that 'Day-O' song, would you?" Sometimes he'll show up to sew my mother's dresses with his longish hair streaked blond and pulled back in a ponytail. "Is the coast clear?" he'll say, making one of his grand entrances, his hairless face expertly made up. "My God—you make a really pretty girl!" my mother once exclaimed. Panchito was not impressed. "I am who I am," he said, with dignity. "If Freddie could see you now," my mother giggled, "he might fall for you."

My mother buys him cosmetics, gives him almost new high-heeled shoes after she tires of them. Uncle Panchito manages to squeeze into her shoes because his feet are so narrow. "Are you sure they're not killing your feet?" my mother asks him, concerned. Uncle Panchito shakes his head, grimly determined to wear her electric blue stilettos no matter what. "His feet are probably killing your shoes," Salvador observes, wryly.

Salvador had absolutely no interest in wearing dresses or stilettos. He was horrified when my mother gave Uncle Panchito some of her bathing suits, the one-piece maillots in leopard, black, and purple my father brought her from Hong Kong. "But Dodi—how can you do that? That's a fortune in swimwear—and you're just throwing it away!" Salvador gasped, calling my mother by the nickname he and Panchito once thought up.

"She is not throwing these bathing suits away—she's giving them to me!" Panchito glares at him. He turns to my mother and smiles.

Salvador holds up one of the skimpy, shimmering swimsuits. "Chito, *puwede ba!* Let's face it, you'll never fit into this—"

Uncle Panchito grabs the tiny suit and stuffs it into his shoulder bag with the rest of his newly acquired loot. "*Hoy, Bruja*, what century are you living in? Have you ever heard of miracle stretch fabric?"

"You'll need a miracle all right," Salvador retorts.

"Puta!" Uncle Panchito is insulted. His mood has soured. I look up from where I've been sitting at my mother's glass vanity table, alert to the sudden tension in the room.

"It's all right, Chito. You look fabulous and besides—I have no use for the damn things," my mother says to him gently. I watch as she touches him lightly on the arm. "What am I going to do with all these outfits? I can't even swim!" she laughs and eases the tension. Salvador grins. "Wear them for Jaime Oliveira," he suggests. Uncle Panchito rolls his eyes.

My mother winces at the mention of the Brazilian ambassador's name. She suddenly notices I am there, in the room with them. "Rio, please go to the kitchen and tell Aida to bring us some drinks and *merienda*." She winks at Salvador and Uncle Panchito. "*Ano ba*—are you ready for scotch and soda?"

My mother the nonswimmer has smooth skin the color of yellow-white ivory. She stays out of the sun. She think it's bad for the skin, that she will age much too fast and have crow's feet and freckles like the American consul's wife, Joyce Goldenberg. My mother uses cold creams, moisturizers, takes daily naps with masks of mashed avocado, mashed *sinkamas*, and red clay from France smeared on her face. She is a beautiful woman who works hard at it. Every couple of months she has Chiquiting Moreno tint her black hair with auburn highlights, just like Rita Hayworth. She yells at me and cousin Pucha not to play in the sun, she warns us about cancer, old age, and the perils of ugliness. Pucha heeds my mother's warnings. I decide to take my chances and disobey her. I love the feel of the sun toasting my skin as I float on my back in the water.

The week before my birthday I am in my mother's room, modeling a new dress for her and her two friends, a red cotton satin dress trimmed with black rickrack. Uncle Panchito has designed and sewn it for my birthday. My mother insists I wear a stiff white crinoline underneath. "I hate dresses!" I blurt out, bursting into tears. "And I don't want a birthday party!" It is no use. I know I will be forced to wear this ridiculous outfit with an itchy petticoat to a party that has nothing really to do with me. It has been planned weeks in advance, invitations delivered to my cousins and to children of my father's business associates, who are strangers to me.

"How can you say that in front of Chito? You're an ungrateful little brat!" my mother scolds, ordering me out of her beautiful mauve rooms. I am not to return until I have apologized and promised to be obedient and wear the red dress.

"She's so strange! So strange!" I overhear her wailing to Uncle Panchito and Salvador as I close the door behind me. I know how much I exasperate her; I know she talks about it all the time with her two pals. *What can I do—enroll her as a boarder at the convent? Why is my daughter so rebellious?* She even complains to my father, who brushes her off. "Rio will be fine," he says, "she's around your weird friends too much, that's all. How can you blame her? You're a bad example for your own daughter," he admonishes her. It was one of their worst fights, I heard it all through the thin walls of my bedroom. My mother turned the tables on him, caught my father by surprise. "Look who's talking," she said, her voice dripping with sarcasm, "Everybody's heard about you and that starlet in Hong Kong!"

There was silence, followed by the sounds of my mother hurling an object, her angry whimpering and my father's gruff voice, muffled in response. Later, I found out from Macario that my mother had not only thrown something but had tried to beat my father's head and shoulders with one of her stiletto heels. My father fended her off with his arms, and ended up spending the night at Uncle Agustin's. Macario told me all this with a slight smile tugging at the corners of his mouth, as if he found the entire episode funny and almost enjoyed hurting me with the details. "It's all true," the chauffeur said, driving Raul and me to school several days later. Lorenza sat in the front seat with him and never said a word. "Your father has fallen in love," Macario announces gleefully. My face burns with shame. Raul spits out a curse. It is the last thing we hear him say for days after that.

I love my mother's mysterious mauve rooms, so cool and softly lit. Whenever she looks in any of her mirrors it is always night and she is always beautiful. She designed the rooms herself, the dressing room with its floor-to-ceiling closets for my father's wardrobe and hers; the special shoe racks and tie racks and drawers just for stockings and lingerie, the closet doors with their full-length mirrors. The dressing room adjoins the bedroom, with its massive bed covered in a quilted mauve bedspread. In one corner there is a rattan settee with two armchairs on either side, where my mother has her manicures on Fridays and my father reads his Raymond Chandler novels at night.

The windows are boarded up and painted over, the air conditioner blasts twenty-four hours a day. There is never any sense of day or night in my mother's rooms, or of the glaring heat outside her mauve sanctuary. I spend hours here, watching her dress and undress, talk in hushed tones on the telephone to Isabel Alacran or Mimi Pelayo, or give orders to the servants. While she gossips with Salvador and Uncle Panchito, I perch on the velvet-upholstered stool in front of her vanity table, mesmerized by her perfumes, her jars of creams and ointments, her gleaming tubes of lipstick in red and lavender shades, her jewelry boxes inlaid with pearls and carnelian, her tortoise-shell combs and brushes, the round boxes of scented talcum, and a black lacquered music box from Japan. A Christmas gift from Jaime Oliveira, it plays a Chopin étude when wound up. That same Christmas, Jaime Oliveira gave me an onyx good-luck charm in the shape of a fist from Brazil, Raul a tennis racket, and my father gold cufflinks with the initials "FG" from the same jeweler in Brazil. Jaime Oliveira and my father like each other, and my father was pleased with his gift. He doesn't notice the music box on prominent display in the center of my mother's vanity table.

I can tell about Jaime Oliveira. I study him around my mother, at Christmas parties at our house or at the Alacrans'. He always brings his wife, who's a very nice woman. Sometimes he brings his two daughters, but they're much too old to talk to me. They tease my brother Raul and flirt with cousin Mikey, who's intimidated by them. Jaime Oliveira hardly speaks to my mother at these parties; when there's music, he asks *Tita* Florence or his own wife to dance. Or he'll sit in a corner somewhere with my father and *Tito* Agustin, deep in conversation about who knows what—probably the perils of being a diplomat, life in São Paulo versus life in Manila, golf versus tennis— just the kind of chitchat my father relishes. If the General shows up the men will all get very jolly and drink more, competing with each other for the General's undivided attention. No matter what, Jaime Oliveira is solicitous of his wife and daughters, and always compliments Pucha and me on how pretty we are. Pucha melts under such flattery, and puts Jaime Oliveira high on her list of sexy old men.

My mother laughs a lot when the ambassador's around, but she never talks to him either. She caught me staring at her once, and shot me one of her sharp looks. When she's in a carefree mood, she calls me *precocious*, an uneasy pride in her voice. I looked *precocious* up in the mildewed Webster's that used to belong to my grandfather Whitman. Cousin Pucha has no idea what the word means. "Am I precocious too, *Tita* Dolores?" she asks my mother. "Sort of," my mother replies, changing the subject quickly by commenting on Pucha's elaborate hairdo, one of Jojo the New Yorker's recent masterpieces. My mother feels sorry for Pucha, that's why she keeps inviting her to our house to spend weekends with me, in spite of the fact that Pucha gives her a headache. My mother worries about Pucha's influence on me. I'm sure my mother secretly thinks Pucha is obnoxious and hopelessly boy-crazy.

Uncle Panchito worries about my mother. He has never understood why she had all the windows in her room boarded up. They argue about it, sometimes. "It's creepy," he complains, "I never know what time it is! It isn't healthy living like this. *Dios ko*—your house feels haunted!"

My mother smiles. "Of course it's haunted." The room, she goes on to explain, is designed to soothe her. "Like a womb."

"Like a tomb," Uncle Panchito corrects her.

I hold the crystal stopper soaked with "Mystere de Rochas" up to my nose, inhaling its dark, rosy fragrance. I close my eyes. "I can still see my angel-gorilla to this day!" my mother is saying. Salvador grunts in response. "He visits me while I'm napping," she continues, "I can feel him in the bedroom, watching over me. He's quite naughty. Why sometimes, that angel-gorilla has the nerve to sit on my lap while I'm riding in the car. Freddie sits in front with Macario, of course, while I sit in the back, all alone with my guardian angel. I never say a thing, even though he's so heavy, I can't breathe! Can you imagine," she laughs, "if I told my husband? He'd be the first one to put me away. He complains about me all the time to that family of his. *Temperamental*, he calls me. Makati Medical—that's where he'd send me. He'd have me locked up downstairs in the psycho ward . . ."

"Mimi Pelayo's son is still there," Salvador says, "after all these years. *Dios ko naman*—he must be thirty by now! She still can't stop talking about him."

"I know just what you mean," my mother says, "Did you know she visits him every weekend? I went with her once. I felt sorry for her and went along to make her feel better. He was all drugged up. His face was bloated. He shuffled around the visitors' lounge in this smelly old bathrobe, like an old man, bumming cigarettes from everybody. 'Did you bring any smokes?' he kept asking Mimi. He kept calling her Benedicta. He didn't even recognize his own mother. He certainly didn't recognize *me*. I gave him my pack of menthols—*naku*, he was so happy! Poor Mimi. I left them sitting there, I pretended I had to go to the bathroom, and never came back. I made up an excuse later about feeling sick."

Salvador holds up another bottle of nail polish: "Silver Moonlight" by Cutex. "How about this, Dodi?" My mother shrugs.

Uncle Panchito looks up from his magazine. "Don't use silver on her—it's tacky!"

"I'll have you know, this is Isabel Alacran's favorite shade," Salvador informs him.

"It's still tacky," Uncle Panchito says. He is not fond of Isabel Alacran, whom he considers overrated. He holds up another page from *Vanidades* so everyone can see. I stop trying on my mother's perfume and look over to where they are sitting. So far, I've put on "Mystere de Rochas," "Shalimar," "Joy de Patou," "Mitsouko," and "Fleurs de Rocaille" by Caron.

"Now there's a woman!" Uncle Panchito exclaims. Anita Ekberg is poised with her mouth open, her head with its mane of blond hair tossed back in an arrogant gesture. She is a lioness; she is obviously not ashamed of her enormous breasts, which threaten to pop out of the plunging, heart-shaped cleavage of her strapless evening gown. She's been photographed by the paparazzi at the premiere of a scandalous new movie, *La Dolce Vita*. Rita Hayworth is at the same party, standing in the background with some man, whose face is obscured by Anita Ekberg's voluminous hair. "Oooh," my mother croons, "let's go see this when it comes to Manila—"

"*Puwede ba*—maybe in five years, if we're lucky," Salvador says, applying the first coat of silver polish on my mother's nails. "That movie will never make it to Manila. Didn't you hear? It's been condemned by the Archdiocese."

"Put that down before you break it!" My mother warns, her eyes flashing. I had just begun sniffing her latest acquisition, something musky and awful by Coty.

Uncle Panchito comes to my rescue. "Rio, do you want me to fix your hair? I'm an excellent haircutter—"

"I wish you would do something with that straight hair of hers," my mother sighs. "I've been thinking of taking her to Chiquiting Moreno's for a permanent."

I look at Uncle Panchito, aghast. "Permanents are tacky," he says to my mother, "there's nothing a little trim won't fix. Come on, Rio—how about the Audrey Hepburn look?"

Salvador starts in again. "I knew you'd say that. There's nothing wrong with permanents, Chito. Little girls look adorable with curly hair."

"I am not a little girl," I remind him.

"Your idea of a little girl ended with Shirley Temple," Uncle Panchito adds, in my defense. They all start laughing while he rummages around my mother's mauve rooms, making a mess of her beautiful things, practically knocking over her precious perfume bottles in a futile search for a pair of scissors. My mother keeps laughing and doesn't seem to mind.

High Society

When my father's mother Socorro Pertierra Gonzaga visits from Spain, we all have to put on our crinolines and white shoes and be on our best behavior. We call her *Abuelita*; she is a widow like my mother's mother, Narcisa Divino Logan, whom we address as *Lola*.

My parents host *bienvenida* parties in *Abuelita*'s honor, and the entire Gonzaga clan in Manila attends: Uncle Agustin and *Tita* Florence, Pucha and Mikey, my father's other brother, my antisocial Uncle Esteban and *Tita* Menchu with their grown-up sons, my cousins Eddie, Ricky, and Claudio, who we call "DingDing." Plus Eddie's wife Nena and Ricky's wife, Cristina. Nena smokes too many cigarettes, is painfully thin, and is considered one of the best-dressed women in Manila, second to Isabel Alacran. She survives on a diet of ice-cream and TruColas, which she has for breakfast, lunch, and dinner. Ricky's wife Cristina is a warmer person, very pretty and fleshier than Nena, but not very smart. My mother calls her "Nena's shadow." Cristina clings to her side at parties, smiles brightly, and never says a word. She keeps trying to get pregnant. Cousin DingDing is in his early twenties, always comes alone to our parties, and leaves early. He entertains my mother with obscene jokes. My father avoids him. Everyone in the family suspects he likes boys; no one discusses it openly. Uncle Esteban isn't close to any of his brothers. We only see him when *abuelita* is in town, which is usually during the Christmas holidays.

Sometimes Uncle Cristobal accompanies *Abuelita* Socorro from Madrid and stays and stays, driving my mother crazy. Sometimes he travels alone to Manila for one of his many operations. He's the richest Gonzaga, and also the most frugal. He prefers making the long journey to Manila, halfway around the world from Spain, just so he can save money on hospitals and doctors. He's never married, the bane of *Abuelita* Socorro's existence. My mother says he doesn't like boys, he just can't bear the thought of sharing his fortune with anyone. He adores his mother, and like most people I know, is infatuated with mine. My mother is the only one who seems to touch the soft spot in his heart. Once, to everyone's amazement, he actually brought my mother a *pasalubong* gift from Spain. In front of everyone, my mother opened the elegantly wrapped box to find a large ceramic ashtray with a matador and bull painted on it, and the words "TO-LEDO ESPAÑA." "Thank you, Bitot," she said, calling him by his nickname. "Just what I need for the living room! How did you guess?" Uncle Cristobal blushed with pleasure. My mother never once lost her composure.

My relatives make me sick sometimes, kissing and fawning over *Abuelita* Socorro like they do. *Tita* Florence and Uncle Agustin think *Abuelita* Socorro will die soon and leave them her sizeable fortune. My mother, who's the only one who treats her like a regular person, says none of it matters. She predicts *abuelita*'s going to die when she's good and ready, and when she does, she's going to will all her money to the Church. As for Uncle Cristobal, he's going to arrange for his money to be buried with him.

Abuelita Socorro and Uncle Cristobal usually stay at Uncle Esteban's house, which is twice as big as ours and boasts a round swimming pool which no one uses. Every day at noon, mother and son show up without fail at our house, inviting themselves for lunch and usually staying for dinner. Uncle Cristobal calls Pacita "the best cook in Manila." He keeps trying to hire her away from my mother, and makes no attempt to hide it.

At our Christmas parties, Pacita cooks sumptuous feasts under my mother's direction. *Abuelita* Socorro prefers rich foods covered with creamy sauces; she loathes vegetables and fruits of any kind, and never eats anything raw or green. "I feel like a *cunejo*," she says, waving away the bowl of salad which Aida mutely holds out to her. "All that lettuce gets stuck in my throat—" *Abuelita* Socorro makes the sign of the cross, makes clucking sounds with her tongue at her own revelation. Everyone at her guest-of-honor's table, especially decorated with a red tablecloth and a Christmas-tree centerpiece of blue tulle sprinkled with fake snow, falls silent. My *abuelita* seldom speaks, and then almost always in the lisping Castilian Spanish Uncle Cristobal has to translate for us: this time she has spoken in English, and it sounds bizarre to us. My father pats her on the arm to reassure her. "Enjoy yourself, Mama—eat whatever you want," he says to her in Spanish. He is the only one, along with my mother, who does not call her "Mommie Darling." "That's right, Freddie—Mommie Darling can eat whatever she pleases," Uncle Agustin chimes in.

When *abuelita*'s in town, Pacita roasts baby *lechon* and bakes three-tiered cakes oozing custard, guava jelly, sugar, and cream. She calls them "Gonzaga cakes." Pacita also makes the best *leche flan* in the world—not too sweet, not too eggy, but firm with the bittersweet flavor of her burnt sugar syrup as the perfect counterpoint. *Abuelita* Socorro practically swoons when she eats it. *Leche flan*'s all I can stand to eat at these family parties. I help myself to three or four servings. I refuse to eat *leche flan* in other people's houses; I never order it in restaurants. After Pacita's ethereal concoction, all the rest is a disappointment.

"You're crazy," Pucha says, piling her plate high from the buffet table with thick slices of pork *lechon*, crispy pork skin, mounds of rice with *lechon* gravy, and more pork. "Why don't you eat real food?" she asks me. What she doesn't know is that when most of the guests have gone home and only the older family members sit out on the candle-lit terrace reminiscing over coffee and cognac, I will say good-night to all of them, including Pucha, and go to the little room behind the kitchen for a secret midnight feast with *Lola* Narcisa. We'll eat with our hands: rice, *lechon, kangkong adobo,* and more *leche flan.*

The Gonzagas are a carnivorous family. My mother says so, sipping her Johnny Walker Black on the rocks, smiling her brittle smile as she orders the servants to bring out more and more food. My mother doesn't eat; she nibbles. She sips her drink, elegantly poised in one of her taffeta cocktail dresses, some Balmain replica Uncle Panchito has copied from one of her foreign magazines. A silk cabbage rose is pinned to one side of her waist. To appease my father, she pushes the food around her plate, anticipating every wish of *Abuelita* Socorro's and acting absorbed in Uncle Cristobal's rambling conversation. She knows how to give great parties—warmer and more intimate than the extravagant spectacles organized by Isabel Alacran, and just as memorable. There is a photograph of her sitting at *Abuelita* Socorro's table, her head cocked slightly to one side. She is smiling what seems to be a genuine smile. My *abuelita* is looking down at the food on her plate. There is a man with a twelve-string guitar serenading their table; his eyes are covered by dark sunglasses. Behind the singing man are four more men dressed in identical *barong tagalog* shirts and sunglasses, playing guitars and bandurias. They are singing something sweet and romantic—I can tell by the look on my mother's happy face. The musicians are all blind; my mother hires the same blind musicians every year. *Abuelita* Socorro requests *"La Paloma"* and *"Malagueña."* The blind musicians know all the Spanish ballads, they sing in impeccable Spanish, even Uncle Cristobal is impressed.

Abuelita Socorro has silver hair. She drenches herself in "Maja" perfume, wears her perpetual black widow's dresses with sheer black stockings and black suede pumps. She has thick ankles, a thick waist, and always wears two strands of pearls. Sometimes she puts on her tiny emerald earrings, the ones her husband gave her, which *Tita* Florence covets. *Abuelita* applies a bit of red rouge on her thin lips, and constantly fans herself with a scented, white lace fan depicting hand-painted flamenco dancers in ruffled red dresses. She fans herself and prays. She prays before eating, after eating, and when there is a lull in the conversation and she forgets we are all there. She makes the sign of the cross as an exclamation, or to ward off the devil. She mutters to herself in Spanish and what my mother swears is Visayan. When everyone is talking at once and she is temporarily forgotten, *Abuelita* Socorro pulls out her miraculous rosary, the kind with beads that glow in the dark. Under her black dress, she wears a scapular pinned to her brassiere, with a remnant from the Shroud of Turin blessed by the Pope. She's the only Gonzaga who's ever been to the

Vatican. My father says she was very pretty when she was young, a mestiza born of landowning parents in Cebu. I wouldn't know. There are no pictures left from her youth. All her photo albums were destroyed in a mysterious fire which burned down the original Gonzaga mansion, right before she and my grandfather left Manila to settle in Spain. "It's a sign from God," was all she said to my father after the disastrous fire in which nothing was left. My *abuelita* is a woman of few regrets.

You'd never know it, but *Abuelita* Socorro is Filipino just like my *Lola* Narcisa is Filipino. My father's father, Don Carlos Jose Maria Gonzaga, was born right here in Manila, near Fort Santiago. But he and his wife considered themselves Spaniards through and through.

We used to call him *Abuelito*, before he died of emphysema. *Abuelito* scared Raul and me to death when he was alive. He had a scornful face and chain-smoked cigars. That's probably what killed him. He only spoke Spanish, and never smiled. He came back to Manila to die—which some people thought was strange. *Abuelito* was buried with great ceremony at Manila Cemetery, in the Grecian-inspired Gonzaga mausoleum. Everyone came to pay their respects: Severo and Isabel Alacran, Jaime and Jacinta Oliveira, General Nicasio Ledesma without his wife. At the funeral service, my brother and I sat with my mother. All the Gonzagas sat together. My father looked like he was about to cry, but never did. My mother cried just a little. She cries when anyone dies, even someone she dislikes. My brother and I were dry-eyed and unsure how we were supposed to feel. We pinched each other to stay awake. As far as we were concerned, an unfriendly stranger had died.

Abuelita makes an effort, but she is a foreigner to me, just the same. She treats me with gingerly affection, and is much warmer toward my brother. She always insists Raul give her a big kiss. "Like you mean it," she will say. She drags us with her to Baclaran Church for her boring Wednesday novenas. She prays for all our souls. We are polite; we try to please her. Sometimes Pucha comes along. I don't think *abuelita* is too fond of her, but she pretends to be, for Uncle Agustin's sake.

When *abuelita* kisses me, I always think of funerals. Maybe it's her overpowering Spanish perfume, watery eyes, pearls, and black dresses. Maybe it's the miraculous rosary she clutches in her hand. I don't exactly look forward to her visits. Every year, it's the same. Sometime around Christmas. "Be nice," my mother Dolores hisses, "otherwise your father will blame me, as usual . . ."

Surrender

Lolita Luna is on her knees. She is trembling, trying hard not to scream. It is always more exciting when she restrains herself. Nicasio Ledesma stands over her. He holds her head up by her mane of unruly hair. He loves her hair—its weight and coarse texture alive in his hands. He dreams of making love to her hair, but doesn't risk offending her by confessing his dreams. You could never tell with Lolita. She would act as if everything was a joke; she would boast of being game for anything. Then, without warning, she'd turn on you. Act just like a prim schoolgirl from a convent run by nuns. Act just like his wife.

The General gazes at her hardened young face, the face he worships. She is still beautiful, her body still firm and voluptuous in spite of years of abuse. His favorite image of her: flushed like a flower in bloom, coming toward him where he waits in the dark shadows of her bedroom.

It is excruciating. Lolita's scalp aches with the pressure of her hair slowly being pulled. She shivers. "Enough! You're hurting me."

They play this game often. The General arrives after lunch, unwraps the *balut* covered with brown paper, and pours himself a shot of rum from the cut-glass decanter Lolita keeps filled for him. Lolita is alone—it's part of her arrangement with the scrupulously discreet General that when he is expected, her servant Mila is always given the day off. Lolita watches him crack open the first egg, sprinkling a little rock salt inside. She grimaces as he swallows the *balut* juice, then chews and swallows the duck embryo. "*Ay,* you're making me sick—" Lolita whines, turning away. "How can you eat that? You're really *baboy.*" "Pure protein," the General chuckles. "You must try one, *hija.*" Lolita shudders at the thought. "I wish you wouldn't bring that stuff in my apartment," she pouts. "Who pays the rent?" the General snaps. He never lets her forget she is a kept woman.

The General takes another *balut,* pours himself another shot of rum. When he is finished fortifying himself, he asks her to sit on his lap. The potent rum affects him immediately. He is not a man who drinks; he only drinks around Lolita. Lolita starts to sit on his lap, then jumps up as a thought occurs to her. "Wait! Let me put on some music first." She can never do anything without the proper ambience, the music piped in at just the right level. Everything for her is a scene from a movie: zooms, pans, close-ups, climaxes and confrontations followed by whispered clinches. The General finds her habits greatly amusing—"What costume are you putting on for me today?" he wants to know.

She fiddles with her Japanese stereo system, a gift from another admirer. It is a constant reminder to the General that he is not the only one. If he had his way, he'd throw the damn machine out the window and execute his rival. But his rival is a powerful friend, and he'd surely lose his Lolita. With her, he must always stay one step ahead, must never reveal the real depths of his jealousy.

Lolita flicks a switch and the music fills the room, something old, sad, and sexy by Dinah Washington. Then she disappears into the bathroom. "I'll be right back," Lolita promises, blowing him a kiss. She locks the door behind her and stays inside a long time. The General knows what she is doing and it infuriates him. *What a waste of a girl,* he thinks to himself. "*Hoy,* Lolita! Come out right now before I shoot down that door!" he shouts. The door finally opens. The General seethes with anger, but gasps when he sees her standing in the doorway. Lolita Luna is definitely high—her eyes are cloudy and there's a curious leer on her face. She is also gloriously naked.

Sometimes he slaps her around just a bit, enough to lightly bruise her complacent face or the insides of her ample thighs. He makes her promise to be faithful, and she readily agrees. She means no when she says yes. She enjoys it when he weeps in front of her, a broken-down war hero, a broken-down old man with a young man's body, too many moles on his face and a reputation as an expert torturer that intrigues Lolita. "Tell me about it," she pleads, a child begging for a bedtime story. "Is it true what they say? Do you like it? What else do you do in that camp of yours?"

The General is horrified by her perverse fascination. "It's wrong," he tells her, "absolutely wrong. Why do you ask these morbid questions?" *Lolita*, he warns her, *you must be careful. You must try to be more discreet.* It is the only time she is genuinely afraid of him. He senses this, and regrets the change in her mood. He compliments her on her latest movie, which he has just seen. He insists that she promise not to accept any more gifts from Severo Alacran. "It's all too incestuous," the General complains. "Don't you have any respect?" Lolita giggles. She asks him to pay for a dress she has ordered. "You'll like it," she assures him, "It's very tight and very French. I'll let you fuck me while I wear it." The General is annoyed; he dislikes it when she talks this way, but agrees to give her the money. Sometimes he feels like she is the daughter he never had.

"And how is your wife?" Lolita Luna asks, too high to care or remember that he has forbidden her even to mention his wife's name. The General frowns. "*Putang ina,*" he curses softly. "What have you been snorting and smoking? Let me see your arm—" He lunges at her, but Lolita pulls away. "Come here," he commands. She starts to retreat to the sanctuary of her bathroom, but the old man is too strong and too fast for her. He grabs her in his arms, staring fiercely into her sleepy eyes. She crumples beneath him. They thrash on the floor, the old man on top of her. "I love you," the General finally reveals to her. She wonders how it will all end, and when.

AVILA ARRESTED IN HUMAN RIGHTS RALLY DISPUTE

Senator Domingo Avila is in trouble again, as illegal assembly charges were filed against him and seven others by the police.

Senator Avila and Sister Immaculada Panganiban from the Sisters of Mercy Order were the alleged primary organizers of a "mock trial" held by human rights activists calling themselves "the court of the common people." The group met in front of the American Embassy on Roxas Boulevard on August 29. After several speeches, which attracted hundreds of spectators, the group enacted a "trial in absentia" on a makeshift platform stage. Several prominent Special Squadron officials, including Lt. Col. Oswaldo Carreon, were accused of human rights violations.

Along with Senator Avila and Sister Immaculada, the following were also arrested: Senator Avila's wife, UP Professor Maria Luisa Avila; Senator Avila's niece, Clarita Avila; Quezon City Councilor Baptista Magalona; Ramon and Baltazar Montano, Jr: and Father Conrado Igarta of Tondo. Senator Avila and Sister Immaculada were detained at Camp Dilidili and later released on their own recognizance, while the others were taken to Camp Aguinaldo for questioning.

The "people's justice case," as it has come to be known, was filed by Brig. Gen. Armando Reyes, Metro Manila Constabulary and Police Chief; Lt. Col. Oswaldo Carreon of the President's Special Squadron Division; and Chief of Staff Gen. Nicasio Ledesma.

During the mock trial, Senator Avila, his wife, Sister Immaculada, the Montano brothers, and Father Conrado Igarta acted as members of the "people's jury," while the senator's niece and Councilor Magalona played the roles of "witnesses to crimes against the people."

When finally reached for comment, Lt. Col. Carreon accused Avila and Panganiban of "creating a negative atmosphere of hatred and disrespect for law and order." He also claimed the rally was held without a permit. "I have no choice but to sue the senator for defamation of character," Carreon said. "These are very serious charges Avila and his leftist cohorts are making against government officials. If found guilty, the senator faces a maximum sentence of ten years in prison. We fail to see the humor in this situation."

—The Metro Manila Daily

Sleeping Beauty

Before her twentieth birthday, before she marries a foreigner in haste and just as hastily leaves him, before she is given the name *Mutya* by her guerrilla lover in the mountains, Daisy Consuelo Avila is crowned the most beautiful woman in the Philippines, our tropical archipelago of 7100 known islands. We are serenaded by mournful gecko lizards, preyed on by vampire bats and other *asuwangs*, protected by *kapre* giants crouching in acacia trees, enchanted by malevolent spirits living in caves and sacred termite-dwellings. The humid landscape swarms with prehistoric, horned warrior beetles with armored shells, flies with gleaming emerald eyes, and speckled brown *mariposa* butterflies the size of sparrows. Eagles nest in mountain peaks; in certain regions and seasons the sky blackens with humming locusts and flocks of divebomber cockroaches. Invisible mosquitoes lurk in the foliage, said to infect children with a mysterious fever that literally cooks the brain, causing hallucinations, insanity, or death. Inoculations against the fever have not proved effective, according to an alarming study recently published in the National Institute Of Health's annual report by the eminent medical duo, Drs. Ernesto and Emilia Katigbak.

The latest national survey reports that eighty dialects and languages are spoken; we are a fragmented nation of loyal believers, divided by blood feuds and controlled by the Church. Holy wars are fought in the combat zones of our awesome archipelago. Senator Avila declares that our torrid green world is threatened by its legacy of colonialism and the desire for revenge. He foretells more suffering in his eloquent speeches, which fall on deaf ears. He is ridiculed and vilified in the government-run newspaper. The underground circulates a pamphlet of his writings, "The Suffering Pilipino": "We Pinoys suffer collectively from a cultural inferiority complex. We are doomed by our need for assimilation into the West and our own curious fatalism . . ." "Fatalism is fatal," begins another influential essay. He describes us as a complex nation of cynics, descendants of warring tribes which were baptized and colonized to death by Spaniards and Americans, as a nation betrayed and then united only by our hunger for glamour and our Hollywood dreams. Is it a supreme irony then, when such an otherwise wise man as the Senator allows his gullible daughter to participate in a government-endorsed beauty contest run by the First Lady?

Daisy Avila is the demure and solitary eldest daughter of the opposition leader Senator Domingo Avila and his outspoken wife, the controversial professor of Philippine history Maria Luisa Batungbakal Avila. Daisy is the adored sister of the unremarkable adolescent Aurora Avila, and the beloved cousin of the infamous painter of erotic infernos, Clarita Avila. She is also the dark-horse contender in the Young Miss Philippines annual pageant. The other contestants include Baby Ledesma, a niece of the famous General, Baby Katigbak, Baby Abad, the Congressman's youngest daughter, and the disappointed runner-up, Severo Alacran's stunning niece Girlie. There is intense and immediate speculation as to how and why Daisy Avila wins over the panel of judges headed by General Nicasio Ledesma. Some say Congressman Abad had rigged the contest in favor of his daughter, and now wants his revenge. Some say the perverse General is solely responsible for convincing the other judges to vote for his enemy's daughter. The choice puzzles even Daisy's family. *Tsismis* ebbs and flows. According to a bemused Severo Alacran, richest of all the richest men and therefore privy to most of the General's secrets, the best *tsismis* is always inspired by some fundamental truth.

General Ledesma has been overheard saying Senator Avila should have been assassinated long ago. In public, the General and the Senator are polite and even cordial. Their wives attend the same church. The fact that Daisy's father is still alive is exploited by our wily President. "You see? This is a free country—just ask Domingo Avila," the President reminds his critics. "He's a dear man—one of our closest friends," the First Lady has said in the numerous interviews she grants foreign correspondents. "Domingo Avila is one of our elder statesmen, one of our living national treasures," she gushes, totally without guile and meaning every word the second she utters it. At the beauty pageant, she turns to nod at the Senator, acknowledging his presence in the row behind hers. She has always found him a handsome man. The Senator's worried frown does not escape her, and it amuses her when the Senator cringes during the talent competition. The shy Daisy recites two florid sonnets by Elizabeth Barrett Browning from memory, and also sings a tentative *"Dahil Sa Iyo."* For her grand finale, she parades up and down the runway in a modest bathing suit with such natural grace that even the worst shrews in the audience have to applaud.

Her mother has refused to attend the coronation, calling her "a disgrace to the Avila name." She forbids Daisy's sister to watch the televised proceedings. Daisy begs her father to escort her to the Magsaysay Pavilion, and he cannot refuse his favorite daughter. Embarrassed, he slumps in the second row of the VIP section, an honored guest seated behind Severo Alacran, General Ledesma, Congressman "Cyanide" Abad, and the preening First Lady.

The open-air pavilion where the pageant is held is known for its terrible acoustics and hungry mosquitoes; it is one of the First Lady's unnecessary monuments, a morbid pile of gray stones crumbling slowly on a hill overlooking Manila Bay. Sequined purple, red, and yellow banners flutter gaily onstage. Said to benefit the Sisters Of Mercy Orphanage and Shelter For Street Children, the pageant advertises SPORTEX, TruCola, and Intercoco Investments, "first names in modern living." Oswaldo "Pepe" Carreon is the last spectator to enter. The newly appointed Special Assistant to General Ledesma and son-in-law of Severo Alacran hurries alone into the pavilion to find his seat. He is the only latecomer to appear without a bodyguard. Often the last to arrive at public functions, he complains that there are too many social obligations associated with his new job. He is a very busy young man. His ailing, pregnant wife Baby is home watching the disorganized event on her new twenty-seven-inch Sony color TV, one of her wedding gifts.

Thousands of spectators jostle each other on the parched lawns of the public park at the bottom of the hill. The ubiquitous vendors in their torn *kamisetas*, short pants, and rubber thong slippers make their way expertly through the tight mass of people. They hawk cigarettes, bottles of warm soda pop, Chiclets, and *balut*. The nonpaying public has stood in the unrelenting sun for hours to catch a glimpse of their idols, their movie stars, even the real *Macoy* himself and the First Lady. In the front row closest to the steps leading to the Magsaysay Pavilion stands Santos Tirador, a man of thirty with restless eyes. Earlier that day, the fortune-teller La Sultana meets with him in the interior of her rusting Mercedes-Benz sedan, permanently parked on a side street near Paco Cemetery. She is guarded day and night by four of her vigilant followers. Some people regard her as a faith healer and soothsayer; her followers visit daily for detailed reports on her nightly talks with the Virgin Mary. She is totally dependent on her followers' charity for food and clothing. La Sultana has never been seen leaving her sacred Mercedes-Benz; she claims to lack the need to urinate or defecate, thanks to a miracle performed during her sleep by the Virgin Mary. She sits in the back seat smiling, waiting for her visitors, reciting the rosary. Even the First Lady drops by for advice. Others denounce the fat old widow as a crackpot, but Santos Tirador decides to visit her just for the hell of it. He gives her his last one hundred pesos. La Sultana prophesies the wild young man will meet a dark queen by chance, "someone from afar." He will wreak havoc in her life, and the price will be high. "For this you will die," La Sultana tells him, smiling wider and showing him her rotten teeth. "But never fear," the widow reassures him, "you will die a happy man. For this, you must be thankful."

One Christmas in a Mountain Lodge up in Baguio, Date Unknown:

If what you say is true, that Senator Avila and General Avila are actually distant cousins, and you've finally admitted Nicasio was promoted to Chief of the Armed Forces and Special Intelligence mainly because *he's* the President's first cousin, then why can't all these men patch up their differences? Aren't they all the same— just one big happy Ilocano family?
    —Dolores Gonzaga to her brother-in-law, Agustin

Que magulo! That's why I moved to Spain.
    —Cristobal Gonzaga

Si, si, si.
    —Doña Socorro Gonzaga

Si, si, si.
    —Florence Gonzaga

very busy young man. His ailing, pregnant wife Baby is home watching
the disorganized event on her new twenty-seven-inch Sony color TV,
one of her wedding gifts.

Thousands of spectators jostle each other on the parched lawns of
the public park at the bottom of the hill. The ubiquitous vendors in
their torn *kamisetas*, short pants, and rubber thong slippers make their
way expertly through the tight mass of people. They hawk cigarettes,
bottles of warm soda pop, Chiclets, and *balut*. The nonpaying public
has stood in the unrelenting sun for hours to catch a glimpse of their
idols, their movie stars, even the real *Macoy* himself and the First
Lady. In the front row closest to the steps leading to the Magsaysay
Pavilion stands Santos Tirador, a man of thirty with restless eyes.
Earlier that day, the fortune-teller La Sultana meets with him in the
interior of her rusting Mercedes-Benz sedan, permanently parked on
a side street near Paco Cemetery. She is guarded day and night by
four of her vigilant followers. Some people regard her as a faith healer
and soothsayer; her followers visit daily for detailed reports on her
nightly talks with the Virgin Mary. She is totally dependent on her
followers' charity for food and clothing. La Sultana has never been
seen leaving her sacred Mercedes-Benz; she claims to lack the need
to urinate or defecate, thanks to a miracle performed during her sleep
by the Virgin Mary. She sits in the back seat smiling, waiting for her
visitors, reciting the rosary. Even the First Lady drops by for advice.
Others denounce the fat old widow as a crackpot, but Santos Tirador
decides to visit her just for the hell of it. He gives her his last one
hundred pesos. La Sultana prophesies the wild young man will meet
a dark queen by chance, "someone from afar." He will wreak havoc
in her life, and the price will be high. "For this you will die," La
Sultana tells him, smiling wider and showing him her rotten teeth.
"But never fear," the widow reassures him, "you will die a happy
man. For this, you must be thankful."

Epiphany

Our country belongs to women who easily shed tears and men who are ashamed to weep. During the days following her extravagant coronation, something peculiar happens to Daisy Avila, something which surprises and worries everyone in her family except for her indomitable mother. Each morning, as Daisy struggles to wake from her sleep, she finds herself whimpering softly. Most of her waking hours are spent crying, or trying in vain to stop. Her eyes are continually bloodshot and swollen. The once radiant beauty cannot pinpoint the source of her mysterious and sudden unhappiness. "It will pass," her mother says curtly, in a clumsy attempt to calm her daughter. Meanwhile, the Avila house is besieged by increasingly aggressive fans and the press. With a nose for scandal, Cora Camacho attempts to bribe the Avila chauffeur Celso and Daisy's former *yaya* Candelaria (now Celso's wife) to give her firsthand information, but to no avail.

Daisy shuts herself in her bedroom, where she can avoid her younger sister's morbid curiosity, her father's pained and pitying glances, and her mother's sharp, I-told-you-so looks. Daisy dreads falling asleep. She is terrified of the weeping which begins while she dreams. She tries to stay awake, swallowing bitter, black Batangas coffee along with the tabs of yellow amphetamine she begs Candelaria to steal from the secret desk drawer in her father's study. In spite of these potent stimulants, Daisy somehow manages to doze off just long enough to wake up once again, drowning in misery. "What are you crying for?" her sister Aurora grumbles, impatient and unsympathetic. The star-is this about a jungle?" Cora Camacho inquires on her TV show, *Girl Talk*. "Does our foremost nationalist family consider us common *Pinoys* nothing more or less than a bunch of savages?" When Senator Avila politely turns down Cora's insistent demands for an exclusive interview, Cora is outraged. "*Aba!* Who does he think he is?"

The First Lady appears that same week as Cora's special guest. When Cora sweetly suggests taking away Daisy's crown and title, the First Lady's eyes, as if on cue, fill with tears. She stifles a sob and pulls out a handkerchief, which she dabs carefully at the corners of her eyes. "*Walanghiya!*" Senator Avila scowls at the extreme close-up of the First Lady's anguished face. "Daisy Avila has shamed me personally and insulted our beloved country," the First Lady sobs. She blows her nose. The camera discreetly pulls away. Aurora Avila runs up the stairs to knock on the closed door of her sister's room. She is shrieking with laughter. "Daisy! Daisy! Come out and see! You're going to hell for sure—you've made the Iron Butterfly break down and cry!"

The hungry pack of journalists, photographers, and fans maintain a twenty-four-hour vigil on the sidewalk outside the gates of the Avila property. Daisy cringes at the thought of confronting them. "Don't worry—even this will pass," her mother repeats, sighing. The weariness on both her parents' faces disturbs Daisy and makes her feel twice as guilty. Candelaria warns her that bets are being placed by the bored predators outside the gates. Who will be the first among them to spot the reclusive beauty queen through the drawn blinds of her windows? Who will capture her tarnished image with the powerful zoom lenses of their Japanese cameras? *Tsismis* quickly circulates in Manila: Daisy Avila is pregnant with Tito Alvarez's baby, Daisy Avila is secretly married to the President's only son, Daisy Avila is a junkie, Daisy Avila is a junkie slowly dying of a sexually transmitted disease.

Through the partially open blinds of her bedroom window, Daisy squints at the African flame tree, the garden of plumeria and bougainvillea bushes growing below. She cannot remember the last time she has been outside in the sun. Overwhelmed by the dazzling light, Daisy hastily draws the blinds before crawling back under the covers

Breaking Spells

On her birthday a week later, Daisy Avila makes a significant decision. She grants Cora Camacho an exclusive interview on her live television special *At Home with a Beauty Queen*.

The entire country tunes in, even those in the remote reaches of our tropical archipelago, places where one battered TV is shared by an entire village. Cora promises an intimate look at Daisy's life, loves, and wardrobe.

The moment Cora asks her first question, Daisy seizes the opportunity to publicly denounce the beauty pageant as a farce, a giant step backward for all women. She quotes her father and her mother, she goes on and on, she never gives the visibly horrified Cora a chance to respond. She accuses the First Lady of furthering the cause of female delusions in the Philippines. The segment is immediately blacked out by waiting censors.

Everyone in the country is elated by the new and unexpected scandal. Daisy refuses to grant any more interviews. "*Hija*, you surprise me," the Senator compliments his daughter. "She doesn't surprise me at all," his wife says.

Daisy becomes a sensation, almost as popular as her father. The rock band Juan Tamad records a song dedicated to her, "Femme Fatale." Banned on the radio, the song surfaces on a bootleg label, Generik. It is an instant underground hit. Condemned as NPA sympathizers, band members are rounded up by plainclothesmen from the President's Special Squadron Urban Warfare Unit. They are detained at Camp Dilidili, a brand new complex of buildings with all the best in modern conveniences: hot and cold running water, toilets that flush, and clean, windowless cells for solitary confinement.

A foreign banker named Malcolm Webb calls Daisy on the telephone. "I saw you on television with that gruesome woman," he says. "Would you like to go out to dinner with me?" Against her better judgment, Daisy immediately says yes. She has never before been out without a chaperone. "How did he get our number?" her mother wants to know. He turns out to be so charming, however, that even the steely professor softens when she meets him. "How can I help but fall in love with your brave daughter?" Malcolm Webb says to Daisy's mother. "A handsome shark," Daisy's father calls him, but he is charmed just like his wife. Daisy is smitten by Malcolm Webb, in spite of *tsismis* that the playboy banker is an old boyfriend of Lolita Luna's, and may even be the father of her blue-eyed son.

The furor over Daisy's TV interview dies down slowly, as other scandals usurp the limelight. Juan Tamad members are released from incarceration on condition that the band never plays again. "That means you can't play in other bands either," the General's tough special assistant informs them. "If I catch any of you in any type of public gathering, and gentlemen—I use that term loosely," Pepe Carreon pauses for effect, "if I catch any of you even fingering a guitar, I'll . . ." He was inventive with his threats, and always polite with his victims. He offered them cigarettes and coffee, even chilled bottles of TruCola. "I am sorry we're out of straws—you'll have to drink straight from the bottle," he apologizes, with a look of genuine concern on his face.

Daisy marries Malcolm Webb in a quiet ceremony with only her family in attendance. She gladly abdicates her title to runner-up Girlie Alacran. There are those who welcome the news of Daisy's marriage with relief. "She'll finally settle down," they predict. "Besides, she's probably pregnant." Tabloids publish unsolicited photographs of the storybook couple, dubbing them "The Rebel Princess and Her Playboy." "How long can this marriage last?" Cora Camacho speculates cattily on *Girl Talk*.

Hounded in public by autograph seekers and other fans, Daisy Avila retreats once again to the safety of her family home. "Fickle Daisy in Hiding!" is the title of a *Celebrity Pinoy* item. Malcolm Webb soon tires of the hysteria and no longer finds the publicity useful. He blames his naïve wife for turning his life upside down; she retaliates by asking him to leave her once and for all. Malcolm Webb returns to England. Daisy now becomes the butt of many jokes. ANO BA, CAN'T SHE MAKE UP HER MIND? scream the headlines.

In the Artist's House

Tired of being cooped up in her family's house for weeks, Daisy decides to visit her cousin Clarita. Daisy and Clarita are like sisters; their mothers are childhood friends and maintain a close relationship, even though their husbands have been feuding off and on for twenty years. "I've never trusted him," Domingo Avila once said about his brother Oscar, "he'd sell his own family down the river for the right price." Oscar Avila, on the other hand, had this to say when asked about his famous brother: "Fuck a saint who thinks his shit doesn't stink."

Clarita's father was a gambler, a small-time con man oozing with charm, a fussy, handsome man too vain to sweat or dance. When he felt the need to be legitimate, he supported himself and his family with odd jobs he obtained by using his brother's name. Domingo Avila had washed his hands of him years ago, when Daisy and Clarita were still infants. The Senator was always kind to his niece however, and helped out with her schooling and medical bills whenever necessary. Sometimes Clarita called the Senator "Papa." There was even a time when Clarita lived with Daisy's family, right after her father ran off to Pampanga with one of his mistresses and her mother Delia was institutionalized. Clarita moved back to her own home when her father returned and, shortly afterward, her mother was released from the hospital. Clarita's father swore, for the umpteenth time, he would mend his ways. Everyone knew better.

Clarita Avila began painting when she was six years old. Her Uncle Domingo paid for her sketchpads, her watercolor sets, her charcoal pencils, her brushes. On her twelfth birthday, he bought her a more durable easel, and paid for drawing lessons with the old painter Horacio. Clarita lived for the afternoons spent at the old man's studio near Mabini. She would later describe her childhood and adolescence as relatively happy times, in spite of everything.

Her mother Delia was a woman who had suffered so much she seemed to be physically shrinking away. She spent long afternoons chatting with her daughter while she painted. Delia Avila would talk about the incessant heat, the oncoming Christmas holidays, and the latest book she was reading. She would describe each chapter as if she were reading the story aloud to an enchanted audience, discussing each character as if they were real people in her life. "Poor Cathy," she would sigh, going over one of her favorite English novels, "she should really let her feelings show for that pitiful Heathcliff." She read voraciously anything she could find; she said books helped her maintain some semblance of sanity. Her daughter brought them for her as presents: novels in Spanish and English, anthologies of Tagalog poetry, spy thrillers, westerns, historical romances, and biographies. The Brontë sisters and Jose Rizal were Delia Avila's current favorites.

Although they were the same age, Daisy Avila sometimes felt younger than her cousin. Perhaps it was her tragic life and her talent that impressed Daisy so about Clarita, Clarita with the waist-length black hair, sallow complexion, stocky body, and twinkling eyes; serene Clarita with the sly sense of humor, who painted shocking miniature landscapes of bright yellow demons with giant erect penises hovering over sleeping women. Perhaps Daisy equated Clarita's great talent with her suffering. She wasn't sure, but she knew it was something powerful that drew her away from her own privileged life.

Clarita's mother was ashamed of her daughter's images and pretended they didn't exist. When they talked in Clarita's studio, Delia Avila's gaze rested on her daughter's face or on the wall above her. Clarita's father was condescending and indifferent. Daisy's mother the professor was the only one in the family with nerve enough to say, "She may be a genius, but that girl is deeply disturbed."

Daisy loved Clarita's pictures. She saw herself lost in the jagged   *113* blue landscapes, painlessly smothered in a leering, yellow demon's embrace. It was that same unsettling feeling, that same shock of recognition she experienced the day she walked into Clarita's studio and saw Santos Tirador.

With his coarse hair and feral face, he seemed an elegant animal trapped on the lumpy sofa, surrounded by mismatched furniture and Clarita's lurid canvases. Clarita's mother, sitting next to him on the sofa wearing the expensive dress Clarita had bought for her, smiled a big smile when Daisy entered the room. Daisy bent to kiss her aunt. Rising from the sofa, the young man held out his hand. Daisy smiled warmly at him. "I've come to see Clarita's new paintings," she tells her aunt. The young man introduces himself. "I am Santos, Horacio's son." Daisy looks surprised. She turns to her cousin. "You never told me Horacio had a family." "He didn't, really," Clarita retorts, annoyed.

Excerpt from the Only
Letter Ever Written
by Clarita Avila:

Santos is good, one of those rare good men with an unpredictable, exuberant sense of humor . . . I can tell the poor bastard's smitten, but who wouldn't be—with that sweet face of yours? Take care to keep up with him, or stay at least one step ahead. My mother has taught me men always adore women they love *in the beginning* . . . Santos is very smart, and because he's a few years older than you he can teach you things. He hasn't had our privileges, and whatever education Horacio provided for him was largely improvised. The old man was a miser, and not very generous when it came to his son, who in fact he barely acknowledged . . . And you've never been an intellectual, though your sophistication will get you through . . . I must warn you—Santos now believes he's on some sort of mission, which can be very dangerous these days. Do you understand? Your note disturbed me at first, but then I thought . . . well, this is good for Daisy. You must remember you are also your father's daughter, so Santos is risking quite a lot by taking you with him. Still, he's already endured so much in his life, he can probably handle anything. Reckless girl. You may be envious of my art, but now I'm envious of your love affair. (*Joking-joking lang.*) I'll miss you. Forgive the way this letter is written—I hope you can read my scrawl! And forgive my bad manners. My mother accuses me of being rude, and I am perfectly aware I haven't been very nice to anyone lately . . . You must know how much Mama and I love you. We always think of you, Uncle Domingo, Tita Luisa, and Aurora. Don't worry about them— they'll eventually understand. And if they don't . . . Here you go again, Daisy—disrupting our lives! Cora Camacho is going to enjoy every minute of this. You know that, don't you? Be prepared for the worst. I really will miss you. Enough of my sentimental garbage, okay? You asked for my opinion—you got it. I must tell you, after that last fiasco of yours, your taste in men is improving. Of course! No doubt about it! Run away with him. Just don't be shocked by how much you're going to suffer. After all, you're still a married woman in everyone's eyes . . .

Jungle Chronicle

The most insignificant circumstances become omens which were almost always unfortunate. The song of the tic-tic, *the appearance of a snake in the house, the shriek of a rat or a little lizard immediately caused a feeling of melancholy and gloom. . . .*

—*Jean Mallat,* The Philippines *(1846)*

PART TWO:
THE SONG OF BULLETS

The sleep had lasted for centuries, but one day the thunderbolt struck, and in striking, infused life . . .

—*Jose Rizal*

The President's Wife
Has a Dream

In the middle of the Pacific Ocean, a large white plantation house with imposing white pillars stands on a tiny island round as a pancake. The waves are still, the water glistens in the blazing sunlight. The island seems deserted, the house pristine and perfect in the silence. She thinks of starched white shirts, sharply pleated white sharkskin trousers, the gleaming blade of a knife.

She walks to the edge where beach meets water. She is dressed in her lavender *terno*, the one with stiff butterfly sleeves intricately embroidered with sequined flowers. She dives into the water in her beaded gown. Her thick black hair is swept up and rigid even in the water the lacquered helmet stays pinned and fixed on her head

It seems effortless at first. But as she swims the distance to her white island house keeps changing: first near then far the camera lens zooms in and out

The house becomes a speck on the horizon. She is panting, struggling to maintain her strength and energy. Her arms plow through the water water thick as syrup water resists her she aches with exhaustion she hears herself groan and gasp for air she momentarily panics someone waves to her from the balcony of the house

Is it her daughter? A faceless woman in a wedding gown clutches a torn veil in one hand. She waves the veil like a banner above her head her movements become increasingly frantic are there sharks in the water? She swallows syrup her eyes sting with salt she heaves her body through syrup she doesn't care she's going to give up any second now and drown

There. She's on the white verandah of the white house. Someone is playing a piano the music drifts from an open window the chords of a haunting mambo the opening chords played over and over again slow and deliberate it's a funeral march where notes keep changing one mambo blends into another a mambo so familiar and elusive

She is in the lobby of the Waldorf-Astoria in New York City. She wears a scarlet beaded silk *terno* an opulent black tulle bustle accentuates her plump buttocks as she struts confidently toward the elevators

She is alarmed. She realizes she forgot to put on stockings and shoes no one else seems to notice

Her entourage of crones dressed in pastel blue walk behind her at a respectful distance. They drag her luggage hundreds of Vuitton suitcases in all shapes and sizes black steamer trunks pale pink hatboxes assorted plastic shopping bags one empty birdcage three pearl-handled English umbrellas and several sets of brand-new American golf clubs the women chatter among themselves their bursts of laughter annoy her she can't understand a thing they're saying suspects they're talking about her

Which of course they are. She turns suddenly to reprimand them but they've vanished the lobby of the Waldorf-Astoria is deserted except for chairs lawn chairs stools armchairs stacked on top of one another wrought-iron garden chairs wooden chairs chairs upholstered in medieval tapestry

Cristina Ford comes out of the first elevator. She wears a nun's habit and veil. "Ciao, bella——" Cristina greets her warmly pulls a cigarette from the deep fold of her pocket and lights it she inhales greedily exhales the smoke with a sigh of contentment "look, darling—— I managed to keep it," she says, pulling off her veil shaking out her leonine mane of peroxided hair she takes another puff on her cigarette before disappearing into a second elevator

It's a perfectly choreographed moment. The third elevator's door slides open without hesitation she steps in she holds up her long *terno* skirt to keep her precious beads from dragging on the floor she looks down at her bare feet the red polish on her toenails is chipped the skin between her toes is cracked and blistered streaked with dirt she is horrified she drops the skirt quickly she can smell her own blood how could it be it's been years is she menstruating?

The elevator operator turns to smile at her she jumps she hadn't noticed he was there oh good it's George Hamilton immaculate tuxedo starched shirt blue-black eyeliner a perpetual tan on his cartoon face it's oh George his white teeth gleam like a knife like a knife she remembers oh he is lit from within when he smiles he's an archangel "WANNA DANCE?" he yawns at her his voice a warped record the elevator comes to a sudden halt doors slide open to reveal a dark suite before she can answer with her usual

Before she can answer with her usual "I'm a woman always ready to dance" she finds herself alone in the hotel room there is a man asleep in a coffin his lips painted a vivid red no it's a large bed she is alone and she is exhausted the bed is freshly made up she is surrounded by enormous bouquets and vases of flowers the bed is freshly made up the crisp white sheets look inviting *she is obviously expected* a box of chocolate seashells lies on her pillow the blankets are turned back in such a way a pile of chairs the temperature so cool the lilting strains of a melancholy mambo piped in through invisible speakers nothing too loud or obnoxious a mere suggestion of music for her sleeping pleasure a pile of garden chairs the temperature so cool all she wants to do is crawl

The curtains are drawn the bed is cool she is hot and terribly horny she removes her scarlet gown which falls in a red heap on the carpet she is pleasantly surprised the mirror reflects a taut adolescent body she munches her chocolates stark naked there is no one in her suite she makes sure of that first she knows now she can do anything she feels incredibly powerful exhausted by jet lag all she can do is fall luxuriating in the iciness of her sheets she's so hot she's burning up this must be purgatory

Pope John XXIII is in her room hiding behind the drawn drapes oh good John her favorite pope her favorite fantasy his plump face friendly and comforting she writhes slowly on her bed of ice she can't believe her luck there is no one there to stop her she can do anything make the pope disappear she opens her legs Pope John puts a finger to his lips shhhhh shhhh his fleshy lips turn up in a guilty smile he's a jolly fat man her Father Confessor her father the bureaucrat her father the old jolly Jesuit Father Manuel

It's a jolly Italian no it's her Ilocano husband leering at her with those painted lips she's enraged by his intrusion "The lipstick doesn't suit you" she snarls at him *"Buwisit! Buwisit!"* "WANNA DANCE?" he yawns at her a warped record left too long in the sun he's a prune he's a raisin he's a pile of garden furniture in the middle of her bedroom something's wrong

She sits up. A lizard emerges from the shadows sluggish clumsy movements a comic Godzilla she is relieved at first it's only a cartoon the lizard's scales are opalescent plastic sequined eyes the color of her scarlet *terno* it's a halloween parade in excruciating slow motion

She sits up in terror. Where's the salt? Pass the salt and pepper please pass the salt and do you by any chance have any Tabasco? the American consul once told her salt on slugs makes them fizz up and disappear a harmless cartoon

This is not a slug. This is a papier-maché iguana. This is some sort of prank some sort of halloween coup d'état is she awake? do iguanas have teeth? *Iguanas taste like chicken* the American consul informs her the American consul is a diplomat who eats anything he's been to Mexico stationed in Uruguay or was it Bolivia? "I am a girl who's ready to dance" she informs him in that coquettish way of hers the American consul whispers in her ear *Iguana stews are heavenly* really sometimes peasant cooking is so inventive *I'm a celestial traveler* she whispers back

She's perched on her throne of bananas she reigns from a mountain of coconuts she wears a nest of lizards in her hair WHERE IS THE POPE? WHERE IS GEORGE HAMILTON? IS THIS ANOTHER ONE OF MY HUSBAND'S PRACTICAL JOKES? She is aware of the weight of her pendulous breasts it's starting to snow in New York City in the name of the Father the Son and the Holy Ghost WHERE IS THAT BITCH CRISTINA FORD?

MAN WITH A MISSION

The popular General Nicasio V. Ledesma has announced his latest strategy for dealing with the growing popular support for insurgent rebels in the Mindanao region.

Speaking at the Manila Press Club yesterday, General Ledesma described his anti-rebel campaign as "a personal mission" which will involve organizing and talking with local people in the remote villages, listening to their grievances against the military, and undermining their support for the leftist guerrillas by distributing food, clothing, and medicine in the areas most devastated by the war.

"It is an incredible challenge," General Ledesma emphasized, "but I am confident that we can win this war if we can win the people's hearts and minds." He joked with reporters and posed for the cameras, dressed in camouflage fatigues and combat boots, smiling alongside his Special Assistant Lt. Col. Carreon. Carreon will accompany General Ledesma on his tour of the Mindanao provinces.

When asked about the seven people killed and nine people wounded in front of Quiapo Church last month, the General claimed the charges of arbitrary killing made by Senator Domingo Avila were grossly exaggerated. "Our men are the finest soldiers in the land," he said, in reference to the elite secret police, the Special Squadron Urban Warfare Unit. "They are trained to be cautious, and to be just. Let's face it—since the revival of the plainclothes government force, law and order has finally been restored in our nation's capital."

General Ledesma is staunchly supported by the President and First Lady, who honored the war hero with a banquet held last night at Malacañang Palace. Among numerous celebrities in attendance were actress Lolita Luna, debonair jet-setter George Hamilton, and pianist Van Cliburn, who danced all night with the First Lady.

Looking healthier than ever despite rumors of failing health, the President toasted a beaming General Ledesma. "Thanks be to God, we can all sleep better knowing Nick Ledesma is in charge of halting the growth of cancerous Communism in our country," the President said.

Absent from the gala proceedings was Senator Domingo Avila, an opponent of the use of Special Squadron units and an outspoken critic of the tactics employed by General Ledesma.

—*The Metro Manila Daily*

Romeo Rosales

First, I have to check out my shirt. The new blue one Trinidad bought me. Made in Hong Kong. One-hundred percent acrylic. According to Trinidad, Miss Know-It-All as my cousin Tomas calls her, acrylics are the best buys. They're easy to keep clean and you don't have to bother ironing. Sounds like heaven to me. What I like best about this shirt is the pale silver thread woven into the shiny blue fabric. The combination sets off my smooth complexion, my blue-black hair. So what if I didn't win the last contest. As Trinidad would say, it just prepared me better for this next one. Plus she heard that contest was rigged, I didn't have a chance. I love my hair

And that damn guard yesterday at Mabuhay Studios! I mustn't think about him, the shit. "DO YOU HAVE AN APPOINT-MENT?" he grins at me. I don't like it. I can't see his eyes behind those corny sunglasses. Who does he think he is, Clint Eastwood? You puny fuck   I could kill you easy with my strong arms my swift Batangas switchblade   I bet your *titi*'s an inch long   that's why you need that goddam gun   goddam asshole

My smile is glued to my face. I remember my mother's face she worships me   I need to write her a letter   how long has it been

"I want to see Tito Alvarez. Tell him Romeo's here—"

The guard motions with his gun. "*Puwede ba!* Get out of here, punk! This is private property—" The grin widens on his dark face. I don't like that sinister moustache of his   greasy fuck   look   he's got a gold tooth   just like Trinidad

I act humble.   I know that's what he wants. "*Sige* naman, *'pare*—"
call him *kumpare*, comrade, brother   you shit asshole

"You know how it is," I plead. "I went to school with Tito, we're
from the same town in Batangas, he's my buddy . . ."

The guard is really laughing now, he can't believe it. His bony
shoulders shake up and down, his sunken chest contracts with laughter.
Skinny fuck   I bet I could really make you squirm just by sitting on
your face   you bastard son of a whore from Tondo

"*Your buddy!*" He acts incredulous, he is toying with me. "My,
my! WHO DID YOU SAY YOU WERE AGAIN?"

"Romeo. Romeo Rosales. Tito said he'd recommend me for a screen
test—"

The guard looks at me with exaggerated surprise. For a moment
I think he's really interested, but I can feel the contempt in those
shaded eyes   bastard son of a whore

"*Talaga!* Big time! Tell me, Romeo—can you sing?"

"Yes," I nod, eagerly. "I was on *Tawag Ng Tanghalan* recently."
"Did you win?"

The question jolts me, and it's the guard who wins. I'm gonna get
you yet   someday   just watch me   you're the loser you impotent
prick

The guard spits on the ground. "You'd better go, you're really
bothering me now . . ." His voice has changed, no longer playful.
His right hand strokes the holster that rests on his hip.

Mother dear,
I leave   but I'm not disheartened   and I won't forget. Trinidad
thinks I'm nuts   but she's the best thing in my life   it's okay with her
whatever I do things are great since her new job at SPORTEX   I've
got to take you there one day you should see all the great clothes she
buys me   she gets discounts on everything
Today I'm trying out a new song for my audition   the theme from
the movie Serenade   *have you seen it? What a stupid question   I*
shouldn't have asked! There aren't any movie theaters where you live
you should get Uncle Turing to take you to the capital in that jeepney
of his   watch out the way he drives   the movie is great   you'll love
Barbara Villanueva   she sings like an angel   when was the last time

you saw a movie?   That time I was a little boy probably   when Uncle
Turing and Auntie Mila dragged us all to see one of those Dolphy movies
you didn't think he was very funny   you hated the provincial theater   it
was too hot and dirty   Mama guess what   the theaters in Manila are
all air-conditioned

The song I've chosen is number one   on the hit parade   "Not
One Single Happy Moment"   maybe you've heard it on the radio at
Uncle Turing's   it's a beautiful ballad   everyone was crying when
Barbara Villanueva sang it at the end of Serenade   I gave Trinidad
my hanky   she's so sentimental!   We've seen the movie three times and
she always cries at the bittersweet ending

I'm sorry I haven't been writing   but I've been so busy with my
job at the country club   you should see all the people I am fortunate
enough to serve   the Archbishop of Manila   Congressman Abad his
wife and beautiful daughters   plenty of movie stars   some of them even
call me by my first name   and of course the big boss Mr. Alacran   he's
always very nice   he's hinted at the possibility of a promotion   from
waiter to desk job!   but I'm not sure I'll accept   I know I'll have the
opportunity to do my screen test soon with the help of my good friend
Tito Alvarez   but don't tell anybody please   you know how gossips are
in that small town   everybody gets so jealous!   that's why I left   you
have the patience of a saint to put up with all those ignorant people

Trinidad's a good girl   a hardworking girl   but neither one of us
is interested in marriage right now   she wants to pursue her studies as
a schoolteacher at U.P.   Trinidad's so smart!   I just want to concentrate
on my show business career   then I can think about settling down   if
I win this next contest then I get a chance to record on Apollo Records
you don't know them   but they're the best   they do all of Barbara
Villanueva's albums   somehow Apollo is connected to Mabuhay Studios
that's what Tito was just telling me   everything's connected   I don't
quite understand it but even Mr. Alacran has a hand in the movie business
that's why I'm so glad I work where I work   Trinidad says I'm "rubbing
elbows" with the right people   first   a record contract   then a screen
test   at the end I get the starring role   that's my two-year plan   it's
always been my destiny

I'm going to close now so I can make it to the post office   it's
always so crowded   here in Manila   any time of day   long lines
everybody with their paketes and letters   I better get going or I'll be
late

I feel lucky today   I've been rehearsing all my moves in front of *the mirror   Tito says it's not just about singing well   talent scouts are on the lookout for the way you dress   the way you talk   if you're a natural dancer* thank god I am! *It's something both Tito and Trinidad call "karisma"*

Trinidad took me to a fortune-teller   please don't get angry, Mama! I know you think it's the work of the devil   but in this case it's not true La Sultana is a very religious woman who lives in a car She's given up her worldly goods and devotes her life to the Virgin Mary Trini also takes me to evening novenas at Quiapo Church   she claims St. Jude and the Virgin Mary always grant her wishes   guess what Mama   I go every Wednesday! Now do you approve?   La Sultana says   I have a great future ahead of me   all the cards point to the "Silver Screen" Mama don't laugh   you know it's what I've dreamed about   all my life

Stop working so hard   get Uncle Turing to help you run the store or that lazy kid brother of mine   how is he doing?   Tell him I didn't forget his birthday   when Auntie Mila comes to Manila I'll be sending him a regalo *through her   OK? I don't trust the mail   last time I sent you and Ping those Christmas presents   they never got there   re-member?   poor Ping   he thought I was making things up   my own brother doesn't trust me*

Keep me in your prayers   I'll not fail anymore   like in the past I sure was kawawa! *Don't worry so much about me   as you can see from the enclosed snapshot I am FINE   give my love to everyone there*

God bless you always
with much love from
your son
ORLANDO

Paradise

The Manila International Film Festival is the First Lady's latest whim. She orders the city and slums rejuvenated with fresh coats of paint, windows and doorways lined with pots of plastic flowers, the streets swept and reswept by women in red and yellow sweatshirts with "Metro Manila Aide" printed in big black letters on the back and front. Even Uncle's shack gets the treatment. Funny thing is, it all looks fake. Painted scenery in a slum no one's going to bother visiting—but what the hell, we all get a big bang out of it. Uncle laughs the hardest, shaking his head in disbelief. Fucking crazy bitch, he calls the First Lady. *Talagang sirang ulo.*

A bunch of new buildings have been built right next to the Magsaysay Pavilion on Roxas Boulevard. She's calling the whole thing a *cultural center*, whatever that means. Movies, ballerinas, and opera *daw*. The workers are busy day and night, trying to finish the complex for the film festival's opening night, which is scheduled in a few weeks. Toward the end, one of the structures collapses and lots of workers are buried in the rubble. Big news. Cora Camacho even goes out there with a camera crew. "Manila's Worst Disaster!" A special mass is held right there in Rizal Park, with everyone weeping and wailing over the rubble. The Archbishop gives his blessing, the First Lady blows her nose. She orders the survivors to continue building; more cement is poured over dead bodies; they finish exactly three hours before the first foreign film is scheduled to be shown. *Hoy*—I'm impressed. Someday, maybe I'll stroll over there and see it for myself.

Along with other honored guests of the government, the German director is flown in, first class, on Philippine Air Lines. He is housed in some big shot's three-story mansion in Forbes Park, right next door to the Alacran estate. Arriving in Manila early in the morning, the German cruises CocoRico later that same night, looking for action. The hairdresser Chiquiting takes him around, introducing him to Andres. Chiquiting's in his glory. He swoops through the door of CocoRico, making sure everyone sees him dragging the German by his elbow. "Darlings! Look who I've brought for you this evening!" he announces. You'd think he was the German's fiancé or pimp.

The German spots me right away, spinning my records. He is intrigued, watching me dance with myself in front of mirrored walls. I'm the best dancer I know; I don't like dancing with other people. What's the point, anyway? Even with partners, we dance alone. That's why I hate playing slow songs; sentimental love songs make me sick, I hate watching the desperate way people grab on to each other in the dark. If Andres insists, or someone gives me a tip, I'll play one or two ballads a night. That's all I can stand. I know I have to do it—Andres gets so pissed off when I don't. He won't admit it, but he loathes real rock'n'roll. He only tolerates it because of all the money he's making. If he could have it his way, you'd be dancing to "The Way We Were" or "I Will Survive" all night long.

I'm on display. The German is watching me from the bar, pretending to listen to Chiquiting blither in his ear. I'm high, lost in the music and moving cool and sexy. During my break, Chiquiting comes up to me. Trying hard to conceal his resentment, he says some important foreigner wants to meet me, buy me a drink. "Joey," Andres informs me, as soon as he gets a chance, "you'd better take advantage of the situation—that guy's famous!" We call Andres the Minister of Information around here, for good reason. He's sure if I play my cards right, the German director will cast me in his next movie. All my problems will be over, ha-ha. Andres is visibly excited, fussing over the famous director. Every time Andres pours him a drink, he wipes up the counter with one of his rags.

I slide onto a stool next to Prince Charming. Andres gives me one of his looks. "Your usual?" he asks me casually, pulling out the Remy Martin. I nod. Andres pours me a double, trying to maintain his composure. I'm following his script tonight. Andres has urged me to order cognac around foreigners, so he'll make more money and they'll be impressed by my expensive taste. "Instead of that cheap rum you're always drinking," he nags. What the fuck, tonight's the night. I'll try anything once. I turn to face the German, real cool, taking my time. He shakes my hand, introduces himself as *Rainer.* "Like Grace Kelly's husband," Andres gushes, "how unusual . . ." He gazes at the German with reverence. Not exactly, the German says, with an embarrassed smile. "Rain or shine, *di ba*?" I tease him, flash him one of my killer grins.

He's around forty, who knows. Pale and flabby, baggy clothes, a drooping moustache and the smell of cigarettes, straggly reddish-blond hair. I'm not sure I can bear to see him naked. It's one thing if he was just an old man. I'd expect to see his flesh hang loose like an elephant; I'd be prepared. That's when I imagine I'm in my movie. I'm the strong young animal—I'm the panther. Or else I'm the statue of a magnificent young god in a beautiful garden. The old man with elephant skin drools. Maybe he's God the Father, lost in paradise. He can't get over how perfect I am; he can't get over the perfection of his own creation. He falls in love with me. They always do. I'll admit, I can get off with some old man that way. I need my own movies, with their flexible endings. Otherwise, it's just shit. Most sex is charity, on my part. I'd rather dance alone.

There's something different about the German. It bothers me. I can't understand his seeming lack of vanity. With all the money he's making, how can he let himself go? It confuses me. He's too young to play my old man with elephant skin. I should get off the stool and go back to work, but I don't move. His eyes pry into mine; alert eyes that don't fit in with the rest of him, so flabby and forgettable. "I hope you fall in love with me," he suddenly says, just loud enough for me to hear. "Why should I, rain or shine?" I chuckle. "Because

I am the most corrupt human being you will ever meet," he says, in that soft voice of his. "Are you bragging?" I challenge him, rolling my eyes to show him I've heard it all before. Poor guy probably thinks I'm stupid, just because I'm poor and pretty. They usually do, at first. I live for that look of surprise on their faces. These foreigners, especially—they think they can say anything off the top of their heads, that I'll let it go by me and won't remember later. They're the dumb fucks, if you ask me. "What can you possibly teach me?" I ask the German, the smile gone from my face. It's time for me to go back to work, and I'm restless. I am not playing now, and the German knows it.

"It's okay, Joey. Roy can fill in for a while," Andres says. He and Chiquiting hover near us, their eyes and ears wide open. Chiquiting interrupts to ask Rainer about his movies, which all sound weird to me. "*Dios mio*, I wish I could see them!" Andres keeps exclaiming. He's beside himself, acting intellectual and grand, pouring generous drinks. "I saw one of your movies in Tokyo," Chiquiting brags, "the one about the blond girl and the Negro." Andres raises one of his bushy eyebrows. "Really? What was it about?" he asks the German, who shrugs. "Did you like it?" Rainer asks Chiquiting. "I was terribly moved," Chiquiting replies, "even though I didn't understand a thing." The German bursts out laughing. Chiquiting looks pleased by his response; he bats his long eyelashes at the foreigner, his eyes glittering with the black eyeliner he sometimes uses. Actually, Chiquiting's not too ugly. I just wish he wouldn't shave his eyebrows—his face looks ghostly and unfinished. He thinks he's divine, a man with glittering eyes and the face of an egg. Always boasting how "advanced" he is, he's the first guy I know to flaunt three earrings in one ear and cut off all his hair. He's doing okay, running the most expensive beauty parlor in town. He takes long vacations and likes to come back with his trophies: surfers from Australia, drifters from Amsterdam, one or two farmboys from Iowa. All blondies. That's what Chiquiting and Andres have in common—they worship blondes.

Last New Year's Eve, Chiquiting showed off his latest acquisition at CocoRico. Some Dutch boy with ringlets and bad teeth. Chiquiting picked him up in the Tokyo airport, then paid for the Dutch boy's trip to Manila, just to show him off! Next thing I hear, the Dutch boy and Chiquiting were both beaten up by the President's son Bambi and his goons, at that boring disco in Makati. Right there, with hundreds of people watching! I wish I'd seen it. The Dutch boy lost his front teeth and was deported a few days later. Chiquiting won't discuss it to this day. The First Lady is his main client, after all.

Rainer downs shot after shot of chilled vodka, something with peppers in it. He does a funny imitation of the First Lady, who had danced with him earlier at the festival's opening night party. Andres is aghast. I'm howling with laughter at the sight of a flabby white man pretending to do a dainty cha-cha in high heels. Chiquiting joins in with his *tsismis*, entertaining the German with stories about the First Lady's "edifice complex," plus her unnatural obsession with personal hygiene. "Perfume here, there, and *there*—" Chiquiting smirks, pointing delicately to his crotch. I bet it's all made up, part of Chiquiting's revenge, but who cares? None of us have had this much fun in a long time.

"They wouldn't dare show my films regularly in this country," Rainer complains. "Why did they bother inviting me for one night?" "Who gives a shit," I say. "All expenses paid—*di ba*?" Chiquiting shakes his head. "Shut up, Joey. You're really *bastus*." He apologizes to the German. "Even if we didn't have censorship, your movies would flop in Manila. They don't have enough action," he explains, "and they're full of unhappy people." Andres leans over the counter to speak more intently to the German. "Did you know how many workers were crushed to death when part of your film center fell on top of them?" "It's *your* film center," the German protests feebly. Andres is panting, quite drunk now. I hope he doesn't have a heart attack. He ignores the German's remark. "They were rushing to build that so-called cultural center where your censored films are being shown— for the first and probably the last time—to a big-shot audience," Andres continues. I am watching him with curiosity. I've never known him to be bitter, or to give a shit about a bunch of workmen. "When the festival ends next week, you and the others will fly back to your countries and remember our hospitality with such fondness . . . We'll all still be here, of course," Andres says, "nothing will change. Your brilliant movies won't make any difference."

"Opiates of the people," Rainer murmurs, wearily. What Andres says makes him sad. He holds out his empty glass. *"Talaga—sayang, ano?"* Chiquiting Moreno agrees, a faraway look in his eyes. We are all silent for a moment.

Here comes that bottle of Stolichniya again. Andres pours it straight up for the German. I just can't drink that shit—I don't care how expensive Andres says it is, or where it comes from, it tastes like chilled gasoline to me. I hold out my empty glass to Andres. "How about another Remy?"

"I apologize for what I said. I didn't mean to offend you," Andres says to the German. "You are a guest, after all—"

The German cuts him off with a wave of his hand and a rueful smile. "It's all right, Mr. Alacran," he says.

"Cristina Ford flew in yesterday. I'm scheduled to do her hair and the Madame's, tomorrow morning," Chiquiting announces, "I guess there's another big party tomorrow night." You can never tell which side Chiquiting is on. When it suits him, he'll go on and on about how fabulous his fabulous friends are, especially the Madame. Then he switches gears on you, with his contempt for everyone.

"I must admit, opening night was impressive," Rainer says.

"Siempre! Built on a foundation of flesh and blood," Andres snorts.

"You're jealous because you weren't invited," I tease him. Andres starts to say something, looks at the famous German director, then shuts up. If looks could kill, I'd be dead.

"They say ghosts of dead workmen haunt the place," Chiquiting says, "you can hear them howling, late at night."

"Perhaps it's the wind from the sea," the German suggests.

"The wind? *Puwede ba*—don't you believe in ghosts?" I ask him, laughing.

"After your festival, the building will stand unused. Wasted, like all her other monuments, those ridiculous resort hotels with their empty rooms. *Di ba*, Chiquiting?" Andres turns to our inevitable source of *tsismis* for confirmation.

The German gives him a cynical smile, which intrigues me. "All haunted by ghosts?" Andres nods.

"Never enough guests," the German says, "just ghosts."

Chiquiting squeals with delight. "*Ay! La Bamba!* Watch out—*La Dolce Luna*'s here!" Lolita Luna makes her noisy entrance, her Coca-Cola figure poured into a short, tight dress. It's all cleavage and caramel-colored thighs. She wobbles drunkenly in her high-heeled sandals, the only woman in the crowded room. There's a genuine crazy bitch—everyone turns around to look at her. We are all aware of her connection to the General; I wouldn't mind fucking her myself, one of these days. She's trailed by that has-been Nestor and that phony new muscleman, Tito Alvarez. They're the center of attention, pushing through the tight crowd to get to the inner circle at the bar, yelling hello to Andres and the purring Chiquiting. Now it's all wet kisses and loud displays of affection. "Am I the only girl here?" Lolita asks coyly, pretending to look amazed. "We're all girls, *di ba*?" Chiquiting snaps back. They're a real comedy act; Tito Alvarez looks annoyed.

What a hot night. One of those nights that will linger in Andres's memory, something he can talk about for the rest of his life. *Remember the night the German walked in?* I can hear him saying.

Lolita lays a hand possessively on the German's arm. Her long silver fingernails graze the rough fabric of his shirt sleeve. "Why did you leave the party so early? I was looking for you—" she pouts. Without acknowledging me, she squeezes her formidable body into the cramped space between us. "You look so serious. What are you talking about, Rainercito?" Andres lights her cigarette. "It's our favorite topic," Andres says, "*Madame. Alam mo na*, I was just filling him in on all her nasty habits."

"We call her the Iron Butterfly," Lolita says to the German.

"I know that," he says.

She totters on four-inch heels, silver toenails peeking out of her flimsy silver sandals. I appreciate her flamboyant style—she's dangerous, a dangerous bitch who isn't just drunk, I can tell. Andres tells me she loves her quaaludes. Can't do without them. "Rainercito," she whines prettily, "how could you leave me alone at such an awful party? I thought you were a gentleman . . . I was so bored!" When Rainer doesn't respond, she takes a sip of his vodka. "Would you like a drink?" Andres inquires. She doesn't seem to hear him; she's only got eyes for the German. Maybe she wants to star in his next movie, like me. "I'm so glad we found you! Did Andres give you all the gory details?" she is saying. "Did you know she has her perfume custom-made in gallon-size bottles? *Talaga!* 'First Lady,' it's called. Pretty clever, huh?"

Nestor is appalled. "Lolita—you're embarrassing our guest. He's also the guest of our government—"

She smiles. "Oh, Nestor, *please* . . . Why don't you and Tito go dance or something. James Brown! My favorite—Rainercito, would you like to dance?"

Tito Alvarez is furious. "I don't dance with men."

"Well, it's never too late to start! *Di ba*, Chiquiting?" she giggles. She's obviously got some brains left in her head—she's already figured Tito's bullshit out.

She winks at Chiquiting, who exchanges meaningful glances with Andres. "Nestor can teach Tito a thing or two," Lolita continues, a smirk pasted on her gaudy face. Tito's eyes harden.

"Hoy, puta—" He makes a move toward her, but is blocked by the German, who steps in his way.

"Showdown," I murmur, grinning.

"Have another drink—on the house," Andres says, pouring Tito a double shot of Remy. Chiquiting steers Tito carefully away from where Lolita stands, swaying. She's so pretty—all purple pouty lips, purple cheeks, and charcoal-smudged eyes.

"Nestor, you're so quiet—" she says, turning her attention toward our reigning has-been.

Poor Nestor. He looks like he's going to be sick.

"Nestor has refined tastes," Lolita tells the German, oblivious to the fact that he's just saved her life. "I think CocoRico's too tame for him. Is it too tame for you?"

"I'm delighted to be here," the German answers.

"Nestor would rather be somewhere else—watching his shower dancers perform. He finds them more exciting. Why don't you take Tito to Studio 54?" She suggests sweetly to Nestor.

Nestor looks grim. "I think you'd better leave Tito alone."

"*Cuidao*, Lolita. Tito's a hothead," Andres warns.

"Did you say *hop*head?" Lolita giggles. "I'm a hophead!"

"You're a bitch," Nestor says, so angry he looks like he's going to cry. Lolita appraises him coolly, then tosses her head in contempt. "I'm a dog in heat," she corrects him.

Chiquiting Moreno saves the day. "I've been to the *real* Studio 54—the last time I went to New York, with Madame's entourage. You should see the pink lights in the toilets! Sooo flattering! *Naku*, I ran into Bianca Jagger coming out of the men's room with Halston. *Dios ko*, I was speechless . . . 'Bianca,' I said to her, 'you look fabulous.' 'Do I know you?' she said to me. *Talagang bruja! Aba*, I gave her the same look, up and down. 'Everybody knows me,' I said, 'everybody who's anybody knows Chiquiting Moreno . . .' "

"*Itsura lang*," Nestor chimes in, relaxing a little.

"*Bola ka naman*, I don't believe a word you say," Lolita says.

"*Ay, hija*—that's your problem," Chiquiting sniffs. We all laugh, including Lolita, the tension temporarily broken.

"Where's that Tito? Did I drive my poor escort away?" Lolita scans the crowded dance floor. She pats Nestor on the shoulder. "I'm sorry for being such a bitch, darling." She lights another cigarette. "Now—what was it we were discussing, Rainercito?"

"Perfume."

"That's right! Madame's custom-made perfume. Hides her smell very well, *daw* . . . She has her own private perfume factory, tucked away in the rice terraces . . . Near Baguio," Lolita adds, making it up as she goes along. "You must visit Baguio while you're here, Rainercito! The seventh wonder of the world—those rice terraces! Or is it the eighth? *Dios ko*, which is it? Baguio or Banawe? I'll be more than happy to take you on an excursion. I'm a very good tour guide—*di ba*, Chiquiting?"

"*Very. Hoy*, isn't it time you went home?" Chiquiting says. I guess the General's waiting for her, but she couldn't care less.

"We'll get a special dispensation from Madame herself, to tour her high-security perfume factory," Lolita rattles on. "Why, Chiquiting here can arrange it. Chiquiting's *in* with Madame, *di ba*?"

"I think you'll need a special dispensation from the Pope himself if you don't get home soon," Chiquiting reminds her. She continues to ignore him.

"The perfume factory's run by—I can't remember! Who is it run by, Nestor?" Her cigarette burns to an ash in her hand. That's what I imagine—she's so high, she doesn't even know she's burning.

Nestor shrugs. "An order of blind nuns."

Lolita whoops with glee. "That's right! An order of blind nuns— blessed with an incredible sense of smell, and absolute discretion! Did you know Filipinos possess an incredible sense of smell? Why are you smiling like that, Rainercito? Don't you take me seriously?" Lolita nudges him playfully with her elbow.

"Of course I do."

She dismisses him with a gesture. "I don't believe you, Rainercito, but never mind. My friends here will testify to the seriousness of my artistic intent. Did you know I was educated in a convent—"

"Run by blind nuns," the German finishes her sentence for her. Lolita howls with delight. Her black eyeliner is smeared around the edges, but it only enhances her sultry appeal.

"I'll take you home," Chiquiting says to her, quietly.

"I'm not ready to go," she insists, angry for a moment, then softening again. I've been staring at her all night. She avoids my eyes, pretends I'm invisible. I don't mind. She's just another wild cartoon I can watch up close. I don't take her slighting me personally. I'd like to fuck her, one of these days. Then I can say, "My list is complete. I've fucked a *bomba* queen." What do I care—the night is young. She can play her silly games, act like a movie star. She can dance for him, make him laugh, touch him all she wants, but I already know the German's mine.

* * *

Rainer signals Andres to pour me another drink, a gesture which doesn't go unnoticed. Lolita looks at me with curiosity for the first time all evening, then turns her back on me abruptly, to make a point. "Hi. I'm Joey Sands," I introduce myself. She turns back around, a fresh cigarette in her hand. "Light my cigarette," she says, leaning toward me. "Let's go, Lolita—" Chiquiting's voice is firm. Lolita pauses for just a second. This time she winks at me. "Good-night, boys—" she says, blowing her famous kisses at everyone in the bar. She turns to look at the German one last time. "Good-night, Rainercito." He bows for her, a true gentleman.

Tito's disappeared. *Where is Tito?* Andres keeps asking. Nestor spots a Chinese mestizo who's just walked in the door. I watch him too— I've never seen him around here. He's wearing tight jeans, a black T-shirt with the faded white SPORTEX logo stretched tightly across his chest. Not bad. Nestor licks his lips, pulls in his fat gut. Donna Summer's "Bad Girls" blares out from the giant speakers, an old hit that's played every night, no matter what. Andres calls it his theme song.

I want to laugh. Nestor restrains himself from approaching the boy too soon. I watch him watch the boy watch the crowd. He stands with other onlookers on the edge of the dance floor, while the roomful of men bob their heads and gyrate their hips, letting go with shrieks and whoops of pleasure.

"Is it true? What Lolita said about the perfume factory?" Rainer asks me, his eyes also on Nestor.

"Probably." I shrug, indifferent to his question and irritated by the song Roy is playing.

"She douses herself from head to toe. She orders perfume by the gallon—it's true," Andres says, pursing his lips like a disapproving old dowager.

"We call it *Vagina de Regina*," Nestor rhymes, shouting to be heard above the music. Mercifully, the Donna Summer song ends. I am glad my break is over, glad to replace Roy at the turntables. I'm in control again, the most advanced DJ in Manila. I'm as advanced as Chiquiting the lizard, Chiquiting who snakes his way through the world, playing both ends against the middle. Let's clear the air. "Bad Girls" is a sorry anthem for sorry queens. I'm going to put on something different, something dangerous. What Andres calls my psycho music. He thinks it's all too loud and deranged. I don't give a fuck. This is for my German's benefit. I know he's watching. I know he understands.

I go home with Rainer in the chauffeured BMW the government has provided. It's past four in the morning. We've left Andres behind, nursing his last brandy while Pedro cleans up. We've left Nestor sitting in a booth, negotiating with the sullen boy of his dreams. Tito Alvarez is long gone, Lolita safe in the arms of the General, thanks to Chiquiting. Everybody's happy.

I've never been in such a fancy car. I've never been to a mansion in Forbes Park. I guess I've scored with the German. Next to him, Neil is nothing, some stupid memory. And what is that worth? It is suddenly easy to forget all those months I waited to hear from Neil. Almost a year since that stupid postcard from Las Vegas. I erase him from my mind.

Rainer breaks the silence with a question. I hope he doesn't pester me with questions all night. "What are shower dancers?" he wants to know. They all want to know. Then they want to see it for themselves.

I wonder what the chauffeur is thinking, if he lives with the other servants at the mansion, if he eavesdrops. I chuckle softly, tell Rainer about Boy-Boy and his job at Studio 54, how the club is located at 54 Alibangbang Street, how the owner is a cop who's never been to New York. It's a gold mine, a kinky haven for the likes of has-beens like Nestor. Hungry young boys crowd the stage, lathering their bodies with soap while an audience watches. Some of the boys soap each other, all part of their routine. The shower dancers rinse themselves off with sponges dipped in buckets of water, taking their sweet time. The music's always good.

"Are they hungry or greedy?" Rainer asks. I look at him, perplexed by his question. "There's a difference, you know," he adds, gently.

What a pain in the ass. "Hey, man. How should I know? Boys

are hungry, so they perform. Audience pays to sit there, greedy to watch—" I shrug a lot when I'm around him. He wants to know if I've ever—I shake my head. "Not my style," I say.

"Is that all they do? Rub soap on their bodies?"

"I told you. How many times do I have to tell you? It's a dance—"

"Do they do it slowly?" The million-dollar question: "Are they hard? Do they come onstage?"

"Some."

The German is incredulous. "Some? Not all? What about your friend, Boy-Boy? Does he like it? Such a wonderful name, Boy-Boy." The German stares at me in the darkness. I recognize myself in the absence of light in his eyes, the junkie in him. And something else, something that bothers me. I remember the same doggish look about Neil, how it always made me angry, how my anger always fueled the American's desire.

Finally, I speak. "Boy-Boy likes it, sure. He can't help himself." I chuckle again.

"Tell me what it's like for him. What he's told you," the German pleads.

I sigh, suddenly very exhausted. I try to recall things Boy-Boy has told me. It is very late. "Aren't we there yet?" I grumble, peering out the car window. When you get right down to it, the German's turning out to be just like the rest of them, with their stupid questions. "Some are already hard—before they appear onstage," I begin, wearily. "Some work themselves up in front of the audience—" I wish I were high. If I were high—"Some are ashamed of their erections. They don't want to be out there, like that—"

"Like what?"

"Ashamed."

"You mean vulnerable. They touch themselves?"

I hope I'm getting paid for this interrogation. "I told you, rain or shine. That's what it's all about. The dance. That's what the greedy audience pays to see." I wonder if the driver understands our soft-spoken English. Will the German pay me in dollars? Get me high?

"How long does it take?" His voice is persistent, his gaze probing.

"What? The dance? Fuck, man. It depends—two or three songs.

Fifteen minutes maybe. Shit. You wanna go there and see for yourself? I can arrange it. Nestor's probably there, by now. Lots of foreigners go—you won't be the only one. Maybe we'll even run into that other asshole, Tito Alvarez."

"When? Right now?"

"Right now, man. You're asking too many questions. You're driving me crazy with your questions. Just get me high first, okay? I know where we can get the best stuff, we can go right now, it's on the way. So I can stay awake. So *you* can stay awake. We'll make the breakfast show—" I smile a sick, lopsided smile. I touch him lightly on his outer thigh, grazing his pants in the same offhand way the movie star grazed his arm with her silver fingernails.

"What makes you think I do drugs?" the German asks. He leans back against the soft leather upholstery, gray to match the metallic silver color of the car. He shuts his eyes. He seems to age even more in the dark, his face drawn and haggard. I have the sudden urge to kiss his dissipated face, just for an instant, surprising myself with the force of my desire. I recoil.

"No more nightclubs," he murmurs. "I've had enough for tonight. We'll go later this week—maybe. But tonight—I want to be alone with you tonight."

"Sure. Whatever, rain or shine."

"I'm scheduled to be here one week. You'll stay with me every night, won't you? I'll take good care of you."

"Sure, maybe." He's got too many ideas. I want him to back off, just a little. "Is there a swimming pool?" He nods, opening his eyes to look at me. "I want to swim in the pool," I say, "tonight. As soon as we get there."

"Yes, of course. We'll swim in the pool all night, if you want."

The car slows down as it approaches the wrought-iron gates that lead to a winding driveway. The house still seems far away, hidden behind bushes and trees. I roll down the car window, stick my neck out and take a deep breath. I pretend the whole world is mine—dark, perfumed, and peaceful, the only sounds the purr of the fancy car's engine and the steady clicking chorus of *kuliglig* in the trees.

The driver honks the horn. A sleepy security guard in blue uniform with a holstered gun unlocks the gates. "Will he kill us with bullets or tetanus?" I joke, pointing to the big, rusty looking gun. "I wouldn't want to find out," Rainer says, smiling faintly. Maybe I'm talking too loud. Maybe I'm being too obnoxious.

We are driven past the guard to the front entrance of the magnificent house. The guard salutes us as we drive by. I salute back at him. A light comes on as a female servant opens the front door. She wears a baggy dress as a nightgown, holding it close against her sturdy body in a gesture of modesty. I want to tell her, "Relax, Inday. It's me—Joey Sands. You can take off your dress and show me your tits—I'm not interested." An invisible dog barks from somewhere out back. Another dog joins in. The servant turns on the lamps in the sprawling living room, which goes on for miles and miles. She stands there, waiting for us to give her some orders. It must be at least five o'clock in the morning by now. Outside the sliding glass doors, an aviary is visible. I spot four giant parrots with long red tails, and some other birds, all sleeping. A spotlight is turned on to show a still and inviting pool, an oasis surrounded by palm trees. Rainer thanks the servant, dismissing her with a curt goodnight.

In the guest bedroom, we wait for the house to settle once again, snorting a combination of the German's pharmaceutical cocaine and what's left of Uncle's heroin, which I pull out of my pocket. "So, rain or shine. You don't do drugs, heh-heh." The German is silent. He pours us two large snifters of cognac, from a bar which has been set up at one end of the room. He seems pleased. "This is perfect, isn't it, Joey?"

"Sure, Rainercito."

"Don't call me that." He bristles, angry now. I rub coke on my gums, help myself to one of his high-class English cigarettes.

"Okay, okay. Relax, rain or shine. I don't mean to offend you. We're in paradise now." I grin at him, sipping the cognac slowly, like Andres taught me to do. I'm not sure I like it any better than I do that gasoline vodka, but what the fuck. It works—cuts the edge off the coke without putting me to sleep. "Let's swim," I say.

"Call me Rainer, please—"

"Sure. Rainer."

He cocks his head, listening for something. "There—I think they're asleep."

"Who?"

"The servants. They're curious about us, don't you think?"

"The driver, maybe. Fuck it. Relax, man. Let's party."

"That's the problem with these colonial situations of yours—"

"No problem, man."

"Rainer."

"Okay. Rainer—" I pause, letting the sound of his name sink in. "What the fuck are you talking about?"

"Servants. They end up knowing your secrets, they always end up knowing too much. It's a kind of insidious power—"

"Servants can't do shit to you, boss. You're being paranoid. They're paid, *di ba*?" I wish we'd quit talking and go swimming. I don't get what he's so worked up about.

"Back in my country, I don't live like this. I live alone, and I like it that way. In a warehouse, with only my cats for company. Don't you get it, dear boy?"

"I'm not dear boy. The name's Joey."

"Did I offend you?"

I'm higher than I've ever been, sick to death of his questions. "Sometimes I shit, Rainer. Sometimes I shit all day long. I wonder where all my shit is coming from, especially when I don't eat. I don't eat for days, sometimes. How come I shit? It's scary at first. Then it feels good. Good shit cleans out my system. I get rid of everything." My gaze meets his, sure and steady.

The German gets up from where he's been sitting on the bed. Matter-of-factly, he steps out of his rumpled clothes. I avoid looking at his heavy body. I'm aware of his overpowering scent, the scent of sweat, liquor, and too many cigarettes. I undress fast, glad to be out of my own damp clothes. "Let's go swimming, Joey." The German says my name carefully, tenderly.

Without hesitating, I dive into the turquoise water of the long pool. The impact of my body hitting the lukewarm water is a soft explosion, the only noise for miles around.

Happily, I float on my back, serene under the canopy of stars in the black sky. A coconut tree bends in a graceful arc over the pool. I could die right now, I feel so good.

The German swims languidly beside me, a big white fish with anxious eyes. "Your father—he was a black American, yes? Andres told me."

"Andres talks too much," I say, though I don't really mind. "He was stationed at Subic Bay—that's all I know about him. Not his name. Not anything." I swim away from him.

He swims after me. We do a couple of laps, then drift toward the shallow end, resting our heads against the black and white tiles that line the pool's edge. "Look," Rainer points to the high fence that encloses us, a tangle of barbed wire and broken glass on top of cement walls. I say nothing. I'll poke around later, while he sleeps. See what I can pick up as souvenirs. Next door, the king of coconuts snores in his sleep, wrapped around that skinny wife of his. Wait till I tell Uncle and Boy-Boy. Wait till I tell Andres—"There I was, your rich cousin's neighbor!" Me, Joey Sands. Andres has never been within three feet of his own relative's house.

"Who does all this belong to?" I ask the German.

"I was told some rich doctor and his wife, also a doctor. They're away on vacation. You like it?"

Of course I do, who wouldn't. I shrug in response.

"Will you stay with me, Joey?"

"All week?"

"Yes—night and day. Don't leave me for one moment." He stops talking long enough to peer at my face, trying to read my mind. "A government official offered to loan me his private plane. I could call him tomorrow, accept his offer. We'll take a trip—we'll have a wonderful time. We'll fly to the jungle. You'll show me waterfalls and volcanoes—"

"Waterfalls and volcanoes? You're crazy. Let's go somewhere fun. Let's go to Las Vegas."

"You've never been out of Manila, have you? How terrible. All the more reason, then. We'll explore your country. Joey—please. Stay with me."

"I work. I have a job, remember?"

"Don't worry about money. Come on, I'll talk to—what's his name. Your boss, Andres. He's a reasonable man. I'll call him today. He can get a substitute for a week, can't he? What about that other guy last night? Don't you know someone?"

"Not like me. No one's as good as me. I'm the best DJ in Manila. Andres will tell you that."

Enjoying myself, I play my stubborn games, reminding the German over and over how good I am, how much Andres depends on me, how I'm indirectly responsible for the club's success. When I've got him where I want him, I finally and reluctantly give in. "All right, all right—one week. But you'd better fix it with Andres. I don't want any shit from him after you leave."

I climb out of the pool. "Where are you going?" Rainer asks, grabbing my ankle. I wiggle my foot, loosening his grip on my leg. I give him a cold look. "To bed. I'm going to bed. How about you?"

I feel the heat from the morning sun, slowly rising. Without looking back, I walk through the patio to the bedroom, the German at my heels.

The day he leaves Manila for Berlin, we have an early breakfast in the coffee shop of the Intercontinental Hotel. The German prefers the coffee shop to having breakfast at the mansion. He's never gotten over being uncomfortable in the presence of servants. Me, I don't give a shit. When I feel their eyes on me, I stare right back. So what. If I stare long enough, they drop their gaze and go about their business. It's simple. I know them and they know me.

The German carries his shoulder bag, the canvas one filled with his most precious possessions: drugs, passport, plane ticket, notebook, pens, toothbrush, comb, and dollars. He's paranoid, dragging his bag with him wherever we go. "You don't need your passport at Studio 54," I've told him. He wouldn't listen. "You never know, I might need to make a quick getaway—"

"You think like a criminal. Are you a criminal or an artist?" I tease him.

"Both," he answered, smiling that dumb sad smile of his.

What a weirdo—seems like that's all I meet these days. What the fuck. He's so generous, I can't complain. I just have to put up with his crazy shit a few more hours.

After breakfast, we're going back to the house and pick up his suitcases, then off to the airport for one last time in the fancy car. "I don't care about my clothes or shoes," Rainer says, as we sit down at a booth in the coffee shop. "But I can't afford to lose this—" He slides the bag under the table, between our feet.

"Joey."

We're drinking coffee. The German drinks his black, with plenty of sugar. I like mine with plenty of milk. Except for another foreigner with eyeglasses reading a newspaper across the room, the coffee shop is empty. I love the interior of our booth, all striped garish upholstery, tiny mirrors, and bright plastic banners like a loud, gaudy jeepney.

"JOEY. I'm talking to you."

"What."

"Have you ever been in love?" the German asks, shyly. I remember the American and his postcard, pouring myself more coffee from the steel coffeepot the sleepy waiter has left on our table. It isn't even six thirty yet; I've slept a few hours, but I feel like I've been up all night.

"Joey. Did you hear me?"

"Yes. And the answer's no."

"I'm a little in love with you, I think."

He confuses and exhausts me. I've grown to like him too, but I'll never admit it. "A little? How can you be a little in love?"

"Are you sorry I'm leaving?"

"Sure, Rainercito."

"I told you, goddammit. RAINER."

"Okay, Rainer. You want me to be sorry? I'll be sorry."

"Whoretalk. You're too young to be so cynical, Joey. You enjoy hurting me, don't you? This is foolish, I suppose. I'm much too old for you, anyway." He pauses. "Would you like to order breakfast now?"

I thought he'd never ask. I look for the sleepy waiter, who scurries

over when he sees my signal. He must be a hundred years old, a
bent man with faded eyes. He wears a limp *barong tagalog* over black
uniform pants, shiny and threadbare from too much use. His thin-
soled, imitation-leather shoes with pointy toes are gray with dust.
There's nothing sadder than cheap shoes on a man. "Yes, sir——" the
waiter is ready with pad and pencil.

I order a big breakfast: scrambled eggs over garlic-fried rice, side
of *longaniza* sausages and beef *tapa*, *kalamansi* juice, and fresh pineapple
for dessert. My last good meal for the next few days . . . The German
is amused.

I feel his eyes boring holes into me, watching every move as I eat,
as if he'll never get enough. "It's a picture I take with my mind, so
I won't forget you." I wish he'd stop. I don't mind when he takes
real pictures of me with that fancy camera of his, which he's done all
week: *Joey Swimming. Joey and Cup of Coffee. Joey Lighting a Cigarette.
Joey Bored. Joey Brooding.* The man has titles for everything! I can't
stand those imaginary snapshots he takes, especially when I'm eating.
"Stop staring at me! You're bugging me, man. You're spooky——" I
stress my words, narrow my eyes to make my point. Crazy. He keeps
it up. I give him an exasperated look, then give up and go back to
my food. I'm too tired to fight. Let him look all he wants—he's paying
for every second.

I eat my rice, my *longaniza*, slices of *tapa*, and fluffy scrambled eggs.
Lots of ketchup and Tabasco sprinkled on everything; it all tastes
incredibly delicious. I'm still hungry. I could eat a whole other plate
of the same thing; I can't wait for dessert.

The German refuses to eat. He orders more coffee and just sits
there, smoking, staring at me. His sad, stupid smile—just like Neil.
I keep my eyes on the crumbs on my plate. Ask the old waiter to
hurry up with the dessert. If I keep my mouth busy, I won't have to
think. Should I ask the German for more money? Should I ask him
to send for me? Whatever it is, I don't have much time.

The foreigner reading the newspaper looks up and recognizes the
German. He waves, getting up from his table to come over to us.
"Oh, shit," the German groans, waving back. Turns out the man's
an American journalist covering the film festival, a big fan of the

German's work. I get up from our table. Rainer looks alarmed. "Joey! Where are you going? Don't leave me alone with this bore—"

"Relax. I need cigarettes. Want some?"

"Have the waiter get them. For godsake, Joey. I don't even know the man's name! He'll bore me to tears—"

"The shop in the lobby's still closed. It's too early," I lie smoothly. "I have to go outside, find a street vendor . . . Don't worry, Rainer. I'll be right back—"

The American journalist approaches our table, grinning with plea-sure and holding out his hand. I wait until Rainer gets up to greet him and his attention is diverted. While his back is turned, I quickly reach under the table for the bag. It happens very fast, the only way it could possibly happen. I walk out the door without looking back, sorry to have missed the fresh pineapple, which the waiter is just now bringing to our table.

I'm fast, slippery, and calm. I'm out the door and in the lobby, walking quickly but not too quickly across the thick red carpet toward the hotel's main entrance. I know better than to run and arouse suspicion, though it's still so early in the morning that no one's at the front desk, everyone else is yawning and sleepy, not paying much attention.

It's okay. I take out the packet of drugs and money and slip it into my jeans pocket, casually leaving the bag with Rainer's passport and airline ticket on the couch facing the registration desk. Maybe Rainer gets his stuff back, maybe not. This way, he has a chance.

It seems strange, there's no one around and it's so quiet. There are two exits on either side of the main entrance. I move toward the door on the left just as a car pulls up in front of the hotel. Long and dark and important-looking, the car's navy blue or black. I'm not sure. I hesitate at the doorway, curious. Where's the doorman? The driver steps out, walks over to the passenger side, and opens the door. I hold my breath—I instantly recognize Senator Domingo Avila. Dressed casual yet businesslike, he looks just like I once saw him on TV, being interviewed by that slimy Cora Camacho. She asked all the wrong questions and didn't get any answers. Shit, Cora. Get to the point! A man like him would be fun to interview. I would've said:

"So, Senator Avila—what makes you fearless? How come you're still here? Everyone else is leaving town . . ."

The bastard would've said what he always says. "Joey, the hand-writing is on the wall."

Not bad for an old man, that Avila. Tall and trim, with a flat stomach, gray crew cut, horn-rimmed glasses. Unaware of my presence, he walks briskly toward the lobby, as if he was late for an appointment. It only takes a second for the noise, quick spurts of explosion I recognize immediately. I dive for the concrete sidewalk, hoping to be swallowed up by benevolent, unseen forces, hoping to come out of this alive. Something tells me I should've known better, I should've known all along, everything was too quiet and empty back there and now, I'm going to die. I'm going to die for something stupid, because I am a witness and I am a thief, I took the German's fucking drugs and money and I don't care about his loving me, I know the Senator's dead like I know my own name, I want to look behind me into the lobby, see his blood—

His blood, oozing bright and dark on the carpet. I wait for another burst of noise, wait for them to catch me outside on the pavement where I shouldn't have been, wait for the cold steel to press against the back of my bent head. I see everything. I want to scream, concrete sidewalk pressed against my face, my face twisted as I snatch one more glance at the blood in the lobby, imaginary gun pressed against the back of my head by imaginary assassins, my flesh bursting open—

The eerie silence lasts only a moment. Just as dangerous, just as unbearable. I hear screams come out of nowhere. The desk clerks, the bellhops, the drowsy waiters, the invisible doorman are all suddenly here in the lobby, bending over the dead Senator. Everyone's busy being hysterical, no one's seen me crouching on the ground outside. One of the desk clerks gets on the phone. She's the only one acting calm, unaffected by the Senator's bullet-ridden body sprawled on the carpet in front of her.

I know it's begun. I've seen the Senator's long, dark car speed away. There was another car. Something else I don't want to re-member. I scramble up to my feet and start running, I don't look back. I run. I run, I almost fly down the street, I disappear around the corner before the faceless men with dark glasses show up, before the shocked American journalist and the German wander out, dazed and confused by the noise and the blood, bullet holes in the walls, the Senator's lifeless body, so much blood from one man spattered everywhere, before the German Rainer, my Rainer, calls my name.

The Weeping Bride

There it is, the centerpiece on the presidential table: a twelve-tiered, gold and white cake trimmed with silver sugar doves. No. It's a twelve-tiered, white and silver cake with white sugar doves and gold filling, created especially for the occasion by the Alacran family dentist, Dr. Benita Zamora. Her son is a poet of the underground, and *she is not at the wedding*. The perennially smiling dentist has been detained by four unsmiling members of the Special Squadron Urban Warfare Unit while on the way to her car after baking the splendid cake. The car, a modest gunmetal-blue Toyota, is still locked and parked in front of the Makati Dental Center's steel and glass building. A half-eaten ham sandwich lies on the back seat, wrapped in wax paper. There seem to be no witnesses to the sudden event. *Dr. Benita Zamora is simply not at the wedding*. Her son's whereabouts are also unknown. According to *The Metro Manila Daily*, the poet's mother has been placed under house arrest. Or rather, she was placed under office arrest. The popular, affluent dentist, dentist to the stars, has chosen to spend the rest of her days within the confines of her professional environment. "It doesn't matter anyway. I only go home to sleep. . . . I'd rather die in my office," the dentist reveals under torture. She refuses to disclose her son's whereabouts.

No. It's actually a twelve-tiered hallucination, a golden pound cake with white vanilla and rum icing, white marzipan doves with silver candy eyes, sculpted white chocolate bows attached to silver filigree butterflies imported from Spain. No. Actually, the silver filigree butterflies were carefully constructed by sixteen blind nuns from the Convent of Our Lady of Perpetual Sorrow. The silver filigree butterflies are a gift from the First Lady, filigree butterflies suspended by invisible wires, filigree butterflies flying out of the bottom tier of the phenomenal cake.

The dentist is dead. The dentist never existed. The unforgettable wedding cake has actually been designed and baked from scratch by the bride's glamourous mother, Isabel Alacran. "I never knew she could cook!" the First Lady exclaims, visibly impressed by the intricacies of the edible sculpture. "My wife was trained to be an architect," Severo Alacran whispers confidentially to the First Lady and the President. The beaming President grunts with admiration. He hardly moves at all, swollen and rooted to his chair. He and his wife are guests of honor at the wedding.

Holding hands under an arc of violet, spun sugar flowers, the bride and groom figurines are balanced on a bed of buttery roses on the top tier of the cake. The First Lady groans with pleasure. She is served the first slice, and takes a healthy bite. The President shakes his head, points to his stomach, and refuses the cake offered to him. The First Lady signals for more. A young waiter with Elvis Presley hair rushes to serve her.

Senator Avila once said: "Food is the center of our ritual celebrations, our baptisms, weddings, funerals. You can't describe a real *Pinoy* without listing what's most important to him—food, music, dancing, and love—most probably in that order."

So the Senator once said, so even his enemy the General agrees. So the weeping bride dreams the night before the Senator's assassination: cakes melt in her mouth, tomatoes and onions ooze out of the slit bellies of grilled *bangus*, silent women baste the roasting flesh of pigs with honey, then smother the lacquered baby pigs under a pile of banana leaves.

She wears a floor-length white veil crowned with a wreath of garlic. "I insist!" her beautiful mother insists, hanging a necklace of garlic bulbs around her daughter's neck for additional protection. "You can't be too careful nowadays," the sinister groom says to the bride, flashing his canine teeth.

It's the pungent vinegar perfume of pork and chicken *adobo* the weeping bride smells, the pungent vinegar perfume a man rubs against his skin before pressing a woman closer to him. Taxi dancer, whore, blondie—a man's home away from home. "What's the matter, blondie? Can't stand my cologne?" the President laughs, rubbing more garlic and vinegar behind his ears. His bodyguards laugh with him. He's definitely one with a taste for blondes—although he likes them all, actually. Dark or fair, fat or thin, nubile or matronly. His personal physician's put him on a strict diet, and it's all for his own good. No pork, no cake, no women. It's all just a memory to him now, some image he pulls out of the night while he strokes himself down there, all dry and crusty between the legs.

The weeping bride wonders if her father will outlive the President.

Senator Domingo Avila has been shot dead.

Mourned by his stoic wife Luisa, by his missing daughter Daisy, the beauty queen rumored to have fled to the mountains with her guerrilla lover, and by his bewildered teenage daughter, Aurora; now mourned by his resentful brother Oscar, Oscar's wife Delia, and his only legitimate daughter, the artist Clarita; now mourned too by the weeping bride, Rosario "Baby" Alacran, who has married Oswaldo "Pepe" Carreon. She does not know why she married, or mourns.

She is not a political person. She is not someone who knew the Senator well. She is not someone who knows anyone well. Baby recalls the Senator's kindness to her once—no, maybe twice in her brief past, when she was a solitary child. Some generous gesture on his part, some friendly comment which even she finds hard to remember—but it happened, just the same. It's the essence she holds on to as she mourns his death at the hands of unknown gunmen, in spite of herself.

In spite of herself, she had longed to invite him to her spectacular wedding, and made the mistake of mentioning it. She was ridiculed, as usual. She was dismissed. The weeping bride knew better, of course. It was impossible. It was silly. She had no control over the situation. Even if he had been invited, the Senator wouldn't have shown up.

* * *

The wedding banquet never stops. A nauseating feast for the eyes, as well as the belly and the soul. Ox-tails stewed for hours in peanut sauce, egg custards quivering in burnt sugar syrup, silver tureens filled to the brim with steaming hot, black *dinuguan* . . . It's the black blood of a pig she pours on her head, the black pig's blood stew she bathes in, to mourn the death of a man . . .

"Imagine," she once confessed to her cousin Girlie, "I've been eating and enjoying *dinuguan* for years, never even considering—*dugo* is *dugo, dugo* means blood! My god, it's the black blood of a pig. My mother laughed when I told her—my mother doesn't eat *dinuguan*. Now I can't eat it anymore, without feeling sick—"

"You're making a big deal over nothing," Girlie Alacran said to her younger cousin, with no understanding but some sympathy.

Senator Avila has been shot dead by unknown assailants. The weeping bride has been in bed for the past week with a mysterious illness: aching bones, lack of appetite, occasional chills, and frequent nightmares. "Maybe it's the flu," she tells her mother on the telephone. The weeping bride apologizes for being ill, as she apologizes for most things in her life. Her mother says nothing. She is more annoyed than concerned with her only child's precarious health. Her daughter immediately senses this, and gets off the phone.

She has not said anything to her mother about her skin. The tiny, itchy, watery blisters that have suddenly reappeared on her fingers after so many years. She tries not to think about it, and applies more ointment from a tube she keeps under her pillow. Her furtiveness is unwarranted. Her husband is never home. He makes flimsy excuses, blames it all on his new job. Somehow, she thinks he may be telling the truth. *His job*, he has told her with pride, *is his whole life*. She never forgets anything anyone says. Her brain is a file cabinet, stuffed with snatches of conversations and vivid memories.

She remembers her servants. How quietly they enter and exit, bringing her hot *kalamansi* juice, chamomile tea, aspirin, icebags for her headaches, hot water bottles for her sore muscles. They take turns massaging her, saying very little. They pretend not to notice the blisters on her hands. She has the whole house to herself, ghostly servants on tiptoe, at her beck and call. She imagines they must mourn the dead Senator, and wonders if he is their hero. She is ashamed of feeling connected to them, and somehow feels unworthy. She tries, once again, to think of something else.

Her husband has been gone for two days this time. She isn't sure, but she suspects something ominous is occurring, something to do with this new husband of hers and the General. She picks up the remote control, turns on the color TV. It's time for her favorite daytime show, *Maid in the Philippines*. The jovial face of the host appears on the twenty-seven-inch screen to the familiar, comforting sound of a noisy laugh track and live applause. A servant named Lorna is telling the host her troubles, all about the family she has to support back home—"My *nanay*, my *tatay*, my three younger sisters, and one brother who wants to enter college." *Enter college*, that's exactly what she says. "Tell us what you're going to do for us in the talent competition," the host inquires with professional concern. The female contestants, all servants, are judged by the audience on the basis of their sad stories and showbiz talents. "I'm going to recite my favorite stanzas from *Florante at Laura* by Balagtas," Lorna informs him. The host whistles through his teeth. "Wow, Lorna *naman* are you kidding? *Bilib na bilib kaming lahat!*"

If her mother knew she was addicted to this show, she'd make another one of her snide comments. Talent shows and Tagalog soap operas are something the weeping bride has learned to watch and enjoy in secret. A furtive, innocent life—that is how she spends her afternoons, lying in bed.

Someone else starts to sing, someone named Naty, a ballad of unrequited love in Tagalog. The audience claps and claps, it looks like Naty might win. The weeping bride is unable to concentrate and finds the TV images suddenly depressing. It's all so sad and vulgar, just as her mother always said. Why doesn't she listen to her mother? She is suddenly afraid. She does not want this baby. She wonders if it is too late to see a doctor. She fantasizes phoning her worldly cousin Girlie. Surely Girlie knows a competent abortionist. If not in Manila, maybe Tokyo or Hong Kong. Money is certainly no object.

The weeping bride chokes on her tears, turning off the noisy TV.

Lying back against the sweat-drenched pillows, she closes her eyes. The weeping bride invents a cleansing ritual for herself. She makes it up as she goes along, this movie starring herself, this movie that goes on and on, this movie that is the only sure way she knows to put herself to sleep.

Senator Domingo Avila has been assassinated.

Dinuguan—it's the black blood of a pig the weeping bride pours on her head, the black blood stew of pale pink pig entrails she bathes in, mourning the death of a man she never knew.

Last Chance

There are no traffic lights working on this wide avenue, only an angry policeman gripping a whistle tensely between clenched teeth. Holding one arm rigidly out, he barely keeps the mess of honking cars, glittering jeepneys, pedicabs, and lopsided tin buses at bay. His other arm waves the jostling crowd along, a parade of bright colors crossing the boulevard. A few pedestrians are wearing battered straw hats, while others hold up flowered nylon umbrellas to shield themselves from the blazing noonday sun. It's exactly twelve noon on a sweltering day, the worst possible time for a nervous policeman to be directing traffic at the busy intersection. He is new at his job, and curses continuously when he is not blowing his whistle at the crowd rushing by him.

Romeo Rosales steps off the curb on his way to SPORTEX to meet his girlfriend Trinidad Gamboa. As usual, they are going to share a hasty lunch of salted *balut* and warm Cokes, or barbecued cubes of meat-on-a-stick from a street vendor, the sort of food Trinidad claims to abhor but devours heartily. "They always tell you it's pork," she complains about the barbecue, "but for all we know, we could be eating dog meat." He shrugs. "It tastes pretty good. Anyway," he teases her, "I like dogs better than pigs."

Romeo hurries to keep up with the brisk pace of the crowd. He sees the impressive façade of SPORTEX looming from a distance, promising air-conditioning, escalators, seductive displays of imported merchandise, and innocuous, piped-in Muzak. The bored salesclerks intimidate Romeo, with their crisp black and white uniforms and polished black shoes. The employees are not allowed to wear any

159

jewelry except watches. It is part of their job to reflect the SPORTEX image of austere elegance, a concept which Romeo finds alien and disconcerting. "Why can't you wear what you want to wear?" he asked Trinidad when she started her new job. "Everyone looks like they're going to a funeral," Romeo pointed out, perplexed.

He hated being in the store. He always dreaded meeting Trinidad in the dingy employee's lounge located in the dark and dirty recesses of SPORTEX's vast, subterranean basement. The store never failed to make him feel poorer and shabbier than he actually was, especially when the salesclerks seemed to make a point of ignoring him the few times he ventured into the men's department. "You're so paranoid," Trinidad said, irritated, "no one's making *irap* to you—they're just busy!" "If they're so busy, why are they just standing there, staring at their nails?" Romeo argued.

Trinidad loves her job, holds dear the small prestige associated with being an Alacran employee. She works long hours without any breaks, isn't paid overtime, rushes through her lunch in less than forty minutes, and gratefully accepts her meager salary. There are no fringe benefits or medical insurance attached to her job, aside from the twenty-percent discount on "all SPORTEX items purchased." For her, the discount is valuable and the job is fulfilling, keeping her in constant touch with the amazing lives of the rich and their wives.

"Mrs. Alacran was in the store yesterday, making one of her surprise inspections. Imagine, she called me by my first name!" Trinidad imitates her boss's famous wife by lowering her voice. " 'Trini, how are you?' *Naku!* She was wearing a genuine Oscar de la Renta, I almost fainted it was so beautiful! It's a good thing I just got a perm and manicure and my counter was spic and span. *Alam mo na,* I'm always wiping away with my rags and my Windex! They fired Nora last week for having dirty nails. Mrs. Alacran had a fit when she saw them—she screamed at Nora in front of the customers, it was horrible *talaga.* Poor Nora, I don't know how she got careless like that, she worked at SPORTEX longer than any of us . . . *Ay,*" Trinidad sighs with exaggerated relief, "Mrs. Alacran hinted I might be getting a raise this Christmas as a reward for my big sale to the *Hapon*—"

Romeo is unimpressed. "You deserve a bonus and a raise for waiting on those Japs," he grumbles. His father, grandfather, and uncle were all tortured by the Japanese soldiers during the war, a fact Romeo has never forgotten. "Why don't you ask for a promotion? It seems like you've been working at that place forever—"

"Forever? I've only been here a few months. And what will they promote me to—department manager? No thanks, I'd rather die. If stuff doesn't sell, you get blamed for everything. Whatsa matter with you, darling? You're in one of your moods *nanaman*." Oblivious to Romeo's mounting anger, Trinidad tells him about her plan to study conversational Japanese under Mrs. Alacran's sponsorship, so she can sell more goods to the hordes of Japanese tourists who shop at SPORTEX. "Look at Carmen. Last month, she was voted Miss Sportex, and she got a real Seiko as a prize for selling more than anyone else in the entire store!" Trinidad's eyes are glowing. Romeo nods, not really listening to her chatter. He interrupts suddenly to ask her to start meeting him outside the store's main entrance. Trinidad is baffled by Romeo's insistence. "Okay, okay, but why? Don't you like coming inside and seeing our latest displays?"

"We never have enough time together," Romeo answers. "This way, if we meet outside, it will save us precious moments." Trinidad smiles warmly at him, flattered.

On this sweltering day, Romeo wonders if there's a painless way to tell her he can no longer see her. The sight of SPORTEX up ahead makes his stomach queasy. Romeo has never loved Trinidad, but he respects her enough to want to leave her with some semblance of dignity. He does not want to be late for their last appointment.

Perhaps he'll tell her he finally got a bit part in a movie with Tito Alvarez and he's leaving immediately to shoot on location in Hong Kong. She'd never believe him of course, and if she did, Trinidad would manage to borrow the money and invite herself along. If he was more of a bastard, he wouldn't explain himself at all; the most he'd do would be to write her a good-bye letter before disappearing completely from her life.

Romeo has decided to do the best he can; he has purposely chosen this brief lunch period in which to tell the gold-toothed, loyal salesclerk the relationship is over. She will be furious and upset, but he knows her well by now and is sure she will not have hysterics in front of her beloved SPORTEX.

His conscience nags him, tells him he may be a fool, may be giving up a sure thing; he hears his mother's bitter voice ringing in his head. "The only stability in your life has been that woman. Don't end up like your father—wasting his life chasing after empty dreams! Who do you think you are, my son?" His mother had broken down and wept during his last visit with her. "Enough of your big city *kalocohan*! Trinidad is a devoted woman—I can tell from everything you've told me about her, you'll never find anyone else like her, believe me . . ." His mother had pleaded with him. For the first time in his life, Romeo felt repelled by the sight of this old, terrified woman.

"I don't understand you, Mama. Don't you want me to better myself? Don't you want me to try?"

"*Ay*, my son—of course I do! That has nothing to do with Trinidad. Can't you see she's trying to help you? She works hard, she's ambitious and practical, she's always on your side no matter what—"

"She's a fool," Romeo blurted out, surprised by his own bluntness.

His mother shook her head. "Ahhh," she sighed, "so that's what you really think of that poor girl."

She was getting on Romeo's nerves. Wasn't she supposed to be on his side? "You don't know her, Mama. You've never met her. And she's no girl—she's much older than me. Why do you think I've never brought her home to meet you?"

His mother gave him a long, appraising look, as if seeing her son clearly for the first time. " *'Sus Maria*, Orlando—I am only repeating what you said about her in your letter. You had nothing but praise for her."

"You don't know Trini. She can be conniving and manipulative—"

"*Dios ko*, such big words! Ugly words!"

Romeo's voice grew louder. "You don't know her! If you knew her like I do, you'd agree she's not for me."

"So you've just been using this poor woman all along and now you're ashamed to bring her home—"

It was his mother's turn to lash out at him. Romeo's sullen silence answered the widow's question. "I don't love her," he finally said, "and that's that. I can't imagine life with a woman like her, who clings to me like she's drowning, choking the breath out of me—"

"I read between the lines of your letter, trying to separate the truth from what you wished me to believe." She paused briefly to acknowledge with sadness the look of surprise on her son's face. "Orlando, you are a good son. You've been a good example to your brother. I know you want me to think highly of you, just as you want the whole world to recognize you someday. From everything you say, even things too good to be true, I gather Trinidad only wants the best for you. She is willing to help you in this so-called 'career' of yours—don't get angry, my son. You're lucky to have found her." The widow was already resigned to the situation. What a fool her eldest son was turning out to be, filled with delusions just like her husband. Yet she chose her words carefully, so as not to hurt or further alienate him.

"I don't love her," Romeo repeated grimly.

"Sometimes it's not about the kind of love you've learned about from those silly movies and songs you like so much," the widow said, looking away.

"I don't want it any other way."

"Wake up, my son! You'll grow old and one day find yourself alone. Don't cheapen a woman's devotion. You're lucky—"

"She's bad luck." Romeo cut her off before she could continue, before their visit became even more painful and burdensome to him. His rudeness to his mother made him feel brutal and ashamed; he was unable to look at her, furious with her for revealing his shortcomings and so much of her own suffering.

Abruptly, he got up and walked out the door. The bus back to Manila wasn't due for another hour and a half. Romeo decided to hang around the *sari-sari* store downstairs and wait. He couldn't stand

163

being in his mother's accusing presence for one more minute. The widow kept staring out the window and never called him back. It was the last time Romeo saw his mother, and secretly he blamed Trinidad for causing the rift between them.

As the widow Rosales feared, Romeo had no success competing on the numerous talent contests on radio and television. He tried them all, sometimes not even making it past the preliminary auditions. He despised Trinidad for being the only one who still believed in him. She showered him with an endless supply of flashy discount shirts and pants from her new job, encouraging him in that optimistic way of hers to keep trying. "Your time will come," she kept saying. Trinidad's blind faith only made Romeo doubt himself even more. He was driven to ask his supervisor at Monte Vista for a promotion.

Romeo corners the house manager, Mr. Chen, in charge of all waiters, busboys, and maintenance personnel at Severo Alacran's country club. "Excuse me *lang*, sir—eh, ah, *puwede ba*, Mr. Chen, may I have a discussion with you?" The terrified Romeo is not sure how to properly address the aloof Mr. Chen, who raises an eyebrow haughtily, trying to fix a name to the obsequious young waiter. "Discussion? About what?" Mr. Chen speaks in English. The aggression and contempt in Mr. Chen's booming voice alarms and embarrasses Romeo, who looks quickly around the deserted Monte Vista verandah to make sure no one else hears the exchange. He clears his throat, swallowing hard.

"My job. My promotion, sir. *Ay*, sir—Mr. Alacran said maybe someday a desk job would be available in the lobby. I've been here exactly two years and four months—"

"Is that so?"

"Yes, sir. I have a high school diploma—my highest grades were in English and spelling. I'm not a bad typist—"

"Is that so? Young man, you're lucky to have this job at all," Mr. Chen replies, smiling coolly and moving past the blushing waiter.

As he watches Mr. Chen walk away from him toward his office, Romeo mutters to himself, *Yes, Mama. I guess I'm just a lucky fuck.*

The house manager turns abruptly to confront him. "Did you say something, young man?"

Romeo shakes his head. "No, sir."

"Are you sure? I thought I heard you say something behind my back."

"No, sir."

"What did you say your name was?"

"Orlando, sir."

"Orlando. Orlando WHAT?"

"Rosales, sir."

"Rosales, if you don't watch it, I'll promote you *down* to a caddy or ditch boy on our beautiful golf course. How would you like that?" Mr. Chen chuckles, but his eyes remain hard and cold as he studies the young waiter. "Just think—you can live on your tips! I think I'll call Mr. Alacran right now, get his opinion—"

Romeo's eyes widen in panic. "Please, sir—"

"What is it, Rosales? Any other complaints?"

"No, sir. Please—" Romeo takes a deep breath. "I'm a very good waiter, sir. I like my job."

"Is that so, Rosales? I'll ask around, keep my eye on you from now on. Mr. Alacran is anxious for current evaluations of all our employees—we're cutting back after the holidays, Rosales. In the meantime, don't think I'm deaf or stupid. And shut the *fack* up when I'm in the room!" Mr. Chen turns away from the humiliated waiter and walks briskly across the lobby to a door marked PRIVATE.

One humiliation after another. On the sidewalk outside SPORTEX, Romeo exhales, feeling miserable. Tonight in the Monte Vista's main ballroom, there will be a special banquet and awards ceremony in honor of Mabuhay Studios' fortieth anniversary in the movie business. Tito Alvarez is sure to attend. Romeo refuses to give up hope, though his phone calls and urgent letters to his childhood friend have gone unanswered. Romeo plans to sign up for night duty, since extra waiters are needed for the banquet anyway. He will corner his friend and ask him a favor—beg him for a screen test, a bit part in his next movie, anything. How could Tito deny him? They had promised to be loyal and watch out for each other, part of being two boys from the same home town, part of Tito's *utang*, his blood debt to Romeo for all the years he'd covered up for Tito's petty crimes. As a last resort, Romeo is resigned to offering himself as Tito's chauffeur and personal bodyguard. Romeo has always had a certain expertise with the *balisong* knife, a talent his old friend should remember and appreciate. Romeo is also convinced that the sinister role of bodyguard has more prestige in the world than the demeaning, servile role of waiter. Romeo is through with being a nobody.

He has to get rid of Trinidad; in Tito's eyes, Trinidad will never do. When it came to women, shoes, and guns, Tito was an expert. Romeo fondly remembers him as the most critical man in the universe, a man of impeccable taste and sophistication, blessed with perfect timing and the luck of the devil.

Tonight's the night—Romeo's last chance to confront Tito and salvage his own uncertain destiny. The prospects of living out the rest of his life as a waiter at the Monte Vista or as an underpaid office clerk loom large before him.

The sun beats down on Romeo's unprotected head. He sees the slight figure of Trinidad leaving the SPORTEX building and standing on the pavement out front. Romeo slows down to give himself time to think. Sweat mixed with his perfumed hair grease drips down into his ears and drenches his collar. He adjusts his imitation RayBans, another recent gift from Trinidad. His forehead glistens. Romeo pulls out a handkerchief and wipes his face. He feels a rushing sensation, a tingle in his stomach he interprets as a good sign. He has made the right decision. He will break off with Trinidad—maybe he will simply be honest with her. He will be cool and efficient, just as he will be cool and efficient tonight at the banquet, when he calmly approaches his old friend for a job. He must choose for himself and finally live the life he has always dreamed of, even if, as his widowed mother has warned him, he chooses unwisely.

Trinidad Gamboa hurries out of SPORTEX, her eyes sweeping across Epifanio de los Santos Avenue for signs of Romeo. Impatiently and out of habit, she checks her cheap watch. It is only 12:29, one minute before their scheduled meeting. Romeo isn't technically late, but she is unbearably hungry. Yesterday, Romeo never showed up at all. When she phoned him later at his job, he scolded her for doing so and told her he wasn't feeling well. "Why didn't you call me? I stood around out front like an idiot, and never had my lunch," Trinidad said. Romeo sighed. "Trini—we're not allowed to use the phone at Monte Vista."

"You should have called me the night before."

"Trini—I don't have a phone, *di ba*?"

"Well. You could have gone to the drugstore downstairs—asked to use their phone—"

"Trini—I've got to hang up. You're going to get me fired."

Trinidad prepares a list of complaints in her head. Her stomach gurgles. Time is slipping by, the precious forty minutes she has for sharing lunch with her lover. She eyes the vendor with his makeshift barbecue stand across the plaza. She paces up and down the pavement in her sensible, low-heeled shoes, trying not to think about food.

Romeo hesitates one block away, frozen by indecision. He wonders if he should wait until he confronts Tito Alvarez and works things out. What if his mother is right? Perhaps he is being too hasty.

At first, Romeo does not see or hear what is happening not far from where he stands. He stares off into space, the other people on the sidewalk a blur of colors and sound. The screams grow louder. A man in a torn T-shirt is running through the crowd, toward Romeo. He is shouting and shoving people aside. His words are unintelligible, his frantic eyes bulging with fear. The crowd panics and runs in every direction. People take up the screaming and shouting until it becomes one huge sound, a siren of terror echoing through the streets. Traffic is halted, car horns honking and blaring. There are other men running after the man in the torn T-shirt, men waving guns in the air. The man in the torn T-shirt rushes past Romeo. The traffic cop is yelling and blowing his whistle, and it is this shrill sound that snaps Romeo out of his momentary daze.

He is knocked down by several shrieking men and women. Romeo picks himself up and starts to walk toward SPORTEX. It is automatic, this response, the direction he takes in spite of the pandemonium around him. Trini, SPORTEX, Trini. *Dios ko*, he prays, *'Sus, Maria, Josep*, if I can just reach Trini. He can almost see her frowning face, hear her petulant voice. "You're late, Romeo—as usual." As usual, of course, darling. He would agree. But Trini, this is the last time you'll have to put up with my tardiness. Or maybe he'll take her in his arms, tell her they will never part. He imagines the puzzled look on her face, the way she cocks her head to get a better look at him. She'd think it was one of his stupid jokes. "Never mind, let's hurry— I'm dying of hunger," she'd say, in that bossy way of hers.

It is then that the bullet hits him, and he falls. Stunned, Romeo is not sure why he has fallen. He tries to get up but can't, and the look of astonishment on his face is suddenly replaced by fear. He thinks he hears Trinidad calling his name. Then the world goes momentarily silent and falls away from him. He is floating on a slab of concrete, suspended above the wide avenue strewn with broken umbrellas, smashed cars, and bodies trampled by a panicked crowd.

Romeo wants to laugh. Something pains him, and he worries that if he doesn't drag himself off the street, the oncoming cars will kill him. Why isn't anyone there to help him? Where is Trini? Romeo turns his head at the sound of footsteps approaching. The pain is unbearable. "That's him," one cop says to another, pointing with his chin. Is it the guard from Mabuhay Studios? "*Sigé*, I'm sure of it." "*Putang ina mo!*" the other man curses, pointing a gun at Romeo's head. Is it a soldier? The men are wearing khaki pants and shirts, outfits busy with significant trimmings and insignia. Romeo is afraid to look at the men's faces too directly—he is sure they are ready for any excuse to shoot him again.

DATELINE: MANILA
by Cora Camacho

In spite of intermittent rains and the ongoing gas crisis, Mabuhay Studios' *Serenade* continues to be the biggest hit of the season. It chalked up close to a million and a half pesos on opening day, and has outgrossed even the new Lolita Luna sex drama *A Candle Is Burning*.

Speaking of *La Luna*, she doesn't deny the fact that she doesn't like upcoming young starlet Bootsy Pimentel, daughter of veteran character actress Patsy Pimentel. "Blame it on chemistry," Lolita said to me during a recent phone interview. In fact, Lolita and Bootsy have a running feud that's the talk of the town, and not just because newcomer Tito Alvarez has all the women hot and bothered! Apparently, Bootsy has been keeping *La Luna* waiting on the set of the new movie they're making, *Ulan*, a Tagalog version of that Lana Turner–Richard Burton potboiler *The Rains of Ranchipur*.

Funny. Not too long ago, it was our Lolita who made cast and crew wait endlessly. While doing *A Candle Is Burning*, *La Luna* disappeared for weeks. She just felt like leaving the country, *daw*—her exact words. Director Max Rodriguez, one of *La Luna*'s ex-boyfriends, walked off the picture and announced he would never work with her again. After three months of expensive delays, director Tirso Velasco was called in to finish the picture . . . The movie's a hit, and it's a good thing Severo Alacran runs Mabuhay Studios . . . or Lolita Luna might've been in a lot of *trouble*.

Now, it seems that Bootsy is doing a Lolita and Lolita is furious. It's the first time the two tempestuous beauties have been teamed up, under the sure-handed direction of our own renaissance man, actor-director-producer Nestor Noralez. This time, Nestor's also written the script, and it wouldn't surprise me if someday Nestor was declared one of our national treasures . . . It was his unique idea to cast *La Luna* and ingenue Bootsy in this film. Whatever Nestor wants, Nestor gets . . .

Bets are being placed on whether Nestor will ever complete this project. According to our sources, *La Luna* has also taken to showing up late on the set these days, and when she does turn up—she can't remember her lines!

—*Celebrity Pinoy*

Movie Star

The Aiwa tape deck is blasting. Now Grace, now Chaka . . . "Just one more time, please . . . Oh, come on . . . You don't really think it's too LOUD, do you, Nicky? *Dios ko 'day*, if you think this is loud . . . wait till I play you some real rock'n'roll! What opera? I don't understand Italian! *Hoy*, Nicky—relax *lang*. 'This is high-class mood music for grown-up girls!' " Lolita cheerfully quotes an Englishman she once knew. She is not sure what he meant exactly, but she enjoys irritating the General.

The Englishman had brought her the latest releases from London. He insisted on fucking to black music. The scion of a family of stodgy civil servants completely unaware of their son's colonial obsessions, the Englishman often told Lolita how much she reminded him of Tina Turner. When her son was born, the Englishman said he would love to bring Lolita back to London and marry her, if only . . . He had a problem finishing sentences, and Lolita was afraid to press him further. She still misses him.

The General hates it when she's high and defiant, floating around the room, ignoring his presence. She moves to the hypnotic music, a repetitive blur of incomprehensible lyrics to the General's ear. He asks her to turn down the volume, but she pretends not to hear him.

At one time, it was enough that he was a powerful man who wanted her more than any other woman. She punished him with her beauty; in the beginning, she was in total control. Things changed gradually after the first year. Lolita realized she had deceived herself, became more uneasy and unsure of him. He, in turn, became more possessive and demanding. She wonders why she is unable to break free of him; perhaps the thought of losing the protection and material security he provides her is too terrifying. She is a talented actress, but she does not know it. She agrees with those who attribute her success to her flagrant sexuality and magnificent body; she is limited in her thinking, as usual. She is a movie star who thrusts her hips and tongue out at the General in that privileged, mocking way of hers, complaining: "You're always telling me what to do, Nicky."

When she is high on her drugs, what she calls her "vitamins," Lolita Luna entertains her delusions more openly. She is convinced the General will help her fix her papers and pay for her passage out of Manila to a foreign country, some place where she can start all over again. Lolita Luna is paid well for her movies, but she's always broke. She dreams of Los Angeles and New York, somewhere she can study acting and stop playing so much, somewhere she can indulge her passion for shopping. Clothes, shoes, lingerie, cosmetics, chocolates, household appliances: it doesn't matter, Lolita always buys at least two of each.

"We can't go. The President needs me," General Ledesma tells her gruffly.

"We haven't gone anywhere in almost a year!"

"There are more important things in life than your vacations—"

"This is not a vacation, this is a new life. You're always telling me to change, so now I want to change. I can't do it by staying in Manila—why don't you arrange it so I can leave?" She stares at him, trying to shame him into submission. He gazes back at her coolly.

"You're in the middle of making a movie, remember? Don't invite trouble by leaving town. Gossip about you and your crazy antics bothers me. It bothers me deeply," the General repeats for emphasis. "What about that shopping trip to Hong Kong a few months ago? Wasn't that enough? Don't you consider that a vacation? You left town without telling me. I had to hear about it from Nestor—"

"I'm not discussing vacations. I'm talking about leaving Manila, permanently—"

The General's laugh is soft and derisive. He sits erect in an oversize wicker lounge chair, quietly picking at the food set in front of him. The servant Mila has left a tray with sandwiches, cold bottles of TruCola and beer, and assorted Chinese pastries. While he eats, he observes that Lolita never does, notes how black and luminous her eyes are, how restlessly she moves around the room. He thinks: It's that shit she's on again—she can't fool me. If I ever catch that dealer of hers, by the time I'm through, he's going to beg me to kill him.

"You have everything you want, right here in Manila," the General says. "Why don't you straighten out and behave? You're a lucky girl—do you know how many others dream of being in your position? Just remember—I don't want to hear anymore *tsismis* about you from Nestor—"

"Nestor is an ass and a liar! He's jealous, and wishes he was me. Of course, you'd rather listen to his vicious gossip than believe me— all I did was go shopping with Girlie for the weekend! I just had to get out of here for a few days—but I'm sure Nestor made it sound like a juicy scandal!" Lolita pouts. He loves it when she gets angry and sticks out her lower lip. He finds it amusing when she sulks.

Lolita saunters over to the tape deck and presses the rewind button. The same song blares out of the speakers a third time. The General calmly finishes his chicken sandwich, then reaches for a black bean cake. "You shouldn't be seen too often with Girlie Alacran."

Lolita stops fiddling with her hair and looks at him, annoyed. "Why?"

"She's nothing but a whore, that's why. It's common knowledge in Manila," the General replies, almost prim. The sudden prudishness in his manner makes Lolita smile.

"Girlie Alacran doesn't need money," Lolita argues, "she's an Alacran! She's Junior Miss Philippines! Why should she—"

"Because she likes it," the General snaps, "just like you like your drugs. It's a thrill for her—making men pay. Especially when she doesn't need the money. You understand that, don't you?"

The General bites into the sweet, round bean cake, which crumbles in his hand. Lolita watches him chew and is reminded of a plodding *carabao* with dusty eyes, submerged in muddy water, chewing grass.

"Did you kill the Senator?" she suddenly asks, taking him by surprise.

The General takes his time, pouring TruCola into a tall glass filled with ice. "Haven't you read the newspapers? We caught the assassin."

"You're really disgusting," Lolita says quietly. She gets up from her seat and paces around the room.

The General takes a long drink from his glass. "You must thank Mila for me, darling. She really knows how to take care of me—"

"Why don't you have another sandwich, then? It's such a shame to waste food," Lolita sneers. She needs a smoke so badly, she wants to scream. Her eyes frantically scan the room for a pack of cigarettes, finally resting on a butt left in one of the ashtrays. Whose? Maybe her dealer's—he was over last night, demanding more money. She picks up the butt and lights it, inhaling gratefully.

The General wipes his mouth carefully with a paper napkin. "I thought you quit smoking."

"I did." Lolita shrugs, stubbing out the last of her cigarette in the ashtray. He had asked her not to smoke. It was bad for her health, the General said, and it stank . . . She smiles at the old man. The air conditioner emits a low, steady hum in the white room. The tape comes to a stop. Lolita walks over to the sound system given her by Severo Alacran. She presses the eject button.

"It's about time," General Ledesma murmurs. He is not prepared for the next tape she inserts, "Pull Up to the Bumper" by Grace Jones. Lolita turns up the volume another decibel. The General groans. "Turn it down NOW," he orders her. When she ignores him, he gets up and kicks the machine with his foot. The machine is destroyed with two swift hard kicks. The silence that follows is deafening.

The General sits down again to eat, saying nothing. He is extremely angry, yet outwardly calm and impassive; he puts away enormous amounts of food. He considers his next move. If he were a wiser man, he would leave her. The affair with Lolita Luna is a messy one, and he cannot afford to waste time and emotion on messy situations.

She does something contrary to her nature. She gets down on her knees before him. She begs him to arrange her visa and lend her the money to leave. She promises to pay him back as soon as she is able, as soon as she is settled. She tells him how important it is to her, how she will lose her mind if she continues living like this, how she is tired of being a movie star, but can't explain why. She does not tell him how trapped she feels, alone with her watchdog servant in her white apartment. When she is finished, he tells her he doesn't believe her. He accuses her of being stoned and of toying with him.

She is stunned by his chilly response. She has planned this moment, aware it excites him to see her kneeling like this, dressed only in her underwear. He has never seen her beg; he's been waiting a long time. A giddiness comes over her. "I swear I'm not high," she whispers to him. "I don't want you to go anywhere," the General finally says, tenderly. "I don't want you out of my sight. I want you here in Manila, where you belong." The General is almost moved to tears when Lolita starts crying. Then he wonders if this is another of her cheap movie tricks, this ability to cry at will.

"If you're so determined to leave," he says, "why don't you ask your patron saint Alacran to give you the money? Or one of those foreigners you like so much? Maybe Alacran will even go with you— I hear New York's his favorite city. A man like him can take off whenever he wants." It pains the General to admit his awareness of her treachery, but he can't help himself.

"Fuck Alacran! Fuck the men you've removed from my life!" Lolita yells. Herself again, she stomps angrily around the room. "Look what you've done to my stereo! You son of a bitch, you better buy me another one—" She whirls to confront him where he sits unmoving, a toad buddha on his wicker throne. "I want to get out of here, Nicky! I want to get out of here before I get killed!"

He looks disgusted. "Why would anyone want to kill *you*?"

"Because I'm your mistress. Because they all know—"

The General is curious and alert now. "What do they know?"

"Oh, nothing. You never know," she adds quickly, "I might get killed by accident, in one of those demonstrations—"

"I didn't know you were such an activist."

"I'm not!" Lolita pauses. "Max has been getting threatening phone calls."

"Max Rodriguez is an avowed leftist troublemaker. He deserves what he gets—"

"What do you mean? Max is a movie director."

"Max deserves what he gets," the General repeats, with the same bland look on his face.

"Nestor told me Max has been blacklisted. He can't even get a job directing plays, or teaching at the university—"

The General shrugs. "Max should be pleased. He's so busy organizing protests and defending human rights, he doesn't have time to direct anything."

"I like Max."

"I don't like *baklas*."

"You like Nestor."

"Nestor's useful."

Lolita longs for another cigarette. She considers asking Mila to run the errand for her, then remembers Mila is gone for the afternoon. She is always gone while he visits. It's never bothered Lolita in the past, but today she wishes she wasn't alone with the old man in her white apartment. The polished chrome and glass, the white abstract paintings and the regulated temperature strike her as ominous and all wrong.

"Is it true Daisy Avila's been captured?" She asks him. "They say she came back to town when her father died to try and see her family, and they found her in some hideout." She knows better than to pry, but questions keep pouring out of her.

"Who told you that—Nestor?" The General casually picks up a bottle of beer. He sips from the bottle, which surprises her. He is normally a fastidious man.

"No one told me. You know how it is on the set. There's a lot of waiting around—people make *tsismis*. I hear all sorts of things—"

"Ahhh," the General sighs, "*tsismis*. I forget—this country thrives on misinformation." He pauses for an instant. "And what exactly do you say, when you hear this kind of *tsismis*? How do you react? Do you add fuel to the fire?"

"I don't say anything, Nicky. I just listen."

He watches her face closely, sees exhaustion crease her brightly made up features. He knows she is lying. "I've always known I could trust you," he says.

She forces herself to smile at him, an effort that doesn't go unnoticed. Once again, the General's pride is wounded.

He wants to make love to her. He dreams she will come to him out of desire—not for drug money, rent money, or access to his power. Not because of her son, who is indirectly supported by the General. The General knows he is a fool, but he holds out his arms in spite of himself, gesturing impatiently for her to come to him.

Lolita Luna realizes that the conversation is over and she is not going to get what she wants. She will rot in Manila for the rest of her life, or else he will have her killed; it is that simple. It is a revelation for the movie star, and almost invigorating. Pulling off her lavender panties, she bursts out laughing. She flings them at the bewildered General; they land on his left shoulder, hook onto one of his epaulets and hang there, a forlorn and frilly flag. "If you're not going to help me, then leave my house," she says with contempt.

"Once again, I must remind you, darling—the lease is in my name."

She storms out of the living room and locks herself in the bathroom. Like the rest of the apartment, the bathroom is white, the walls and ceiling mirrored. The white tub is sunken, the floor around it carpeted with a plush white rug. The effect is both antiseptic and sexual. The bathroom is her favorite room, her hideaway. The sight of her naked body in the mirrors excites her. Transfixed by her own image, she caresses herself, then remembers the old man waiting in the other room.

Disgusting old shit. She can imagine only too well what he's up to—stuffing her panties in his pocket, one more souvenir of one more disgusting situation. They were all the same, these old men. Even Severo Alacran, with all his high-class manners and expensive cologne. Carrying around her used panties as if they were a fetish, like a piece of her they had carved off, like her skin. She offered them some glimpse of immortality—she knew this in her own stoned, fuzzy, instinctual way.

Lolita Luna has one more option. One of Severo Alacran's partners has approached her about an unusual movie deal, what he refers to as "experimental art films." These art films would involve lengthy close-ups of Lolita Luna's vagina, shot by professional cameramen in living color and in a variety of simulated violent settings. "We will only allude to violence," the man reassures her. Her vagina teased by the gleaming blade of a knife, for example, or perhaps a stubby black pistol. Or by the edge of a samurai sword, in a script featuring grinning Japanese villains. When the movie star looks offended, the producer hastens to calm her. "Simulated and suggestive—fear as an erotic stimulant—that's all we're after. You'll be surprised how much people will pay to see you, *La Dolce Luna!* It's not a movie for the average taxi driver, of course. He could never afford the price of admission. This is art! Think of your European counterpart! If you wish, there will be no actual penetration," he adds blithely.

She is asked to name her price, a request which intrigues her. "You're our biggest star after all," the producer says. She wonders if Severo Alacran is involved, and decides not to ask. She is told the movies are privately screened for select audiences. "We only use top directors and performers," the producer continues. "Max Rodriguez and Nestor Noralez have already agreed to direct our projects." Lolita is stunned by the information. The producer tells her to take her time making a decision, and leaves her an engraved business card with his name and phone number.

More shoes, more drugs, her own ticket out of the country. Her debts paid off, once and for all. Her four-year-old son's future finally insured. Her child lives with her parents in Zambales. Strict Catholics, Lolita's mother and father have not spoken to her in years. They are ashamed of their daughter and refuse to see her popular movies. Her mother claims the child as her own. Lolita sends home generous monthly stipends for her son, who is clearly mestizo. She cannot decide who the father is—maybe the Englishman who married Daisy Avila, maybe some American. It's not important. She loves her son and is convinced he is better off with her parents. Lolita has not seen him since his second birthday, as her mother's grim countenance makes all visits unbearable.

She is fascinated by her dark and brazen image in the mirror, by the way her flesh glows in the midst of such impersonal splendor. The General bangs his fist against the locked door, twisting the brass knob and calling her name. He apologizes and pleads with her, promising her a plane ticket one moment, then threatening to kick in the door when she doesn't respond.

The old man's voice is hoarse with shouting. Lolita Luna tears herself away from her mirrors. "All right, all right, calm down, Nicky!" she shouts back. She hesitates, her hand on the doorknob, then she dismisses her fears. The General is just another old man. She opens the door.

Golf

In Girlie Alacran's dream, the caddies are dark, barefoot boys with reddish-gold streaks in their long, uncombed hair. They live in caves beneath the palatial country club, which is perched on a cliff overlooking a jungle of banana, *narra*, tamarind, coconut, and indigo trees. Wild orchids, red and pink *gumamela* flowers sprout miraculously from the clusters of serpentine vines that cover the jungle floor.

It is dusk when the boys creep out stealthily from their subterranean shelter. The unsuspecting guests sip rum cocktails on the open-air verandah; they wear bathing suits with fluffy towels draped around their necks. Languid in their rattan lounge chairs, they gaze blankly at the spectacular jungle view, not talking to each other.

Everyone is present who matters: Uncle Severo and Auntie Isabel, cousin Baby, Girlie's dead mother Blanca, her blind father Pacifico and fat brother Boomboom, her past lover Malcolm Webb, even the President and the First Lady. They are all sitting in separate areas, unaware of one another, when the front flap of cousin Baby's maternity bathing suit is blown up by a sudden gust of wind, revealing the bright yellow beach ball concealed underneath. "That's all there is," cousin Baby starts singing. "Sprinkled with stars / that's all there is / sprinkled with shining stars!" She closes her eyes, repeating the inane lyrics with rapt concentration, her face glowing and ecstatic. "Santa Rosario, Santa Rosario, where is your husband?" Malcolm Webb asks, running up to her. He is wearing a waiter's jacket and bow tie over his swimming trunks, and carries a tray of assorted drinks. When there is no response from cousin Baby, he climbs up on the railing and dives off into the jungle, the tray of drinks still balanced on one hand.

Girlie's blind father taps a rhythm with his cane. "Sprinkled with little / tiny stars," he joins in the singing, his voice feeble and strained. He is almost drowned out by cousin Baby's unwavering soprano.

"Tiny / tiny stars / sparkling stars!" sings an enthusiastic chorus led by the President and First Lady. They love to sing, and the First Lady is radiant with happiness. The song ends abruptly; they force Girlie to kneel on the edge of the verandah. She is blindfolded, her hands tied behind her back. "You frauds! You chickens!" Girlie screeches. Cousin Baby starts to sing again. "Fried little stars / fried little chickens," Baby warbles, and her sweet, lilting refrain soars above the vast green abyss of the jungle below.

When they attack, the caddies are armed with golf clubs. They swing their deadly weapons, striking anyone in their path with sleek and shiny putters, number-two irons and number threes, clubs with massive, wedge-shaped, wooden heads. "I GONNA KILL YOU WID YOUR OWN SHIT! ARNOLD PALMERS! JACK NICK-LAUS!" the dark boys roar in unison. The leader grabs Girlie by the hair. He rips off her blindfold so she can see what is happening to her. "You must be mistaken," she says, meekly. She says this several times, until she realizes it is a waste of time, no one is listening. She begs and pleads for her life while the growling boy drags her around the verandah by her hair. She is a carcass, a prize trophy, but he is unsure about killing her and Girlie senses it. "I don't even like golf!" she yells, in desperation.

An even younger caddy, still a child, threatens her with a set of Ben Hogans. He picks up the heavy golf bag with ease, swinging it up high and aiming it at Girlie's head. "It's my brother you want!" she cries. "Not me! Not me!" She is a coward and a traitor, she doesn't want to die. In a final, pathetic attempt at saving herself, Girlie arches her back and thrusts her hips in the air, offering her body to the surly boys. They are not interested. It is the main thing Girlie will remember about the dream.

* * *

Her Saturdays are spent idly, sitting on the terrace of the Monte Vista with a group of young men. She has not been able to reach her married lover by telephone, and Girlie Alacran is irritated.

"Who's that?" Tito Alvarez cranes his neck to get a better view of a woman running across the lawn. Boomboom Alacran screws up his nose in distaste and looks away. Joselito Sanchez smiles. "Manicurist. She works downstairs in the salon," he says.

"*Achay.*" Pepe Carreon dismisses her with a wave of his hand. "You can do better than that, can't you?" he teases the actor. Boomboom Alacran giggles.

"Oooh—who's that?" Tito Alvarez whistles softly. He has just won the first round of golf with his friends, and he's exuberant, itchy to get laid. Almost anyone will do. The movie actor strokes his new black mustache, assessing the middle-aged foreigner in the short tennis outfit.

"*Kano*, I'm sure," Pepe says, not bothering to look.

"Wow," Tito murmurs in admiration, "nice boobs." He hisses at the foreigner, then winks at her knowingly. The woman hesitates, embarrassed. She looks around nervously for someone she knows, but the only other people present are a table of little children with their *yayas* and the waiters hovering nearby. The matron walks hurriedly past Tito's table, pretending not to notice him.

"Watch it, *pare*. She's the wife of the German ambassador," Joselito warns him.

"So what. I can tell she's hot for me." Tito grins.

"You should shave off that dumb mustache," Joselito says, "it doesn't suit your image. I thought you wanted to start playing good guys in the movies—"

"Women love it." Tito turns to Girlie Alacran. "Doesn't a little beard feel good, . . . down there?"

"I wouldn't know." Girlie is unable to meet his eyes.

"This guy is really something," Joselito complains, indicating the smug actor to the rest of the table. "Remember that French model I was showing around Manila?" Pepe Carreon nods. The expression on Joselito's face is a combination of admiration and disbelief. "I invite this guy along, one day—and you know what he says to her right after I introduce them? 'HEY! YOU WANT TO FUCK ME TONIGHT?' That's it, man—no *arte*, no class, no style!"

The men start snickering. "And what did she say?" Pepe Carreon asks.

Joselito Sanchez cracks up. "She said: 'The bed's not big enough!' "

"He's got it all wrong," Tito Alvarez insists, happy to be the center of attention. "She said: 'NO THANK YOU, monsieur. The bed's not big enough!' "

"*Ay!* I'm hungry—" Girlie Alacran announces, yawning. *Daw*, she says to herself, unimpressed with Tito's boasting. An image of her own wide mouth gapes open in her mind, the expression DAWWW stretched out to convey her unspoken contempt for what has just been said.

Pepe Carreon snaps his fingers and a waiter appears. More drinks are ordered, a bowl of peanuts for Girlie. Pepe lights a cigarette. "The man confessed," he says, suddenly. His eyebrows go up and down in Tito's direction, to emphasize the significance of what he is saying. "*Alam mo na, brod*. The methodology of our Urban Warfare Unit—*talagang* effective!" Pepe looks pleased with himself.

"What are you talking about?" Girlie asks, sitting up straight in her chair.

She is ignored. Tito smirks, helping himself to Pepe's pack of imported cigarettes. "I told you—it would all work out, *di ba*?"

"What are you talking about?" Girlie repeats, louder. Tito smiles one of his seductive smiles. He slips a hand casually under the table, resting it on her thigh. "Shhh," he says, in a mock whisper.

Girlie turns to Pepe, who finally speaks. "Just a guy. Someone we've been after for a long time." He is annoyed. He finds her presence an intrusion, as he does with all women. Barely able to keep up a civil front, Pepe avoids looking at Girlie. He wonders if Boom-boom is responsible for inviting her along.

The drinks and a bowl of peanuts are set on their table by a distraught waiter. He hands Tito a note from someone requesting his autograph. Tito gladly obliges, then waves the waiter away when he is finished. Girlie picks at the oversalted peanuts while the men gulp down their drinks.

"Where's Baby?" Tito asks Pepe, with a sly look. Pepe shrugs and looks bored, his standard reaction when any reference is made to his pregnant wife. "Home asleep—where else! I never knew a woman could spend so much time in bed—sleeping."

"You don't know about women," Tito Alvarez tells him, moving his hand further up Girlie's thigh. "They need TLC, man . . . *Alam mo ba ang TLC?* Tender Loving Care! Every day of the week, like brushing your teeth. I guarantee the results!"

"My cousin's expecting, any day now—" Girlie mutters, pushing the actor's hand away from her crotch as discreetly as possible. She isn't sure why she doesn't just get up and leave. The men wouldn't even miss her.

"I know that," Tito snarls at her, "everyone knows that!" His flushed face betrays his anger, but he grins hastily, flashing gleaming white teeth. Girlie is disgusted by and afraid of him, but it is as if her body has grown heavy with fatigue and become part of the chair; she cannot move. She fights with herself to get up, to tear herself away.

Boomboom giggles again. A large round version of his sister, he is a pink-faced mestizo with light eyes and thinning hair, his enormous paunch protruding under the tight T-shirt he wears over his Madras-plaid bermuda shorts. You are a big baby, Girlie wishes she could say to her brother. A man with soft, pudgy hands, Boomboom's never worked a day in his life; he lives off a monthly allowance. Girlie gazes at her brother and wonders if she is any better. She quickly finishes her drink.

She takes a deep breath and pushes herself out of her chair. "I have to make a phone call," she says, to no one in particular. Without excusing herself, she walks away from the table. She almost starts running but stops herself, relaxing only when she has passed the sign by the guard post which reads:

YOU ARE NOW ENTERING THE MONTE VISTA GOLF & COUNTRY CLUB MEMBERS & GUESTS ONLY PLEASE DEPOSIT ALL FIREARMS HERE

The men watch with some curiosity as Girlie walks away, taking in the sway and curve of her generous hips, the angry click of her high heels against the tiled floor. "Your sister is sexy," Tito Alvarez observes, winking at Boomboom this time. "Ever tried her?"

Boomboom's face remains bland and impassive. "Your sister's pissed off," Joselito Sanchez remarks. No one pays attention to him.

Tito pours himself another beer. He has just finished his third shot of Jack Daniels. "What did I say? I didn't mean to offend her—"

"Women," Pepe Carreon mutters. He is glad she is gone, and hopes she won't return. The men sit in silence, the afternoon light soft and flat on the golf course before them. The children and their *yayas* have long gone.

Severo Alacran, Pepe's father-in-law, appears in the green distance, intent on a game with two Americans. In their torn and muddy Converse sneakers, the caddies lag behind respectfully, hauling cumbersome leather golf bags and oversized golf umbrellas on their bony backs. Severo Alacran waves absently as he passes the younger men sitting on the terrace. "Are you going to play another round?" he asks, not waiting for an answer. Pepe smiles automatically and waves back.

Tito looks around for the waiter. "*Ano ba, pare*—the service stinks. You'd better tell your in-law."

"I'll inform the Secret Squadron," Pepe quips, but no one laughs.

Silence hangs heavy over the deserted terrace, broken only by the low, rustling hum of cicadas. Tito wonders if Girlie will come back. She's a little too touchy, but what the hell. He'll apologize for his behavior, offer to buy her dinner. If he persists, he knows he can persuade her to go with him to a nearby motel and finish off the hot, tense afternoon. Tomorrow promises to be grueling, the start of work on a new movie. Tito prays for Girlie's return. A day without sex is inconceivable to the movie star. Satisfying his desires comes easily to him, and he doesn't give up until every whim is gratified. He remembers the manicurist running across the lawn, her long black hair streaming down her back.

Boomboom Alacran is happy, content to listen to his friends brag about real or imagined exploits. He hopes the afternoon goes on forever. The identity of the man who confessed, the confession itself are inconsequential to Boomboom. All Boomboom craves are the details: the look on the man's face as Pepe's meticulous agents or Pepe himself prodded and probed in their search for answers, the exact number of seconds, minutes, or hours before the man finally succumbed.

Pepe Carreon rubs his stomach. "*Pare*, if you offered me a bowl of the purest cocaine on one hand, and a bowl of my cook Francisca's *adobo* on the other, and I had to choose—" Joselito Sanchez rolls his eyes. Tito Alvarez begins to laugh. He knows the punchline, but he plays along with the earnest military man. "You'd choose a game of golf!" Boomboom blurts out. Tito slaps Pepe on the back as the other men join in the laughter. Pepe looks at them with suspicion. He does not appreciate being the butt of anyone's jokes, especially the jokes of a fool like Boomboom Alacran. It only takes some slight insult, real or imagined, to set him off, and he makes sure everyone knows it. Fortunately, the alcohol has relaxed him; Pepe's tight, thin lips break into a reluctant smile, then his mouth falls open with the force of his high-pitched, hooting laugh.

For one drunken moment, Tito Alvarez is terrified by the man shaking with laughter in front of him. He is convinced Pepe has been transformed into a salivating dog howling on the terrace of the Monte Vista. The hallucination only lasts a few seconds. Tito's hand trembles as he brings another cigarette up to his mouth. The acrid taste nauseates him, and he quickly puts it out. He rubs his burning eyes, and feels badly in need of a bath. "I better go home," he says, "I don't feel well."

"You need another drink. *Hoy!*" Pepe shouts belligerently, looking back toward the shadowy, deserted hallway, "Is anybody there?" The table is littered with empty beer bottles, too many glasses, ashtrays crammed to overflowing, and a half-filled bowl of peanuts. A warm breeze scatters ashes on the white tablecloth. Pepe Carreon curses under his breath and smashes his fist on the table.

INSECT BOUNTY

MANILA, Philippines (IP)—The police commander in a trash-filled district of Manila has offered to pay residents $5 for every 1,000 flies they capture.

Lt. Col. Romeo Maganto, who is well known for going after suspected communist assassins in the slum district of Tondo, said the bounty is part of his area's effort to prevent an outbreak of insect-borne diseases.

"If we cannot do away with this garbage, I think it is better to eliminate these creatures that bring sickness," said Maganto. He said inmates in his station's jail have been assigned to count the flies before they are burned.

Tondo is the site of Manila's dump, called Smokey Mountain, where officials say 300 tons of garbage is dumped daily. The bounty project is being funded by several civic and business organizations.

—Associated Press

Hunger

GUILTY MOTHER was the first jeepney to slow down and stop for Joey on Epifanio de los Santos Avenue. Joey didn't care which direction the jeepney was headed. All he wanted was to get away as fast as possible from what he had just seen.

Across the windshield, a smaller, hand-painted sign boldly proclaimed in bright blue letters: FOR CHICKS ONLY. Joey gave the driver money and squeezed in between two women obviously on their way to market, carrying their straw and plastic *bayongs*. Next to one woman sat a chubby boy of six or seven, his bristling crew cut shiney with pomade. Dried mucus encrusted the boy's nostrils. His khaki pants were neatly pressed, his starched shirt embroidered with the fleur-de-lis emblem of the San Antonio de Jesus Academy. He stared at Joey with sleepy curiosity. Joey forced himself to meet the boy's gaze, trying to appear at once friendly and detached. Children made Joey nervous. He attributed to them too much power, the uncanny ability to see through other people's disguises. Joey shifted uneasily, trying in vain to settle himself comfortably in the jeepney's cramped space. The boy's mother moved her bags away from Joey, frowning. The child kept staring, his mouth slack and partially open. Joey looked away.

Across from Joey sat a row of triplets, their jaws moving as they chewed betel nut. They appeared to be in their nineties, two men and one woman. The brothers were dressed in identical soft *camisa* shirts and loose brown cotton pyjamas, and leaned forward on carved, pearl-inlaid walking sticks. Their slightly hunchbacked sister sat in the middle, regal and delicate in a handwoven camisole with butterfly sleeves worn over an ankle-length, rainbow-striped skirt. She smiled prettily at Joey, her sunken eyes like glittering beads, her teeth stained red with betel. Resting at her feet was a magnificent white rooster in a bamboo cage. An omen or a sign perhaps, Uncle would say. The white rooster surely meant death, but the triplets might bring Joey luck. His heart beat wildly.

Turning slightly, Joey faced the back of the jeepney driver's head. He looked like an ordinary man, with long black hair and an orange TruCola T-shirt that showed off his muscular chest and tattooed arms. He was whistling along softly with Kool and The Gang on his transistor radio, his eyes shielded from the glaring morning sun by futuristic wraparound sunglasses. Joey felt the driver watching him in the rearview mirror, which was adorned with scapulars, assorted medals, a single rosary, and a rabbit's foot keychain from the Manila Playboy Club. Joey sat up straight, preparing himself to jump out at any time.

The fat schoolboy made a face and stuck his tongue out at Joey. Joey's first reaction was to lunge at the boy, but he smiled feebly instead, as if he were amused. The boy's mother scowled, pinching his arm. The child grimaced in pain but never made a sound, giving Joey an evil look. The ancient triplets studied Joey and the schoolboy curiously. As GUILTY MOTHER pulled up to a busy intersection, Joey jumped out.

He knew he was somewhere in Cubao, and the unfamiliarity of the area was a great relief to him. Joey felt safe enough to wander around and clear his head. He even considered showing up for work later at CocoRico. He'd surprise Andres by showing up on time; he'd say hello to the boys, make some money, forget all the bullshit that went down. No one would connect him to the assassination at the exclusive hotel. Anyway, Senator Avila would've been murdered sooner or later. He was always saying his days were numbered on those stupid TV interviews. What the fuck, Senator Avila had asked for it. Someone had to shut that big mouth of his.

Joey wondered if he should tell Uncle. He desperately wanted to tell someone. The matter-of-fact brutality of the murder seemed unreal, like a gangster movie, but he was unable to erase the vividness of the actual moment from his mind, the Senator's body sprawled in a pool of blood on the plush carpet, the blood so red it vibrated black in Joey's buzzing mind. And the holes in the wall behind the reception desk—there must've been dozens of holes, maybe hundreds. How many times can you shoot a man? Joey decided making him a witness was God's peculiar way of punishing him for his sins.

He had been to church only twice in his life. For Joey, God was definitely a white man, Charlton Heston in robes, with flowing white hair and matching beard. He toyed briefly with the idea of finding sanctuary in the church across the street—he could interrupt the morning service and demand to see the parish priest. Was the parish priest also the Father Confessor? Joey wasn't sure. "Father," he would say, "You've got to listen to me. I don't know what I'm doing here . . . I don't know how to confess but I have to confess, now. I don't think I'm baptized, but if I have to die I want to go to heaven. I've only been to church a couple of times—one time was to bury my mother. I don't remember much about the service—I think I fell asleep in the arms of an old man called Uncle. The second time was a catechism class some nun was teaching. She found me on the streets, selling cigarettes. She kidnapped me, dragged me into the parish hall of a church in Malate where she had all the other street kids rounded up. We held open bibles and little *stampitas* she handed out, with dreamy pictures of the Virgin Mary ascending into heaven on the front, and a prayer on the back . . . I saw Boy-Boy and Carding, giggling in the back of the room. 'Have you had anything to eat?' the nun asked me. She was a foreigner or something, with very white skin and red cheeks. She pointed to a passage in the bible. 'I can't read, goddammit!' I yelled, throwing the book on the floor. The other kids laughed, cheering me on. The nun was petrified but she slapped my face, and when I tried to hit her back this priest came running in and took me to another room filled with statues. Jesus Christ stared at me from the cross, his face all twisted and bleeding. The priest pushed me down on my knees and ordered me to pray for penance. 'Or else I will call the police,' he said. Fuck penance. I had no idea what penance meant. I ran away as soon as the priest left me alone. I told Uncle later, and he laughed about the foreigner nun. Slum missionaries, he called her and her kind. He warned me to stay away from churches. 'They round up all you lost children,' he said, 'and brainwash you in special slum missionary camps far, far away.' Father, my name is Joey Sands. I'm a whore and the son of a whore. I just saw Senator Avila murdered. How come I feel guilty?''

A plane appeared to float in the clear blue sky. Slow and majestic, it flew in a sure, straight path. Joey's heart fluttered and sank. What time was it? Did Rainer make it to the airport? Or was he looking for him this very minute, looking for his missing cash and his drugs? Perhaps someone had actually spotted Joey lying on the curb in front of the Intercon. General Ledesma's infamous secret police were probably on his trail, with Rainer leading the pack. "Yes, Sergeant," Joey imagined the German saying politely, "I know the man who did this. He stole my wallet—" Rainer's sad, hangdog expression would never change. He had expected Joey to betray him, as others had betrayed him so often. The Sergeant would be wearing the dark uniform of the Special Squadron's Urban Warfare Unit. Joey could picture him clearly, grinning obsequiously and shaking the famous German director's hand. When the Sergeant removes his futuristic wraparound sunglasses, he reveals that he is the tattooed jeepney driver with the Prince Valiant hairdo. "Okay, boss! Okay! Now Mr. Rainer, where did you say the suspect lived?" the Sergeant would inquire, his manner friendly and efficient. Rainer would gladly cooperate. Momentarily lost in his own fantasy, Joey swore at himself—he had told Rainer everything, down to detailed descriptions of Uncle's shack and its exact location.

Joey shivered in the heat. He tried to shake off the ghostly apes that squatted down on his shoulders, blaming the phantoms on the unexpected violence he had just witnessed and on Rainer's coke. With enough rest and some food, the mournful *kapre* would surely disappear. Cautiously, he approached a man carrying a briefcase and rolled-up newspaper. The man was dressed in the gray slacks, cut-rate shoes, and conservative tie of a bank teller or office clerk. A passing van advertising holiday sales blared Nat King Cole crooning "Chestnuts / roasting / on an open fire . . ." from loudspeakers set up on the van's roof. Joey made an effort to sound casual. "Excuse me, *pare*—what time is it?" The man slowed down, gave Joey a suspicious look, then glanced at his watch. Joey's eyes were bright with fatigue. "Ten to eight," the man said, hurrying away to catch his jeepney. *"Salamat!"* Joey yelled his thanks. Knowing the exact time solved nothing: it set artificial limits on the hours that stretched out before him, but the dreadful emptiness and confusion were still there, along with the fear.

He wandered aimlessly, block after long block, waiting for night to fall. He blended into the crowds rushing to offices and schools, to modern department stores with garish window displays of paper lanterns, plastic reindeer, and Santa Claus in a sleigh. MALIGAYANG* PASKO*MERRY*XMAS is sprayed in fake snow on the glass.

Joey walked and walked, avoiding eyes. When he got too tired to walk, he found alleys and back doorways where he could snort up minuscule amounts of Rainer's powerful coke to keep him going. Smelling the pungent odors of cooking from open windows and the *ihaw-ihaw* stalls in the market place, Joey salivated. Garlic, vinegar, chocolate meat. Pig entrails stewing in black blood. He gagged at the thought of his favorite dish. It was better, he finally decided, just to keep walking.

The world resonated around him, incomprehensible and steadily more terrifying as the day wore on. People brushed lightly against him as they hurried to their destinations, the trailing sound of their laughter and conversation startling his overloaded senses. The delicate phantoms on his shoulders stirred, pressing their weight down upon him. Like him, they were afraid. He had to get to Uncle. When it finally got dark, Joey jumped into another jeepney, this one going in a specific direction. The jeepney's hood was ornamented with gleaming metal horses and multicolored streamers. The fancy handpainted sign across the windshield boasted SUPER BAD in gothic letters.

"Disappear," Uncle said. The old man studied Joey with wary eyes. From time to time, he patted the dog curled on the floor beside him.

Joey buried his head in his hands, too wasted to respond. He hadn't expected this reaction from the old man. "You shouldn't have come here," Uncle said, "I'm implicated, now. Guilt by association—you know what I mean? I never thought you'd be this stupid."

"I didn't ask to be there when it happened," Joey said.

The old man was indignant. "Of course not! But there you were, boy—wrong place at the wrong time—just because you were greedy for some foreigner's dope."

"Dope *and* money," Joey corrected him in a weary voice.

There was a flicker of interest in Uncle's eyes. "Dollars, I hope. How much did you get?"

"Not much," Joey mumbled, evasive.

"I hope it was worth the trouble, you stupid son of a whore! *Not much?* What do you mean by that? Do you remember who you're talking to? Bullshit, Joey—*talagang* bullshit!" The old man waved a fist at him.

Joey said nothing. He ached with fatigue and hunger, his head pounding. He hadn't eaten since breakfast with Rainer, and even that seemed like a dream.

"He fuck you good and treat you good," Uncle hissed, "then you forget all about Uncle—Uncle who raised you, who fed you and buried your no-good mother. Uncle who teach you everything—how to fuck good and steal good, huh Joey?" The old man was seething with rage, a little drunk from the cane liquor he'd been drinking.

Joey remembered Rainer's dope, stuffed in his pocket. A dull pain throbbed in his body, his brain hummed. "You want some of this?" Joey asked him, taking the packet carefully out. His smile was uncertain. "It's first-class."

Uncle made a dismissive gesture with his hand. "I got my own dope." He paused. "I ask you about the foreigner's money."

Joey sighed. "A hundred U.S., in cash. Some German bills and coins," he lied. "A few traveler's checks. You can have those—"

Uncle stared at him in disbelief. "Traveler's checks? Very funny, Joey. VE-RY FUN-NY." he chuckled. "It's okay. I can wait until you come to your senses, heh-heh. You liked that foreigner, didn't you? He fuck you good and treat you good, like the American? *Alam mo na*, Joey—us *Pinoys, basta puti*—" The old man's voice dripped with sarcasm. Joey looked away. "Better than the American?" The old man was incredulous. "Oh boy, Joey—you musta hit the jackpot! Is he going to send for you anyway, now that he knows you're a thief?"

Uncle lit an unfiltered, brown *Matamis*, inhaled deeply, then began coughing. "*Putang ina*, I'm going to die soon, Joey." The wracking cough subsided. Uncle sat back in his chair, taking long drags off the sweet, harsh cigarette.

"Have you seen a doctor?" Joey asked, with real concern. The old man laughed, then started coughing again. He uncorked a bottle of local rum, taking a generous swig. He pointed the unlabeled bottle at Joey. "My medicine. Want some?"

Joey unfolded another foil of coke. Using the long nail on his little finger, he dipped into the powder, snorting up a couple of healthy doses. He leaned back against the wall in satisfaction, his eyes tearing. He knew the high wouldn't last very long, but for now, it was fine. The dread had vanished, lurking in the shadows somewhere behind him, nameless and hazy. But he would have to watch out for the signs. The dread was insidious and cunning, like Uncle. It could come out of nowhere and sit on his shoulders, a menacing evil. Joey's laugh was bitter. He took the bottle from the old man, wiping the rim before taking a swallow. Uncle was amused. "*Puwede ba*—I'm not contagious."

"That's what they all say," Joey retorted sharply, feeling like himself again. He handed Uncle back the half-empty bottle. He was strangely glad to be in the old man's company. What better place to be on edge than the edge? Joey settled back into the darkness, his fear and hunger temporarily appeased. *Bahala na*, Uncle. *Bahala na*.

The assassin Joey described to Uncle was wiry and tall, with the pale, blemished skin of a mestizo. "I couldn't see his eyes," Joey said, dipping into the coke once again. "Those goddam regulation sunglasses! You can't see eyes—you don't know anything."

The old man nodded, sober now. "That's why the bastards wear them. Would you recognize him again? Come on Joey—think! This might save you in the end—"

"I don't know. I'm not sure. There were five or six others with him. Shit—I wasn't really counting."

"What about the gunman? Would you recognize him from a photograph?"

"Who knows—it all happened so fast. I could be wrong—"

"I don't think so," Uncle said, a grim look on his face. The dog jumped in his sleep, dreaming dog dreams. Uncle bent over to scratch his neck.

"Uncle—I was scared shitless. There I was—lying on the ground, pretending to be invisible. There might've been a hundred more of them, for all I know! Everything happened so fast, faster than you could imagine. I waited for them to shoot me next—just make it fast and sweet, I prayed. A million guns seemed to go off at once—" Joey started to laugh, then stopped himself. "I guess they wanted to make sure he was really dead, huh? They didn't even see me. There was too much going on. I realized I was alive and crawling away—" Joey paused to reflect for a moment. "This skinny guy I told you about. He seemed to be in charge. I dunno why I think so, but it hit me the minute I saw him."

"Why? What was it about him? Think!"

"I dunno why, Uncle. Look—I'm telling you the truth." Joey suddenly thought of food. Something in a brown, tangy sauce poured over hot, steaming rice. Some kind of spicy meat, maybe chicken or goat. He thought of how the rice would fill his burning stomach, easing the pangs of hunger he was beginning to feel again.

"I know you're telling me the truth," the old man said amiably. He was thrilled by Joey's disclosures but tried not to show it, his ravaged face a mask of calm. After a moment's silence, he began questioning Joey again. "Trust your instincts, and they will lead you to the truth—what made you single out this man? What was it about him?"

The old man's persistence wore Joey down. He snorted more coke before attempting to answer the question. "This man was the leader because he shone," he finally said. "The others all looked the same to me, except for him—"

"What about his voice? Did he say or shout anything?"

Joey shook his head. "Did he carry a weapon you recognize?" Uncle raised his voice in excitement.

"I don't know anything about guns," Joey said, irritably. He took a deep breath. "Okay—he carried something like a small machine gun. And his face—it was a long face with bad skin. That's all I remember, okay? Is that enough?"

The old man nodded, satisfied. He rose from his chair and went to a corner of the room where boxes were stacked on the floor. The dog woke at the sound of his master's movements and leaped up to follow Uncle, wagging his tail and expecting food. The old man shooed him away. Joey watched Uncle rummage through the boxes; when Uncle found what he was looking for, he handed Joey a flat envelope. "Here—you need to sleep. It's almost morning, and you're going to have a long day ahead of you. Merry Christmas, Joey."

Joey looked at the envelope in his hand. "I can't, Uncle. I—feel sick," Joey stammered, hunching his shoulders as if to ward off a chill. He was starting to panic. "I don't think I need to sleep. I think I need to eat." Joey shut his eyes and gritted his teeth.

"Well, there's nothing here to eat except the dog," Uncle said, "and you know I'd kill you first, heh-heh . . ." He gazed at the sick young man crouched on the floor, listlessly holding the envelope of precious heroin in one hand. When the old man spoke, his gruff tone softened into a soothing one. "Joey, listen to your Uncle. There's nothing to be afraid of—you're home now, remember? You just did a little too much of that foreigner's coke. Plus you haven't eaten— I haven't eaten myself, since yesterday! Dog eats better than me—I make sure of that. *Ay*, Joey my boy. What you want for Christmas? What you want that's going to make it all better for you? Uncle will do his best to help you," the old man said, carefully removing the package from Joey's limp, sweaty grasp. "Don't worry—Uncle will do all the work. You'll feel better—I'll fix some for both of us. Then you can sleep. Sleep till tomorrow, with this. All day, if you want. You're safe here, *di ba*? Uncle will take care of everything, lay out the mat for you . . . When you wake up, we'll go out and eat—that little place you like. You'll be refreshed! One-hundred percent better!"

The old man bustled about the one-room shack, getting the works ready like a chef about to cook a gourmet meal. "You need sleep bad—anyone can see that," the old man rattled on. "I go out later, do some business, pick up some food for Taruk. No one will bother you—I promise."

Joey felt too weak to resist. "Don't leave me," he pleaded.

"I'll be right back—you know Uncle always does his business quick. You'll be asleep, won't even know I've come and gone," Uncle chuckled again.

"They'll come here," Joey insisted. "They're looking for me. They know where you live—" He was delirious, rocking from side to side, crouched on the floor. He hadn't moved from where he sat in hours. The dog looked up, growling.

"No one will come here," Uncle grinned, shaking his head. "You're well protected. No one will bother you, ever. This is Uncle's house," he reminded him, in the same soothing, maternal tone of voice. Uncle leaned closer to Joey, breathing heavily. The old man stroked Joey's arm, and tapped the young man's veins with a certain tenderness.

It was early morning, before the first rush of traffic and noise from the highway. Uncle tied the mongrel up with a long chain attached to his front door. Joey had finally drifted off to sleep, sucking his fist, curled tensely on the mat Uncle had laid out on the floor. The dog howled as the old man hurried down the alleyways and disappeared.

Sergeant Isidro Planas wasn't surprised to see him enter the café. Like the Metrocom cop, the old man was one of the Ideal Café's regulars. "*Ano ba, pare?* Good morning—come join me for coffee!" Sergeant Planas called out in a booming voice.

Every morning, bright and early, Isidro Planas was the Ideal's first and most enthusiastic customer. The proprietor was a surly, rotund widow named Mrs. Amor, referred to as "Missus" by most people.

The old man sat down at the Sergeant's table. Wearing a shapeless housedress and threadbare, beaded velvet slippers on her swollen feet, Mrs. Amor took her time wandering over with an extra cup and saucer. "Are you eating, Uncle?" Sergeant Planas asked.

"Uncle never eats," Mrs. Amor said matter-of-factly. She ignored Uncle's mumbled greeting. She set down before him an economy-size jar of Nescafé, a thermos jug of hot water, and a bowl of sugar. Waving flies away with her other hand, she then brought over an extra spoon as well as a small can of evaporated milk which she put down in the center of the plastic-covered table, making as much noise as possible. After she left, Sergeant Planas shook his head. "Strange bitch—but what a great cook! They say she poisoned her poor husband. Did you know he was a cop?"

"*Siempre*. Everyone knows that. So—she sent him to an early grave, huh?" The old man stirred Nescafé into his cup of boiling water.

"You bet. I put up with her, though—we all do. She can put a hex on you," Sergeant Planas whispered. He resumed a normal tone of voice. "You should eat, Uncle. You're getting too skinny in your old age."

"Graveyard food. No thanks."

"C'mon—the food's great here! I just ordered breakfast—" Sergeant Planas did not like to eat alone.

The old man sipped his coffee. "I'm in a hurry. I need to contact someone—maybe you can help."

A thickset man with a bushy mustache and a perpetual smile, Sergeant Planas told himself something was up with the wily old man but he'd better play dumb. He pulled out his pack of Winstons with a flourish and offered it to Uncle. "Go on," he urged, "help yourself— U.S. brand! That's all I smoke . . ." He licked his teeth. "You know how it is—local brands give me a sore throat."

Uncle put two cigarettes in his shirt pocket. "For later," he said.

"You know Bobby in customs? Gets me all I need. Charges me almost nothing," Sergeant Planas boasted. The old man nodded, bored.

"You know Bobby?" Sergeant Planas asked again, after a moment of uneasy silence. The old man shook his head.

"My wife's first cousin. Big shot at the airport. A good man to know. Just tell him you're my friend—"

Uncle shrugged. "I don't hang around airports," he said, drily.

Mrs. Amor appeared with a tray of food. She set the plate of runny eggs, rice, and greasy sausages in front of the policeman and started to walk away. Sergeant Planas took one look at his food and called out to her frantically. "Missus! Missus! What's this?" Mrs. Amor turned around slowly, a profoundly indifferent look permanently fixed on her moon face. She said nothing. "Missus, I ordered *tapa*," Sergeant Planas said, his face flushed. "And sardines—*tapa*, sardines, and garlic-fried rice. NO eggs. NO sausages."

"*Tapa*. Sardines." Mrs. Amor raised one grotesque, thinly penciled eyebrow. "I don't have *tapa*, Sergeant Planas. I'm out of sardines. If you want garlic, I'll bring you a bowl of it. Fresh garlic! Chopped, cooked, or raw—how would you like it? I'll make it special, just for you—" The widow's body shook as she laughed.

The Metrocom cop was bewildered. "Why didn't you just say so, Missus—back then when I ordered my food?"

The widow pursed her lips and silenced the Sergeant with one of her withering looks. She disappeared behind the thin curtain that separated the tiny kitchen from the eating area. Defeated, Sergeant Planas sighed and dug into his food, shoveling the unappetizing-looking mess into his mouth. He spoke to Uncle with his mouth full. "What a witch that woman is! Ummm . . . Not bad," he grunted. "Garlic—my ass! I'd like to smear garlic all over that *puta*'s face before I make her *sipsip* me, goddammit, she can't talk to me like that! I'll bet this is some of her dog meat—you sure you don't want some?"

Uncle tried to conceal his mounting impatience. "I need your help, Planas. It's very important—"

"Maybe it's *lapchong*—" Sergeant Planas said, "Chinese sausage."

"Planas—I have to see Carreon," the old man said, quietly.

The fat cop slowly lowered his fork and spoon, a gleam of interest flickering in his speckled eyes. Two other men, also in Metrocom uniform, entered the café. They sat down a few feet away, nodding to the Sergeant. He barely acknowledged their greeting, keeping his gaze focused on the old man sitting across from him. "How can I help you?"

"Set up the introduction," Uncle said. "Tell Carreon I can be trusted."

"Carreon! That's big-time, *pare*—too big-time for me. Don't forget, I'm just a policeman," Planas said, with fake humility.

"Come on, Planas—I don't have time for your bullshit. You're not just some cop. You work for Carreon. You work for Carreon and you love it." Uncle enjoyed watching the fat policeman squirm under his scrutiny. "I'm an old man with vital information. Information that could affect national security. Carreon trusts you—pass the message along." Uncle was conscious of the two men watching them with curiosity and talking softly to one another.

Sergeant Planas's eyes were no longer friendly. "What kind of message?"

Uncle smiled. "In my younger, psychic days, Planas—I would've warned you about the perils of too much drinking, eating, and too many *putas* in your life. You're going to die of some new and deadly venereal disease, if your liver doesn't go first."

"*Putang ina mo.* Do you want me to kill you right here?"

"You can't kill me yet, Planas. This information is valuable to you—*confidential*, boss. *A matter of life and death.* Don't forget to mention that to Carreon." The old man savored the English words coming out of his mouth. "Confidential" and "a matter of life and death," just like the clipped dialogue he remembered from old American gangster movies. Paul Muni or Paul Henreid, George Raft or James Cagney—it didn't matter if he mixed them up. The phrases still rang in his ears, after all this time. It suddenly occurred to him that he hadn't been to a movie in over thirty years.

An amused look crossed Sergeant Planas's sweaty face. He shook his head slowly in mock admiration. "Uncle, Uncle, Uncle—you pimp son of a dead whore, you bastard! May you burn in hell for eternity, and may the Blessed Virgin Mary squat over your burning body and piss the hot piss of hell on your face, goddam national security my ass!"

"Sounds divine," Uncle murmured. Sergeant Planas slapped Uncle fondly on the back. "You pimp," Sergeant Planas said, "what are you involved in now? This stinks like big-time trouble." He paused, lowering his voice. "Look, old man—I'm a cop no matter what you say. I'm a cop with a greedy wife and quite a few children. I have to think of myself, *di ba*? In risky situations like this, I have to think of me. What's in it for me?"

"You'll be rewarded," the old man interjected swiftly. "I have something planned for you . . ."

"Oh. Is that right?" Sergeant Planas let the old man's words sink in. This was going to be an extraordinary day. My goodness, he would later exclaim to his wife, when you least expect it! Good fortune comes in the most shocking disguises. Take that old bastard Uncle, for example. Sergeant Planas was sure he was handling things well, sure his enormous greed wasn't apparent. "I don't want trouble, old man. You got me in trouble once before." Sergeant Planas was smiling.

"I got you out of it, didn't I?" Uncle snapped, his voice rising.

Sergeant Planas glanced quickly at the two men nearby, who were busy eating. He shot a warning look at Uncle, who gazed back at him with undisguised hatred.

"Things got nasty. Things got out of control," Planas said, evenly. "You almost cost me my job—maybe more. I don't want that kind of trouble again. When Carreon's involved, the stakes are going to be high."

"It's worth it," Uncle assured him, "I guarantee that, Planas. You know I keep my word. I'm the one sticking my neck out. You don't even have to get involved, except for giving Carreon my message. It's a fucking easy way to make money—"

Sergeant Planas frowned. "You're not going to tell me more?"

"It's for your own protection," Uncle said smoothly, "it's better you don't know anything yet."

"How much? I have to think of me."

"I'll make it worth your while."

"How much?" Sergeant Planas was eager now, a hunter circling his prey. He sat very still as Uncle leaned over to whisper in his ear.

The widow Amor pulled the curtain aside and peered out of her kitchen. It was now 7:35 in the morning. Her eyes rested on the old man called Uncle and the greasy policeman Isidro Planas. *"Hoy!"* She yelled at them rudely, "You want something else, or you want to hurry up and pay me now?" Her broad hands rested on her hips as she stood facing the table. Sergeant Planas seemed preoccupied, picking at his teeth with the edge of a matchbook. He handed the widow a wad of pesos. "Keep the change, Missus," he murmured absently. The widow Amor looked momentarily startled. Then, un-impressed with his sudden generosity, she gave him one last disap-proving look before waddling away.

Redemption

Joey woke in a pool of sweat. The light bulb dangling from a cord above his head glimmered faintly. In Uncle's hot, windowless room, Joey had no sense of whether it was day or night. He sat up panting heavily, jolted from his dreamless sleep by the dog's incessant barking outside the door. Joey's head was still sore, a dry metallic taste in his mouth. Unbearably thirsty, he reached for a dirty glass half-filled with water on the floor beside him.

He looked slowly around the room, trying to remember and rearrange events in his dazed mind. A collage of pornographic centerfolds covered Uncle's walls, making the room feel even smaller and more claustrophobic. Joey shut his eyes to close out the sprawling, leering images of painted girls and blank-eyed boys with erect penises fondling each other without enthusiasm. Joey knew he was one of them—the ominous and holy children of the streets. "Scintillating Sabrina and Gigi." "Boys at Play." "Bangkok Bombshells." "Lovely Tanya and Her Sister."

He reached up and unscrewed the light bulb. No light came in from two rectangular openings Uncle had sawed near the ceiling, the only sources of ventilation in the small room. It was definitely night, Joey decided, unnaturally quiet except for the dog's rustling movements outside the front door. How long had he been asleep? In the distance, Joey heard the sound of a man's voice calling out to someone. Then laughter, followed by the buzz of more male voices and footsteps walking by Uncle's shack. The dog barked; a man laughed again. It could've been one of the gangs out for the night, on their way to hang out in front of the *sari-sari* store to drink *tuba* or *basi* and exchange stories about ghosts and women. It could've been Jojo or Junior, gang boys who sometimes bought dope from Joey and Uncle. Through Uncle's paper-thin walls, all sounds seemed to come from the same darkness Joey was sitting in. The dog was restless; Joey could hear every panting breath and low growl as if the animal was in the room with him. The footsteps and voices faded away. Joey was overwhelmed by loneliness.

He bit down hard on his lower lip, wanting to cry out for help but restraining himself. He knew the friendly sounds outside could just as well have come from Metrocom or Special Squadron agents sent to find him. He realized the old man had tied the dog up outside to prevent him from leaving. *Fucking Uncle*, Joey cursed—the old man was always one step ahead of him. The adrenalin coursing through his body made him want to jump up and run. Fucking Uncle, fuck it. He could just say *fuck it*, take his chances with the damn dog and run. Joey gulped at dry, dead air. He felt sick but there was nothing left to vomit.

He crawled to the chair in the center of the room, clutching it for support as he pulled himself up to his feet. His hand brushed over the objects scattered on the table next to the chair, finally curling around Uncle's Eveready flashlight. Exhaling with relief, Joey switched it on. A path of dim light opened up in the stifling darkness. Without being seen from the street, Joey had to find Uncle's cache of drugs and whatever cash he might have lying around before making his escape.

The old man was going to kill him, or have him killed. Joey felt too weak to laugh. He had been waiting for this all his life—this moment of betrayal from Uncle. It had been his destiny, and he welcomed it. He wondered how the old man had figured it all out. Uncle never ceased to amaze him. For the right price, he was capable of anything. Who would he blackmail, now? The man with the lean, pockmarked face? The bait, as usual, would be Joey. Uncle was more than willing to sacrifice his surrogate son.

The revelation was almost a relief, but in spite of himself, Joey felt hurt. He had expected betrayal, but was not ready for despair and anger at being betrayed. In his way, he loved the old man. *Zenaida, Zenaida,* Joey whispered to himself, *Mother of God, my god, the bastard buried you.* He had not said his mother's name in years, and steeled himself against the tears welling up inside him. He was disgusted by his own sentimentality; he had never considered himself capable of self-pity, terror, or yearning for his long-deceased mother. He had always felt cheapened and humiliated by the memory of her, Zenaida, and his unknown father. And so his litany went: *GI baby, black boy, I am the son of rock'n'roll, I am the son of R and B, I can dance well, you can all go to hell! Putang Ina Ko!*

Mother of a whore, his phantoms chanted, whore of a mother, son of a whore! They beckoned to him: Once a whore, always a whore! Was the German home in Germany, safe in his warehouse full of art and cats? Joey's tears were blocked by the force of his growing rage. He knew he had to escape, somehow. Past the growling dog to somewhere safe, somewhere safe and anonymous. He needed food and shelter—for how long wasn't important. He knew he wanted to live: it was that simple and basic. Joey was not going to let the old man or anyone else kill him.

There was no time to lose. Joey ransacked the room, flipping through Uncle's neatly folded clothes, overturning the cardboard boxes Uncle used for storage. He found a case of bullets, but no gun. Joey whimpered and cursed in frustration, flinging Uncle's possessions around him: a useless iron with no plug, two towels, a black rosary, letters bound in twine and addressed to "Ismael Silos" in beautiful, faded handwriting, a water-stained photo album with all the pictures removed, three cans of Vienna sausages and one tin of Spam, one black Converse sneaker without shoelaces, and a pile of Uncle's treasured collection of foreign magazines. The old man had paid a small fortune for black-market copies of *Hustler, Lolita, Spartacus, Penthouse,* and *High Society*—some still unopened and wrapped in plastic. The raunchier, the better. "You know I like to look," Uncle used to gloat. The sight of Uncle poring over glossy pictures of naked white women had always made Joey feel ashamed and sad.

Feeling ludicrous, he tore up as many magazines as he could; in a final fit of malice, he unzipped his jeans and pissed all over Uncle's strewn possessions.

Joey never found money or Uncle's cache of drugs, but inside the Converse shoe he came upon the sleek butterfly switchblade Uncle had brought back years ago from Batangas. "Guns are efficient," Uncle used to say, "but knives give you more satisfaction." He preferred knives, he said, because sometimes things got personal; you simply had to make that kind of grisly contact with your victim's flesh and bone. "When you stab someone, you look him in the eye. Always look him in the eye," Uncle told him, "and let him know exactly who you are . . . It's a way of paying your final respects."

Joey had never killed anyone. There had been a moment once, with a customer. Joey had been thirteen, wise enough to carry a knife for protection. The man had gotten out of hand, and things had threatened to get ugly. Something sparked in Joey's eyes; his body tensed and shifted. The man realized he'd gone too far; he backed off, murmuring apologies. Nothing else had to be said. Joey was paid a little extra. The moment passed quickly, and was just as soon forgotten. He never saw the man again.

It was extraordinary, how Joey had managed to sidestep the violent encounters common in the lives of everyone else around him. He'd never been arrested or had to pay a bribe to get himself out of a jam. "You're a lucky boy," Uncle often marveled, "I knew it when I first took you in. You bring *me* luck."

Joey pressed himself against the door and softly called the dog's name, "Ta-ruk," imitating the coaxing tone the old man used to lure his pet. Cautiously, Joey opened the door just wide enough for the dog to see and smell the piece of Spam he held in one hand. The dog whined in anticipation, wagging his tail as Joey undid his chain and let him inside the shack, bolting the door carefully behind him. Joey watched as the animal lunged at the canned meat thrown on the floor.

There was nothing to keep Joey from escaping now. The dog was preoccupied; Joey could easily slip out the door. But he felt another rush of anger; the switchblade opened like a gleaming fan in his hand.

Omens, signs, Uncle's language of the spirits . . . He had to leave a message the old man would understand.

It was essential to act immediately, without thinking. Emitting a muffled scream, Joey grabbed the scruffy fur at the back of the dog's neck and held on for dear life, thrusting the sharp blade below the dog's right ear. Blood spurted everywhere as the dog jerked in response. Joey kept stabbing the animal, the queasiness in the pit of his stomach rising to his throat. Once again he tasted metal on his tongue. The dog yelped and whined with each thrust of the knife, horrifying Joey. He began to weep, furious with the dog for not dying quickly. His anguished cries and the animal's became one and the same. His arm grew numb with the effort of killing, but Joey wouldn't stop until the shuddering dog finally lay still.

The smell of blood in the dark, airless room was unbearable. Joey stripped off his T-shirt but kept on his jeans, now stained and splattered black with gore. He wiped the sticky knife blade on his shirt, then folded and slipped the *balisong* into his back pocket. Using water from the giant oil drum Uncle kept in a corner, Joey washed up hurriedly. Shivering in his damp jeans, he bent down to lap at the water in the drum, trying to quench his terrible thirst. That done, he took a clean T-shirt from one of the overturned cartons. It was the best he could do; Uncle's pants would never fit him. Leaving his bloody shirt and the butchered carcass of Uncle's dog behind as souvenirs, Joey slipped out the door.

The balmy night air hit him in the face. Fresh and unexpected, the almost sweet scent of rotting food and open sewers mingled in the night breeze. Joey darted in the shadows, past makeshift squatter's huts leaning at precarious angles over the fetid canals where oversized rats foraged and swam, ignoring him. He crossed the open field that led to the main highway. The moon was full. Joey guessed it was late, perhaps past midnight. He no longer had Rainer's money; it had vanished with the old man. What was left was a worn hundred peso bill and Rainer's coke, wrapped in foil next to the knife in his pocket. His best bet would be to find Boy-Boy at Studio 54. Ask to spend the night. Maybe Boy-Boy would cook for him. One good night's sleep and hot food—then he could make plans, devise a strategy.

Boy-Boy was like a brother to Joey; he could be trusted. He never asked too many questions, or passed judgment. Joey suspected Boy-Boy was also infatuated with him, and decided to take advantage of the situation.

He walked to 54 Alibangbang Street, which wasn't too far away. On the sidewalk out front, a group of young men loitered, staring curiously at Joey as he approached. "Hey! Joey Sands! What's happening, boss? It's me, Dodoy—" one of them greeted him, grinning widely. He was a Chinese-Filipino with a spikey haircut and a tight T-shirt, cut off to reveal his midriff. "Hey," Joey nodded, smiling uneasily. He could not for the life of him remember Dodoy, if he'd actually ever met him. Something about the eager young man felt instinctively wrong. Brushing past him, Joey pushed open the unmarked door and started up the narrow stairs. Music drifted down to the street below, the urgent, nasty rhythms of James Brown's "Sex Machine." He was stopped by the insistent voice of the unfamiliar young hustler. "Hey Joey—you got anything?" Dodoy touched Joey's arm. "We'll trade you downers, boss—" His voice was loud and obsequious, but his eyes were hostile, appraising Joey coolly. Cigarettes loosely dangling from their pouting lips, the others encircled Joey, hopeful and menacing. Ears pierced with gold hoops, studded with gold crosses and fake diamonds, their lean young bodies were tense with nervous, undirected energy. The boys waited for Dodoy to give them the signal to pounce on Joey, who kept smiling. "Not tonight, guys—" Joey said, "I'm all out. Maybe tomorrow—" He paused, focusing on Dodoy with an unswerving gaze. "How about a cigarette?" he asked, taking the hustlers by surprise. With obvious reluctance, Dodoy handed Joey his pack of local Marlboros. Joey swiped a couple, saluting his thanks as he bounded up the stairs toward the pulsating music. Dodoy stared sullenly after him, gathering his thoughts. *You're safe for now*, he said to the retreating figure silently, *but I'm not gonna forget, motherfucker*. Then he shrugged, a display of false nonchalance for his friends.

Upstairs, Joey waited in merciful darkness next to the stage of the crowded nightclub. Boy-Boy and the shower dancers were going through their routine, the third and final set of the evening. "Sex

Machine" segued into a slower, more agonizing, sexual funk. The audience was riveted by Boy-Boy's performance. Lighting one of Dodoy's Marlboros, Joey forced himself to relax.

Facing the empty street, the young hustlers resumed their idle positions, leaning against the unmarked façade of Studio 54. "*Putang ina,*" Dodoy muttered, unable to restrain himself, "Who does that nigger think he is?" The others howled with laughter, their raucous male voices jarring the night's heavy silence. The air smelled of rain, the impending typhoon that heralded a tropical Christmas. Somewhere in the distance a rooster crowed, signaling the approaching dawn.

Jungle Chronicle

Children who die very young are crowned with white flowers, dressed in their finest clothes and like adults, are brought to the cemetery in an open coffin; music precedes the coffin to the church, and the part of the cemetery especially consecrated to them is called, at least in Paco, the "Angelorio," that is to say the place where the angels are buried. Instead of crying, the family makes great rejoicings, because they are considered as enjoying a privilege that no man can share with them, that of their children dying without sin.

—Jean Mallat, The Philippines *(1846)*

The Famine
of Dreams

(The Colonel who arrested her has a baby face. He speaks to her politely in English. They arrive in an unmarked car at the recently renovated military complex. It is after midnight. Colonel Jesus de Jesus holds her by the elbow in a deferential manner, as if he were a gallant gentleman escorting her to a formal ball. "Contemplate your sins and your crimes here at our cozy Camp Meditation," Colonel Jesus de Jesus chuckles. He takes her on a brief tour as he leads her down the maze of corridors toward the General's special interrogation room, what some survivors jokingly refer to as General Ledesma's "VIP Lounge"—for very important prisoners. "Here," the Colonel points out proudly, "our state-of-the-art computer area, where vital information is processed and transmitted to our other headquarters. And here—the men's room on the left and the newly painted women's restroom on the right— for our occasional guests as well as our staff," he adds, giving Daisy another smile. In the next building are recently installed shower facilities that can accommodate hundreds. And the food isn't bad, he assures her with a wink. He flirts with his eyes and touches her freely every chance he gets, bending over to sniff the nape of her exposed neck. "Beautiful," Colonel Jesus de Jesus sighs. The guard opens the door. "Good evening, *hija*," General Nicasio Ledesma greets her.)

At magandang gabi sa inyong lahat, ladies and gentlemen. Tonight's episode of *Love Letters* is called "Diwa." Brought to you by our sponsors Eye-Mo Eyedrops, TruCola Soft Drinks, and Elephant Brand Katol Mosquito Coils, "Diwa" stars the one and only Nestor Noralez as Ponciano Agupan, with Barbara Villanueva as Ponciano's

wife Magdalena, and Bootsy Pimentel as their daughter Rosalinda
. . . Patsy Pimentel portrays Doña Ofelia, and Glenn Magpantay
appears in a cameo role as Don Gregorio. This week's special guest
star is Tito Alvarez, who plays the mysterious drifter, Real.

(In the foreground, the clatter of dishes and utensils being set
on a table. In the background, the soft chirping of nocturnal
insects underscored by a sweet, strange melody played by
mandolins.)

MAGDALENA: (anxious) *Dios ko!* Where is your father?

ROSALINDA: Stop worrying, Mama. You worry too much,
and you'll get sick again. (pause) Why don't
you start eating?

MAGDALENA: I'll wait for your father. You know he hates to
eat alone. *'Sus Maria!* Where could he be? It's
so late!

ROSALINDA: (concerned) Stop it, Mama. Sit down and get
away from that open window. You'll catch cold
in the draft.

MAGDALENA: Wait! (pause) Rosalinda, what was that?

ROSALINDA: What? What are you talking about, Mama?

MAGDALENA: (stage whisper) Shhh! Be quiet. (pause) Rosalinda—did you hear that?

(The General turns up the volume. "Do you like these melodramas,
hija? Kind of sentimental, don't you think?" Daisy stares back at
him. "Your late father and I shared a mutual respect for the
remarkable culture of this country," the General says, gazing at
her fondly. He is sitting with his hands clasped on the desk, the
radio on a shelf behind him. He nods to Pepe Carreon. "Would
you care for a cigarette?" Pepe asks Daisy. "A glass of water or
coffee? Have you had any dinner?" Daisy refuses to sit down.)

More than an eyedrop. A trusted friend for over twenty-five years.
Too much sun? Too much smoke getting in your eyes? Try gentle
Eye-Mo for instant relief! (Followed by the merry Eye-Mo jingle.)

The Merry Eye-Mo Jingle

When you don't know
What to do
And your tired,
Burning eyes
Make you blue
Sigé na, go get
Your Eye-Mo
You'll feel better
With gentle Eye-Mo
Sigé na, sigé na
Gentle Eye-Mo!

(**A burly man is introduced as Dindo. One of our President's trusted aides, the General explains. He has some questions for you. The questions are innocuous at first. Daisy stifles an urge to laugh. "When is your birthday?" "When is your sister's birthday?" "Does your mother attend church?" The burly man's face glistens with sweat in the air-conditioned room. "Have you been in contact with your cousin, Clarita Avila? What about your husband, the for-eigner?"** *Malcolm Webb,* **the General corrects the burly man. "I'm fussy about details," the General says. The burly man apologizes. "How did you meet Santos Tirador? Did you commit adultery with any other man before or during your relationship with Santos Tirador?"**)

(The sound of a door opening and closing. A chair scrapes on the floor.)

ROSALINDA: Papa! What happened?

MAGDALENA: (sobbing) *Dios ko,* Ponciano—my god, what have they done to you? Why . . . (gasps) There's blood on your shirt!

ROSALINDA: Papa! Mama! What's going on? (The sound of moans in the background) You look terrible, Papa. Why don't you lie down?

PONCIANO: (groaning) No, no. I'm—I'm all right—

(As Magdalena speaks, there are sounds of clattering dishes, faucets being turned on and off, water running into a basin.)

213

MAGDALENA: (angry) *Dios ko, 'Sus Maria Josep!* Ponciano— why didn't you listen to me? I knew something was going to happen to you—that dream I had last night, filled with dreadful omens . . . (tearfully) Didn't I warn you? Sit down, my husband. Here, let me wipe your face with this damp cloth—

PONCIANO: (groaning with relief) Ahhh—*salamat*, Magdalena—I feel—much better. Much. Better. Already . . .

MAGDALENA: Where have you been? You didn't go to the river again, did you?

(Ominous music in the background.)

PONCIANO: Magdalena, please. I . . . I don't want to talk about it—

ROSALINDA: Papa, what are you trying to hide?

MAGDALENA: (accusatory) You did, didn't you? You did it again—

("One of your father's favorite songs," the General tells her, "was 'White Christmas' by Bing Crosby. He only liked the Crosby version. Not too many people knew he was a sentimental man, with sentimental taste in music and movies . . . 'Give me Eartha Kitt, give me Benny Goodman!' I used to say to him. This was in the old days, when your father socialized with me more often," the General smiles. He shakes his head slowly at the memory. "Your father was a stubborn man. He believed in moral lessons. He wanted everyone to be perfect, to consider him as an example. That stubbornness might have contributed to his downfall, *di ba?*")

Thirst-quencher to the stars. The thinking man's soft drink. After a long hard day at the office or at school—TruCola! For that quick jolt of energy, that fizz-boom-pop! That sunbeatable combination of sunkist oranges and caramel soda!

TruCola Calypso

Ay, ay, aray! Bili
mo ako nang

Ice-cold TruCola!
Sa-sa-sarap ang TruCola
De-de-Oh! Delicious!
De-de-Oh! Delicious!

(The announcer's voice returns while the TruCola calypso is
still playing, to remind listeners about Diet TruCola and Cherry
TruCola, now readily available at supermarkets and *sari-sari*
stores everywhere.)

("Are you aware of Santos Tirador's involvement in the recent
ambush on PC troops near Sagada on November second?" the
burly man suddenly asks Daisy. His tone is no longer courteous.
Daisy has been momentarily lulled by the voices on the radio.
Surprise and dismay show on her face. "All Souls' Day," the
General murmurs. "All Souls' Day," the burly man echoes. "There
were very few survivors among my troops," the General says to
Daisy, "which is very upsetting to me. You understand me, *hija?*"
Daisy vows to remain silent, no matter what. She imagines she is
not pregnant with Santos's child, that somehow she will steal the
General's pistol and open fire on all the men in the room. She is
barely showing, and wonders if the General suspects her condition.
"The poet who sheltered you—Zamora," the General pauses, then
looks at the burly man. "Primitivo Zamora," the President's trusted
aide hastens to tell him. The General nods. "Yes—Primitivo Zamora. How long have you known him?" When Daisy still does
not speak, the General seems disappointed. "*Hija,*" the General
speaks softly, addressing her as daughter in tender Spanish, "I
must warn you. Even I can do nothing about my men's excesses—"
He motions to Colonel Jesus de Jesus, who hands him the Polaroid
snapshots. "Here, *hija*. Look at these—so terrible, don't you think?
A terrible, terrible fate. Terrible, really." The General sighs. He
points out the young man's mashed testicles, the close-up of his
gouged-out eyes. Throughout, the General keeps sighing, making
clicking sounds with his tongue against his teeth. Daisy's tears flow
hot down her cheeks; she tastes the salt in her mouth. She tries in
vain to stop crying, but her tears keep streaming down. "Look—"
the General shoves the last snapshot in front of her averted face.
"Look—my men rearranged him totally. A styrofoam cup where
his brains should be—isn't that ingenious?")

(A knocking sound at the door. There is tension in the music, percussion and a taut plucking of strings.)

MAGDALENA: (alarmed) Who could that be at this time of night?

(More knocking sounds, this time more urgent.)

ROSALINDA: I'll go see—

MAGDALENA: No! Don't!

PONCIANO: I'll go—

MAGDALENA: No! Shhh! (pause) Who's there?

MUFFLED VOICE: Real. I'm here to see Ponciano Agupan.

PONCIANO: Let him in, Rosalinda.

MAGDALENA: (frantic) Who is Real? Wait! Rosalinda—

(Sound of door creaking open, and footsteps. Magdalena gasps. The music builds to a moderate peak.)

(Colonel Jesus de Jesus asks to be first. He assaults her for so long and with such force, Daisy prays silently to pass out. Her prayers go unanswered. The other men crack jokes, awaiting their turn. "Lover boy *talaga*," one of the officers grunts in admiration. When he is finished, the baby-faced Colonel licks Daisy's neck and face. "My woman," he announces, heaving himself off her. The room starts to stink of sperm and sweat. The President's aide is next. Only Pepe Carreon and the General refuse to participate, preferring to stand in one corner and watch. While the burly man thrusts into her, the General leans over to whisper in Daisy's ear. He describes the special equipment set up in another room, a smaller room where the General plans to take her after his men are through. "We can finally be alone," the General says. He calls her *hija* once again, exclaims at her extraordinary beauty. He promises to make her dance.)

Bananas
and the Republic

Madame reveals: Her unabashed belief in astrology, the powers of psychic healing, Darwin's theory of evolution, and the loyalty of her homosexual constituents.

Her faith in a nuclear freeze.

Her respect for Oscar de la Renta.

To make a point, Madame removes one shoe. She holds it up for the foreign journalist's benefit. "Local made! You see, Steve—they say I only buy imported products. But look, *di ba*, my shoe has a label that clearly says: Marikina Shoes, Made in the PI! You know our famous expression, *imported*? It's always been synonymous with 'the best,' in my country—" She pauses to glance around the room at her hovering female attendants, all dressed in blue. Madame turns her attention back to him. "They accuse me of being extravagant, but I've owned these shoes for at least five years! Look at the worn heel . . . And this beautiful dress I'm wearing is also local-made, out of pineapple fiber, which we also export. I use top Filipino designers exclusively for my clothes and my shoes . . . Valera, Espiritu, Ben Farrales . . . And Chiquiting Moreno is the only one allowed to *touch* my hair! I am a nationalist when it comes to fashion," she smiles. She has been lying to him cheerfully all morning, and they both know it. He smiles back.

She shows him the mother-of-pearl heel of her custom-made peau-de-soie pumps. "I have big feet for a Filipina," she sighs, "all my shoes have to be special ordered." Pale blue, sky blue, virgin blue, happy blue, mother-of-pearl blue shoes. Her own designs, she tells him proudly. Her favorite color, blue. A color which for her signifies harmony, peace, her serene oneness with the universe.

Queen of beauty queens, Miss Universal Universe, Miss *Bituin*, Madame Galactica, Madame International, *Maganda*, Pearl of the Orient, Pacific Rim Regina, Mother of Asia, Land of the Morning, Miss *Bahay Kubo*, Miss Manila, Lunaretta, Moonlight Sonata, *Binibining Pilipinas*, Jet-Set Ambassadress of *Adobo* and Goodwill, whose unwrinkled face reflects the shining love, the truth burning in her heart . . . Mother of Smooth Alabaster Complexions, Hairdo of Eternity, Calculating Mother of Noncommital Mouth and Eyes . . . O Perennial Indifference! O Lizard-Pouch Chin! Defiantly held up for the cameras, every photo opportunity seized . . .

Madame uses her favorite American expression as many times and as randomly as possible throughout her interview. "Okay! Okay! Okay *lang*, so they don't like my face. They're all jealous, okay? My beauty has been used against me . . . I've been made to suffer—I can't help it, okay! I was born this way. I never asked God—" she sighs again. "Can you beat that, *puwede ba*? I am cursed by my own beauty." She pauses. "Do you like my face?"

The reporter tries not to look astonished. His tape recorder running, he also scribbles down everything she says in his notebook. She appraises and dismisses him swiftly, noting his hairy arms, cheap tie, limp white shirt, and dreary wing tips.

He avoids answering her sudden question, affecting a light attitude which rings false. "You're turning this around, Madame—don't forget, I'm interviewing you," he grins, but she does not smile back. He hopes he only imagines that her eyes harden. "Don't worry, Steve, I never forget." She looks back at her blue women and smirks. The reporter keeps his voice steady. "What about the young man arrested by Ledesma's men earlier this week?" He glances down at his notes. "I believe his name was Orlando Rosales. Are any formal charges being made?"

Madame shakes her head slowly. She affects a look of sadness, which she does well. "You should interview General Ledesma and Lieutenant Carreon about that. These are terrible times for my country, Steve. Do you mind if I call you Steve? Good." She pauses. *"Ay!* So much tragedy in such a short time! It's unfortunate, all this violence. Thanks be to God for our Special Squadron, a brutal assassin has been apprehended . . ."

"Orlando Rosales was shot down in the middle of a busy intersection, in broad daylight. He was taken immediately to Camp Dilidili, and no one was allowed to see him. His fiancée claimed he was an innocent man, on his way to see her for their regular lunch date. He had no known political affiliation, and since giving her testimony, his fiancée has disappeared," the reporter says, in a neutral voice.

Madame looks surprised. "Is that so? No one's told me anything about it." She decides he reminds her of some sort of insect, with his long legs and arms and bulging brown eyes enlarged by thick, wire-rimmed glasses. Is he Jewish? She sniffs in distaste. Her face remains a cordial mask. "You know, Steve—Orlando Rosales had a gun. How do you foreigners explain that? The same gun that shot Senator Avila! He was also shooting back at the police."

"He was a waiter, wasn't he?"

"That was his job, yes. His assumed identity. Oh, he was brilliant, Steve. Quite a brilliant, sophisticated young man. What we call here a genuine 'intelektwal,' " she smiles. "This had been planned for some time, planned very carefully. Even this whole business with that poor fiancée of his—she was his unwitting accomplice. How do you say it? His 'foil,' *di ba*?" She looks pleased with herself. "General Ledesma was aware of a plot, but no one was sure when the assassin would strike. We tried to warn Senator Avila, but—" Madame sighs deeply this time. "Orlando Rosales had everyone fooled, including his own mother." She describes an investigation after the assassin's arrest, linking him to a known group of subversives based in the Cordilleras. She laughs. "Steve—you know the latest joke? NPA—for nice people around."

"What about Daisy Avila? Rumor has it she's been captured and detained."

There is a brief, tense moment of silence. "I am unable to discuss Daisy Avila," Madame finally answers. "It is a matter that pertains to our national security. But I will tell you this, okay Steve? As far as I know, Daisy Avila is still in the mountains. Another poor girl, led astray by that evil man! You should really interview General Ledesma about all this. Okay, Steve?" She brings up her favorite movie in English, *The Hunchback of Notre Dame*. "I feel like the poor hunchback. Here was this ugly man, okay? But such a beautiful spirit! I know Anthony Quinn quite well, Steve. Do you know Anthony Quinn?"

"No, but I saw him in *Zorba the Greek* on Broadway." He does not know why he responds, and feels foolish.

"*Ay, talaga!* You're from New York?" She visibly warms to him, and becomes more animated as she talks. "I should've guessed—you look like a New York *intelektwal!*" she giggles. "Didn't you think Anthony was better in the movie version? Tony was much younger then, *di ba?*"

Madame confesses: How privileged she feels, as the wife of the leader of an emerging and prosperous nation and as the mother of such intelligent, unspoiled children. "My daughter is at Princeton," she reminds the journalist. Her laugh is bitter. "People talk about corruption. That is what you're implying, isn't it, Steve? Okay, you say. We are a corrupt regime—a *dictatorship. Dios ko!* We've been accused of throwing our bananas in the garbage to purposely rot while children starve. We make deals with the Japs. Our sugar rots in warehouses, *daw.* Meanwhile, everybody's starving. We take your precious dollars and run—but where will we run, Steve? You can run but you can't hide, *di ba? Naku!* I wouldn't look like this if I were corrupt, would I? Some ugliness would settle down on my system. You know the common expression—'ugly as sin'? And I don't mean the Cardinal—" Madame giggles girlishly again. One of her blue ladies pours her more tea and refills the journalist's coffee cup. "There's truth in common sayings, *di ba?* If I were corrupt, I would look like that other movie, *Dorian Gray. Di ba,* he got uglier and uglier because of all the ugliness in his life?"

He decides he will leave her sentences unedited when the interview is over. Her convoluted thinking intrigues him, her appropriations of

American English. She is fond of words like "coterminous," which he will later have to look up in an unabridged dictionary. But he is aware that her romance with Western culture is not what is at stake. He fights the cynicism that threatens to engulf him whenever she speaks. He knows he must see the interview through to the end.

Coiffed and complacent, Madame sits on her exquisite armchair inlaid with intricate mother-of-pearl designs. "Handcarved by Muslim craftsmen," she informs him proudly. "Have you been to our Mindanao region, Steve?" She offers him the use of a government plane. With one shoe off, her stockinged foot is visible to him. She rubs it against her other ankle. He notices her toenails are manicured a glossy peach color, with white half-moons in the center. He averts his eyes from her foot, aware she is toying with him. "*Ay,* I'm so tired," she murmurs. She signals one of her attendants. "Would you like a snack?" He politely refuses, and feels more foolish than ever.

She slips off her other shoe, squirming to rearrange herself in the elegant chair. Crossing her legs, she smooths her *piña*-fiber skirt demurely over plump knees. "I'll tell you something, okay Steve? There are no real issues. Issues are conflicts made up by the opposition to further tear my country apart. The opposition is envious and greedy and impatient. The opposition is ugly, Steve. They want to take things away from me and my husband—there's nothing brave or noble about the opposition! That's something you foreigners stir up, to cause trouble. To create news. Sensationalism, *di ba*? The noble opposition is a bad dream. God save us from the day when my husband steps down as the leader of this glorious country! Then you'll witness real bloodshed—unless we make adequate preparations to protect ourselves from being overrun by wild dogs fighting among themselves for a chance at power. The fighting will go on for years—" She takes a deep breath. "Don't you think we know there is hunger and poverty still rampant, in spite of all our efforts? We never denied it, okay? People look at me. Because I happen to look great—they assume—they put two and two together—they accuse me of stealing food from children's mouths. Absurd, *di ba*? No way! Okay—these people have nothing to begin with. Who am I to steal from those who have nothing? Why should I? Nothing can be gained from nothing, *di ba*? Common sense, Steve—the opposition lacks common sense."

He is exhausted by her tirade, too drained and exhausted to argue with her. It is not his place to argue. He is conducting an interview, after all. He will let her go on and on. He will construct from this an intimate profile of Madame, startling and amusing. Even so, a whirl of images nags at him. Bananas and mounds of coconuts, fields of sugar cane, grainy black and white footage of sobbing women, women kneeling over open graves, graves piled with the corpses of mutilated men and children. The chubby-faced waiter Orlando Rosales with his pathetic Elvis pompadour—out-of-sync and dated, but certainly innocent.

"Do you have anything more to say about the late Senator Avila?" He asks her a predictable question and expects a predictable answer. He must wind up the interview in some coherent fashion, turn off the tape recorder. He must pack up his briefcase, thank her profusely, and leave as soon as possible. The air-conditioned conference room is chilly; his underarms are damp with nervous sweat. "A terrible thing," Madame replies. "We warned Senator Avila to stop consorting with the left. He was always trying to make deals with the NPA. My husband told him, many times—'Domingo, there are no deals to be made.' Domingo was a stubborn man. Just as we predicted, they double-crossed him. Set him up and executed him to exploit the situation. Of course, they knew we would be blamed. We're convenient targets, *di ba*? Domingo Avila was expendable to those bloodthirsty goons—what a waste of a fine man! You tell me about sympathy, Steve. Now that is an issue, okay? Sympathy versus empathy—I know the difference, for I am blessed with the capacity for both. My critics accuse me of being too emotional," she adds, wryly. "Perhaps I am actually cursed."

"What do you mean?"

She sends one of the women out of the room to fetch her gold pen and some paper. "It's very clear, what I mean." Her voice is impatient. "I will draw you a picture, Steve. If you like, for your benefit, so you can better understand. Okay? For the benefit of the grieving widow Avila and her family, all those who accuse me of being heartless and lacking in human emotion. Don't you think I've been a victim too?"

She does not expect an answer. He decides he will not ask her any more questions about the war in her country. He has no stomach left for her games. In a sense, she has won. There is no war in her mind— as there is no real threat that could possibly exist in her husband's mind. It must be the only way, the weary journalist decides, the two of them could function sanely from day to day, conducting interviews and posing for pictures in the gloomy grandeur of their haunted palace on the edge of a swamp.

Madame starts to draw. "I've been accused of being a great dreamer. Oh yes. I dream not only at night when there are moon and stars, but I dream more so in the daytime . . . I admit, I dream awake, my eyes wide open. I could be dreaming right now, *di ba?* I believe in the power of dreams and the power of tears." She draws a large crescent moon. The moon she surrounds with dozens of cartoonish, twinkling stars. She does not stop drawing. She fills every inch of the yellow, legal-size pad with stars and moons of all shapes and sizes. Her face earnest and intense, she bends over the paper and forgets everyone in the room. The foreign journalist is stunned. He keeps the tape recorder running in the silence.

Big round moons, thin wedges, moons with smiling faces, moons obscured by fat and fluffy clouds. She draws stars as ornate and fantastic as Christmas ornaments, stars with tails; at the bottom of the paper she draws jagged blades of grass. When there is no room left on the paper for her drawings, she looks up. Madame remembers why she is here, all dressed up in the immense conference room of the palace, with the bug-eyed foreigner staring at her. *The journalist.* He has been pleasant enough, not too unkind with his questions. Her feet still hurt. She is relieved the journalist came alone, without the usual photographer in tow. She is not in the mood today, and does not feel like putting her shoes back on. Enough. She smiles at the foreigner coquettishly, more out of habit than anything else. She decides he is definitely not her type. "Is there anything else, Steve?"

she asks, implying that the interview is now over. Her face looms before him, a glamourous powdered sponge, a slice of white angel food cake, a white moon. "I should have been a singer," she says, wistfully. "I could have been an actress in one of those romantic musicals, back in the days when movies were movies and everyone loved romance! *Ay*—where is romance, these days? Off the record, Steve. What would life be without movies? Unendurable, *di ba*? We Filipinos, we know how to endure, and we embrace the movies. With movies, everything is okay *lang*. It is one of our few earthly rewards, and I longed to be part of it! I was going to call myself Rose Tacloban, as a joke." She shrugs. "Obviously, God had greater things in mind. I met my husband, and our destinies entwined. Together we served our country, and together we sacrificed everything. We were chosen by God to guide and to serve—" Her braceleted arm sweeps over the room, over her blue women, the imposing furniture, and her scattered blue, mother-of-pearl peau-de-soie pumps. "What greater destiny could there be? Everything you see here is God-given. I don't know how to explain it any better, Steve. I am simply here to carry out our Lord's wishes. It really isn't about me personally. You can tell your readers Madame is simply fulfilling her destiny. There is nothing she wants for herself. Absolutely nothing."

Rising from her elegant chair, she holds out her hand. The reporter shakes it, conscious of his own clamminess. One of the blue women picks up her shoes. The reporter thanks Madame for such an illuminating interview, and apologizes for taking up so much of her precious time. She does not apologize for anything. He is already forgotten.

Followed by her attendants, she glides down the hall in her stockinged feet, toward another set of double doors. She turns suddenly to face him, as if a thought has just occurred to her. "Excuse my husband for not being available, okay? This is one of his golf days."

The foreign journalist nods. She is gone in a matter of seconds. He turns the tape recorder off, packs his tools into the worn leather briefcase. Notebook, pen, pencils, the fancy German microphone. The recorder he slings by a strap over his shoulder.

Terrain

Boy-Boy has arranged everything, surprising Joey with his seriousness and his plans. He hides Joey in his tiny apartment for weeks until the height of Christmas and New Year's celebration; Boy-Boy counts on the cops being drunk and sloppy, more likely to look the other way. He tells Joey this with apparent confidence and experience. Joey is impressed.

For what seems a tedious eternity, Joey spends agonizing days and nights pacing Boy-Boy's two rooms. He is insomniac and nauseous, subsisting mainly on tepid cups of powdered Nescafé with plenty of condensed milk and too much sugar. He chain-smokes the cigarettes Boy-Boy brings him. There are books scattered around which Joey cannot read; to pass the time he watches television. Boy-Boy's secondhand, nine-inch black and white set does not meet with Joey's approval. "*Ano ba, pare*—did you find this piece of shit in the *basura*?"

What Joey misses most is his easy access to dope, which Boy-Boy brings him on increasingly rare occasions. "It's time you quit," Boy-Boy said one morning. "Where you're going, they won't allow this." "Are you sending me to hell?" Joey grumbles. He's not sure what's worse—withdrawal or boredom. "How long do I have to stay here?" he constantly asks. "At least you're alive," Boy-Boy tells him. His optimistic manner infuriates Joey. "If I spend one more day like this, I'm going to kill you or kill myself," Joey threatens. Boy-Boy grins. Joey is pale and sick and thoroughly unconvincing.

Boy-Boy insists Joey watch the news on television with him. "What for? They're all lying—you told me so yourself! It's the government station, *di ba?*" "Read between the lines," Boy-Boy says. He has learned to ignore Joey's moods; he knows Joey is itching for a fight. Boy-Boy concentrates on what the anchorman is saying in Tagalog on the tiny screen. The sudden excitement in Boy-Boy's voice rouses Joey from his surly stupor. "Did you hear that? *Shit!* They've let Avila's daughter go!"

Joey's anxious and impatient, craving a hit. Sometimes his body shudders uncontrollably; invisible worms crawl under his skin. He wonders if he'll ever lose this terrible need. It is Sunday. "Get ready," Boy-Boy tells him, "my friends are coming for you tonight." Joey is sullen. "Who are they? Can't you tell me their names? Where the fuck am I going?"

Boy-Boy ignores his questions. "Don't worry. You'll find out soon enough." When night falls, a car pulls up in front of Boy-Boy's apartment. A woman is driving. Boy-Boy, who has been watching for the car since the late afternoon, turns to Joey. "They're here. Let's go—"

"Who is she?" Joey wants to know, peering over Boy-Boy's shoulder through the blinds. "Come on—you're wasting time!" Boy-Boy glares at him.

He leads Joey to the waiting car. The woman does not acknowledge Boy-Boy, but says hello to Joey in a friendly voice. Joey barely glimpses her face before he is shoved in the back seat by Boy-Boy. There is a man sitting in the back, who blindfolds him. "What the fuck do you think you're doing?" Joey starts to struggle, but the man is strong. "Relax, Joey. I told you this would be necessary," Boy-Boy says in a low voice. After a brief pause, Boy-Boy pats him on the shoulder. "Goodbye, Joey," he says, shutting the car door. "Let's go," the man says, brusquely.

"Why didn't Boy-Boy come with us?" Joey asks, his voice shaking. He is trying to stay calm and trust these strangers, as Boy-Boy advised. The man beside him smells of musty sweat and old clothes. Joey takes a deep breath. *Okay*, his mind's voice speaks to him now, in an urgent whisper—*so far, so good, Joey Sands.*

"Boy has things to do in the city," the woman who is driving answers. "He's needed there."

They reach their destination a short time later. Joey tries to guess—Pasay City? Quezon City? Greenhills? Maybe they drove around in circles, to fool him. Maybe he's back at Boy-Boy's little apartment, above the dress shop on a narrow, unlit street. Joey is led out of the car by the musty-smelling man, through a gate, on to a flagstone path, up two cement steps, through a damp passageway and up a flight of stairs. A sharp right, more stairs. A door is unlocked. Someone else is there, Joey can smell him. His loins tingle with excitement, he desperately needs to piss. "*Puwede ba*—" Joey hesitates. The woman laughs softly. Everyone talks in a low murmur. The blindfold is removed. Joey blinks at the fluorescent light in the square, sparsely furnished room. A tall young man with short hair and eyeglasses shows him the toilet.

The place is shabby but clean, one large room with adjoining kitchen and toilet. There are no pictures on the walls, no telltale souvenirs of any kind, no attempts at decoration. There is no shower or bathtub, just a toilet. The walls are cracked and peeling, painted a depressing pastel blue. There is a wooden table, and four mismatched chairs.

The toilet reeks of disinfectant. A single light bulb emits a weak yellow glow. Joey zips up his jeans, the clean ones borrowed from Boy-Boy. A large brown cockroach scurries across the floor, and for a moment Joey panics. He leans against the wall and shuts his eyes, taking slow, deep breaths to pull himself together like Boy-Boy taught him to do when he was crazy and sick.

Joey hears them talking in the other room, unable to make out what they are saying. He hears his name mentioned, and flushes the toilet. The three people turn to look at him when he steps out into the main room. The woman smiles. "Call me Lydia," she says, graciously, as if she were a hostess at a party. She holds out her hand. Joey takes it, feeling foolish as he shakes her hand. She moves with swift self-assurance, her dark eyes darting and curious. "Would you like coffee? You have a long trip ahead of you," she tells him.

"Maybe I should just sleep," Joey says.

"Not yet," the woman says, shaking her head. "We all have to be alert in case anything happens—" The other two men are smoking cigarettes and drinking coffee, sitting in a cluster with Lydia at the table. She motions for Joey to sit down as she introduces them. "This is Rudy," she says, pointing to the young man with eyeglasses, "and this is Edgar." She gestures toward an older man who bows his head mockingly in Joey's direction. Rudy puffs languidly on his unfiltered cigarette, ignoring Joey. The man named Edgar wears his stringy black hair tied back in a ponytail with a leather cord. A wispy mustache droops around his mouth; there are scars and keloids on his neck and arms. "Hello, Joey—*kumusta*?" he grins.

They are waiting for one more person, the woman explains. Joey yawns. She hands him a thermos cup of bitter coffee. "We don't have any milk," she apologizes. Edgar notices Joey flinch at the taste. He gets up from the table and rummages around the kitchen, finally finds a jar of white sugar in one of the empty cabinets. "I don't know how long it's been sitting there," the woman says. Edgar shrugs, handing the jar to Joey. "Sugar's sugar."

The woman tells Joey their names are all made up. Edgar looks annoyed, but says nothing. "I've always loved the name Lydia," the woman confesses, "I hate my actual name! What about you, Edgar? Rudy?"

Rudy looks infinitely bored. Edgar shrugs again, staring at Joey. "The reason we change our names," the woman continues, "is quite obvious. That way, if any of us is captured—"

"Tell us what you saw," Edgar interrupts. Rudy perks up, shaking himself loose from his boredom and smoke-filled reverie. Joey squirms in the hard wooden chair; his ass hurts. The woman pours everyone more coffee. "I can't help myself," she exclaims, "I'm everyone's mother! Drink some more, Joey. *Sige*—we'll be going soon."

When Joey finishes his story, there is silence. The silence is broken by the sound of Edgar's quiet laughter, a laugh of recognition. He slowly shakes his head, amazed by what Joey has told him. He leans over and touches the woman named Lydia, briefly and sympathetically. She looks away. Rudy is agitated, and gets up from the table. He peers between the slats of venetian blinds that cover the window facing the street. "Where is that fucker?" he mutters to no one in particular.

When the other man finally arrives, he is introduced as Tai. Joey is blindfolded again and led down to another vehicle, something with more room, like a truck or van. He is wrapped in canvas and blankets, instructed to lie on the floor. "If we're stopped, lie very still," Lydia tells him. Rudy stays behind, murmuring goodbye to Lydia before retreating back into the dark shelter of the anonymous building.

Edgar is driving. Tai sits with him in the front seat. Lydia sits behind them, the bundle wrapped like a cocoon lying under the seat at her feet. "We'll make good time," Joey hears Tai saying.

"You were late," Edgar says gruffly.

The road is winding and bumpy. Joey falls into a half-sleep; he dreams he is dancing on stage at Studio 54. The audience is booing. He is lathering soap all over his bloody clothes. He looks down at his body, which is flabby and fat. Uncle is sitting in the front row, the only one smiling and waving, a proud parent. Joey realizes there are other men onstage, behind him. The audience claps and cheers for the chorus line of dancing men grinding their hips. They wear khaki uniforms. They soap their uniforms. It is all unbearably funny; Joey wonders why he is the only one laughing.

He is four years old. He is in a fancy hotel room with his mother. She has long black hair and a sturdy body, and calls herself Lydia. She bends over to kiss him. She is not his mother—she is the hermaphrodite Eugenio/Eugenia. She wears a beaded flapper's dress, her face garishly painted and her hair marcelled. He turns away from her kiss, and she begins to cry. She is not his mother—she's Andres Alacran. He sits down on the bed next to Joey and shakes his finger at him. "Bad boy," Andres reproaches him, "bad boy."

He is back in the nightclub, dancing with soldiers. He is not Joey, he is Boy-Boy. His T-shirt is ripped, his jeans torn and splattered with blood. The soldiers wear lipstick and dangling earrings, they are a gang of hoodlums led by Dodoy, they encircle and menace him without missing a step. They dance closer and closer to him, pantherine and graceful. Joey wakes up, suffocated by the blankets loosely covering his face. He fights off his dreams, forcing his eyes open. He is groggy and exhausted. The blankets smell of mildew and mothballs. Joey's muscles are cramped. They have been driving for hours.

He feels the woman prod him gently with her foot, as if to reassure him. The vehicle comes to a complete stop. The silence that follows is eerie, as if the world and they themselves are in suspended animation. Even the insects hush. Joey imagines the doors of the van flung open, the soldiers dragging him out and throwing him on the ground. Lydia sighs; Edgar starts up the motor. Joey almost pisses on himself in relief. He hears a muffled conversation between Tai and Edgar. Lydia joins in.

Joey is hungry. The woman starts humming and singing to herself, a lilting wordless melody, a lullaby. Joey reminds himself these curious strangers are somehow responsible for him. "They're the only ones who can help you," Boy-Boy had said. The vehicle swerves, narrowly missing a truck carrying gasoline on the lonely country road. "Goddam gasoline," Edgar curses. Tai laughs. Lydia keeps singing. Joey drifts back into his nervous sleep. "*Pare*—I think he was carrying diesel," Tai jokes.

"Who gives a shit—he almost killed us," Edgar says. Joey's body twitches from time to time, with the force and terror of his dreams.

Just after sunrise they stop, somewhere up high, where the air is cool and thin. Joey is helped out of the van by Tai and Lydia. He rubs his bleary eyes. Up ahead, there is a bamboo hut with a thatched roof, built to blend in perfectly with a grove of trees. Joey feels enveloped by intense greenness, the dizzying effect of the lush vegetation and dense foliage that surrounds them. He shivers from the chill of the morning air. "It's invigorating, isn't it?" Lydia says to him, breaking into a wide smile. For an instant, she is almost beautiful. Joey grins shyly back at her.

A toothless old man appears in the doorway of the hut, greeting Edgar in a nasal, clicking dialect. The old man's voice is whining and insistent. Edgar listens carefully, nodding from time to time. Making signs for the others to do the same, he follows him into the hut.

There is another man there, squatting on the dirt floor. He is middle-aged like Edgar, and carries an M16 slung over his shoulder. He nods curtly at Edgar, and spits some of the betel nut he's been chewing on the ground. He is not introduced. He calls Edgar "Boss." He will drive the vehicle back down the mountains. He leaves immediately, without saying good-bye. It seems to Joey that for them, this is routine, this dangerous journey back and forth, from city to mountains to jungle, over precarious and awesome terrain. With a sinking feeling, he hears the engine start up. Lydia sees the look on his face. "It's not a bad hike," she says to Joey, amused. "There are trails."

The old man squats comfortably on the ground; they follow suit. He addresses Edgar in the singsong rhythms of his dialect. Joey notices his broad, calloused feet, toes splayed out, caked with white dust. "He wants to know if we're hungry," Edgar interprets. Joey nods, eagerly. Edgar turns back to the old man, responding with uncanny fluency.

The old man leaves and returns with strips of dried, salted meat. There is water from a nearby stream, and sweet, small, overripe bananas. Joey wonders about the tough meat, decides not to ask. He devours the food while everyone watches. He guesses he is chewing on the flesh of a *carabao*; he is too hungry to care. The old man grunts with amusement as Joey finishes the last of the bananas. He makes a sign. Edgar jumps up. "Time to go," he says.

The old man guides them up steep, winding mountain trails, his toes gripping rocks and stones with the sure and expert grace of a goat. Joey sweats and pants with the effort of keeping up; overhanging branches from trees and prickly, serpentine vines cut into his face and arms. He shudders, imagining he sees snakes coiled and waiting. The heat is sweltering by midmorning, the air humming with dragonflies and mosquitoes. Joey's exposed flesh is stung; insects dive into his hair. He slaps at invisible creatures. The sweat dripping from his forehead stings his eyes. He imagines with horror how, without warning, leeches will drop on him from the wet foliage, like dew. Birds screech and whistle; Joey imagines they are pteradactyls from some movie, gliding smoothly by.

They trudge and stumble up to where the trail seems to end, but the impatient guide urges them on, through a thicket of giant ferns and more trees. The sun casts a shimmering path of dusty light through the shadows of the humid jungle. They walk in silence, Joey way in the back, struggling to keep the rest of them in sight. At one point, Lydia slows down to wait for him. She touches his arm, pointing out two monkeys peering down at them with insolent faces, perched on their leafy trapeze. Their long, glorious tails curl up like plumes.

Joey is overwhelmed by a sense of fear and wonder. His life in Manila is only a memory now, the faces of Andres and Uncle blurred and distant.

A clearing suddenly emerges out of the tangle of twisted vines, the moist blades of leaves and prehistoric trees. There is a camp, a smoldering fire. A barefoot boy runs up to them. Joey stands still, frozen by the sea of faces turned toward him, wary yet curious, young men's faces. "Lydia!" one of them calls out. The woman embraces him, says something in greeting no one else can hear. The old guide squats down by the fire. Lydia and the man look back at Joey. Tai and Edgar disappear into a solitary tent propped between two trees. The barefoot boy offers Joey water.

Tai and Edgar emerge from the tent with a wiry man and a beautiful woman. The man carries an M-16 across his back, and holds his hand out to Joey. He is introduced as a priest. "Father Francisco," Edgar calls him. "Call me Tikoy," the priest grins. He and the beautiful woman are dressed in drab colors. The woman is wan and thin. She is embraced warmly by Lydia, then led to where Joey is standing. "My cousin," Lydia says proudly. "She calls herself Aurora." The woman glances sharply at Lydia. She reprimands her. "You shouldn't have said that—" Lydia is dumbfounded, embarrassed. She turns abruptly and walks away. The beautiful woman's dark face softens. She will apologize to her cousin Clarita, later. Her eyes remain fixed on Joey. "I want to know about my father's killer," she says. He suddenly recognizes her face.

Weeks later, when she has grown to trust him, she will describe the absurd terms of her release from Camp Meditation, how she was granted a pardon by the President on condition she remain in permanent exile, how she was escorted to the airport by a military convoy with wailing sirens. Her plane ticket is paid for by her mother, she says with bitterness. Her mother and sister accompany her to the airport; her mother spends the entire time mute and dry-eyed, holding on to her terrified sister. She has not heard from them since. She hopes they have already left the country, thinks it will be better for them if they have.

She herself returns home as soon as possible, under an assumed identity, with the help of powerful friends. She arranges her journey back into the mountains, to the refuge provided by her comrades. She laughs sadly when she uses the term "comrade." There is a tinge of irony in everything she says. Except for her cousin Clarita, her comrades are her only family, now. "I claim responsibility for everything I do," she says to Joey.

They will get drunk together on cane liquor one night. She cries while Joey describes his mother, what he remembers of her. She reproaches herself, and apologizes for being sentimental. She will not cry when she describes how her lover was captured while she was in detention, or how her unnamed baby girl was born premature and dead. They are together all the time. She teaches him how to use a gun.

Luna Moth

My mother hosts a farewell luncheon for the American consul's wife, whom she despises. With the help of our cook, Pacita, she plans an innovative menu combining American and Filipino dishes. She and Pacita shop the day before the luncheon; they go up and down the air-conditioned aisles of the SPORTEX Stop & Shop, the awesome new supermarket located on the first level of the SPORTEX complex.

"Made in de USA!" The cheerful cashier jokes as she totals the enormous cost of my mother's purchases: small cans of Libby's succotash, Del Monte De Luxe Asparagus Spears, two bottles of Hunt's Catsup, one jar of French's Mustard, Miracle Whip Sandwich Spread, Kraft Mayonnaise, Bonnie Bell Sweet Sliced Pickles, Jiffy Peanut Butter, packages of Velveeta, party-size bags of Cheez Whiz, one box of Nabisco Ritz Crackers, and several boxes of Jell-O gelatin in lime and cherry flavors for my brother Raul. At the last minute, my mother throws in one canister of Johnson & Johnson's Baby Powder. "For me," she says to the puzzled Pacita.

Her local items include: one large bottle of Rufina *patis*, one gallon of Kikkoman Soy Sauce, several bushels of fresh *kalamansi*, one head of lettuce, two cases of TruCola, several cloves of garlic, three pounds of tomatoes, one pound of dried *dilis*, one jar of shrimp *bagoong*, one twenty-pound sack of rice, and several pounds of frozen, boneless *bangus*.

My father is home in bed, recovering from his first heart attack. A mild case, Dr. Ernesto Katigbak assures us. My mother is not convinced. My father is still a young man, why is he sick like this?

Dr. Katigbak leaves our house, and I hear my mother speak in a harsh, accusing tone to my father. "You eat too much," she says, "it's going to kill you . . ." She complains the only exercise he gets, besides fooling around, is sitting on his ass, gambling long hours at the poker table. "I'm too young to be a widow," she declares, with a tremor in her voice.

He tells her she gets on his nerves, she should leave him alone to rest if she really wants him to get better. He ends by asking her: "And what do you do all day for exercise, except move your mouth up, down, and sideways, making *tsismis* with your queers?"

My mother exits grandly, slamming doors behind her. The door to her bedroom, the door to her sitting-room, and so on. I don't see her again until her guest of honor arrives.

The American consul is being transferred to Saudi Arabia. His wife is not thrilled with the situation. Howard and Joyce Goldenberg are both Jewish, from Pasadena. Their daughter Trixie is enrolled at my convent school as a special student. The nuns excuse her from attending Catechism class, Holy Mass, and Benediction at our chapel; she is treated with cautious deference, like a Martian or a person with a contagious disease.

Mr. Goldenberg is a very tall man with curly hair and rumpled good looks. Absentminded and friendly, he is popular with everyone. His wife Joyce suffers two nervous breakdowns while she's in Manila. She is sure they are being transferred to Saudi Arabia as part of an anti-Semitic conspiracy. She talks about anti-Semitism so often, I finally ask my father what it means.

"*Ay, que* cute!" Pucha moans in feigned despair, every time Mr. Goldenberg walks by us toward the living room, where the adults spend most of their time playing cards, munching crackers, and drinking large amounts of alcohol. He is amused and flattered by Pucha's adolescent flirting, and never patronizes her. My parents tease him mercilessly. Only Mrs. Goldenberg is flustered and annoyed, intimidated by my nubile cousin's blatant desire for her mild-mannered husband.

Older men are one of Pucha's preoccupations. The summer before the Goldenbergs leave, my parents invite her to spend a week up in Baguio with us in an imitation Swiss chalet they are renting for the summer with the consul and his wife. Baguio is wonderfully cool, its elevated mountain terrain dotted with forests of pine trees. In Pucha's imagination it's the closest thing to America. We are both eager to show off our pastel orlon cardigan sweaters, which we wear draped over our shoulders, under single strands of tiny pearls. Pucha's pearls aren't real, mine are. No one can tell the difference. We affect the casual teenage glamour of Gloria Talbott in our favorite movie, *All That Heaven Allows*. Trixie Goldenberg wears jeans and her father's old shirts. Pucha thinks Trixie's a lesbian. She and Trixie just don't get along. When Pucha's in Baguio, Trixie Goldenberg spends as much time as possible away from the summer house.

All week, Pucha and I find everything unbearably romantic. We shiver in the alien cold weather; we inhale the sharp scent of evergreen that permeates the thin air. While the adults shop for souvenirs at Baguio Market or go drinking at the Baguio Country Club, Pucha and I practice tongue-kissing in front of the rustic fireplace. "Quick," Pucha says, "before that Trixie comes home." She is always Ava Gardner or Sandra Dee, and always insists I'm Rock Hudson. The adults return late in the day bearing gifts: carved ashtrays and book-ends ornamented by Igorot fertility gods with erect penises or drooping breasts, woven baskets and cloth depicting lizards, fish, and other fertility symbols. Pucha giggles when she sees them. My mother and Mrs. Goldenberg put their purchases away and bring out the alcohol for cocktails before dinner. Mr. Goldenberg shows my father how to build a proper fire. Trixie shows up for dinner late and pointedly ignores us. "Where have you been, young lady?" her mother asks, but goes back to her conversation with my mother without waiting for an answer.

I have started menstruating. To celebrate, I cut off all my hair.

Pucha examines my head, frowning with displeasure. "You look like a boy! You look terrible—like Joan of Arc! Who cut your hair?"

"Uncle Panchito."

She gives me one of those I-feel-sorry-for-you looks, just like her mother. "*Ay, prima!* I don't want to be seen with you! How could you have let that man touch your hair? He's a dressmaker. Why didn't you just get a perm? Perms are adorable. Look at you—you look like a plucked chicken—"

"It's the rage. Audrey Hepburn. Everyone's doing it, in Hollywood and Rome."

Pucha's unimpressed. "Oh, sure. And when was the last time you were in Hollywood or Rome?"

"*Sabrina*—we saw it two months ago, remember? Starring Audrey Hepburn and William Holden."

"*Ay, puwede ba!* Audrey Hepburn's flatchested."

"She's beautiful," I stammer, blushing.

"Boring, *prima*, boring," Pucha groans. She stresses the word *boring*, one of Trixie Goldenberg's favorite expressions. It has replaced *corny* as the most frequently used English word in my cousin's limited vocabulary.

"This salad is unbelievable," Mimi Pelayo says with enthusiasm, stabbing another piece of canned asparagus with her fork.

"Where did you get the asparagus?" Sylvia Abad asks.

"It's a malicious contradiction!" Mrs. Goldenberg interrupts. "How could they possibly send us to Arabia?"

"It's *Saudi* Arabia, darling," Isabel Alacran corrects her, smiling one of her icy smiles.

"Whatever it is, I don't want to be there!"

My mother changes the subject by asking Isabel Alacran about the shoes she's wearing. The women stop eating long enough to peer under the table. My mother claims Mrs. Goldenberg is a madwoman. Functioning, but crazy all the same. She is tolerated because she is the American consul's wife and her powerful husband intervenes on behalf of my parents.

The time my grandfather Whitman was dying, for example. He was kept alive by intravenous feeding, and the doctors prescribed for him some special astronaut food available only in North America. We had no access to this exotic miracle diet, and my mother went into hysterics. Mr. Goldenberg arranged for a U.S. army plane to fly in the cartons of powdered food every two weeks. It cost my father a thousand U.S. dollars a month, but it was apparently worth it; my American grandfather survived three extra years. After he died, the remaining boxes of priceless orange space food stayed stacked in the pantry, collecting dust and cobwebs. When Pacita opened one of them, tiny black bugs swarmed over her hand. My grieving mother finally ordered the astronaut powder fed to the pigs.

When my *Abuelita* Socorro fell down and broke her hip during one of her annual visits from Spain, Mr. Goldenberg arranged for her to stay at the American Hospital, which was technically only for Americans. My father was grateful, and showered the Goldenbergs with gifts in return. A membership to the Monte Vista Country Club, boxes of Tabacalera cigars, cases of aged Spanish brandy, and gleaming tins of pale yellow Mango Tango ice cream, Mrs. Goldenberg's favorite. When she was released from the hospital, my *abuelita* thanked the Goldenbergs profusely, offering a special novena for their souls. Privately, she took my father aside, curious whether the Goldenbergs were real Jews.

The Day of the Dead. All Souls' Day, 1959. Or 1960—why is it so difficult to recall? Why didn't I write it all down, keep diaries and journals, photos arranged in chronological order in a fat picture album? When Uncle Cristobal insists the Gonzagas make an effort to trace their genealogy, my father is the only member of the family who isn't interested. Even my mother ridicules the Gonzaga's genealogical chart as another example of their self-aggrandizement. "We are direct descendants of Christopher Columbus," Uncle Agustin used to boast. "Well—I was named after him," Uncle Cristobal would remind us. "Really, Bitot. You're taking yourself too seriously," my father tells him on the telephone. It's one of those rare occasions when stingy Uncle Cristobal calls us long-distance from Spain. The two brothers argue over the phone, my father finally hanging up in a fit of petulance. To our surprise, Uncle Cristobal stubbornly goes ahead and spends his own money to hire a genealogist to work on our family tree. He squanders a fortune on this endeavor. Years later, after Uncle Cristobal dies, his lawyer sends us copies of our genealogical chart. Uncle Agustin and Uncle Esteban have theirs bound in leather. As soon as he receives his copy, my father purposely misplaces it.

I do not know my paternal great-grandfather's name, or my great-grandmother's. I've been told she was Chinese from Macao, that Uncle Cristobal burned the only photographs of her so there is no remaining evidence. And where was my maternal grandfather from? Somewhere in the Midwest, my mother shrugs and tells me. I am ashamed at having to invent my own history.

The only thing I know for sure is that my mother's grandmother was the illegitimate and beautiful offspring of a village priest. My mother can never remember her name, and *Lola* Narcisa refuses to disclose it. The only thing *lola* has reluctantly told me is that her mother had blue-gray eyes, in startling contrast to her brown skin. The father of my blue-eyed great-grandmother was a Spanish missionary, and to speak his name was absolutely forbidden in my *Lola* Narcisa's house.

We are in the bamboo garden, my *Lola* Narcisa and I. She points out the fragile, transparent snakeskin shed at the base of the bamboo grove. I am fascinated by its pale, ghostly texture, the ridges of serpent vertebrae so clearly etched in the abandoned shell it makes me shiver.

On the terrace above us, the women huddle over their elegant lunch. My mother Dolores, the guest of honor Joyce Goldenberg, Isabel Alacran, Mimi Pelayo, and Congressman Abad's wife, Sylvia. Mrs. Goldenberg laughs too loud and chatters non-stop throughout the entire meal. The servants balance platters of grilled *bangus*, artfully arranged on beds of fresh parsley and sliced *kalamansi*. "Is it true," Mimi Pelayo is saying to Isabel Alacran, "that your husband's bringing over Anita Ekberg to do the new SPORTEX campaign?"

"No, no! Isn't he bringing over that other one, Claudia Cardinale?" my mother Dolores says.

"Who's Claudia Cardinala?" Joyce Goldenberg wants to know.

"Cardinale," Isabel Alacran corrects her again. Her voice is steady, soothing, filled with authority. A hush falls over the women as she speaks. I shut her out, picking up the snakeskin to examine it more closely. *Lola* Narcisa bends toward me, making one of her interested sounds. Since my grandfather's death she talks in sentences only when absolutely necessary. Otherwise she groans and clucks, hisses or chuckles very softly, to imply pleasure or amusement.

"RIO!" my mother shouts, alarmed. I look up, distracted. "What's that you've got in your hand?" She makes a move to get up from the table, a frown on her face.

"Snake," I answer, without thinking. Joyce Goldenberg squeals in terror; the other women stop eating. My mother stands up, but doesn't come any closer.

"What in god's name are you doing?" She glares at her mother, angry now. *Lola* Narcisa gazes calmly at her.

"It's only skin, Dolores. It can't hurt anyone," *Lola* Narcisa says in careful English.

My mother keeps glaring at her, but speaks to me. "Put that thing down right now and wash your hands," she commands, before going back to her food.

1960. Joselito Sanchez's younger brother Tonyboy brings me back stacks of records from America: 45s, 78s, 33 LPs. Little Richard, Chuck Berry, Fats Domino, Ritchie Valens, Chubby Checker, Joey Dee and the Starliters. I'm in bliss. Tonyboy teaches me the latest dances. The Madison, the Twist. Even though he's dark, Pucha thinks he's okay because he's so rich. He shows me how to slow-drag, rubs his groin hard up against my crotch. Or we join Raul and watch television, the big box of dreams my father brings home one day as a surprise. *Tawag Ng Tanghalan*, *I Love Lucy*. When my brother's out of the room, Tonyboy asks if I need a lesson in French-kissing. I ply him with questions based on material I've gathered from my treasured *Photoplay* and *Silver Screen* magazines. Pucha and I have just seen *Imitation of Life*. Is it true about Lana Turner's daughter killing that gangster? "When I grow up, I'm moving to Hollywood," I announce to Tonyboy. "Oh yeah sure," he murmurs, burying his face in my neck. I'm impressed with his American accent, the way he says "Oh yeah sure" with such confidence.

"I can see it now," Tonyboy says, with a hint of sarcasm, "giant billboards in Quiapo advertising INDAY GOES TO HOLLYWOOD, starring Rio Gonzaga. We'll get Tito Severo to produce it as a musical—" We are slow-dragging expertly to something mournful by Frankie Lymon. Tonyboy makes a clumsy attempt to fondle my nonexistent breasts. I slap his hand. "Stupid—you don't believe me? I'm going to make movies, Tonyboy. Not act in them!" I look at him angrily.

"What an imagination!" Tonyboy laughs, sticking his tongue in my ear.

Maybe 1960 or 1961. *West Side Story* plays to a standing-room-only audience at the Galaxy Theater. Pucha and I are seated in the balcony. Rosemary Garcia and her sister Belen are sitting in the row in front of us. We are chaperoned by a sullen Raul, who would rather see his idol, Jack Palance, starring in *Bazooka!* at the rat-infested theater in the Escolta; he would rather be anywhere but here. He is embarrassed and bored by our movie, making loud wisecracks every time Natalie Wood opens her mouth to sing. "Look at those fillings! The girl's got cavities!" He hoots in the darkness, he curses at the screen, calling the lithe, dancing actors a bunch of *baklas*. The audience titters at my brother's remarks. I sink lower in my seat. Someone in the orchestra section yells at Raul to shut up. "Come and get me, you bastard!" Raul yells back, enjoying himself now. "*Dios mio*, Raul—" Pucha mutters, making faces at me in the darkness. Defiantly, Raul lights a cigarette. A timid usher shines a flashlight in our direction, but makes no move to stop him.

This is how my brother meets his first love, Belen Garcia. She turns around and gives him a withering look. She is very pretty, with long hair and freckles on her nose. My cousin Pucha finds Belen's freckles strange and repulsive, but I have long ago stopped taking her opinions too seriously. "You're ruining the movie for everyone," Belen Garcia says to Raul. "Why are you so rude?" She seems to feel sorry for my brother, which confuses and intrigues him. He has never been confronted so directly by anyone so attractive. He is silenced, and apologizes to her quietly when the movie is over.

Belen Garcia becomes Raul's first wife. They marry young, but so

241

does everyone else we know. She bears him three children in rapid succession, all girls. My parents argue: *Females will be this family's curse. Girls are fine. Girls are a burden. This isn't China! No, it's worse.*

My brother and Mikey are often stopped for breaking curfew. They joke with the soldiers who stop them; they bribe them with cash to avoid being sent off to Camp Meditation. Mikey gets sent there once, arrested for drunken driving and speeding with Joselito Sanchez. "It wasn't so bad," Mikey brags to my brother. "They had us pulling weeds and mopping up toilets." My father bails Raul out of several sticky situations during martial law; he threatens to disown Raul, but my brother doesn't take him seriously. Belen Garcia gives up and leaves him, taking her babies with her. My brother meets another woman, named Erlinda. She bears him two more girls, and they are married in a civil ceremony. "They are living in sin," *Tita* Florence says to my mother, who doesn't respond. The names of Raul's daughters are: Filomena, Raquel, Josefina, Esmeralda, and Dolores, after my mother.

Abuelita Socorro dies in Spain. She goes into a coma, and never gets to say goodbye to anyone. No one is sure what really ailed her. Maybe her insides just gave up after all the rich foods she ate. No greens in her long life, no fruits or vegetables. My father retreats into his bedroom and weeps privately. Uncle Cristobal flies her body back to Manila, so she can be buried next to her husband. Her funeral is more lavish than *Abuelito's*.

My mother has been right all along. *Abuelita* Socorro leaves everything to her priest and her church. She is buried wearing her black dress and matching pumps, her strands of pearls, and her black rosary wrapped around her wrist; her brilliant emeralds dangle from her ears.

Mr. Goldenberg and his wife survive Saudi Arabia. Years later, my mother receives a letter. Mrs. Goldenberg has divorced her husband and manages an art gallery in Florida. Trixie Goldenberg has married twice and is infertile. Mr. Goldenberg has retired from his diplomatic career and lives in New York. He is writing a book of memoirs, and is often nostalgic for Manila.

"How are you and Freddie?" he writes my mother. "I miss your wonderful dinner parties, and all that incredible food. I assume Pacita is still with you . . . And what about your son, Raul? Is he working yet? Last but not least, your daughter Rio, and that wild cousin of hers, Pucha . . ."

Pucha's first wish is granted. She marries Boomboom Alacran as soon as she graduates from high school. *Tita* Florence and Uncle Agustin are elated and orchestrate an elaborate wedding which my father helps pay for. Pucha starves herself for a month and manages to lose ten pounds. She squeezes into a frilly white gown even though she is no longer a virgin. Chiquiting Moreno is sent for to do her hair. I am one of her bridesmaids, dressed in a dreadful concoction of pastel pink chiffon and lace. Pucha insists on a pink and white wedding— we're straight out of one of her storybook fantasies, and she cries with happiness.

It is a terrible marriage, which barely lasts a year. Boomboom is insanely jealous, and locks Pucha in the bedroom before paying his daily visit to the Monte Vista, where he sits around all day drinking and gambling. Because he is an Alacran, he never has to work. He accuses Pucha of countless betrayals, he beats her frequently. With the help of her terrified servant Ramona, Pucha finally engineers an escape one night while Boomboom is out getting drunk with his friends. Clad only in her nightgown, Pucha and Ramona hail a taxi to Uncle Agustin's house. The scandal that ensues drags on for weeks, with Boomboom threatening to kill himself on Pucha's front lawn. Mikey comes home from Bicol to defend his sister's dubious honor. Pucha never speaks to Boomboom again. My cousin is forced to get her foreign divorce in the end, but she continues to use the name Pucha Alacran.

My mother begins painting shortly after her fiftieth birthday. Except for occasional drawing lessons with Horacio, she has had no formal training in art and is ignorant of its history. She paints and paints; with furious energy, she covers immense canvases with slashes of red, black, yellow, and mauve. She uses the same colors in different combinations. "My bleeding bouquets," she calls them. She moves into Raul's now empty room and converts it into her bedroom-studio. My father acts as if everything were normal, even when Uncle Agustin says, "Your wife has slapped you in the face."

Without warning, she cheerfully announces she is sending me to school in America and moving there with me for an indefinite period. I am ecstatic, at first. Everyone else is stunned. My father cannot stop her—my mother has inherited money from her father and pays for our passage to America. We settle first in New York, then Boston. I convince myself I am not homesick, and try not to bring up my father or brother when I speak. My mother actually sells a few paintings. The months turn into years. "Are we going to stay here forever?" I finally ask her. She looks surprised. "I don't know about you, but I love the cold weather. Go back to Manila if you want. Tell Raul I miss him more than he could ever imagine." She smiles one of her cryptic smiles. "But he'll have to visit me here if he wants to see me—" her voice trails off.

Raul writes me letters in red ink, polite letters quoting from the Scriptures and inquiring about my health. He achieves local fame as a spiritualist healer and preaches to his followers in the countryside. Erlinda and the children follow close behind, his loyal family of believers. He distances himself from the rest of the Gonzagas, who are ashamed of his newfound fundamentalist Christian ministry. Only Pucha, of all people, visits him regularly. She writes me notes on Hallmark greeting cards:

Oye, prima—que ba, *when are you coming back? Tonyboy asked about you, I saw him at SPORTEX boy he still looks grate! I think he left his wife you dont know her shes a forinner from Austria or Australia you know he told me you really broke his heart when you left plus you never answered any of his letters,* pobrecito naman! WOW! *I saw Raul yesterday at that new apt. of his I brought him new clothes for the kids, theres so many! Erlinda's pregnant again. I didnt stay two long, he was in one of his moods you know how Raul gets. Hes always complaineing you dont write anybody and its true. Write him, okay? And send your mother my regards I hope shes not mad at me. Thanks be to God my parents are okay. Uncle Esteban had another operation, in case you didnt here. Mommie says HELLO! She and Papi had merienda with your father last Sunday. Mikeys getting married. AT LAST. Why dont you come to the wedding?*

Love & prayers,
PUCHA

When I finally come home to Manila to visit, my father warns me not to bother visiting our old house. "You'll be disappointed. Memories are always better." Smiling apologetically, he tells me reality will diminish the grandeur of my childhood image of home. I take his picture with my new camera, which later falls in the swimming pool by accident. The camera is destroyed, along with my roll of film. I decide to visit our old house in Mandaluyong anyway, borrowing a car from Mikey. Pucha goes with me; she loves riding around in cars and doesn't need any excuse. "After that, let's go to the Intercon Hotel and have a drink," she says, a gleam of mischief in her eyes. "Put on some makeup," she bosses me, "you look tired." I laugh. Pucha is up to her old tricks. She applies thick coats of blue eyeshadow on her heavy eyelids, studying her face in the mirror with rapt concentration.

My father is right. The house with its shuttered windows looks smaller than I remember, and dingy. The once lush and sprawling garden is now a forlorn landscape of rocks, weeds, and wild ferns. The bamboo grove has been cut down. "Let's go," Pucha whispers, impatient and uninterested. An old man with bright eyes introduces himself as Manong Tibo, the caretaker. He unlocks door after door for us, pulling aside cobwebs, warning us to be careful. Rotting floorboards creak under the weight of our footsteps. "My bedroom," I say to the old man, who nods. I am overwhelmed by melancholy at the sight of the empty room. A frightened mouse dashes across the grimy tiled floor. Pucha jumps back and screams, clutching and pinching my arm. "Let's go," she pleads. "Wait outside. I'll be there soon," I say, trying to conceal my irritation. I am relieved finally to be alone, in this desolate house with only Manong for company. He studies me with his bright eyes. "You live in America?" His niece is a nurse in San Francisco, California, he tells me with pride. Someday, he hopes she'll send for him.

I stay another hour, walking in and out of the dusty rooms in a kind of stupor. The shutters in the windows of the kitchen, Pacita's kingdom, are hanging from their hinges. The gas stove and refrigerator are gone. "Thieves," Manong shrugs, when I ask him. Broken glass is scattered on the floor. He tells me the house will be torn down within the month and a complex of offices built in its place. The property and the squatters' land adjoining it have been bought by the Alacran corporation, Intercoco.

I say good-bye and thank the old man. "See you in America!" Manong Tibo says, waving farewell. Pucha is slumped down in the front seat of the car, irritated, hot, and sweaty. "I wouldn't do this for anyone but you," she grumbles without looking at me, then peers into the rearview mirror. "Look at my makeup!" She gives me an accusing look. I slide into the driver's seat, fighting back tears. Suddenly, I grab her hand. She stares at me, puzzled. "Are you okay?" It seems an eternity, but I pull myself together. Pucha hands me her lace handkerchief, drenched in perfume. "Watch out when you blow your nose—okay, *prima*?" She teases. She squeezes my hand, uncomfortable with our display of affection. I start the car, turning to look at her before we drive away. "I really love you," I say, to her utter amazement.

My cousin will find happiness with a man, once and for all. He is a stranger to us, a modest man from a modest family, someone we never knew in our childhood. The Gonzagas breathe a collective sigh of relief. Pucha lives with her new husband, childless and content; she never leaves Manila.

My *Lola* Narcisa lives to be a very old woman. She is the main reason for my frequent visits to Manila; I dread not being there when she dies.

*   *   *

I return to North America. I save all Raul's letters, along with my father's cordial birthday telegrams and Pucha's gossipy notes, in a large shopping bag labeled FAMILY. I move to another city, approximately five thousand miles away from where my mother lives and paints. We talk on the phone once a week. I am anxious and restless, at home only in airports. I travel whenever I can. My belief in God remains tentative. I have long ago stopped going to church. I never marry.

In my recurring dream, my brother and I inhabit the translucent bodies of nocturnal moths with curved, fragile wings. We are pale green, with luminous celadon eyes, fantastic and beautiful. In dream after dream, we are drawn to the same silent tableau: a mysterious light glowing from the window of a deserted, ramshackle house. The house is sometimes perched on a rocky abyss, or on a dangerous cliff overlooking a turbulent sea. The meaning is simple and clear, I think. Raul and I embrace our destiny: we fly around in circles, we swoop and dive in effortless arcs against a barren sky, we flap and beat our wings in our futile attempts to reach what surely must be heaven.

Pucha Gonzaga

Puwede ba? 1956, 1956! Rio, you've got it all wrong. Think about it: 1956 makes no sense. It must have started sometime around 1959, at the very least! You like to mix things up on purpose, *di ba? Esta loca, prima. Que ba*—this is cousin Pucha you're talking to . . . *Doña*, we grew up together like sisters, excuse me *lang*! I'm no *intelektwal* as you've pointed out loud and clear, but my memory's just as good as anybody's . . .

Hoy, what are you trying to prove? Your *kalocohan* I don't understand. We got movies late in those days, don't you remember? They advertised them as "first-run," but it wasn't like it is now; back then, the movies were as much as two or three years behind the times, and I don't think that one was in color, that one you keep describing with Rock Hudson. *Oye, prima*—Rock is *still* my idol, I should know! And that one with Shelley Winters and Liz Taylor—I don't remember saying Shelley deserved to die, I would never say anything like that— even if she is really *sin verguenza*, she let herself go to the dogs and get fat, did you ever see *The Poseidon Adventure*? I tell you, I never saw that movie in my life! If you're gonna talk about the past, don't say I said horrible things I never said, *puwede ba*, how could you do that to me? I don't think it's very funny, not at all. I never went to movies condemned by the Church. *Chica*, I may be a divorced woman like you say, but I don't spit in the eyes of God and willingly commit sin! You're mixing me up with someone else.

I may not remember all the details, but I certainly should know
WHO was making eyes at me in the Cafe España that fateful after-

noon! It was my first husband, Ramon Assad. *Puwede ba*, he was never fat, not ever in his life—in fact, we used to call him "Ting-Ting"— I think you made that up, you were always good with nicknames. Ramoncito was so skinny he reminded you of a broom, *"walis ting-ting!"* How can you forget that? And he had pretty eyelashes and perfect skin—you used to tease me about it. How can you call him fat and ugly? Look at me—I'm fat now, but still sexy. He was crazy for my boobs and my hips—he liked his women big. Ramoncito was never fat, he could eat and eat and he made me eat with him; he never gained a pound. My mother thought he had tapeworm. Plus he never beat me—the reason I left was because I was tired of supporting *him*. How could you mix him up with that *baboy* Boomboom Alacran?

Well, you never liked Ramoncito, and he knew it. For once in your life, you were probably right. He was a lousy husband, except in the sack. My mother warned me: "You can't live on kisses alone." I almost did, but God brought me to my senses. I just want you to get my damn history straight, Rio—*puwede ba*, it matters to me.

Maybe the movie was in color, maybe not. That's not what's important. *Oye, prima*—this much is true, you'd better wake up and accept it: 1959 was many years ago. Your mother's father is alive. Your *Lola* Narcisa is dead. Our *abuelito* and *abuelita* are alive and well and living in Mallorca with *Tito* Cristobal. Your father isn't poor—how can you lie about such big things? Belen Garcia is still married to your brother, who works for your father at Intercoco. Your mother and father are still together. Nobody's perfect, Rio— but your parents stayed married no matter what, through thick and thin and your father's *kalocohan*, thanks be to God.

Pobrecita naman, Isabel Alacran died of cancer in 1967—but everyone else is fine, I'm telling you!

Nothing is impossible, I suppose, with that crazy imagination of yours. I'm not surprised by anything you do or say, but if I were you, *prima*, I'd leave well enough alone.

Kundiman

Our Mother, who art in heaven. Hallowed be thy name. Thy kingdom come, thy will be done. Thy will not be done. Hallowed be thy name, thy kingdom never came. You who have been defiled, belittled, and diminished. Our Blessed Virgin Mary of Most Precious Blood, menstrual, ephemeral, carnal, eternal. Rosa Mystica, Black Virgin of Rhinestone and Velvet Mystery, Madonna of Volcanoes and Violence, your eye burns through the palm of my outstretched hand. Eye glowing with heavenly flames, one single Eye watching over me, on earth as it is in heaven.

Dammit, mother dear. There are serpents in your garden. Licking your ears with forked tongues, poisoning your already damaged heart. I am suffocated by my impotent rage, my eyes are blinded by cataracts blue as your miraculous robes, I listen intently for snatches of melody, the piercing high-pitched wail of your song of terror.

Here, clues to your ghostly presence in the lingering trail of your deadly perfume: wild roses and plumeria, the dizzying fragrance of damas de noche, the rotting bouquets of wilted sampaguita flowers you cradle in your arms.

I would curse you in Waray, Ilocano, Tagalog, Spanish, English, Portuguese, and Mandarin; I would curse you but I choose to love you instead. Amor, amas, amatis, amant, give us this day our daily bread.

Our mother who art, what have those bastards gone and done now? Your eyes are veiled and clouded by tears, veiled but never blinded. Dazzle us with your pity, let the scars tattooed on your face be a reminder of your perennial sorrow. Kyrie eleison. Kyrie eleison. Lamb of goddammit who taketh away the sins of the world!

My dim eyes scan the shadows in vain, Ave Maria full of grace. Ita missa est. Manila I was born here, Manila I will die here, tantum ergo sacramentum. So the daughters say, so the sons seek out miracles, so the men will not live to see the light.

Your long monkey toes grip the hairy coconuts strewn at your feet, virgin with one ear pierced by a thorn. Stigmata of mercy, the blood of a slain rooster spouts from the open palms of your monkey hands, stigmata of beautiful suffering and insane endurance, Dolores dolorosa. Spilled blood of innocents, dead by the bullet, the dagger, the arrow; dead by the slingshot of polished stones, dead by grenades, hunger and thirst; dead by profound longing and profound despair; spilled blood of ignited flesh, exploded flesh, radiated flesh; spilled blood of forbidden knowledge, bless us, Mother, for we have sinned.

Our Mother who art in heaven, forgive us our sins. *Our Lady of Most Precious Blood, Wild Dogs, Hyenas, Jackals, Coyotes, and Wolves, Our Lady of Panthers and Jaguars, Our Lady of Cobras, Mournful Lizards, Lost Souls, and Radio Melodramas,* give us this day; *Our Lady of Typhoons,* deliver us from evil, forgive us our sins but not theirs.

Ave Maria, mother of revenge. The Lord was never with you. Blessed art thou among women, and blessed are the fruits of thy womb: guavas, mangos, santol, mangosteen, durian. Now and forever, world without end. Now and forever.

ABOUT THE AUTHOR

Born and raised in the Philippines, Jessica Hagedorn is the author of *Dangerous Music* and *Pet Food and Tropical Apparitions*, collections of poems, prose, and short fiction published by Momo's Press. Her multimedia theater pieces include *Holy Food, Teenytown,* and *Mango Tango,* which was produced by Joseph Papp at New York City's Public Theater. For many years, she was the leader and lyricist for the Gangster Choir band. She is presently a commentator for *Crossroads,* a syndicated weekly newsmagazine on public radio. Jessica Hagedorn lives with the artist John Woo and their daughter, Paloma.